The
Gospel
of Judas

Also by Simon Mawer

FICTION

Chimera

The Bitter Cross

A Jealous God

Mendel's Dwarf

NONFICTION

A Place in Italy

The
Gospel
of Judas

A N O V E L

SIMON MAWER

LITTLE, BROWN AND COMPANY

BOSTON • NEW YORK • LONDON

Copyright © 2000, 2001 by Simon Mawer

First American Edition

The characters and events in this book are fictitious.
Any similarity to real persons, living or dead,
is coincidental and not intended by the author.

Library of Congress Cataloging-in-Publication Data
Mawer, Simon.
    The gospel of Judas : a novel / Simon Mawer. — 1st American ed.
      p. cm.
    ISBN 0-316-09750-0
      1. Bible. N.T. Gospels — Authorship — Fiction.   2. Catholic
Church — Clergy — Fiction.   3. British — Italy — Fiction.
4. Italy — Fiction.   I. Title.

PR9120.9.M38 G67 2001
823'.914 — dc21   00-060644

                    10 9 8 7 6 5 4 3 2 1

Text design by Meryl Sussman Levavi/Digitext

Printed in the United States of America

To Connie—as always

The
Gospel
of Judas

1

Bless me Father, for I have sinned."

A curious structure, the confessional. A cross between a wardrobe and a prie-dieu, a varnished wooden construction that is probably the only piece of furniture never to have awoken the interest of collectors. You'll not go into a precious modern house, somewhere in Islington, say, and find a confessional in the hall and a careless confession by the proud owner that it was "Something we picked up at an auction. We thought it'd go so well just there. Wonderful for hanging coats."

No.

A confessional has other resemblances: a booth in the visiting room of a prison, for example; the place where, for a few minutes a month, the condemned meet the free to exchange platitudes and recriminations.

"Bless me, Father, for I have sinned." A shadow beyond the grille. The intense, anonymous intimacy. The awful fact that a soul is about to be laid bare, that horror may be revealed. "Bless me, Father, for I have sinned." But she was merely suffering from scruples, an affliction of the religious that is just as tiresome as a rash, *is* a kind of mental rash in fact. You scratch and it only gets worse. People go off to Africa to work in the missions because of scruples. They catch real rashes there. "I have doubts," she said.

"Good Lord, my child, we *all* of us have doubts," he told her. "*I* have doubts."

"Do you? What are yours?"

"Who is hearing this confession?"

Was there a suppressed giggle from the far side of the grille? He even stole a glance to his left, but she was no more than a shadow beyond the metal lattice. Outside, the shifting, shiftless crowds of the great basilica; inside the stuffy wooden box, this curious intimacy with a half-seen, barely apprehended silhouette.

A breath of perfume drifted through the barricade that divided them: something musky, something with an underlying hint of sharp fruit. "I'm sorry, Father. Forgive me."

"You must take this seriously or not at all," he admonished her.

"Of course, Father."

"And other than these doubts?"

"I touched myself, Father."

"Was it just once?" One should not get overinquisitive. There was, of course, a sin in that. There was a whole pit full of sins waiting for the confessor, a pit that writhed with the snakes of voyeurism and prurience.

"More than once."

"If it's become a habit then that's one thing. And if it's just an occasional weakness that's another. Which is it?"

She giggled. Quite definitely this time, the shadow beyond the grille giggled. "I'll take the occasional weakness."

"Are you serious about this?"

"I'm sorry. It was the way you said it. As though you were bartering with me. Trading contrition for penance."

"You mustn't make a mockery of it."

"Sorry," she repeated. "I'm sorry."

He said something about the motives for confession, recited some little lecture about true contrition, about the love of God and the forgiveness of sin. "Sin is absence of God. Nothing more, nothing less. If you truly wish to return to God, then confession has meaning. Only then."

"Yes," she said. "That's what I would like."

He noted the careful conditional but let it pass. "As an act of penance say a decade of the rosary and a prayer for my own spiritual well-being. Now make an act of contrition." The rituals of religion, a vocabulary understood only by the initiate: she recited some little formula of self-accusation and pious resolution, and in return he gave her absolution. Then she whispered thanks and left the confines of the box, let slip that curious, transient intimacy that the confessional creates, drifted out of the claustrophobic shadows and into the world.

He turned to his right and slid the other shutter back to reveal another presence, another shadow, another complex of sin and doubt and anguish. "Bless me, Father, for I have sinned."

At six o'clock in the evening he slid both shutters closed and, as a surgeon might peel off his surgical gloves, removed the stole from around his neck. Confessor, surgeon. There was a similar intimacy, the one spiritual, the other physical, and a similar anonymity. The one pokes among the bowels of the patient, the other among the innermost secrets, and both do it all in a spirit of resignation and emotional indifference.

Leaving the confessional box, he walked out into the crossing of the transepts, beneath the awful, vacant dome, beneath the substandard mosaics, beneath that great volume of space that

Michelangelo Buonarroti subsumed into the building in a manner that amounts to grand larceny. Could pure space evoke a sense of the numinous? People shifted around on the pavement like grains of sand drifting back and forth across the floor of a tidal pool—tourists, and pilgrims, and those, the majority, perhaps, that lay somewhere in between. Candles flickered around the balustrade where you stand and look down into the sunken space where the tomb of the Apostle lies. People crowded around like onlookers at the scene of an accident to see if it was really true. Someone even asked him about it; and of course he assured her that it was, that it really *was* possible that the Apostle himself was buried there.

"Only *possible,* Father?" she retorted. "What kind of faith is that?"

And indeed, what kind of faith was it? A poor, dried-out thing, a construct put together of habit and defiance and anxiety. "The material fact is not important," he told her, "and presumably lies in the realm of archaeology, not theology. The spiritual reality is that you are as close to God in your own sitting room as in the basilica; but the basilica has worth if it strengthens your faith."

And then the woman—gray-haired, an accent that he took to be German, a worn and defeated face—said a curious thing: "Does it strengthen *your* faith, Father?"

It was raining outside. Lights glittered in the wet basalt slabs of the piazza and a Christmas tree daubed the space with a smear of northern paganism. The orange glow of the city lit up the clouds like the backwash from a great conflagration. He hurried through the rain to his rooms, and showered and changed for a reception which was to be held that evening in one of the innumerable palazzi of the city, the closing reception of a congress that had been going on throughout the past week.

The reception was a dull affair, a milling of black and gray and navy blue beneath the cavorting nymphs and goddesses of a late mannerist ceiling. Pink breasts and flaccid penises flopped around above the heads of the earnest clerics. There was the occasional splash of color from a bishop, or a lady diplomat doing the duty rounds, or the wife of an Anglican priest (and the boyfriend of another), but the predominant theme was Roman—clerical, introverted and self-satisfied.

"This is Manderley Dewer," someone said to him and he found himself shaking hands with one of the few women in the place. She surprised him by recognizing his name. "Didn't I read something by you in the *Times*? Something about scrolls from the Dead Sea?"

He looked at her distractedly, awkward in the presence of women. "Hardly scrolls. A few fragments. The En-Mor papyri."

"The earliest pieces of the gospels," said the man who had introduced them. "Quite the most important textual find in the last fifty years."

The woman attempted some kind of conversation. "Isn't the point that if the fragments do come from a gospel it would push the earliest date to before the Jewish War in AD 66?"

"That's what the article said," Newman agreed. "Politically it's a wonderful idea."

"Politically?"

He glanced away over her shoulder as though looking for something, escape, perhaps. "Religious politics. Mud in the eye for the scholars who claim that the gospels are late inventions put together by the early Church. But that's not the point, is it? The point is the pieces themselves, the texts, the witness."

She contemplated the idea, her head tilted to one side, a faint smile on her lips. "It excites you, doesn't it?"

The word *excite* seemed threatening. He felt a shifting embarrassment. "What do you mean, excite?"

"The texts. They excite you." There was to her smile a kind of slant that he couldn't read. Eyes can be dead things, charged with expression only by the refraction of incident light; but mouths have their own life. And hers had some quality of irony that he couldn't read.

"Yes, I suppose they do."

What else did he see? What does a celibate see in a chance encounter with a woman? He saw a face of modest proportions, large eyes of indeterminate color somewhere between green and brown, a look of faint anxiety beneath the insouciance. Hair ill-kempt and touched with the tones of autumn. She seemed rather younger than he—in her early forties, he thought, although he had little practice in judging the age of women, or anything much else about them, come to that.

And what, he wondered, did she see? Dull, dry cleric? Something sterile? Something at the dead end of humanity, probably.

There was that silence that so often comes after the first words. What else was there to say, after all? Where could the point of contact be? "Are you here for the conference?" he asked.

"Here or *here?*"

"I'm sorry?"

The confusion seemed to amuse her. "Here is this room, yes. Here in Rome, no." Her husband was a diplomat, she explained. She shrugged as though it was of no interest, and it was her turn to glance around as though for distraction. Somebody remarked on the ceiling (everyone remarked on the ceiling when there was a pause in the conversation), and she looked upward at the dusty swirl of phallic gods and mammary goddesses, before looking back at him and smiling that particular smile, and asking, "Do you think they had scruples, Father?" And in a moment he caught the same drift of scent from her as had come through the grille of the confessional, a sharp touch of citrus that didn't seem to emanate from a commercial perfume at all but rather was something natural and dangerous. And he had a most profane thought: that this was like the way the apostles at Emmaus had recognized Christ after the resurrection, by a mere gesture, by a combination of words, perhaps even by a smell.

He felt himself redden: grave discomfort, sweating with embarrassment under stiff clerical gray. Mercifully the others on the edge of the conversation had moved away to examine some piece of furniture and they were momentarily alone. "How very awkward," he said.

"Do you think so? What about the separation of office and person?" She put her head on one side as though to examine both him and the proposition together, finding them both faintly amusing. "Anyway, I'm the one who should be embarrassed, and I'm not. So I'll give you leave not to be either. You must have heard a lot worse in your time. I must say, I imagined you older."

"And I imagined you younger."

She winced. "Touché. A silly little adolescent, maybe?"

"Something like that."

"I'm afraid confession makes me that way. It always reminds me of school. D'you know, we used to make up sins just to have something to confess? I expect you know that, don't you? I touched Anne-Marie when she was in the shower, I told Matilda that I don't believe in God, I said a rude word behind Sister Mary Joseph's back, that kind of thing. But now I can assure you that I'm much more grown up." She was laughing, as though to deny the assertion at the same time as she stated it. "Anyway, you must come round some time. Where do you stay? You must come round for dinner. Give me your number."

It is not uncommon for Catholic women to befriend priests. It is a kind of patronage. Priests are to be supported materially, while they in turn support the faithful spiritually. If you come from the Protestant tradition maybe you do not see it in quite the same way, but looking after a priest is a kind of good work. If you don't come from any tradition at all, you probably cannot see why there might be a celibate priest in the first place and why, for God's sake, a woman might ever concern herself with such a man.

"I'm sorry," he said, "I didn't quite get your name... Manderley?"

She glanced up from her handbag where she was rooting around for a diary or something. "Madeleine. Madeleine Brewer."

There. Madeleine Brewer. The very first encounter. Thus the chaotic hand of coincidence had its way, like the petulant hand of a child rearranging the pieces on a chessboard.

"Tell me," she said, pen poised over her address book.

Magda—now

The apartment where I live now is in an old Roman palazzo, the Palazzo Casadei. The building stands on the edge of the ghetto: one face confronts the open, Gentile world; the other overlooks an alleyway that winds back among the cramped houses of the Jewish quarter. The apartment crouches beneath the roof of the building: the ceilings slope, the windows are at floor level, the floors are uneven; there is a sense of refuge up there under the tiles, a sense of sanctuary. During the war, it is said, the Principessa Casadei hid Jews in the warren of rooms beneath the rafters.

I work, of course. I can't exist on nothing. Part-time, ill-paid, off the record, I work. The organization for which I work is the grandly named Anglo-American Language School and it occupies the third floor of a block near the main railway station, sharing the

11

building with a trattoria, some offices belonging to dubious import/export firms and even more dubious lawyers, and a *pensione*. For a logo the school boasts the Union Jack and the Stars and Stripes in a clumsy juxtaposition, like battle honors won in some obscure colonial war. *Listed by the British Council,* it claims on a scroll beneath the flags.

I am paid weekly, in used 10,000-lire notes. From the very beginning the director viewed me with suspicion, wondering at the motives of a man of my age taking up casual teaching work; but he guessed, quite rightly, that I have no more interest in denouncing him to the tax authorities than he has in making my employment legal. No references asked for and none given: it's that kind of place. But at least I have a job and can keep body and mind together, if not soul. I have long ago abandoned any attempt at keeping my soul.

And for company I have Magda.

I found Magda. I found her in one of the first classes that I taught at the language school. She was like a piece of flotsam cast up on the shore of the city, one of those bits of debris that drift in from Europe, from the Middle East, from anywhere in the world, really—Latin America, the Philippines, India, anywhere.

Novotná Magda. At first it wasn't clear which was her first name. Novotná Magda, she repeated doggedly when I asked, so *Novotná* I called her and she seemed to accept it. She was tall and silent and dressed in black, as though in perpetual mourning for something, lost innocence, perhaps. Her hair, which to conform to the Slav stereotype ought to have been fair, was in fact or in fiction almost black. It was cut short and ragged and made her appear younger than she was, her complexion giving the game away: heavy makeup doesn't hide a coarse skin. Red lipstick made a scar of her mouth. She was what in France might be described as *gamine.*

"First you tell us all where you live," I announced to the class

in that first encounter. In response I received a litany of the dispossessed and the itinerant: in a hostel; with friends; I share apartment; I move around.

Novotná's legs wrapped themselves around each other like a
lucid black snake coiling around a sinuous sapling, the sapling of
the knowledge of good and evil, perhaps. "With my sisters," she
said. She did not mean siblings, but religious, some obscure order
of Polish nuns.

"And where do you come from?"

"Maroc."

"Burundi."

"Morava," said Novotná. The name evoked a small stir of anguish within me, a little frisson of something like horror.

"And where do you want to go?"

"America."

"America."

"America."

A shrug from Novotná, a gesture entirely in keeping with her
manner, which was one of indifference to much of what went on
around her. "America," she agreed, in the manner of one who
might say "the moon."

We plunged into the lesson. "At customs" was the theme. It
seemed appropriate. The students composed themselves to play
the roles they dreaded, the surly faces of officialdom, the hopeful,
hopeless faces of the dispossessed.

"May I see your passport?"

"Here is my passport."

"Where is the visa?"

"The visa is at the back." Hollow laughter at this.

"What is your purpose?"

"I want to work."

"We have jobs for enthusiastic workers." More laughter. The
hopelessness of the whole thing began to strike them: it tran-

scended barriers of language and culture and became a universal all-comprehensible joke.

"I work as a secretary," said Novotná. "I type good."

"*Well*. You type well."

"I type well. I am willful."

"Probably. But you mean willing."

"I work as executive," said one of the other students. The laughter was general.

Was it after the sixth or the seventh lesson that I invited her to lunch? What would Madeleine have said about that? Probably she would have told me to let the girl alone. What does she want with a dry stick like you? she would have asked. But Novotná treated my invitation as she treated everything in life: with that indifferent shrug and a thoughtful chewing of gum. "OK." She seemed to pause for careful reflection and to gather together bits of fragmented English. "I think if we go to lunch, you call me Magda," she decided.

Magda, Madeleine: the congruity of the names amuses me. In whatever terms you measure the human personality, never have there been two women further apart. Magda is tall and silent and dressed in black, as though in mourning for something; Madeleine was small and ebullient, the kind of person who made her husband raise his eyes heavenward in mock despair. Madeleine was soft and comforting; Magda is anonymous and indifferent. Madeleine was open, Magda is shut. But both named for the same woman, the woman out of whom Jesus cast seven devils, the woman who stood beside the mother of Jesus at the foot of the cross, the woman who saw the stone rolled away from the tomb, the woman who made the first announcement of the resurrection to the disciples as they cowered in the upper room.

"They have taken away the Lord, and I know not where they have laid him."

So we had lunch at Zia Anna, Aunt Anna's, a tawdry trattoria nearby that I have taken to using when I can't be bothered to return to the apartment. We ordered *spaghetti alla puttanesca,* spaghetti with tart's sauce, a concoction of red tomatoes and black olives that brings to mind sin and hellfire and menstruation, and Magda sat across the exiguous table from me, deposited her gum (a momentary glimpse of gray amalgam within the scarlet depths of her mouth) in the ashtray, and ate the dish with the methodical determination of someone who is not quite certain where her next decent meal is coming from.

She used to work in a shoe factory, she told me between mouthfuls, in the design department. Life there was dull and the pay was bad, and she decided that she wanted something better so she came to Italy with a friend, just to see. A girlfriend. She shrugged the girlfriend off. "She goes back."

"And what job do you do now? In Rome there can't be much work."

Magda sniffed. With an unexpected delicacy, almost as though she were touching up her makeup, she used her napkin to wipe red sauce from the corner of her mouth. "I draw." Then she reached down to her copious bag and produced a folder to show me, passing sheets across the table. They were charcoal sketches, skilled enough, the kind of facile things you see in Piazza Navona to attract tourists to have their own portraits done: there was Barbra Streisand, there was Madonna, there was the Pope. She shrugged. "And I do model."

"Artist's model?" I asked.

For the first time she smiled. It was a hurried, perfunctory thing, her smile—a mere widening of her mouth, a momentary expelling of air from her nostrils. "Pictures."

"Pictures?"

She shrugged, as though it were obvious. "Photographs. No clothes."

The noise of the trattoria intruded on our conversation, the clash of cutlery, the scrape of plates, the noise of unheard conversations from the other tables. And I sensed the clash of two emotions, the scrape of two sensations, one that in my previous life was always allowed full rein, the other that was always suppressed: shock and lust.

"Do you want to look at that also?" she asked.

"Perhaps not."

She shrugged indifferently and returned to her food, mopping up the remnants of sauce with a piece of bread, and then ordering *pollo alla diavola* with the eagerness of someone who had just devoured spaghetti with tart's sauce and found that no problem. "And the nuns?" I asked. "What do they think of the work you do?"

"The nuns?" She laughed. "The nuns know nothing."

Three days later Magda was thrown out of her hostel. She was given ten minutes' notice to clear her things. The nuns knew more than she had thought. She spent the night at the main railway station and probably earned 50,000 lire letting someone fuck her in the back of a car. I don't know. I'm not a fool, but I don't know for sure. The next day she came to her English lesson as usual.

"I look for somewhere to stay," Magda announced to the class.

Magda, Madeleine, Magdalen. Mary Magdalene. She has long been a problem, has Mary Magdalene. Mary from Magdala, presumably. That's not the issue. The issue is, who was she? The great sinner of Luke? Mary of Bethany? The woman who anointed Jesus with chrism and thus gave to him the title Christ? But whatever her identification, we cannot doubt the central fact—for she was a woman, and the early Church would have edited the story differently if it possibly could have done so: early on the morning of that first Easter Sunday, Mary of Magdala was the first person at the empty tomb; and, in the Gospel of John, which is likely to be accurate on this point for the very same reason, she was the first person to see the risen Jesus.

Magda standing in the midst of my apartment, a tall black figure: clumsy shoes, black stockings, black skirt (too short), black coat (tossed aside onto the broken sofa), black sweater stretched over small mammary swellings, black hair cut short around her face, red mouth chewing over the situation. An expression of indifference and wariness, a faint suspicion.

I showed her up the steps out of the living room onto the roof terrace. She turned to look. There was a betrayal of emotion here: a short, sharp intake of breath, a faint smile. All around her was the city—the surface of the city that the inhabitants never see as they go about their business down on the ground. The terrace seems like a boat adrift on a stormy terra-cotta ocean, the tilted, tiled rooftops breaking like waves against towers and gables and domes. Madeleine had cried out when she saw the view, she had projected her pleasure, she had exulted. Magda merely smiled, as though she already knew.

"I will draw," she announced. She put her bag down and went inside for a chair. When she came back she stood holding the chair for a while as she considered the prospect. From where she stood she could see, at a rough count, sixteen domes, including the biggest of the lot, the father and mother of all domes, the one that the whole world knows, quite wrongly, as Michelangelo's; but lesser domes as well, artful, baroque cupolas, with lanterns like nipples. The Gothic tradition of the north has always favored phallic spires and a lean, ascetic Christ figure; but in the south the female element in Christianity has ruled: subtle, comforting, seductive, redolent with the scent of other, more ancient cults— Demeter, Ceres, Cybele, Isis. *Mariolatry,* if you want a derogatory, Protestant term for it: *Marian devotion* if you want the party line.

Magda made her decision. She hitched her skirt up, sat down with her feet cocked up on the cross-bar of the chair, pulled a sketchpad from her bag and began. Her hand was sharp and assured, the strokes she made like cuts at a thing of flesh, something swift and surgical; and lines appeared that magicked a third dimension out of the mere two of the paper, so that as she worked the dome of Sant'Andrea della Valle (Maderno) was plucked out of the lucid Roman air and methodically transferred to the sheet in front of her.

"It's good," I told her.

She shrugged. "Maybe I sell." She worked between the ribs of the dome, giving them a curve, a sullen pewter tone; then she molded a ball of rubber and bent forward for a moment, working at the gray. When she straightened up, erasure had paradoxically given something positive, a gleam of sunlight to the leads.

Magda is an artist. The whole panorama encircled her as she worked so that somehow she seemed to be the axis around which all this revolved, this city of domes and bell towers, of guilt and hypocrisy. Magda is an artist and like an artist she seems to possess whatever she observes.

For three days she slept on the broken-backed sofa in the sitting room. She slept curled up with a blanket thrown over her, as one might sleep on a bench in a park or a station waiting room, and in the morning I would find her in the kitchen making a cup of coffee—*turecka,* she called it, although its resemblance to Turkish coffee was minimal—her hair tousled, her face puffed up and creased from where it had been pressed against her arm or the folds in the blanket or the rough, worn velvet of the sofa. She would be wearing a large, shapeless black T-shirt. Her legs were pallid and awkward, as though embarrassed by their nudity. She would acknowledge my presence with little more than a nod, and then she would shut herself in the bathroom and emerge after half an hour wearing her makeup—thick makeup applied to her skin like clotted cream and lipstick like an open wound—and leave the apartment. She would say almost nothing to me beyond the word *ciao,* which perhaps appealed to her because it has been taken up by American youth and smacks of indolence and bubble gum. Each day I thought she might not reappear—her paltry things were hardly hostage against her return—but each evening she was back, the makeup less intense, the manner the same: quiet, introverted concentration. I seemed barely to exist for her.

And on the fourth night, as silent as a nocturnal mammal, she crept into my room and slid into my bed.

Magda knew immediately, of course. I was surprised at the time, but now I understand. Magda knew all about me. She lay curled up in my bed like a cat, indifferent but knowing.

2

 s that Father Leo Newman?" A female voice with that faint and tell-tale accent, the *th* halfway between a fricative and a plosive.

"It is."

"This is Madeleine Brewer. We met at that reception. Perhaps you remember?"

"Of course I remember."

"I told you I'd ring. Will you come to dinner? Is next Wednesday all right? I know it's rather short notice, but . . ."

Of course he would.

The Brewers had an apartment in the Borgo Pio near the Vatican City. It was the kind of place that embassies keep on for their staff, the square meters carefully equated with rank on the basis of some secret bureaucratic formula, their particular rating being high, for Jack was a minister or something. They ate in a large and slightly dusty dining room with photographs of the children on a grand piano and a painting of a saint—female, distraught—above the vast fireplace. Madeleine felt the need to apologize for the place: "It's like living in a sacristy. I think it once belonged to a cardinal and he left all his holy pictures behind and now we have to look after them because they're so valuable and if we didn't they'd just go into some cellar beneath the Palazzo Barberini or something."

The saint over the fireplace seemed pained by the prospect. A monstrance in her hand betrayed her identity to those who could interpret such things. "She's Saint Clare," Madeleine said. "Just up Saul's street." This remark was directed at another of the guests, a journalist of some kind. "Clare's your patron saint," she explained.

"I have a *patron saint?*" He was Jewish—Goldstaub—and looked nervous at the prospect.

"Oh, certainly. Patron saints don't give a damn about your religion. They are highly ecumenical." And Madeleine launched into a little dissertation on patron saints. "There is a typical Catholic logic to the whole matter," she explained. "Saint Lucy had her eyes put out, so she's patron saint of opticians. Saint Apollonia had her teeth knocked out, so she got dentists. Clare is the patron saint of television because popular legend has it that she appeared in two places at the same time. Pope Paul appointed her."

"Pope Paul the *Sixth?*" The journalist seemed aghast.

"The very one."

"They still *do* this kind of thing? You're joking."

"I am deadly serious, aren't I, darling?"

Jack smiled indulgently from the other end of the table. "Maddy is always at her most serious when she is being absurd."

"Now, Saint Lawrence was roasted alive on a gridiron—"

"And got barbecues." The journalist was getting the idea.

"Near enough. Cooks. Saint Stephen is bricklayers. They stoned him. Saint Sebastian, archers."

"Archers?"

"They shot him. A hundred arrows. You've seen the pictures, surely."

"I thought that was Saint Bartholomew."

"He was flayed alive. Patron saint of taxidermists. Oh, and Saint Joseph of Copertino is the patron saint of airmen."

"*Airmen?* But, hell, they didn't *have* airplanes."

"They do now. Saint Joseph used to fly around the place, so they chose him for the job."

"He used to *fly?*"

"Fly. It's quite well attested. He was sometime in the sixteenth century, so it's not all that long ago. Anyway, don't you have flying rabbis?"

"Not in Borough Park, we don't." The man turned to Newman for some kind of authoritative judgment. "Hey, this is your scene, Father. Is all this true?"

Leo Newman, sweating and awkward at the other end of the table, agreed that it was, more or less. "The trick is to treat the absurdities of the faith as genial eccentricities, as proof of the boundless confidence of the believer. It's not an article of faith. You don't have to *believe* it."

"I should hope not."

Madeleine caught the priest's eye. "Does Father Leo believe it, though?" And that was the moment when something turned inside him, something visceral, like the first symptom of disease. That was what made it all the more disturbing, that it seemed so profoundly organic. The cerebral he could deal with. The cerebral he could battle against, had long ago learned to battle against. Mental images were things he could chase from his mind like Christ chasing the money-changers from the Temple (an incident that is generally accepted by the most skeptical of New Testament scholars as genuine, indeed pivotal). But when it was the temple of the body that was under assault, the dismissal was not so easy. No easier to dismiss a cancer. And her glance at him as they sat at the long dining table beneath the benevolent eye of Jack and the agonized eye of *Saint Clare Contemplating the Eucharist,* School of Guido Reni, seemed to plant the first seeds of some disease in his body.

"I don't know," he replied lamely.

"I think you do," she said with that smile. "I think Father Leo is a skeptic." And the word *skeptic* splintered the atmosphere in the room with its harsh consonants, its barbed resonances.

Newman was one of the last to leave that evening. He felt a need to apologize as he was shown to the door. "I've outstayed my welcome."

Madeleine helped him on with his coat, turned him around like a child to adjust the lapels. "Not at all," she said. Others were already going down the stairs, opening the outside door onto the street, allowing a draft of damp winter air to scurry into the stairwell. "We're delighted that you thought it worth staying. You'll come again, won't you?"

"Will I?"

"If you'd like to. I'll be in touch." She looked at him curiously. "I tell you what . . ."

"What will you tell me?"

"Show me your work. Can you do that? That's what I'd like to see."

"At the Institute? It's very dull. Books, documents, nothing interesting at all."

"Let me be the judge of that."

"Look."

They were in the manuscript rooms of the Pontifical Biblical Institute, surrounded by gray steel shelving, lulled by the distant hum of air-conditioning and dust filtering, enveloped in a sterile atmosphere designed to suspend what had been previously suspended only by good fortune: the subtle decay of the texts. The old Dominican who was the archivist fussed somewhere in the background, searching for something spectacular and medieval to show her, something miniated, rubricated, illuminated with its own inner, pious fire.

"Look," Leo said. He had a computer on, the screen live and shining. A dun-colored fibrous fragment hung there behind the glass, a fragment of papyrus the color of biscuit, inscribed with the most perfect letters ever man devised, words wrought in the lean and ragged language of the Eastern Mediterranean, the workaday language of the streets, the meanings half apprehended, half grasped, half heard through the noise of all that lies between us and them, the shouting, roaring centuries of darkness and enlightenment. How was it possible to communicate to her the pure, organic thrill?

"Is this one of your pieces? One of the things you are working on?"

He nodded. "The En-Mor papyri."

"What exactly is En-Mor?"

"A place. A God-forsaken place by all accounts, except that I suppose these finds show that God never forsakes anywhere. I've never been to the actual site. It's just a dig run by the Israeli authorities. And they found these fragments in a cave nearby." He traced the words on the screen with his finger. "*Kai eis pyr*. And into the fire. That's what it says. Possibly from Matthew, a proto-Matthew. Matthew chapter 3, verse 10: 'Every tree that does not produce good fruit is to be thrown into the fire.' Or Luke. They both have the same words."

He could hear the whisper of her breath beside his ear. She leaned forward to see, leaned over his shoulder; and he was enveloped not by the mystery of the ancient script, its perfect characters, its tantalizing context, but by the soft warmth of her presence, by the touch of a stray wisp of her hair, by her scent.

"We're not certain, of course. Nothing's ever certain. But the site is thought to date from the first century. There's the possibility that what we have are fragments of Q." She wanted to know. Her expression told Leo of her interest. Not mere politeness. "Q is *Quelle,* the source," he explained. "The collection of teachings that Matthew and Luke have in common, but which is not found in Mark. Now this phrase actually comes from the preaching of John the Baptist . . ."

"Isn't it extraordinary?" she breathed. Casually, quite casually, she laid a hand on his shoulder as she leaned forward. That physical contact sounded louder in his mind than any ideas. "So these are the oldest known bits of the New Testament?"

"Probably. But it's more than just age. These finds almost prove that the source of the New Testament, *one* of the written sources at least, predates the Jewish War. Now the implications of that . . ."

She seemed to be interested, that was what was so remarkable. She seemed to want to listen to him, whereas Jack would just smile and nod and change the subject with a diplomat's arrogance and a diplomatic unconcern. "Does it really *matter?*" Leo had heard him ask. "In this day and age does it really *matter* any longer?" And Madeleine had answered her husband tartly: "To me it does. To millions of people all over the world, as well. Not the clever ones like you, maybe. Not Her Majesty's bloody Foreign Office, unless it has a political angle. But to *people* it matters."

"So what's the place that you work for called?" she asked him now. "The World Bible Center? Tell me about it."

He smiled, not really knowing himself, not understanding the dynamics of the thing, the apparent random chance of it all, the manipulation of the hand of contingency that might be mistaken for the hand of God. A few months previously, that was all. There had been a telephone call in the middle of a dull morning, the voice of the director of the World Bible Center in Jerusalem wanting to speak to Father Leo Newman please, and was that Father Leo himself, and how happy he, Steve Calder, was to renew an old friendship with Leo after all this time. Leo knew Calder from a conference in California the year before. He remembered hair of perfect platinum and teeth of pearl. He remembered a low-slung villa amid weeping willows and immaculate lawns and an illuminated swimming pool in which a Roman Catholic bishop was swimming in the company of a female Evangelical pastor. He remembered an argument during the evening barbecue about the Jesus Seminar, that group of academics who thought that biblical truth could be approached on a democratic basis, by a show of hands. Calder had been an enthusiastic supporter—"We've got to get more rationality and less faith into the debate," he had cried. "Faith is the enemy of discovery."

Fool or fraud?

"Leo, I want your help," the man had said over the phone. "We've got one hell of a find. A place on the Dead Sea called En-Mor. You know it? Well they've just turned up a whole slew of papyrus fragments. And we need someone of your status to help with these things. I'll give you a look at the material and I'll give you time to think about it. But I know you won't need the time. I know when you see these things you'll be hammering on our door and crying to be let in."

The first photographs had come by courier the next day. There was that anguish of anticipation as he sat at his desk and struggled to open the package, fiddling with the plastic wrapper, tearing the waybill aside and slitting open the inner envelope to discover inside a single photograph, ten inches by eight. Of course he recognized the thing immediately as he slid it out onto the polished surface of his desk, recognized it in a generic sense, that is: a high-resolution photograph of a flake of papyrus. The fragment was five inches by four. There was a ruler laid alongside to give a scale. It was five inches by four and the edges were frayed and the texture of the material, the warp and weft of the plant fibers, was clear; and there were four lines of writing running across it. The text was blurred and scoured as though by a rough eraser, but the lines of writing were as straight as if they had been ruled, with all the exactness of a machine and all the individuality of an artifact. The ink was faded to brown, but the characters were somehow still fresh—bright, live things. Koine. The language was Koine, the demotic Greek of the Roman Empire, the lingua franca of the Eastern Mediterranean, the language that anyone with an education would have spoken in those days, the language of commerce and exchange, the language of administration and law. Jesus would have spoken Koine. He would have talked to Pilate in Koine.

Leo had turned the photograph over just to see, to delay the moment of reading, just as one might savor a childhood treat by deliberately putting it off. On the back was a circular stamp, a stylized globe with the title WORLD BIBLE CENTER, JERUSALEM wrapped around the edge like an atmosphere; and a catalog number.

Then he had turned back and started to read.

It was like solving a crossword clue. One word had stood out. One word had given the whole piece away, a single word that occurs a mere four times in the whole of the New Testament: *gennemata*. Offspring. He checked in his concordance, his hands shaking with excitement as he lifted the volume down from the shelf. Then there were a mere three letters of the following word, but there could be little doubt about them either: epsilon-chi-iota. E-Ch-I.

Echinos, a hedgehog.

He had laughed aloud at the thought, laughed to himself in the silence of his room. Offspring of hedgehogs. He had wanted someone with whom he could share the joke, someone who would have laughed with excitement at the whole thing. But there was no one there. Just the institutional sounds outside: the slamming of a door, the laboring of the elevator as it moved down to the ground floor, music playing in a nearby room. He almost got up from his desk and ran to the door to call someone, anyone to share his emotion, but he didn't.

It wasn't *echinos* of course; it was *echidnon*. Vipers. Offspring of vipers.

The rest had been easy.

"I suppose it was what I'd been hoping for all my life," he told Madeleine. "Concrete evidence that the gospels, at least the source of the gospels, predate the Jewish War, and that therefore they contain genuine eyewitness accounts."

"But surely that's obvious."

"But surely nothing at all. You know what the name Jesus actually *means?*"

"Isn't it just a name?"

He shook his head. "In this business you always start with the name. Names always had meanings. Jesus is the Greek form of Joshua, Yehoshua, and it means *God is salvation*. So you can see it's easy enough to explain Jesus away as just the personification of faith in God, not a historical figure at all. If the earliest manuscripts only come from the first century, if the gospels themselves were written that late—after Paul's ministry, let's say—then it's easy to make the kind of claim that you hear often enough, that Christ was a construct of the early Church, a mythic figure given some kind of historical identity in order to help simple people believe."

"And you've disproved it all."

He shrugged. "It was clear from the start that these pieces were early. Second century for sure. You see those characters?" She watched and listened with that focus that she had, the moment when the bright and ironical became focused as though by a lens. "What we call *zierstil,* decorated style. See the gamma? Second century at least. And then there's the use of the iota ad-script, which died out in the second century, and suddenly I thought, my God, this might be older than the Rylands fragment." He looked around from the picture. "And I realized that this find was sensational. The earliest New Testament text from the Holy Land, probably the earliest in existence."

The images came over the telephone lines. Every few days he logged on to the Bible Center's server and found the pictures wait-ing for him, two images for each fragment along with a catalog number, nothing more. One image would be high resolution and time-consuming to download. The other would be a smaller ver-sion to give the general idea of things. The ragged scraps would unfurl themselves on the screen of his computer and hang there in the luminous rectangle of light like pieces of old, tattered rag; like bunting from a celebration held long, long ago. They gave an illusion of reality. You could see the shadows they cast on the white background; you could see the individual fibers flaking off from the edges. A row of dun-colored flags signaling from the past, a strange and cryptic semaphore:

... *winnowing fork is in his hand and* ... *[he will gather the wheat into]* ... *his granary, but the chaff he will burn with unquenchable fire* ...

Fragments of the Gospel of Matthew, from a site that could probably be dated to the time of the Jewish War and the burning of the Temple. He was reading the oldest gospel texts known; he was doing what, as a child, he had dreamt of doing, when, father-less and alone, he had passed hours in solitary thought in the chapel of the seminary: he was reaching out his hand to touch the Jesus of history.

The *Times* came out with the story first: NEW FINDS NEAR THE DEAD SEA CONFIRM HISTORICITY OF NEW TESTAMENT. The tabloids put it more succinctly: PAPYRUS PROVES GOSPELS. It was a mild sensation, ringing faint echoes around the world in the inner pages of newspapers, meriting mention toward the end of news broadcasts. Leo Newman found himself crammed into a darkened cell in the BBC studios in Rome to talk to a disembodied voice in London who asked questions like, "How does this make the Jesus story more meaningful for the twenty-first century?" A group of American Bible scholars set about trying to prove, using an elaborate computer analysis, that the fragments were not Christian at all but came instead from a long-lost part of the book of the prophet Hosea. The Pope himself made a private visit to the Institute to view the images and confer a shaky blessing on the head of Father Leo Newman. "A lion in the battle for truth," he said. "A voice of truth for the millennium."

Lord, save me from the sin of self-regard, Leo had prayed, while the shock waves reverberated around the globe and trembled in the background, like a distant storm.

He watched as she walked around the manuscript room, a bright splash of color among the gray and brown, a sharp stroke of the profane among the studiously devout. "Isn't there the corrupt smell of ambition in all this?" Her tone was faintly mocking, touched with that astringent irony that so intrigued him. "Isn't there pride and ambition? Shouldn't faith be enough?"

"Perhaps faith is never enough."

"What's that meant to mean? Don't you have enough faith? You're a priest."

"It's not lack of faith, although perhaps there is always that. It's the intrusion of other things, human things."

She waited a moment for him to continue, standing over by the window and watching him with what was left of her expression once the smile had gone, a look of concern and faint bewilderment. Then abruptly she changed her tone. "I must go," she said, making a show of looking at her watch. "I'm afraid I must

leave you to your texts." And she began to gather up her things—
her handbag and scarf. Her umbrella? That had been surrendered
at the entrance to the manuscript rooms. "Thank you so much for
showing me round, Leo. It has been fascinating." Briskness again,
a sharp change of tone, a confusing sensation that one person had
just been replaced by another.

He turned the computer off. "I'm afraid they won't search
your handbag when you leave," he said. "But they ought to. They
don't really know how to deal with women—they can't imagine a
woman coming here and stealing anything."

"But you can?"

"I can imagine almost anything. That has always been my
abiding sin."

"Is it a sin?"

"I don't know. Maybe it is, yes, because you always end up believing the worst of people." He showed her to the main door. The
porter glanced at them through the window of his cell and then
went back to reading the sports paper.

"Do you think the worst of me?" she asked. They stood for a
moment in the entrance. The urgency of her departure seemed to
have vanished.

"I think the best of you."

"That is *very* dangerous." She touched his arm. She might
have raised herself on her toes and kissed him on the cheek, but it
didn't seem appropriate just there, beneath the plaque that talked
of popes and pontiffs, of stern fathers and bridge-builders between God and man. So she just squeezed his arm, a quick sharp
grasp, and told him that she would be in touch soon and turned
and walked away down the narrow street, her shoes clipping on
the stones, her feet wobbling on the awkward unevenness of the
setts. And he felt an absurd and pungent sense of loss.

3

L eo among the women and the coffee cups, with Saint Clare looking down on him with anguish as though appalled to see one of her kind embroiled in the trivial and the quotidian. Leo answering polite questions politely—they had been to see the Roman cemetery beneath the crypt of Saint Peter's—and wanting Madeleine to come and speak to him. He felt like an adolescent, that was what was so galling. He felt like a teenager (horrendous word with its meretricious, transatlantic connotations) trying to attract the attention of some older girl, while she moved through the group of women with a disturbing, adult assurance.

Finally she came over to him. The topic of the Roman burial ground had been exhausted. All around them the women were talking of families, of children and schools, of houses and maids and vacations. "Tell me about yourself," she asked. "Is that allowed? What kind of family produces a priest?"

"You wouldn't want to know about my family," he assured her. "It wasn't like yours."

"What's that meant to mean? Wasn't it happy? All happy families are the same, aren't they? Where does that come from?"

"Tolstoy."

"*Anna Karenina,* that's it. All happy families are the same; each unhappy family is unhappy in its own way. Is it true?"

Why should she want to know? What interest could she have? The women came up to offer thanks and farewells. "You'll stay for some lunch?" she asked him.

"I don't want to overstay my welcome again."

She laughed, and offered no answer. He watched her smiling and laughing, shaking hands, offering a smooth cheek for a farewell kiss, two farewell kisses, one on each cheek, turning the other cheek, a consummate performance. From on top of the grand piano, framed in silver, Jack and the two girls laughed at the scene. He found himself trying to picture the small rituals of her family life, what the Brewers would do and what they would say to one another. His imagination was defective in such matters, a stunted thing with no experience to call on. It was as though he had trespassed into a foreign territory, a place with its own customs, its own language, with all the attraction of the unfamiliar. He was entranced. His own family, his tiny, fragile family was a different organism from hers, a different institution, hedged about with a past it couldn't talk about and an inheritance it couldn't acknowledge.

"Tell me," Madeleine said when the last of the women had left. "You tell me and I'll listen."

So he told her. Confession of a kind, explication and expiation woven together. He told Madeleine of his home life, musty with the smell of a vanished past and cloying with the attentions of a pious widowed mother who brooked no interference from the outside world beyond the inattentive children who came around for piano lessons. Homes have their own smell, their own amalgam of scents and flavors: his had been redolent of incense, gathered devoutly into his mother's clothes when she went to mass each morning and brought back to the house, to be extruded into the heavy, languorous atmosphere. A candle, burning perpetually before an icon of the Blessed Madonna and Child, added its waxen perfume.

"Sounds very Irish," was Madeleine's opinion.

"Not Irish, not anything. A strange creation of my mother's. Her family had been Jewish once—Neumann, Newman. Her mother was a convert."

"But Newman's *your* name." There was a silence. Implications were considered, matters of legitimacy and illegitimacy, those terms that once ranked high in the potency of language. The word *bastard*.

He slid past the obstacle. "I never knew my father. He died before I was born. I was the only male in the house. All the others who ever came seem to have been women: my mother's partners in bridge, her piano pupils, the maids, two distant cousins who called occasionally—spinsters or widows, I never really knew which—all were women." The incontinence of confession. They sat at either end of a capacious sofa, legs crossed, hers demurely with her skirt pulled down to the gleaming disc of her patella, his extravagantly with his ankle resting on his knee. "I've never talked about these things before, do you realize that? Never had the opportunity, I suppose."

"You don't have to now. Not if you don't want to."

"She's dead. One is meant to speak well of the dead."

"Can't you speak well of her?"

"I've never really understood the theological basis for the idea.

Surely there is a greater need to speak well of the living. Let the dead bury their dead, isn't that what Our Lord said?"

"So tell me."

There was a strange intimacy in talking about it to Madeleine, a sense of confession in reverse, her absolution for his memories. "I adored her, of course. I had little choice in the matter. Her rages, her sarcasm, her indifference were terrible weapons. So was her affection. *My lion,* she always called me, *my little brave lion.* She suffocated me, I suppose. With love and affection, of course; and with a history that was not mine, that never would be mine."

"History?"

"You know the kind of thing: ancestors, disasters." There was something receptive about Madeleine, as though she exerted a gravitational pull on him, drawing him toward her: his secrets, his past, his very personality. "Tell me," she said.

He couldn't recall his mother as a young woman. In his memory her eyes were the only thing that retained an illusion of youth: they were as bright and blue as the eyes of a china doll, gazing out in surprise through the decaying mask of her face as though startled to find time passing and flesh decaying. For the rest, she only possessed the relics of good looks, like an aged actress trying to deny the years. The skin of her cheek was soft and waxy and dusted with a fine powdery down like mildew; her mouth, approximately edged with lipstick, held the shadow of a lost sensuality in the way that a painting may show traces of an earlier figure lying underneath. "My manikin, my *Männlein,* come and give your mother a kiss," she would say, and her embrace was heavy with that incense and the rosaceous perfume that she habitually wore. When he was ill he slept in her bed and felt her body, a perfumed presence, a strange melding of the gaunt and the fleshy, close to his. And sometimes the emotion of holding him against her loose breasts (what emotion? what anguish lay behind her cloying at-tentions?) drove her to tears, so that her features would collapse like wet paper, making a grim contrast with her bright, old-fashioned dresses and her brassy hair. A doll left out in the rain, he used to think; and added that to a list of uncharitable thoughts he had to expiate. "What is the matter, Mother?" he would ask. "Tell me the matter?" But she would shake her head bravely and deny that it was anything that Leo had done, or could do, or could even imagine. The unimaginable was what haunted her, and haunted therefore his childish prayers as he knelt beside his bed at night. "Your father, your poor, poor father," she would moan, and from silver frames on the piano, on the sideboard, on the mantelshelf, he looked down at the pair of them, a man of imposing serious-ness, with a face that bore within it the lean, long lineaments of duty. "He watches over us, of course he does. He sees us, he knows our thoughts, he understands our weaknesses . . ."

"How on earth did you survive?" Madeleine exclaimed when Leo described it to her, but the question was meaningless. The person he might otherwise have been did not survive. What did survive was the person he became. What did survive was the man who found himself prostrated on the ground before the altar of a Roman basilica along with three dozen other postulants laid out like so many corpses before the bishop. And his mother watching from a front pew, dressed in funereal black, with a black veil over her head (already out of ecclesiastical fashion) and funereal tears in her eyes.

Elation? Ecstasy? Enthusiasm? A fine, abstruse theological word: French *enthousiasme* or Late Latin *enthusiasmus,* from Greek *enthousiasmos,* from *entheos,* "possessed by a god, inspired." The power of it all, the sense of possession quite as vivid as mere car-nal love, a sensation of climax more potent than paltry orgasm. They had warned him in advance, of course: beware of the emotions, his spiritual adviser had said—emotions bring only pain and deception.

"Why are you crying?" he asked his mother after the ceremony. "Isn't this meant to be a happy moment?"

"I'm weeping for Leo that was," she said. A biblical turn of phrase that ranked with the very best of her utterances.

The Church of the Sisters of Our Lady of Mercy, a church of impressive purity and plainness in a city where the baroque abounds, a church attached to a community that seemed battened against the modern world, against the forces of Mammon and the forces of darkness. During the night the sisters ran a soup kitchen and shelter for illegal immigrants—Albanians, Moroccans, Kurds—and during the day they watched and prayed; and on Saturday evenings they poured out their confessions of peccadillo and scruple in the stuffy confines of the confessional where Leo Newman sat listening. It was a relic pastoral duty that he kept up as though to remind himself of something half forgotten among the texts and the scripts: the point of it all, the love for one's fellow man that was meant to underpin one's vocation. During the week he dissected the words from the past, words from beyond the great divide that was the Jewish War and the destruction of the Holy City of Jerusalem; while on Saturday evenings he put all that behind him and went around to the sisters' convent and put on his stole and sat in a bare room beside a grille and heard their trifling confessions. The next day, shriven and absolved, they doffed their functional overalls and dressed in their traditional habits and sat like a flock of gulls within the confines of the thirteenth-century choir enclosure, while he celebrated mass.

There would always be a few members of the public in the congregation: passing tourists drawn in by the perfect, birdlike purity of the nuns' voices singing in choir; a few pious women who lived nearby; a vagrant or two; a gypsy begging. And one day there was Madeleine Brewer.

She sat far at the back of the church in the shadows of the organ loft, her green jacket like a sharp spot of paint in the gloom, her face without visible expression. She sat motionless for the homily—a discussion of Saint Paul's letter to the Galatians, a record of the first internecine quarrel of the Church—and at the climactic moment of the mass, at the invocation of the Lamb of God who came to take away the sins of the world, at the moment when the sisters' voices floated up from the choir in the communion hymn, she slid out of the pew to join the line of communicants.

The faithful shuffled forward.

"Il corpo di Cristo."

Father Newman raised the host before their eyes.

"Il corpo di Cristo."

Host, *ostia,* one of those vestiges which emerge out of the modern language like half-hidden words in a palimpsest—*hostia:* a sacrificial victim. Once a garlanded bull being led to the altar for ritual slaughter, now a little fragment of wafer that may or may not embody the sacrificed Christ.

"Il corpo di Cristo."

Some communicants held out supplicant hands to receive the wafer; others waited, lips open, for the host to be posted into their mouths. It was a muddle that liturgical reform had created and never resolved.

"Il corpo di Cristo."

The sisters sang of the Lord who has made his wonderful works to be remembered; who is gracious and full of compassion; who has given meat unto them that fear him; who is ever mindful of his covenant.

"Il corpo di Cristo."

And Madeleine Brewer stepped up to the altar rail and stood

before him, with her hands folded demurely before her and her chin up as though to face an awful truth with defiance. Her mouth opened to let the tiny, glistening tip of her tongue touch her lower lip.

"The body of Christ," he announced to her. He spoke in English, and lest there be any doubt, he held up the small disk, a mere flake as light as a butterfly's wing, for her to see.

"Amen," she murmured.

He reached forward and touched the flake to glistening, pink flesh. She drew her tongue back. Her lips closed and the host was gone. For a moment she shut her eyes. Then she gave a small, impersonal smile, turned away and walked down the empty aisle back to her place.

Initium sapientiae timor Domini, sang the sisters: the fear of the Lord is the beginning of wisdom: a good understanding have they that follow His commandments.

At the end of the service he hurried into the sacristy to divest. He hoped—it was a hope so secret that he almost managed to keep it from himself—that she would be waiting outside; but, except for a pair of indifferent tourists, he found the nave of the church empty when he emerged.

Families and the power of families. Families weighed on Leo Newman's mind, the peculiar intensity of families, what they mean and have meant. Families as the natural selfishness of man writ large, man straining beyond the feeble confines of his body in order to possess things beyond his reach—including the future. Families as life, and families as death; families as creation and families as destruction; families nurturing love and suckling hate; families as the beginning and the end.

Families are paramount in the New Testament. There is, for instance, Herod's family against Jesus'. Leo worried at the problem during those days. He worried at the matter of blood and inheritance. Consider this string of facts, this woven circlet of thorns, picked carefully out of the brambles of the New Testament and laid before the students of the Pontifical Biblical Institute: Jesus came from a priestly, royal family; as a newborn infant he apparently risked death at the hands of Herod because he, by way of this family, had some kind of claim to the throne of Israel. When he was in his thirties this claim burst into life through his cousin John, son of a temple priest Zechariah and a woman of the House of David. John started a popular movement in Judaea and Galilee. Religious or secular, the distinction didn't exist in those days— John started a movement and it disturbed the edifice of power. He attacked Herod's son Antipas on grounds that were both moral and dynastic, and for his pains he was flung into prison on the far side of the Dead Sea.

"You may ask yourself why, if John was nothing more than a half-crazed preacher, he should have mattered so much?" Father Newman asked his students. They shifted uneasily in their seats, sensing the sharp smell of heterodoxy. "Salome danced her sinuous dance (we know the name from Josephus, the dance from Mark and Matthew) and called for John's head, and when her wish was granted, it was his cousin Jesus who took up the baton on behalf of the family. 'Are you the one, or do we look for another?' they asked of him."

He eyed the audience with a certain curiosity, as though they not he were on show. "Never doubt the claim," Leo Newman warned them. "It has come down to us through the centuries, through the telling and the texts, through the copying and the glossing and the interpolations and the excisions: there it is in three languages on the titulus above his head when he hung on the cross: THE KING OF THE JEWS."

Some members of the audience crossed themselves.

"That was the claim for which he died. If the whole thing was mere history and the gospels merely historical texts, Our Lord's ministry would be put down as nothing more or less than an attempt to take the throne of Judaea back from the colonial rulers and the satraps, an appeal to the God of Israel, a return to the spirit of the Maccabees."

And he paused at that point, for here the merely heterodox trespassed over into heresy. For the signal fact is that after Jesus' death his brother James inherited the leadership, and the Church admits no siblings in the family of Nazareth, no other children of the perpetually virgin Mary. And yet there it is, in the Acts of the Apostles and in Josephus: John to Jesus; Jesus to James. Inheritance and succession: the Janus feature of families. Inheritance and succession: the grindstones that crush the child to dust.

Family, and the power of family. Madeleine's family had its own curious argot, its own exclusive customs. Like a stranger in a foreign land, Leo Newman, priest of the Pontifical Biblical Institute, began to learn. "Beano," they said, "pass the beano," when they meant wine. "*Issma*" signified "come here" because they had spent some time in Cairo, where Jack was First Secretary; Madeleine was "buffled" when she was confused, and things were "famulus" when they were good, and Jack was "jabber" when he was telling the rest of them off. Jack was brisk and jovial, a man with both brain and brawn, a man who had the word *ambassador* engraved on his heart. The elder of their two daughters, seasonal orphans at a boarding school in England, had been christened Catherine because that was the name of Jack's Oxford college, which was where, he assured Leo, he had come to loathe Anglo-Saxon and love Madeleine. He treated Madeleine with mild amusement—Maddy, he called her, with its faint suggestion of amiable madness—while to his children he granted an impersonal affection, as though there was little difference between the two of them, as though they were both some kind of household pet. The younger daughter, for reasons that were never clear, was called "Boot"; but *acushla* was either of the girls, for it comes from *a chuisle mo chroidhe* and is Irish for "pulse of my heart."

The metamorphosis of a relationship is a mysterious thing, much too mysterious for a simple naming. One may interpret it in retrospect, as a historian will look over the trace of past events and descry a thread, a logical development; but at the time, in time, there is no thread, is there? There is nothing more than the contingent facts of existence, the small moment as significant as the large, the detail dictating to the whole. Leo was an acquaintance, he became a friend. Family outings, the occasional party, a concert or two, that kind of thing. And whereas acquaintance may be shared with others, friendship is an exclusive thing, with its own cryptic dimensions, its own assonance. He would start a sentence and find his own words trampling on Madeleine's identical ones. He would glance at her, and find her watching him with bewilderment there in her expression, as though she was trying to puzzle out words from a language she didn't fully understand. They smiled and watched each other smiling. Casual contact—the merest touch of a wrist, arm brushing shoulder—became something that each was aware of.

"It's a bit like having our own personal chaplain," Jack remarked of his presence one day when they were out walking in the Alban Hills.

"Good gracious, I hope not," Leo protested, and Madeleine echoed his words exactly—"Good gracious, I hope not"—so that the twin supplications stumbled across one another and it was unclear who had spoken first. There was something embarrassing about the coincidence, as though they had been caught embracing and needed to provide some kind of excuse.

"You always laugh at the same things," her older daughter said; and her words, with their tone of accusation, brought a strange silence to the group, as though something had been said that should have been covered up, kept secret, been consigned to the limbo wherein are laid matters of family disgrace.

The thread of contingency is inscrutable. Somewhere above the Dead Sea a ragtag group of students and archaeologists was at work picking over the bones of the past, kneeling in the dust and sifting fragments from the rubbish, and finding there the first hints of disaster. While somewhere in Rome a married woman and a dry and sterile priest shared something fragmentary and ill-defined: a sympathy, a sense of irony, a feeling of doubt, a sensation of discovery.

"May I ask you a dangerous question, Leo?" Madeleine was smiling her small, Irish smile and watching him in that way she had, with her head tilted slightly on one side. Questions in the confessional are dangerous, but this was not the confessional—this was somewhere mundane: the kitchen of the Brewers' apartment, amid a litter of bottles and unwashed glasses. Beyond the kitchen door was the noise of a party. Jack was holding forth about dealings with an Italian ministry, about the absurdities of the bureaucracy, the arcane hierarchies, the subtle obligations and inducements. "It's not so much *who* you know," Leo heard him saying, "it's who they *think* you know."

"May I?"

"Go on."

She paused, as though perhaps building up her courage. "Did you join the priesthood because you don't like women?"

He felt a faint reddening, perhaps a glimmer of anger. "No, of course that's not the reason."

A maid came in with a tray and there was a brief exchange in pidgin Italian. When she had gone he found Madeleine looking at him curiously, as if she were standing before an abstract painting and trying to make sense of it. She seemed to have steeled herself to pursue the matter. "But is it so? That you don't, I mean."

"I'm not homosexual, if that's what you're asking."

She looked away, busied herself with a plate of canapés. "I'm sorry. I shouldn't have asked. I'm sorry if I've made you cross."

"You haven't made me cross."

"Yes I have. I can tell better than you can yourself. I know that expression. But I just wanted to know. You probably don't understand, but I wanted to know."

He watched her go out into the noise of the party, watched the quick and artful way she switched mood as the laughter and chatter greeted her in the other room. He watched her join the party and he thought of Elise. A lifetime trying to banish her image to the depths of his psyche, but still it rose to the surface. Elise, who had come nearest to breaking through whatever barriers he had set up in adolescence; Elise, who had almost upset the strange physics of sublimation that is the key to celibacy. Even after all those years he could picture her still, as though she were sitting out there on the sofa among the crowded adults of Madeleine's party, her knees demurely together, her patent leather shoes carefully parked side by side. He had been nineteen, Elise a mere fifteen. She possessed a pretty and totally mendacious downward cast of the eyes, rosy cheeks that might have been applied with rouge, rather heavy eyebrows, and a faint, dark down at the corners of her upper lip. The little pianist. She used to play "Für Elise," partly because that was her name but mainly because it was also the only piece she could manage at all competently, being too lazy, so his mother said, to practice.

Laziness is next to sinfulness, his mother said.

Remove occasion for sin and you remove the sin, she said.

But the memory? How do you expunge that?

It was one day during the Easter holidays that Elise came around to the Newmans' apartment. Leo had never met her before, never even seen her, had no idea who she was when he opened the front door to her and found her standing there on the doormat that said WELCOME but didn't really mean it. The girl was slightly pigeon-toed—patent leather pigeon-toed. Her blue dress hovered uncertainly between childhood and adolescence, having flowers scattered across its surface and a bow at the back, but also an ample décolletage that lifted and displayed precocious breasts. A pleasing blush touched her cheeks. The blush was, he could feel, reflected in his own face.

"Is Mrs. Newman in?"

"She's out."

"Who are you, then?"

"Her son."

"I have a piano lesson with her."

"I thought she rang to cancel it."

The girl shook her head. "No," she replied. "No, she didn't." And Leo smelled the sour and flinty stench of mendacity, for he *knew* that his mother had telephoned. He had heard her make the call.

"Maybe you should come in and wait," he suggested. His blush deepened, with shame for the girl and shame for himself as he compounded her lie: "I don't think she'll be long." For behind the smell of mendacity there was something else: the subtle, physical perfume of complicity. She *would* be long. His mother's cousin was ill. Her cousin lived somewhere out of London and his mother would be gone until late evening, leaving him all alone to study for looming examinations. Theology. Classical Philosophy. Ancient History.

Remove the occasion and you remove the sin.

Leo Newman, awkward and withdrawn junior seminarian, stood aside and invited the occasion in, and it sat there prim and rapacious before him in the chintz armchair where his mother normally sat, its knees pressed together, its mouth (a dark red bud like the mouth of a Pre-Raphaelite Madonna) pursed in an expression of studied allure, its patent leather shoes settled on the carpet like tiny little coffins; while the crucified Christ watched from the wall above the piano on whose lucid surface the silver-framed relatives (dead father, deader grandparents) watched like a grim jury.

"Tea?" he asked. "Would you like tea?"

Yes, she told him, yes, she would like tea.

Inviting Elise in and assuring her of his mother's imminent return was also the only initiative that he took in the whole of the affair. Every other move—the artful, arch conversation they held over a cup of tea, the promise to meet in the Botanical Gardens the following afternoon, the hot, damp kisses which they finally exchanged two weekends later—all of those were Elise's. Elise was practiced and eager: he was hesitant and shy. "You do *this,* you silly," she said, and he found her tongue, as wet and warm as a tropical fish, flapping around inside his mouth. "And if you touch my bosom I will *not* mind, although you may not put your hand up my skirt, for that is vulgar so early on in our relationship." Her breast was a soft bud of a thing, live beneath his fingers. As he touched it she remained as still as a bird.

There followed a season of assignations without his mother's knowledge, a random collection of walks along the canal, of nervous and distasteful gropings on discreet park benches (once they were moved on by a policeman, another time shouted at by a woman), all culminating in a climactic visit to a malodorous cinema during which Elise reversed her previous proscription. Her breath in Leo's ear was a soft and sultry thing, more sensation than suggestion: "Touch me *there,*" it whispered. And he did, twisting his hand upward and inward (an awkward trick that he could only improvise) over nylon and a curve of bare flesh, past elastic, past gusset, to find the sudden surprise of hair and a soft and malleable wetness, like something that one might discover, groping with blind hands, in a tide pool: something bearded and molluscan.

Excitement? Tumescence? Of course. And revulsion. Elise stirred in her seat, as though in some kind of pain. Leo stopped and withdrew his hand. He felt stained with sin, and his fingers were glutinous with the material evidence of it.

"Where are you *going?*" she whispered.

Remove the occasion and you remove the sin. Remove the evidence and you remove the sin. He was going to wash, in the inadequate benison of cold water, amid the familiar, comforting, ammoniac smell of the men's lavatory. And when he returned she was sitting there in the shadows with her eyes on the screen—Elvis Presley?—and her skirt down to her knees and her mind on other matters. "Did you *do* it?" she whispered as he resumed his seat.

"Shhhh!" a voice urged from behind.

"Do what?" Leo asked. He watched her profile in the light thrown back from the screen. She was smiling. "You know what I mean," she whispered. "If you're good, *I'll* do it for you next time. I've done it to boys before, you know. I know how."

Sin and the occasion of sin. Remove the occasion and you remove the sin. The first and foremost rule of celibacy.

"You have been walking out with Elise," his mother remarked unexpectedly the next day. It was often difficult to judge her tone. Anger? Impatience? Reproach? There was no point in denying the matter. Doubtless one of her friends had spied on them (that shouting woman?) and reported the matter to the head office. She watched him coldly as he sat there blushing, and behind his blush was the remarkable thought that, beneath his mother's skirt, between her bony thighs, couched in ample *directoire* panties, she too was like *that.* Sin was always there, lurking in the shadows, watching and waiting like a rapist.

"You must stop seeing her," she said flatly. "It would not be right if you should become too close, and it is impossible to see much of a young girl without becoming too close." And then she smiled. She smiled across the tea table, the doors open behind her on the exiguous urban garden where sunlight came down in curtains among the glistening shrubs. Her smile was a small banner of triumph hung across her face. "Besides," she said, "Elise Goodman is a Jewess."

"We all of us suffer from temptations of the flesh. Of one kind or another." Thus one of young Leo's instructors in the seminary, facing up to the troubling issue of Elise and her like, pacing around his study as though he might surprise wanton lust hiding among the bookshelves and the armchairs and the prie-dieu. A crucified Christ hung reproachfully on the wall in front of the student's gaze. "Remember that in canon law only a complete man may be ordained priest. Neither eunuch, nor homosexual. So you mustn't worry about such desires, and nor must you dwell on them. My advice is . . ." the priest lowered his voice lest the heresy be overheard ". . . to find relief for yourself if it becomes too much to support." He rubbed his hands briskly, almost as though to show the way. "It is—*was*—my experience that such feelings are transient and superficial and once you have found relief they disappear. Rather like quenching one's thirst. Once you have had a glass of water the matter is closed. Of course, this is only a . . . ah . . . stopgap method. An emergency. A lesser sin in order to assuage a greater. It must not become habit. With discipline and prayer, you should be able to obviate the need for such emergency measures. Remove the occasion and you remove the sin. Sublimation is what the psychologists call it"—he was a self-confessed liberal, this paternal father—"but it is really no more than directing our energies to the service of the Lord." He smiled and patted Leo on the knee encouragingly.

Thus Elise and her kind were banished to hidden parts of Leo's mind. Thus he was reconciled with his mother. Thus he was reconciled with his vocation. The ritual of the liturgy and the demands of faith reestablished their equilibrium. All the answers you may wish for lie within faith, but it demands a complete and incontinent surrender, an immersion as total as any baptism. Indeed baptism is a kind of enactment of the surrender: you bathe in faith, you swim in it, you live by it, surrounded by it, buoyed up by it, engulfed by it. You *drown* in it, for at times it takes your breath away as entirely as any lungful of water. The sheer outrage of it, the boldness of it, the incomparable drama of the fact that the universe, the whole universe, condensed itself into the form of one single man and that he walked this earth and walks it still.

"The word *faith, pistis,* and its derived verb *pisteuo,* occurs more than two hundred forty times in the New Testament. John employs the verb ninety-eight times. Often it is qualified with the preposition *eis,* with the significance *into.* This is the significance given to saving faith, the need to commit body and soul to a union with Christ. Elsewhere it is qualified by *epi,* upon . . ." Thus Leo Newman, a new man, lecturing to a group of young seminarians, and feeling like a soldier who has been to the front line and heard the shells coming down, and is now passing the experience on to raw recruits. Soldiers of Christ, they look back at him with earnest faces, hoping that he will teach them the tricks of survival. It was interesting to find the same military metaphor employed by a former pupil, now a priest running a parish in Liverpool:

I remember your lectures in the seminary, he wrote. *We looked to you as one of the examples to follow, one of the leaders who would show us the way forward into battle, and now see what you have done. How many souls have you dragged down to the flames with you? How many innocent lives are lost?*

All the answers lie in faith; and when you lose your faith you have no choice but to substitute for it a philosophy that deliberately and coldly offers no answers at all.

4

T ake a family group out on a picnic. To Sutri and the Etruscan country to the north of Rome. To woods and sudden gorges, to brown cliffs punctuated with tombs, and hidden, bramble-ridden staircases. Jack was driving the first car, with friends (Howard and Gemma from London, staying the weekend) in the next. Newman was in the back of the leading car, an extra, something sterile but vaguely interesting, like an artifact from some remote archaeological period. There were also the two daughters, newly back from boarding school, seated on either side of him and on either side of the great divide of self-consciousness, the older one, Katz, consumed with blushes and silence whenever he spoke, the other, Claire, stark in her observation of his condition. "You don't *look* like a priest," she said.

"What do priests look like?"

"Priests are just ordinary people," Madeleine put in, glancing over the front seat at the girls.

"No they're not. Priests are boring."

There was laughter from the adults.

"Father Leo's not boring. He's quite famous, really. He writes about the Bible in the newspapers."

Newman tried to change the subject. "The Pope's a priest," he suggested.

"The Pope's boring," the younger child asserted, and Catherine blushed for shame.

"The Pope loves every one of us," Madeleine said. "*That's* what makes him just a teeny bit dull."

Outside the town there was the ancient amphitheater, and rows of tombs in the cliff. They parked the car and went to look. "Where are the dead people now?" Claire asked, peering in the open doorways at damp, bare floors. "Did they go to heaven?"

It was an intriguing theological point. "Where *did* they go," Madeleine asked, "all those millions who could never have known about Christ for the simple fact that they lived before he was even born?"

"We don't know," Leo said.

"Well, we can't just dismiss them, can we? They were, in their time, as real as you and me. Even now, if death has no dimension of time, they remain as real as, say, your dead mother or my dead father."

"Limbo," suggested Jack. "Isn't that the special place you've dreamt up for that kind of problem?"

"Limbo's for babies, silly," answered the older of the two girls.

The little theological debate spluttered on as the group looked around the tombs. The path led along the foot of a cliff and then climbed a moss-shrouded ramp to where a sign announced the chapel of the Madonna del Parto, Our Lady of Birth—once, so the guidebook said, a mithraeum. The place was entirely excavated from the rock: pillars, aisles, a narrow apse, everything. It smelled of damp and age, a sour, claustrophobic smell. "Leo knows all about mithraeums," Madeleine said to her husband. "Or should that be mithraea? He took us to one underneath San Clemente."

Leo found that he wanted her to look at him, that was what was so disturbing. He even talked volubly so that she would. As they poked around the shadows of the cave he expounded on the subject of Mithras, of bulls and sacrifice and the secret rites of initiation into the mysteries, of the bull's seminal fluid impregnating the whole world; and she did look, watching him with a secretive smile that may have been amusement, may have been imbued with something like sympathy. "The way that Christianity won," he told them, "was by abjuring the exclusive, by welcoming anyone, by having nothing to hide."

"What's abjuring?" the elder of the girls asked. "Why do you use big words all the time?" And Jack laughed, and asked, "Why *do* you use big words all the time?"

"Because small ones won't do," Leo said.

They went back to the car and into the town. Leo held the younger child's hand as they walked through the narrow, shabby alleys. "Shall I show you something?" he said to her. "Do you know a man called Pontius Pilate?"

"Of course," Claire said immediately. "He killed Jesus."

"The *Jews* killed Jesus," Catherine corrected her. "It says that in the Bible. The *Jews* killed Jesus."

"The Romans killed Jesus."

"The Jews." It threatened to become one of those ridiculous childish arguments—did, didn't, did, didn't, did.

"Leo's Jewish," said Madeleine.

Jack seemed startled. "Are you?"

Leo tried to shrug the matter away: "Newman, Neumann. There was a conversion in my family early this century. My grandmother." He knew what Jack was thinking. Jack had a sharp diplomat's mind and wouldn't miss a thing like that. As they walked through the town toward the main square, past *alimentari* and bars, Leo felt the cold wind of jealousy blowing through his mind. Why had Madeleine betrayed that fragile, insignificant confidence?

"Did *you* kill Jesus, then?" Claire asked.

"How could a priest kill Jesus, silly?"

"What about Pontius Pilate?"

"He wasn't a priest."

"He was a Roman. And Father Leo's a Roman Catholic."

"So are you."

"I'm not . . ."

"You *are* so."

"I think the children should shut up," Jack decided.

The main square of the town was like a stage set, with fountain and café and municipal building, and a host of extras hanging around as though waiting for the orchestra to strike up and the overture to begin. Leo led the way across to the palazzo on the far side. A stone plaque beside the entrance proclaimed the *Municipio,* the city offices. The building was plastered in rust-red stucco and the entrance archway was decorated with marble fragments that had been turned up in the fields around the town, a litter of bits and pieces hung on the walls at random, like dandruff clinging to a flushed scalp.

"It's here," he said, nervous that it would not strike the girls, for really it was not much, a mere plaque, a mere inscription, a trivial witness from the past. He couldn't judge children, their mixture of innocence and sophistication, their honesty and their mendacity.

The group shuffled around and looked up to where he pointed. And the word *Pontii* stood out from the epigraphic muddle, some reference to a local family, the *gens* Pontii.

"So what?"

What, indeed? The only evidence, if evidence it be, for the Italian existence of a lesser colonial administrator with a chip on his shoulder and a pushy wife: Pontius Pilate. The most famous Roman there has ever been. There's no competition, really, is there? Forget Julius Caesar or Tiberius. How many Christians are there in the world? A thousand million? Apart from the Virgin Mary, Pontius Pilate is the only human being mentioned in the creed. So his name is on the lips of every single one of those thousand million Christians, every time he or she goes to church. That's fame for you.

"This is where he came from. This was his hometown." And added "possibly," sotto voce, lest it ruin his paltry story.

So Leo told the Brewer family and their friends about Pilate on that early spring day at Sutri, when the wind was colder than it ought to have been and he was eager for Madeleine's attention. He talked of Pontius Pilate to the girls, to Madeleine, to Jack if he was listening, to Howard and Gemma if they cared. He gave him some kind of appearance—hair cut short, chin shaved clean: a sharp contrast to his bearded subjects—and sketched out a character of sorts—the kind of man who believed in the virtues of the republic, in the rule of law, in duty to the state and honor to the ancestors. A man who had made a useful marriage and had now stepped onto the first rung in the ladder of imperial ambition. Pontius Pilatus, a knight of the equestrian class, who might now aspire to one of the greatest prizes of all—Egypt. Pontius Pilate, who gained the favor of the Emperor's adviser Sejanus and was sent to Judaea in the summer of the twelfth year of the reign of Tiberius.

"Rather like British India," said Jack, who *had* been listening.

"Exactly like British India," Leo agreed. "The same fat, idle princelings sending their children to Rome or London for education—Herod's children all came here. There were the same strange religions, the same holy men with mad expressions and a dangerous role in politics, the same local politicians with their eye on the main chance. And the same kind of blundering colonial administration."

"You could use it as a case study at the Foreign Office," said Howard.

"Poor Pilate," said Catherine.

"Why poor?"

"Because he had no choice," she said, with the sudden insight of the young. "Jesus had to die, so Pilate had no choice. Neither did Judas."

"And what about Mrs. Pilate?" asked Madeleine.

They walked back to the car, back to the tombs and the amphitheater. "The tradition is that she was called Claudia. Claudia Procula. According to Origen she became a Christian and the Greek Orthodox Church even canonized her. Saint Claudia. But legend also has it that she was Sejanus's mistress and that's how Pilate got the job."

"What's a mistress?" asked Claire. "I thought it was a teacher."

The adults laughed. Sisterly duty overcame Catherine's embarrassment. "A mistress is a lady friend," she said firmly.

"Is Mummy Father Leo's mistress, then?" the younger girl asked. She wondered, no doubt, why her words brought more laughter. Maybe she wondered why Father Leo reddened. Maybe in later years she would remember that incident, and see in its small moments of awkwardness and amusement a strange foreboding.

They had returned to the amphitheater. Jack and the girls and the two guests from London had gone ahead into the center of the circle of rock. The tiers of seats rose up around them. Madeleine and Leo stood at the entrance looking across the grass to where the others posed like figures on a stage.

"Why did you tell Jack about my being Jewish?" Leo asked her.

She seemed surprised at his tone. "Is it a secret?"

"Not a secret, no. But something I told you."

"I'm sorry." She seemed not to understand, as though she hadn't grasped the significance, the secret shared. "I'm sorry if I betrayed a confidence, but I didn't think it was particularly private."

"It doesn't matter."

"I'm sorry, Leo. Is that OK? I didn't realize and now I'm sorry, all right?"

"Let me have war, say I!" Jack cried to the empty seats. "It exceeds peace as far as day does night."

"Why do you get so angry?" Madeleine asked.

"I'm not angry."

"Yes you are."

"— It is spritely, waking, audible, and full of vent!—"

"You just can't accept an apology. God, is that what comes of living the life of a celibate?"

"It's got nothing to do with it."

"Not much."

"Peace is a very apoplexy!" Jack declaimed. The girls ran circles around him and laughed. "A getter of more bastard children than war's a destroyer of men!"

"It's got nothing to do with it," Leo insisted. "Nothing at all." And he told her, there and then he told her, while Jack pranced around the amphitheater of Sutri and the girls screamed with delight at his antics, and Howard and Gemma laughed:

Another picnic, another era, another pair of cars. The main road to the town of Sutri is only asphalted in places now, mere hard-packed gravel in others. But there is the same avenue of umbrella pines, the same modern cemetery (less full now and without electric light) and the same row of Etruscan tombs on the opposite side. Tomb country, this, a landscape of the dead. And the same village on its perch of volcanic rock at the end of the avenue, like a ship about to enter the narrows and confronted by the small flotilla of cars coming toward it.

"Over here!" The leading car is a convertible, an Alfa Romeo, and the sound of the guide's voice can be clearly heard above the noise of engines as he turns in his seat and waves to the left. A white silk scarf billows. "The theater!" He is a young man, narrow and dark, darker than the others, who are clearly his seniors. His car lurches and swerves (no traffic but a donkey cart) and runs off the gravel onto a flat area beside the road, beside the cliff and the gateway that leads into what he has indicated, a rock-carved amphitheater.

A Mercedes follows and draws to a halt alongside the Alfa. The passengers get out. The ladies are in floral-print dresses with square shoulders and narrow waists. They wear wide-brimmed hats against the sun, and platform sandals against the earth, and they pick at this and that like birds. Three of the men are in flannels and soft shirts and white canvas shoes, and look as though they may be about to play some kind of game, tennis or badminton or something. In sharp contrast to them the man in command wears a suit. His only concession to the day, to the sky of untrammeled blue and a sun as sharp and painful as a thermic lance, is a battered and incongruous panama hat. "How can you *bear* it in this heat, darling?" The woman who half admonishes him is blond (hair rolled into an elaborate sausage that frames her face), lean and busy.

"This amphitheater is unique," the young man explains in the manner of a professional guide. "Probably Etruscan in origin, it was of course used through the Roman period."

"The *first* Roman Empire," one of the men says. There is a hint of mockery in his voice, and some, but not all, of the others laugh. The blond woman does not laugh, for example. When the young man speaks she is inclined to look away, to busy herself with other matters, like directing the operations of the fifth male, the servant who takes things from the back of the Mercedes—hampers, a tablecloth, a canteen of cutlery—and carries them through the entrance into the amphitheater. The woman instructs him like a general deploying troops, while her husband—the suited, hatted man—watches her keenly. "Over there. Not here. And those there, so that people can take them as they wish. And put the wine in the shade. We used to picnic in the woods at Buchlov," she explains to the others, as though to justify her orders by claiming great experience in the matter. "Carriages, not cars. And tables, chairs, everything. And my brother would organize games for the children . . ." The white cloth is laid out in the very center of the theater, as though a performance is expected and all these are props—the silver cutlery, the long-stemmed glasses, the white bone china. The servant makes a number of journeys to and fro, from cars to picnic, while a peasant with the donkey cart observes them soundlessly from the road.

What does he make of it? Seven adults and a young boy, all milling around in the spring sunshine, exclaiming at the place, at the rough tiers of seating that rise up and outward from the space in the center like ripples in a pond, all talking in tones he cannot grasp, words that mean nothing. But he knows them as German. That much. *"Ciao, nonno,"* the boy calls to him in accented Italian. He acknowledges the greeting with a toothless grin before thumping his donkey on the flank and continuing along the road toward the village.

"Spätlese," says the tall man, picking a bottle out of a hamper. The label is elaborate with Gothic script, bearing a picture that looks like a scene from *Der Ring des Nibelungen*. The glass is beaded with condensation. "Wonderful."

"I prefer *our* wine," his wife says.

"Absurd. Your wine is Austrian rubbish. This is the finest Rheinwein."

"Not Austrian, Moravian."

"Worse. Nothing but Jews and Slavs."

There is laughter. He draws the cork (this is a picnic: the servants can't do *everything*) and pours the pale wine, and they all take a glass and hold it to the light and sip, and agree with Herr Huber that this is delicious. They sip and swirl and make noises with their appreciative lips. Frau Huber bends down to adjust something on the tablecloth and the young man pauses to watch her skirt's soft rise. She wears silk stockings (rare these days). They are wrinkled slightly at the knee and their seams lead eyes irrevocably upward into the shadows where one can, for the moment, imagine stocking tops and fasteners and the cool, living silk of flesh. Herr Huber notices the young man's glance, and frowns. "I'm afraid we'll have to sit on the ground," Frau Huber says, dropping to her knees as though to show the way. Her legs fold demurely beneath her. The men relax. The servant begins to serve the food, awkwardly, far too much part of the group as he stoops to present the ladies with their portions of *prosciutto crudo* ("not as good as Viennese *Schinken*," Herr Huber says) and green figs, far too close to the ruling class and conscious of it.

And then there is a sound—sudden and intrusive, like the fabric of the blue sky being torn apart. The group pause in their eating—"I prefer Prague ham," someone is saying—and glance upward as something dark and silver, something awkward, cruciform, loud, flashes overhead from behind the fringe of holm oak and streaks over the theater and away over the road and above the umbrella pines, tearing at the sky as though doing it a great hurt.

"*Amerikaner!*" the boy cries in excitement, getting to his feet and running to the entrance to the theater as though he might catch the great, dark machine.

"Nonsense," says one of the men. "Luftwaffe! A Messerschmidt."

"Leo!" shouts the woman after the running child. The noise is background now, a distant, departing roar against the spring day.

"American," agrees one of the men, and Herr Huber begins a lecture, directed mainly toward the youngest of the men, the dark,
Latin one, a lecture about how the great tragedy of the war is that
it has given the Americans an excuse to get into Europe, and
things will never be the same again, whatever happens . . .

Figures in a Distant
Landscape—1943

⌇

T he Villa was built by some Polish count in the nineteenth century during the brief and hopeless flowering
of the Kingdom of Poland. It is a grandiose pile, all pillars and porticoes, cupolas and pediments, as though the architect
had a rudimentary grounding in the work of Palladio but none of
his sense of harmony and balance. But the garden that surrounds
it is another thing altogether: formal and classical behind the
building, it transforms into a Piranesi fantasy below, a temperate
jungle with Roman brickwork (the remains of one of the aqueducts that used to supply the city), falling water, sinuous paths,
damp, vegetable shade. Columbine, clematis, honeysuckle, dog
rose, the heavy scents of jasmine and orange (a small orangerie
with the blossom as white as distant doves among the lucid
leaves), the elusive perfume of box, the vulgar scent of tuberose,

everywhere a litter of Roman marble fragments found during the building of the garden in the previous century and left scattered around, mossy and mildewed, for the passerby to rediscover for himself. Halfway down the hill is a small *tempietto,* modeled on Bramante's masterpiece. The whole is a perfect Roman phenomenon, at once artifact and natural, fantasy and reality, past and present.

Two figures are in the garden. They have made their way from the formal garden on the far side (still ponds, an artificial grotto, clipped hedges, parterre paths) around the side of the building and down the paths of the lower garden. The woman appears to be giving her companion instructions, and the instructions (a shock to any would-be eavesdropper) are in English.

"If you were to overwater the plants they might easily die," she says.

"If I were to overwater the plants, they might easily die," the young man enunciates. Then he repeats the phrase *they might easily die* as though trying to consign it to memory.

Frau Huber pauses to inspect a casual blossom beside the path, a florid fuchsia dancing in the shadows, the Adelaide variety, she happens to know. "To tell you the truth," she admits, "I'm not certain whether it should be *might* or *may.*"

He seems shocked. "You don't know? Are not there rules?"

"You'd say *aren't.* In ordinary conversation."

"*Aren't,* then." He is slightly impatient. "You see, there *are* rules." His face is solemn, bright, made up of contrasting lights and shadows. You might hesitate to use the word of a young man, but he is beautiful. No one would have any hesitation in his own language: *bello. Un bel uomo.*

"Yes, I suppose there are rules. But English is a funny language. Perhaps you could describe it as . . ." The woman pauses, as though the word that has occurred to her is rather shocking

"... *democratic*. So the rules get broken, and then people forget them, or don't bother with them, and . . ."

"I like your definition of democracy. I will remember it. It sounds very like Italy. And yet there *are* right words, because you say I have wronged."

"You say, I *am* wrong." She glances around from the plant. "It's difficult, Checco. It's an *instinctive* language." Her own use of it is almost perfect. A native speaker might wonder about her origins, about the overemphasized vowel sounds and the precision of her consonants, but the wondering would not lead anywhere very much. There are no real clues. Frau Huber. Gretchen. Blond, sharp of both body and mind, possessed of a kind of beauty. You might hesitate to use the word of a woman, but she is handsome. You wouldn't hesitate in her own language: *schön*. "You don't think of the English as instinctive, do you? People imagine them as hidebound and obedient. But they are not. That is the mistake the Germans have made."

"The Germans have made a mistake?"

"You must work on your endings, Checco. It's the great problem with Italians speaking English. *Mistake,* not *mistakah.* Chop the consonant off at the end. Oh, yes, they have made a mistake all right."

"And you?"

"Me? Oh, I've made many mistakes."

"Was marrying Herr Huber one?"

She is silent, perhaps considering the question, perhaps wishing to ignore it. "This flower."

"Fuch-sia," he says.

"In English one says *few-sha*."

"But it is *fuch-sia,* after the botanist Fuchs."

"But in English that sounds rather rude. So it is *few-sha*."

"To be polite. That is typical, isn't it? Instinctively polite."

She laughs. "We grow these at home, do you know that? My father's hobby. We have a *fuchsarium*. Very famous in Moravia." Her hand holds the flower, turning it upward so that the delicate inner parts are exposed, the stamens and the inside of the corolla. "Have, had, who knows what will happen to it?"

She drops the flower and goes on down the path toward the gravel clearing where the *tempietto* stands. The wooden door opens as she pushes it. Inside is swept bare. Light filters down from the lantern at the summit of the cupola, but it is not strong enough to disperse the shadows that collect at the circumference of the floor. He closes the door behind them. Standing inside the cylinder it is as though they are at the bottom of a dry well, cool and damp and secret.

"We had a hut among the rhododendrons," she said. "*Have*. It's still there, I suppose. It was our den, *die Bude*—my brother's and mine. It was . . . oh, dozens of things: a ship, a cave, a fortress, a home." She glances around the drum that surrounds her, the exactly fitted stones, the ribs of the dome, the lights above them. "The light was like this. There must have been some kind of skylight . . . yes, a window in the roof . . . and it gave light just like this."

"And your brother?"

"My brother is dead. He died at Rostov."

They stand still for a moment, and let that fact—a distant, presumably cold death that is difficult to picture in this lush, bright garden, with the paths winding down between the beds, and the sounds of crickets and birds loud in the luminous air—lie between them.

"Why did you marry Herr Huber?"

She looks at him in surprise. "Why is it anything to do with you?"

"Was that a mistake, marrying him?" He talks in German now, and with the change of language his tone is more insistent, as though he is now more confident that what he means is what he says. "He is so much older than you. Gretchen, tell me." And suddenly, surprisingly, he takes hold of her hand, as though almost to shake her into giving some kind of answer—"Was it a mistake?"—while she looks at him with an expression of faint bewilderment. "That is none of your business."

But what is his business? Where do the bounds of intimacy lie? He holds her hand—a narrow, fragile hand—and watches her as though waiting for an answer.

"Please let me go," she says quietly.

"Do you realize what I feel for you?"

"Francesco, don't be absurd. Please let me go."

He lets her hand drop. She stands for a moment looking at him, bewilderment still there in her expression.

"Have I offended you?" he asks.

"Of course not." She smiles. "You have flattered me. But you have trodden on dangerous ground."

"A minefield?"

"If you like. It might be better if you wait here for a while," she says. And then she has pulled open the door and gone out into the sunlight, leaving him alone in the block of light that comes in through the doorway. Her steps are brisk on the path, fading away into the general sounds of the morning.

Magda — now

Far below the apartment, on the *piano nobile,* groups of
tourists shuffle around the relics of the once great past
of the Casadei family, peering at the portrait of the family pope—Innocent the something-or-other—and wondering
when the ceiling will be regilded. Up here beneath the rafters birds
and rodents scrabble in the wainscot. When it rains water drips
through onto the kitchen floor with a dull persistence. A bucket
stands ready and provides an echo of rain long after a storm has
passed on.

Apart from the kitchen—little more than a galley—there is a
living room, a bedroom and a bathroom. The bathroom is awash
with Magda's things: her tights hanging like flayed black skins over
the bath, her panties soaking in the cracked bidet, her pots of face
cream, her lipsticks, her mascara brushes littering the shelves.

Days pass. Spring becomes summer, with that imperceptible shift that brings harsh white out of effulgent amber; and Magda draws, observes, takes domes and roofs and towers and transfers them, with a soft mutation, onto her paper. She draws other things, and paints them as well (the apartment fills with the organic smell of oils and turpentine and acrylic resin, like an artist's studio). She paints the sun, setting like a bloody wound behind the ragged knife edge of the Janiculum Hill; she paints the strange, spiky plants that grow around the terrace (abstract shapes these, like something by Yves Tanguy); she paints the interior of the apartment.

Magda is an artist, and an artist possesses what she sees. It was an insidious possession, step by cautious step: first the view, and then the apartment itself, the random assembly of things within it, the broken furniture, the dusty books, the dirty dishes, the sagging, ruined sofa in the sitting room; and then the occupant: Leo at the stove making coffee, Leo asleep in the armchair (his mouth half open, a thin ribbon of saliva trickling from one corner of his lips; pen and ink with a gray wash), Leo sitting and watching her quizzically and hiding who knows (except Leo) what thoughts? Leo the lion, looking old and ragged, scarred by time and circumstance. Interior with figure.

Magda is an artist, and an artist possesses what she touches. She touches my flesh, with the tenderness of a nurse, the softness of a mother. She touches the slick, waxy skin of my trunk, the frozen waves of lucid skin which lap at my neck, the wax-paper tissue on the back of my hands where the tendons have fused and the fingers are clawed and almost useless. She touches this silently, as though the touching alone may do something for me.

"What happened?"

"Flames," I tell her. "Fire and brimstone."

Fire she understands, but not brimstone. Fire she can understand, but not hell. "You can feel?" Her finger moves down the smooth, morbid tissue. "You can feel?"

My skin is dumb. But I can still feel. I am alive to every twitch and whisper of the world, every movement she makes in the shadows of the apartment, every breath she takes, every murmur of the city outside our walls.

"Tell me," she says.

Leo on fire, squatting like a pope on his throne, like a Bacon pope, Pope Innocent the something-or-other, screaming and burning, his flesh falling like molten wax, dripping like wax, his eyes staring out of his agony as though through a grimy pane.

Magda is an artist and an artist possesses what she sees. She possesses the apartment and all that is in it.

Dear Father Newman, someone wrote, *may you burn in hell.* The letter was anonymous, of course. It was signed "A good Catholic."

You cannot separate belief from context, that is what I have discovered. You cannot divorce what you hold from the circumstances that are holding you. When did the disciples' faith let them down? During the storm on the lake, when Peter tried the same conjuring act as his Master and attempted to walk on the water—"Oh, ye of little faith." Or when the man was being led away, a political prisoner, to a drumhead trial and death: "And they all deserted him and ran away."

So what do I believe now, living as I do in the midst of this rotting, chaotic city, with the centuries piled up around me like so much debris on a rubbish heap? I believe in the one force that is more apparent here than anywhere—I believe in the force of time, the impetus of that dimension that seems to have baffled even the physicists, the power of that force that will, in time, cure every ill, solve every problem, fulfill every nightmare. Time. I see time all about me, like a substance. I see it in the clutter of my apartment, in the fabric of the city, in the lessons that I teach. The tyranny of time, as dictatorial as any god. I see time in the face that stares back at me from Magda's portraits: a grotesque caricature of the fresh and innocent face that started out from the seminary some thirty years ago. Bright and hopeful then; lined and staring now, the elements dispersed and various, as in a cubist portrait. But that is me: once-brown hair now scrubbed to a short, gray brush like a convict's; the whites of the eyes tinged the color of weak tea; the mouth (almost lipless, almost a trap) turned down at the corners and merging in with narrow creases that come diagonally down from the edges of the nose. Leo Newman, now.

And Leo Newman then? How do you get to this strange solitude, with a girl who speaks little English and says more to you through the medium of paint than through speech? What are the territories you cross? What wilderness of stone and thorn, with the jackals lurking in the background and the vultures circling overhead on high, invisible thermals?

On the corner of the palazzo where we live, Magda and I, just where an alley leads back into the ghetto, there is the local grocery shop. I go there every morning for milk and bread; but I go no farther into the depths of the ghetto, fearful of what I might find. The shop calls itself a minimarket, a grandiose title which means simply that you must fetch and carry for yourself and pay at the desk. Usually I go alone. Sometimes Magda comes with me, and the signora treats her with a curious indulgence, as though she might be my daughter, giving her cheese to taste or a piece of ham or some sweets, calling her signorina and smiling on her in the fond manner of a distant aunt. What does she imagine about Magda and me, I wonder? Father and daughter seems unlikely. Man and mistress? Client and customer? Perhaps that. This city has seen everything except heresy, every sin, every failure, every vice; it has learned to accept.

In the shop there is a dusty crucifix on the wall behind the cash desk, a plastic thing of curiously exact anatomical detail— carefully delineated muscles, tendons like cords, blood of autumnal hue running down from palm and foot and lacerated side. So far I have never observed anyone in the shop take the faintest notice of this icon. Certainly it hasn't seen a duster in the last decade. But there it is, a crucifix in this city of crucifixes.

Magda eyes the cross circumspectly. What does she know of it? From her childhood of institutionalized atheism, what has she picked up of the religion of her ancestors?

The True Cross was found by Saint Helena (b. *ca.* 248 Bithynia, modern Turkey, d. *ca.* 328 Nicomedia, now Izmit, modern Turkey), the mother of the Emperor Constantine. The finding is, *was,* celebrated by the Church with the Feast of the Invention of the True Cross, a title that has within it both the etymological history of a word and a pungent, unintentional irony. The feast may have been canceled (by Pope John XXIII), but the relic remains, housed in the Church of Santa Croce in Gerusalemme. Pious legend? But pious legends in this city are almost as old as the events they describe. The remains (mere splinters now) are kept in a modern chapel at the back of the main basilica, but from the main church you can still go down to where the lumps of wood were, presumably, first housed: the chapel of Saint Helena. This and the adjoining chapel of Saint Gregory are rooms of the original Sessorian Palace, where Helena actually lived. Not legend, that. It was this woman who journeyed to the Holy Land (not legend), found the True Cross (legend) and brought it back to Rome, where it was divided up, and fragments were distributed to the churches of Europe as a modern merchandising company might distribute items to franchise holders: baseball caps with the company logo, plastic figurines, that kind of thing.

Helena also brought back the nails of the Crucifixion, part of the titulus that was posted on the cross over Jesus' head, the stake to which he was tied when they scourged him, some rock from the tomb, some rock from the cave at Bethlehem, the stairs from Pontius Pilate's palace, and part of the cross on which the good thief hung. She must have been like an eighteenth-century Englishman on the Grand Tour shipping art treasures back in crates to his stately home.

I took Magda to see the relics. She looked at the bits and pieces with a mixture of atavistic wonder and modern skepticism. "How did they know?" she asked.

"How did they know what?"

"It was the good thief's cross? You said good thief. How did they know?"

The Church has an answer because the Church always has an answer: it has been around too long to be caught out that easily. I explained: "Rather conveniently one of Helena's workmen injured himself. So they put the wound against one of the crosses they had found . . . and the wound didn't heal. So that must have been the cross of the wicked thief. Then they tried the other cross, and as soon as the wood touched the wound it closed up and the pain went away and not even a scar was left. So that was the good thief's cross."

The plank of wood in question was sealed in a recess in the wall, behind thick glass and an iron grille. Would it still stand the test? Magda thought about my answer for a while, and then shrugged. But when we got back to the apartment she began to paint—thorns, spears, blades, a forest of things that pierce and cut, and pieces mixed up with the paint, bits of thorn, a scattering of sand, toothpicks, sharp, abrasive things. And among it a man on fire.

In Jerusalem, in the Church of the Holy Sepulchre at the heart of the Old City, you may also walk down steps from the upper church into a chapel of Saint Helena. You go down steps past rows and rows of crosses scratched into the rock by medieval pilgrims, down into a bare, chiseled space like the bottom of a well. Light filters down into the depths from a window high up in the roof.

The chapel was originally exactly what tradition claims for it: a rock-cut cistern of the early Imperial era. It would have been here when Helena was around. There's a *terminus ante quem,* a date before which it must have been constructed, of 44 BC. The story is that after the Crucifixion they just threw the cross into a nearby well, where it was discovered three hundred years later by the Empress on her Grand Tour. Light comes down from the high window to illuminate the dusty space and it's not difficult to imagine, really. If you've seen laborers at work, it's not difficult to imagine. There would have been swearing, of course. Fucking this and sodding that as they struggled with the rough beams, dragging them this way and that and finally dumping them over the edge into the pit. There is always swearing. Obscenities take on a strange semantic neutrality on the lips of such people, but I suppose they would have made a satisfactory counterpoint to the sound of splintering wood.

Was there, one wonders, an element of cover-up about the whole thing, a desperate desire on the part of the politicians to dispose of the evidence and to pretend that whatever it was that had happened, hadn't happened at all? Politicians haven't changed, have they? And there was politics in this, sure enough. That's the thing that has got lost among the piety—the politics of it all.

The workmen would have been from the very bottom of society, because merely handling such things as a crucifixion tree was a defilement. Probably they would have been slaves. One thing is quite certain: they wouldn't have had any idea of the significance of what they did, or that one day, either in legend or in reality, an emperor's mother would come searching for the planks of wood. Or that two thousand years later men would still be picking over the event like vultures picking over a skeleton in the hope of finding a scrap of flesh.

So, they threw the bits down a well. And the body? Ah, that's the crucial thing, isn't it? What did they do about the body?

"His disciples came during the night and stole him away while we were asleep" . . . *And to this day that is the story among the Jews* (Matt. 28: 13, 15).

And to this day?

Do you need a resurrection? I ask the question in a Socratic sense, knowing my own answer and not willing to give it away. Do you need a resurrection *nowadays,* I mean. Oh, they needed one then, sure enough. Everywhere you go in this city you find relics that attest to the fact that the Romans and the Greeks and every-one of the time needed a sacrifice and a resurrection. Look at Dionysus. But now?

Magda paints, and she possesses what she paints: scarlet like the sunset, crimson like a lake of blood, black as betrayal: Leo on fire, crucified by fire; a blasphemy.

Recital—1943

An elegant evening in the ballroom of the Villa, a long room with a lucid wooden floor and marble-framed windows and curtains of yellow silk. Chairs are arranged in rows. On the shallow stage at one end is a Bechstein grand piano. Seated at the piano in long, black evening gown, blond hair gathered up so that her neckline is exposed to the gaze of all (something startlingly intimate about that) is Frau Huber. She is not quite beautiful. Her face is a trifle too long, her nose possessed of an angularity that distracts from what one might call (many do) a classical profile. She sits erect, with her left foot forward to the pedals, her right tucked beneath the stool. Her back is curved slightly, like a bow.

She is not quite beautiful; but she is potent. Hands poised over the keys, angular talons dipped in blood, head held erect and brow faintly creased, she is potent. The audience is hushed. Then, tentatively and softly, so softly as almost to be inaudible to those at the back of the room, she begins to play. And the notes fall like tears into the spacious room, carefully chosen tears, the place of each one determined with care and precision—Liszt's setting of the Schubert song *Gretchen am Spinnrade*. Gretchen at the spinning wheel, Gretchen at the keyboard, the notes drifting out over the audience like living things, each with a finite life of its own, each with a birth and a death. And the men in the audience, many of them in shark-gray uniform, one or two in black, most of them distant from home and full of *Gemütlichkeit,* feel their eyes glisten with tears; while at the same time (men are capable of such emotional gymnastics) they try to picture the woman stripped of that dress, her limbs lean and white, typical Aryan limbs, her breasts small and loose, her belly swelling slightly, a gleaming blond floss between her thighs—an image that goes with Liszt and Schubert well enough.

The piece rises to its climax in great waves and then dies away into silence. There is a moment of stillness into which a storm of applause seems almost reluctant to intrude. *"Brava!"* they call. *"Brava!"* The *principe* Casadei, one of the few Italians in the audience, rises to his feet and creates a small tide among the others, so that soon all are standing and applauding. And Frau Huber too rises to her feet and looks back at them distractedly, as though surprised to find them there at all. Her head inclines toward the audience slightly, her expression one of faint amusement. When the applause has finished and the guests have subsided, she sits once more, and Liszt takes over completely from Schubert, the *Years of Pilgrimage* flying past, the hands pouncing onto the keys, ambushing them, striking chords from the gleaming lacquered box, snatching notes from the instrument like thieves plucking jewels from a casket, darting with sudden runs up and down the keyboard, great swirls of sound coiling out into the expectant room, racking the audience, racking her slim body, racking the body of the young man who sits in the third row from the front, over on the right-hand side of the room.

Tennis. The tennis court lies behind what were once the stables of the Villa and are now the garages and apartments for the more senior of the servants. Tennis. A rectangle as red as the surface of Mars in the shadow of the ruined Roman aqueduct that runs diagonally through the gardens. The scuff of tennis shoes on the dirt and the sweep of two white figures, virginally white, as white as any pair of androgynous angels. She throws the ball high into the air and serves. As her arm sweeps up and over there is a glimpse of the secret curve of her armpit with its glistening flock of hair. The ball speeds efficiently over the net. He returns it with a neutral stoke. She runs in from the baseline, her feet beating on the dirt, her body poised over the bouncing ball, her racket arm swinging back like a loaded catapult. The drive sweeps forward through the ball, sending it hard into the waiting net.

"No, no, no! You must not make fall your racket head." She teaches him English, he teaches her tennis. "You must try to keep firm your wrist. Let me show you."

An excuse, this? He skips over the net and takes up his position behind her, holding her right wrist and her left shoulder, pressing his body against hers so that they almost become one moving unit. "Like *this,* and *this,* and *this,*" he says, pulling her back and then sweeping her whole body forward into the stroke, time and again, rhythmically, flowingly, the tempo marked con brio. She can feel him firm against her buttocks as he sweeps her forward, pulls her back, sweeps her forward. "You keep the racket head *up* and you sweep *through* the ball. You will practice the shot as a punishment."

He releases her slowly and returns to his side to chip balls over the net for her to sweep regally, imperiously down the sidelines and into the netting at the far end. "*Brava,*" he cries at each successful shot. "*Brava!*"

Then the game continues, she tossing the ball high into the bright air (that glimpse of moist hair) and sweeping through the serve, he returning into the midcourt so that she can practice the flowing, graceful drive again. "*Brava!*" again, and she smiles in delight, while high overhead (they barely pause to look up) a cluster of silver crucifixes draws white lines of vapor across the sky.

He allows her to win her service game, and then he serves (a mere swipe of the ball, but it is clear that the whole thing could be much more hostile, much faster and more angled) and lets her return the ball before sweeping it far crosscourt to send her running for it along the baseline and end up in the netting at the side of the court, where she hangs for a moment, laughing and panting.

"Where is Leo?" The sudden voice is an intrusion. Her husband has appeared at the side of the court, a tall and elegant figure in a pin-striped suit. How long has he been watching? What has he seen, and more important, what does he *think* he has seen?

"My dear, I didn't notice you." Gretchen laughs, although there is nothing to laugh at. "Leo? Leo is in the schoolroom. He is working on . . ." She glances at her opponent for a clue.

"Charlemagne and the Holy Roman Empire."

Herr Huber's face is narrow and finely sculpted. His smile is ornate. "Why is Herr Volterra not *teaching* him about Charlemagne and the Holy Roman Empire?"

"Hansi, you know this is the time when we have our tennis lesson," she says reproachfully. The use of the diminutive is lèse-majesté. Herr Huber frowns.

"Herr Volterra is employed as a tutor, not as a tennis coach."

"Are you proposing to drive him away from me just when I am winning?" She has her hands on her hips, petulantly, almost (but not quite) defiantly. But the young man is already gathering up his things, clipping his racket into its press, picking up towel and spare racket and gathering up the stray balls. "Perhaps later, Frau Huber," he says. "Now I must go." Herr Huber watches him hurry away from the court toward the small wooden pavilion which is the changing room, before glancing back to his wife.

Herr Huber's office, on the second floor of the Villa, above the reception rooms with their tapestries from the Beauvais factory of scenes from the life of Christ. The office has tall windows looking out over the formal garden at the back of the Villa. There are heavy drapes and heavy Bavarian furniture that might be more appropriate in a hunting lodge somewhere north of the Alps. A great desk gleams in the light from the window. A portrait of the Führer in the dun-colored uniform of the SA looks down from the wall behind the desk. It contrives to look over the shoulder of Herr Huber as he sits at the desk and examines the young man before him. He himself is more discreet in his avowal of allegiance than the Führer: his display of loyalty takes the form of a simple lapel button, a bright enamel blossom of red and white and black, the *Hakenkreuz*.

"Is my wife good at tennis? She seems very keen on the game."

Herr Volterra swallows. "She is a good athlete." On the desk there is a silver-framed photograph of Gretchen wearing a dirndl. She is leaning against a gate and laughing at the camera. The sun catches her hair and makes of it a pale cloud, an aureole, a nimbus of light. Behind her is a wooden chalet and, in the background, mountains. Beside it is another photograph. It shows Leo in the uniform of the Jungvolk, the junior section of the Hitler Youth.

"And you are good?"

"I was a quarter-finalist in the Italian championships. The junior class," the young man adds.

"An athlete." Herr Volterra inclines his head a fraction, as though acknowledging a compliment. "So why are you not in the army?"

"I was discharged. Herr Huber, you know all about this. Malaria, contracted in Abyssinia . . ."

"Oh yes, of course. Malaria." Herr Huber's tone is faintly skeptical. He is an imposing figure: tall and slender, with an elegant awkwardness about his movements as though he has spent a lifetime trying without much success to fit his limbs into the confines imposed on him by a shorter world. He takes a cigarette from a silver box and taps it briskly on the desk in front of him. "A cigarette?" But the young man declines the offer. There is a pause as Huber lights the cigarette, holding it almost tentatively between the tips of his second and third fingers, tightening his lips as he takes the end of it into his mouth, drawing deeply on it and letting the smoke out in a thin blue stream. "Tell me, Francesco. What do you think will happen?"

The use of his Christian name is carefully noted. "Happen, Herr Huber?"

"To your wretched country . . ."

The younger man shrugs. "It is difficult. I don't see . . ."

"You may be honest with me," Huber reassures him. "I have been a diplomat all my life, and a diplomat learns to do two things—represent his country whatever his country may do, and protect his sources as a priest protects those who confess to him. Consider yourself under my protection."

Francesco smiles, as though he has been paid a great compliment.

"So tell me. Now that the war is on Italian soil, what will happen?"

"I think . . ."

"*What* do you think?" Huber gets up and strolls around the desk, until he is standing directly behind Francesco. He places his left hand on the younger man's shoulder in an ambiguous gesture that blends friendship and coercion and a certain, tense intimacy. "Tell me what you think."

"I think Italy is just a pawn."

"And which player will take the pawn?"

"The Americans are very powerful."

The two men, the one standing tall and slender behind the other, stare across the desk at the portrait on the wall of the man who, they both suppose, is the other player. Then Herr Huber reaches forward over Francesco's shoulder and, like someone laying out a hand of cards, places six photographs on the desk before him. "These," he says. "Do you know them? I need their names."

Ah, names. Always names. Names and photographs, culled often enough from some family collection snatched from a battered wallet, a bedside table, a desk drawer: young men and young women staring out of the lacquered paper with bright enthusiasm or solid determination, or snapped while astride a bicycle or standing beside a car or sitting at a table. White shirts, gray trousers, bright, floral frocks. Eyes narrowed against the sun. Brave, bright faces without any concept of the future.

"Well that one, certainly," Francesco says, pointing. "That is Buozzi. Bruno Buozzi."

Herr Huber makes a noncommittal sound, a mere grunt. He knows that the photograph shows Buozzi (shirtsleeves, collarless, sitting at a restaurant table), and the young man knows that he knows. The question is this: how much longer can he guarantee only to betray those who have already been betrayed? It is a nice problem. The photograph of Gretchen laughs back at him as though amused at the dilemma.

"And this one?"

The young man shrugs. "I don't think—"

"But you *do* know him," says Herr Huber quietly. Herr

Huber's voice is remarkably soft for his bulk. You might expect a loud, barking voice from such an imposing figure. The gentle, caressing sound is almost a surprise, like small, neat feet on a large man. He squeezes Francesco's shoulder, as though to remind him of the possibility of pain.

"Is this a trick?"

Herr Huber smiles humorlessly. Of course it is a trick. Every single question is a trick. The photograph shows two men and a woman standing against some railings, with a lake in the background. Francesco's eyes narrow, as though he is struggling to remember, when in fact he is struggling to forget. Socialist Party meeting in Geneva, 1937. "Unless . . . I don't know the woman, but I think that man must be Pertini. It's not a very good photo. The other is Paolucci. I think. Giulio Paolucci. He was some kind of official. I'm not sure what—provincial secretary for somewhere in Lombardy, I think . . ."

Herr Huber nods. He keeps his grasp of Francesco's shoulder. The question is, does he nod because the identification is correct and the test has been passed, or does he nod because he has gained a further piece of information? Pertini is nothing, of course. Herr Huber knows Pertini. But the wretched Paolucci?— is he even now languishing in a cell in Via Tasso, with an assumed identity that is about to crumble? Has Francesco Volterra, known to his intimates as Checco, signed another death warrant?

The game continues. Chess? Cat and mouse? Choose your metaphor. Herr Huber smiles occasionally, frowns occasionally, and at the end gives a great sigh as though he has just completed a demanding physical task. "Enough," he says, gathering up the photographs and consigning them to the inside pocket of his jacket. "Enough. Let's talk about other things." He releases the young man's shoulder and crosses the room to the windows to look out across the formal garden, the Italian garden, a complex geometric construct of paths and hedges, boxes of box, triangles and spirals of box, like the intricate cells of an organic whole. "Let us talk about young Leo. How is he doing?"

"He's an intelligent child."

"And he works hard?"

"Hard enough."

A glance around. A rather stiff smile. "You are covering up for him. He is a lazy child."

"But clever."

"You are fond of him?"

"We get on well."

"And Gretchen. You get on well with Gretchen." The use of her Christian name, the *diminutive* form of her Christian name, is disconcerting. Francesco shifts uneasily in his chair. It is warm in the room and beads of sweat glisten on his forehead. The Gretchen of the photograph seems to laugh at his discomfiture, tilting her head back and laughing derisively.

"With Frau Huber, as well. It is, perhaps, that we share a fondness for Leo."

Herr Huber nods. "You are a Catholic, aren't you?"

Francesco agrees that, yes, he is a Catholic. All good Italians are Catholics. Although perhaps he is not a very strong believer.

"Gretchen is also a Catholic, a devout Catholic, did you know that? I expect she has told you. Her mother was English, a *governess*. Do you understand the word?"

"*Una tata?*"

"Is that the Italian word? Someone employed to look after the children, a respectable girl from a respectable bourgeois family, and when the mistress of the house died suddenly—a riding accident of some kind—there was the young governess ready to hold the mourning husband's hand. A clever move, don't you think? Clever also to convert to Catholicism and claim moral purity rather than allow the widower to have her as a mistress. And cleverer still to get herself pregnant so quickly, to provide a half-sister for the children for whom she had been caring."

Francesco perches on the edge of his chair, looking for escape.

"So, despite seeming so beautiful, so perfectly Aryan, Gretchen is actually a mongrel," Huber says. "She is a cross-breed, a genetics experiment from the place where the father of genetics was born." He laughs, and expects Francesco to laugh with him. "While I, on the other hand, am of pure German stock. Like her I was born a Catholic, but unlike her I do *not* believe. And you say that you do not believe either . . ." He smiles at the young man, indulgently, like an uncle smiling at a favorite nephew.

"I believe that there might be a God. Maybe I believed more strongly once, that is all."

Huber shakes his head. "It seems an ever more unlikely proposition, doesn't it? The existence of God, I mean. Nietzsche declared the death of God. For me as for Nietzsche, there is no God, only blood and race. But Gretchen believes and, to make her happy, I accompany her and Leo to church." He looks thoughtfully away from Francesco, toward the window and the garden, and then suddenly, sharply, back. "And in the last weeks she has ceased to take communion. Now why do you think that can be?"

"I wouldn't even try to imagine." There is a rivulet of sweat running down Francesco's temple. "It would be an impertinence, an affront to Frau Huber's privacy even to think about it."

"But I try to imagine." The tall man's voice is quiet, almost reflective. The accent is on the personal pronoun, as though he has a right to know what goes on in the heart and mind and soul of his wife. "*I* try to imagine what the reason might be."

In the schoolroom young Leo, wearing knickerbockers and a Norfolk jacket (we must always keep up appearances, even when there is no one to appear to), bends over his exercise book and takes copious notes about the life of Christ—Christ beating the money changers out of the Temple, Christ arguing with the Pharisees on the Sabbath, Christ being led before Pilate. He looks up at Francesco, blue eyes looking from beneath blond hair at the dark-skinned Italian.

"Explain this paradox to me," the boy says. He has recently learned the word *paradox* and enjoys using it. It sounds absurd coming from the mouth of a child as young as he, absurd and pretentious. "Jesus was a Jew. How could it be that he was so intelligent?"

Francesco shrugs. "It isn't that the Jew lacks intelligence. He may be highly intelligent—for example, look at his well-known prowess at chess. What the Jew lacks is the creative faculty."

"Who said that?"

"Oh, I don't know. Some book I read. But I don't believe any of it. For example, Mendelssohn was a Jew. He didn't lack the creative faculty, did he?"

"*Mutti* no longer plays Mendelssohn. He is *not* creative, that is what they say now. He is *derivative*." Leo frowns at the word, as though he is not quite sure of the meaning. "Yet wasn't Jesus creative? Didn't he create the true religion for the whole of mankind?"

The Italian considers the conundrum for a moment, and then smiles. "It was not Jesus who created it, but God." There is a thoughtful silence. Through the windows come the outside sounds of the garden—crickets, a blackbird singing, a gardener clipping a hedge in the Italian garden below.

"But Jesus *was* God, that is what Father Berenhoeffer says. So God himself must be a Jew . . ."

"I expect so."

"You *expect* so? This is a very dangerous thing to say, Signor Francesco." The child looks at him with disapproving eyes and, having caught him out, a glint of triumph. "Judas I can understand. Judas has all the untrustworthy qualities of the Jew. But Jesus? It is too much . . ."

"I think perhaps you should get on with your work, young man. Or I will report your idleness to your father."

The lesson continues in the bright, sunny room while a fly circles beneath the ceiling light and Signor Francesco reads a book.

After a while the boy looks up again.

"Why do you always look at my mother?"

Francesco feigns surprise. "Why do I *what?*"

"You look at her all the time. Are you perhaps in love with her?" The boy's expression is quite serious: all the seriousness and thoughtlessness of childhood is there.

"I *like* your mother very much. She is a good woman, and she is very much in love with your father."

"I know that, but that is not what I asked."

The office is in shadow, the heavy drapes drawn to keep out the sun. A clock ticks on the mantel. A fly buzzes mindlessly against a windowpane, trapped between curtain and glass, like a specimen in a collection that has suddenly and desperately come alive. From the wall the Führer stares petulantly into the shadows. On the desk there is the silver-framed photograph of Leo in the uniform of the Jungvolk, and the picture of Gretchen wearing a dirndl.

Francesco is at the desk, with the drawers open and papers laid out before him. Francesco is a thief. The question is, what is he stealing? And for whom?

5

T hey don't warn you about it when you join the priesthood, do they?"

"Warn you about what?"

"The loneliness and the boredom."

"I'm not bored. What makes you think I'm bored?"

Her sharp laugh. "You've just admitted to being lonely."

Jack watched, faintly amused. He sat in his favorite armchair, detached from the two of them on the sofa, and he laughed at his wife in the manner of someone amused by a precocious child. "Let him be, Maddy. What did poor Leo do to deserve this?"

"Leo the lion," she said, ignoring her husband. "But you're feline, not leonine. You're just like Percy." Percy was the cat that the Brewers had inherited from the previous occupants of their apartment. It was a gray, solemn beast that sat in the middle of the carpet and did nothing. His Staffordshire pottery act, was what Madeleine called it. The cat was an exemplar, a paradigm. "Just watch him. Not asleep, just sitting. He's like Leo. Nothing to do, nowhere to go, no one to talk to, nothing going on in his mind."

The cat had been, of course, castrated, but Madeleine never referred to that aspect of the analogy.

"He's waiting for mice," Leo said.

"And you? Leo the lion? Waiting for gazelles?"

"I'm not predatory."

"Precisely."

"Precisely, what? What do you mean, *precisely?*"

"There you are: you're reduced to semantic arguments. That's all there is. If you're not careful, you'll slide on into old age and semantics is all you'll have. You'll sit there just like the cat and words will go round in your head and there'll be nothing else."

"Your analogy is breaking down. The cat's mind is empty, you just said so yourself."

"I bet you even rationalize your faith, don't you? I bet you don't *feel* it any longer, not with your emotions, not with your body. I bet it's just words. Liturgy, dogma, creed, words. Sterile. Tell me what you think."

"What I think about what?"

"You, your life, your vocation. What's it for?"

Conversations like this gave him a sharp and curious sense of delight—something that was almost physical, like a guilty pleasure. On occasion he provoked them, willed her to produce these outbursts. "Why on earth do you *live* in these dreadful rooms, Leo?" she asked when she and Jack visited him in the Institute. "What's to stop you moving out, getting a place of your own? If you're not careful you'll end up evolving into a dreadful old fossil just like all these other priests."

"I don't think you *evolve* into a fossil," he answered her. "I think you've mixed your metaphors. Again."

"There!" she cried triumphantly. "That's just what I mean."

She became, of course, the negation of her own argument, his escape from the very evils she accused him of. Her tone, her presence, her manner conspired against him, jostled him out of complacency and compliance. Consciously, unconsciously, he began to change. A metamorphosis. Celibacy is the enemy of change but Leo Newman, Father Leo Newman, began to ease himself reptile-like out of the dry skin of his old life.

"How do you know a *princess,* for goodness' sake?" Madeleine asked when he told her his plans. She bubbled with laughter at the idea. "How on *earth* do you know a princess?"

"She was a friend of my mother's."

"Your *mother's?* I thought your mother was a piano teacher."

"Can't a piano teacher know a princess?"

"A cat may look at a queen," Madeleine said. It was what Leo had come to label one of her "Irish" replies.

She went with him to visit the princess in her castle, the eponymous Palazzo Casadei, a moldering Roman palace that had belonged to the family since the sixteenth century. The family had survived popes and kings, dictators and presidents. It had lived there when Benvenuto Cellini was a prisoner in Castel Sant'Angelo, and when Keats was a young hopeful dying of consumption in a boarding house not far away. It had watched the Garibaldini celebrating in the streets and the French troops marching in to restore the papacy. It had weathered theocracy and monarchy, oligarchy and tyranny but now looked as though it might well not survive democracy. The *principessa* lived on the *piano nobile* amid the fantastic wreckage left behind by bands of marauding visitors: the portrait of the family pope, the paintings of long-dead ancestors, the gilt and guilt of those five hundred years' survival. She resembled her surroundings as a pet resembles its master: she was ancient and decaying, the edges frayed and the prominences shiny and threadbare.

"*Conoscevo tua madre*," she said to her visitors from the outside world. I knew your mother. She used the familiar form of the pronoun, *tua*, as though Leo were a child. "*Una bellissima donna.*" The old woman nodded as though confirming the fact to herself and the fog of memory seemed to disperse for a moment to show distant scenes, forgotten people. "I remember hearing her play, do you know that? She played like an angel. Schubert, Liszt, Beethoven, those great Germans. Ah, *die gute alte Zeit*. And I remember you, oh yes, I remember you. Young Leo, isn't that it?"

Leo and Madeleine sat awkwardly on a threadbare sofa from the last century, an uncomfortable thing with tortured legs and twisted arms. "Yes," he agreed, "that's it."

"And she is dead now?"

"She died eight years ago."

The *principessa* shrugged. What else could one expect? They were all dead, her friends just as much as her enemies. All dead, just as she herself appeared almost to be dead, or at least to occupy some state between the living and the dead, a kind of limbo. She pointed her clawed finger at Madeleine. "And who is this?"

"She is a friend."

"She is not your wife?"

"I have no wife. I have never been married."

The old woman's laugh had within it a rich bubble of corruption. "Why should you? I was never married. I had many friends but I was never once married. Many friends, many lovers." They were there all around her, framed in silver—beautiful young men in wide-lapelled suits and two-tone shoes, beautiful women with wide shoulders and pomaded hair. Edda Mussolini, wearing some kind of turban, smiled out of one frame and greeted *mia cara Eugenia, con affetto*. "And you want to come and live here? You have seen the apartment?"

"The *portiere* gave us the key."

She shrugged. "It's a poor enough place. This whole palazzo is a poor place, old and rotting like me. I am the last of the line, do you know that? Oh, there are cousins of some kind, there are always cousins in an Italian family, but no one that I see. I am the last. My father's only child, and the line dies out with me. Why shouldn't you come and live here, eh? Gretchen's little boy, sterile just like me. Why not?" The idea seemed to amuse her. She began to laugh once more, a laugh that soon transformed itself into a racking cough, so that a female attendant hurried in from the room next door to help her. "Gretchen's little boy," the old woman cried through coughs and laughter, "Gretchen's sterile little boy."

Madeleine and Leo left awkwardly, in the midst of medical ministrations. They went down wide marble stairs past a group of tourists going into the public rooms where dusty things were roped off and approximately guarded. "What a nasty old woman," Madeleine said. "What did she say? The German, I mean. I could follow the Italian, but she said something in German."

"*Die gute alte Zeit.*" Leo laughed at the idea. "It means 'the good old days.' "

They emerged from the staircase into the shadows of the entrance archway. In the courtyard (Giacomo da Vignola, 1558) was sunlight and greenery, a circumference of columns, a floor of sloping basalt, a pond with a clump of vegetation around the central fountain. From the midst of this growth a carved figure peered out at whatever tourists were around, a gnarled and leery satyr dribbling water into a stone bowl like a senile man dribbling saliva into a kidney basin. The vegetation included elegant fronds of *Cyperus papyrus,* the papyrus plant.

They climbed other stairs in the building, the back stairs, stairs that led behind the scenes and had once been for the servants.

"How did the *principessa* know your mother?" Madeleine asked as they climbed. "I didn't realize she lived in Rome. Or was it in London?"

He evaded the question. "It was a long time ago."

"And she remembered you as a child?"

Leo laughed. "Of course she didn't. She's gaga."

"But she knew your name."

"Yes," he agreed, "she knew my name."

The apartment was high up beneath the roof of the building. Leo unlocked the door and stepped inside. The place was more like an abandoned attic than a place to live, a loft filled with rejected, broken furniture. The ceilings sloped toward the floor. The floor itself creaked and flexed. There was the smell of dust, the smell of age, the smell of nameless events in a nameless past. "A lair," she exclaimed, following him inside. "Leo's lair." They went through the cold and empty rooms with something like amazement, something like amusement, something of the pent-up, unspoken excitement of children.

"It'll be hot in summer."

"Unbearable. And cold in winter."

Ancient pipes snaked around the margins of the rooms like relics from the industrial revolution. "But there's heating of some kind." She peered out of a dormer window onto a stretch of broken tiles. There was a short struggle with the latch before the window yielded. She pushed it open and climbed out, calling him to follow, calling to him to share her astonishment. "Good God Almighty," she cried. "Come and look at this!"

He clambered out after her. He must have been startled by the view. Bewilderment, delight, an amalgam of emotions. It must have shown on his face. He stood there in the middle of the terrace with the city around him, circling around him, wheeling around him as though he were the axis and the whole place was his circumference; and Madeleine laughed at him and his new-found independence.

*   *   *

Together with Jack she helped him move his things from the Institute. There were books but little else, almost nothing physical that bore witness to the existence on earth of Father Leo Newman, priest of the Roman Catholic Church: no accoutrements, no furniture, no *things*. Even when he had installed himself in the apartment, the place remained shabby and bare, a mere dormitory. Madeleine helped him buy things for the kitchen, cutlery, some saucepans, things that he had never needed before— sheets, towels, all the stuff of domestic life. "The civilizing of Leo," she called it. They bought him an armchair, to set against the broken-backed sofa that was part of the sparse furnishings. And Madeleine bought him an alarm clock to rouse him in the mornings. It had the words CARPE DIEM across its face.

"Must be like getting a divorce," Jack observed. "You suddenly find yourself out on your own after years of dependence. Not easy, old fellow, not easy."

Leo felt a sense of relief when the Brewers were gone, relief and guilt, just as he had as a child when leaving his mother on his return to school. The solitary was ingrained in him, like a scar burned into the skin. Celibacy means more than mere sexual abstinence: it means that you become sufficient unto yourself, contained, self-absorbed. He walked around the apartment not like a prisoner examining his cell, but like an explorer on a new and limitless island. Below him the traffic noise of the city; up here beneath the tiles a sense of space, of liberation, of solitude. He prayed for an hour, reading his breviary, reading bits from the Bible, muttering words, keeping long silences. He prayed to a lean and twisted Christ figure; he prayed to a God who veered between the patriarchal mythic figure of childhood and an abstract concept as vast as a galaxy, as vast as the space between the galaxies, as vast and nebulous and meaningless as the space that contained all the galaxies and all the spaces. That evening he slept in his clothes, fetuslike on the ugly, lumpy bed, and awoke to a morning that was pregnant with possibility. It was a strange delight to move around the place in his own time, to make a cup of coffee with the *caffettiera* that he had bought with Madeleine, to walk out onto the roof terrace and watch the early sunrise over the Capitoline Hill.

Thoughts? More a sensation. A sensation of possibility.

He was to meet Madeleine and some of her friends at a Roman church, to play the expert guide. In the event it was raining, one of those sudden, surprising storms that strikes the city in early spring, turning dry streets into boiling torrents within a few minutes. The traffic ground to a halt. Cars appeared marooned like islands in the stream. The Janiculum Hill was capped by a gray pall and the dome of Saint Peter's basilica vanished in the murk. He waited in the exiguous shelter of the narrow Romanesque portico of the church that was to have been the meeting place and wondered how long it would be before he would be allowed to escape beyond the wall of falling water.

Thoughts of a solitary priest caught in a rainstorm: he cannot ignore rain, not rain like that, elemental rain, diluvial, Noachian rain. He cannot merely think about the papyrus fragments he is editing for the World Bible Center, those precious flakes whose existence was stirring the world of textual analysis, or the homily that he must deliver at next Sunday's mass. He cannot do all of this when confronted with that rain. And thunder beating over the cupolas of the city, like someone moving furniture in the anteroom of heaven. And lightning illuminating the face of the city with a sudden ghastly pallor, the pallor of arc lights. The questioning of the elements. Where, poor priest with doubts, were you when I laid the foundations of the earth? Has the rain a father? Is it nothing more than a concatenation of static and water vapor and the clash of bodies of air, warm and cold, dissipating the energy of a hydrogen bomb with all the random carelessness of a child? From which direction does the lightning fork? Who carves a channel for the downpour and hacks a way for the rolling thunder?

What did they think when *he* stilled the storm? Did it make them any happier? You get short, sharp storms on the Sea of Galilee. The wind descends from the Golan Heights, the country of the Gadarenes, and rushes down the slope like a herd of wild pigs and crashes against the water. Shifting masses of air, local heating, sudden confusion, just as suddenly quiet. So what happened on that occasion? Did they think everything was going to be plain sailing with this man, who, it seemed, might be able to work meteorological miracles?

Why are ye fearful, O ye of little faith?

And then a figure, some kind of hood held over its head, splashed through the downpour and skidded into the shelter beside him. "Christ, how embarrassing," it said. "Not really appropriate language, is it? Golly, maybe. *Golly*, how embarrassing." She shook water from her hood (now revealed as a plastic bag with a supermarket logo printed on it) and grinned up at him through plastered hair. There was water on her cheeks and a brightness in her eyes, as though, among other things, the rain had washed away some of her years. "I'm afraid there's only me, you see. I tried to phone you to cancel it, but there was something wrong with your line and I couldn't get through."

"I don't think it's working yet. I've rung the company, but you know what they're like."

"So I came."

"And the others?"

"I'm awfully sorry, Leo. I mean, I *did* get through to the others . . . and we canceled. But now that I'm here, I mean we might as well have a look . . ."

He tried to get out of it, tried to suggest that they postpone it to another day, but she insisted. "I really want to see the place, and here we are, for goodness' sake, and so let's. If it's all right for you to be alone with a woman. I must say"—regarding him with a comic, inquisitive expression—"you don't *look* like a priest."

"What's that got to do with it?"

She smiled, pulling a handkerchief out from her bag and wiping her face. "We will not create scandal. Priest alone in church with woman. I don't think the News of the Screws could do much with that, do you?"

"News of the . . . ?"

She laughed. "*World. News of the World.* Goodness, which cloister do you come from? Come on, show me."

So they ran around the corner—a burst of rain, a burst of laughter from Madeleine—and reached the door. On the notice-board inside the vestibule there was a faded announcement giving the times of mass and a poster explaining that it had recently been World Mission Month and that there were many people out there who were very much worse off than any of you here. The inner door creaked open on a pulley system and slammed abruptly behind them. They were inside, in a vault as empty as a sarcophagus—as dusty, as stony, as cold. Gray columns rose up to a dank and shadowy roof. There was a tentative smell of incense, like the smell of mothballs clinging to some long-out-of-fashion dress. A sanctuary light burned dimly in the shadows at the far end, and a frescoed figure stared out of a nearby pillar like a ghost looming in the shadows of a haunted house. Outside the rain came down, an amalgam of noise like the rushing of a great wind, the wind of Pentecost, perhaps.

Madeleine bobbed perfunctorily in front of the altar and clipped in her narrow shoes across the floor—cosmatesque spirals and circles—to the only painting that the place possessed, an entombment of Christ that looked to the untutored eye to come from the thirteenth century but which was actually fifteenth and simply old-fashioned even when it was painted. "So?" she asked, standing before her dead Savior and looking across the uneven pavement at Newman. "Where are the secrets?"

"In the sacristy."

The sacristy was populated by heavily varnished wardrobes and a sideboard with the instruments of the Mass on it. Set into the wall beside the door there was a lavabo with a ceramic Mother and Child above the basin, the work, so a handwritten notice assured the onlooker, of the school of Andrea della Robbia. Surprisingly in this still and dusty place, there was also a human being, an ancient crone hiding in ambush behind a stand of dog-eared postcards. She glared at the couple as though they had already committed some gross act of desecration. Newman wished her *buon giorno,* although all the evidence from outside (a crash of thunder which set the whole building shaking) was to the contrary. The ancient woman remained impassive in the face of the storm and the greeting. "*Mille lire, per le luci,*" she demanded.

Madeleine scrabbled in her handbag. "I must pay."

"It's only a thousand lira."

"It's the principle."

The old crone regarded the money with suspicion. Then she surrendered a rusty key and gestured toward the corner of the room where there was a narrow door that looked as though it might lead into a broom closet or something. "*Giù,*" she said. Down.

The door opened to reveal a narrow spiral staircase descending into the bowels of the city. Madeleine peered into the pit. "How horrible. You go first."

So they wound their way down into the past, like a descent into a tomb, like a descent into Hades, Madeleine's shoes clipping on the iron stair just behind his ear and her voice echoing in the drum of the stairwell. "I don't like this kind of thing," she said. "I hated it under Saint Peter's. I get all claustrophobic . . ."

But there was nothing enclosed about the space below the church where the stairs led, nothing cramped or claustrophobic—it was wide and empty and gray with dust. A string of bare bulbs lit the place with a blank and inquisitorial light. They climbed down onto the dusty floor and clambered over wall footings and around pillars. There were bits of pavement beneath their feet and earthenware pipes and blocks of volcanic tuff. Pillars rose up like stalagmites in a cave to support the roof of the building, which was the floor of the modern church directly above.

"Where are we?" Madeleine asked. She craned to see, her face open with amazement. "*When* are we?"

"About the second century AD. Some kind of public hall converted into a Christian place of worship. People probably worshiped here who remembered Paul and Peter in the city."

The idea stopped her. She stood there in the midst of the urban litter of the centuries like a flame, a bright flame in the gray ashes. What did she think? Did she feel that frisson that comes from an apprehension of the past, that little thrill of propinquity? That is what he assumed. He read nothing more than that into the glance she cast in his direction (hazel eyes, the scattering of faint freckles, the slight frown of concentration). "Can you *feel* them?"

"Who?"

"Those early Christians."

"That's your fey Irish for you."

"It's imagination."

"Do we want imagination?"

She glanced around and up. "If not, why come?"

The smell: a smell of the centuries, dead and airless. Somewhere beyond a low wall a mosaic emerged from beneath the dust like a sore showing through an animal's pelt: the outline of a fish drawn in gray basalt tesserae. He called her over to see. "It's time for your fish lecture," she said. "Go on."

Symbols, signifiers, signs. Fish is a curious one: *ichthys,* a fish.

It is an acronym, in fact, for *Iesous Christos Theou Hyios Soter,* Jesus Christ, Son of God, Savior. They used it as a sign of recognition, casually tracing the design in the dust with an idle, scraping toe, or scrawling it on a wall just as they do nowadays, just as someone had chalked the slogan Dio c'è—there is a God—on the wall of the Palazzo Casadei just beside the main entrance. *Dio c'è.* It's an interesting proposition.

"If you've heard it already, why ask for it again?"

"You're offended. I only meant it as a joke. The others, you know what they say? They say, goodness he's serious."

"Isn't that what you'd expect from—"

"A priest? I suppose so. And they also say—"

"What do they also say?"

She crouched down and brushed her hand over the fish shape, and as she bent her hair fell forward like a cascade of seaweed. Even her hand was like something marine, a pale starfish floating over the fish, tapering fingers with a scattering of freckles like a subtle cryptic coloration. She swept some dust away from the single crude eye so that it could see more clearly. "They say, why on earth did he become a priest? What a waste."

Madeleine looked up and there was something else there, some other sign, perhaps: the silent, eloquent gape of her neckline, her breasts hanging there in the shadow like forbidden fruit among the leaves of a tree, the fruit of the tree of the knowledge of good and evil. "What a waste," she repeated.

That was the moment when there was a crash of thunder outside, a massive explosion from the upper world that intruded even there eighteen centuries earlier, reverberating around the ancient walls like an earthquake. That was the moment when the lights went out and plunged the two of them into an all-consuming darkness.

"Oh, Christ!" Madeleine's voice was shrill with panic. Darkness, total darkness pressed up to the eyes and lay against the skin like a suffocating cloth. It offered no perspective. Only her voice, sharp, momentarily terrified, gave depth to the darkness around them. "Oh, my God. Where are you? Leo? Where are you?"

"It's all right. Don't be frightened."

"Of course I'm bloody frightened." Darkness as a substance, pressing against the cornea, pressing in on the body like a shroud. "Where are you, Leo. Leo?"

"Here. Come towards me. Mind the wall." There was a movement, a scrabbling like rodents among the dust, a suppressed cry as she stumbled; and then something live crept through the mask of darkness and grasped his hand, a small, fragile animal clutching at him.

"There you are." Her voice was suddenly mere inches from his face, just below his chin. The sound of her breathing was palpable in the blackness, a disturbance in the tissue of darkness, as though something were tunneling through it to reach him. "Thank God," she murmured, clambering up and leaning against him in relief, shaking with what he supposed was fear. "I'm sorry," she whispered.

He felt her breath. He put out his hand speculatively into the void and touched her cheek and the soft pulp of her lip. "What is there to apologize for?"

"Don't let me go, Leo," she whispered. "Don't. I'm sorry. Don't." A strange alternation of demand and apology: I'm sorry. Don't. I'm sorry. Don't. Her hair had a scent about it. He half recalled it from the enclosed, airless intimacy of the confessional: a warm mammal smell mingled with other perfumes—the scent of citrus, the scent of musk, the scent of other things that he could not name or imagine. Frankincense and myrrh, perhaps. Scent is dangerous, stirring dull roots. The word *redolent* comes from the Latin verb *olere,* to emit a smell. He had once read that the center in the brain that is concerned with the perception of aroma is next to the memory center, so that the one stimulates the other. Smell recalling the past, the smell of attar of roses and lemon. The first time he had embraced anyone for years. His mother. The distant girlfriend named Elise. No others. Proust with his madeleines, he thought, and smiled through the faint sense of revulsion, the feeling of wanting to push her away, the sensation of something at his throat, clasping the windpipe, constricting the windpipe, choking him and making him want to vomit, closing and opening at one and the same time. Aperient and astringent.

And scent doing something else, something that he would have to come to terms with later, confess to some anonymous priest—for he would be loath to speak of it to his usual confessor, who would tell him what he did not want to hear, that he should put temptation away and never see the woman again. He didn't want an admonition like that. Already he was bargaining with his God. For in that embrace he felt a palpable tumescence. And he experienced the bewildering sensation that the physical may be bound up entirely with the spiritual, so much so that he was uncertain which had happened: had lust dragged down love, or had the spiritual, the cerebral elevated erection to a prayer?

How long before the lights came on? One minute? Ten? There was first a distant twilight and a shout from the upper world—the crone who guarded the souls of the dead coming with a flashlight—and then the bulbs themselves flicked on once, twice, and then remained on, to display the waste of rubble around the clinging couple, stark in their unshaded light. They parted in embarrassment. "Oh God, how awkward," she cried, avoiding his eye and brushing herself down almost as though ridding herself of some kind of contamination. "I really think we'd better be going, don't you?" She picked up her skirt a fraction and examined her knee. "Blast, I've torn my tights on that wall." She didn't look up. She no longer looked at him, no longer caught his eye and smiled in that manner of hers, part irony, part curiosity, part wondering whether she was missing something that others had understood. She didn't look at him. It is said that you can tell when a man and a woman have become adulterers. Before the event they watch each other all the time, steal mutual glances at every opportunity. After they have consummated their passion they avoid each other's eyes.

From that moment in the darkness of the paleo-Christian subterranean Church of San Crisogono, Madeleine Brewer avoided Leo Newman's eye.

A voice on the phone, disturbingly familiar, a faint tone of mockery, a sharp hint of the profane. "Can I come round and see you? I want to talk. Will it be difficult?"

"Here at the flat?"

"Wherever." Outside the open window was the scream of swifts and the distant roar of traffic down the Lungotevere. Inside, within the dull boundaries of his apartment, he sweated. "It's up to you," he said.

"The flat. The lion's lair."

She came at ten-thirty in the morning. He watched her from the window as she walked along the pavement on the far side of the street. She crossed to an island in the stream of traffic, glancing up for a moment at the Palazzo Casadei in front of her, waiting for a break, an eddy in the whirl of car and bus and moped that might let her across to the near bank. A bus stopped to disgorge passengers nearby. She plunged into the flow, a small, determined figure in navy skirt and sensible walking shoes and a bright red jacket. A wide, slightly masculine stride. He watched her disappear directly below.

Fear? Nothing so focused. Confusion. A sense of choking panic. A faint hint of revulsion at the prospect of her smell, her presence, the fragile sound of her voice. And impatience, an impatience that was without direction or focus, just an impatience that the thing should be over.

She apologized as she came in, although it wasn't clear what she had to apologize for. She looked around distractedly and threw her jacket—blood red, a hemorrhage, a clot—across the back of the chair that she and Jack had given him, and said how sorry she was to bother him; while Newman fussed around her, drew up a chair for her to sit, apologized for its discomfort, busied himself making a cup of coffee at the electric ring in the narrow kitchen. Absurdly he found himself ashamed of his room, of the dull furniture and the paltry possessions. These were things of which he had once been proud: proud of their deficiencies, that is.

"I'm sorry," she repeated as she took the coffee. "I suppose you get this all the time."

"What?"

"People opening their hearts to you."

"Is that what you're doing?"

She laughed and looked away, blushing, looking for distractions, finding little in that uncompromising place. "You need flowers in here. I should have brought some. The place needs brightening up."

"A woman's touch?"

"If you like. I suppose the idea would revolt you." She got up from the chair she had hardly sat in and went over to the window, to crouch down and look out on the street, to pick at the curtain, to touch, for no apparent reason, the pane of glass. "Now we see through a glass darkly," she murmured, "then, face to face."

"Why *revolt?*"

"Aren't you allergic to that kind of thing, stuck in your masculine world?" She made a small expression of distaste. Her face was reflected in the windowpane and he could see both, the face and the faint, milky reflection. "I'm sorry. I invited myself here and I'm just being rude. I don't even know whether it was the right thing to do in the first place. I want to talk about Jack, about my marriage, but I don't expect you're the right person to do that with, are you? I need a parish priest. A parish priest might not have personal experience to refer to but he's heard it all before, isn't that the idea? Whereas you . . ." He let her talk. A small flood of words, neither one thing nor the other, neither social chat nor true confession. "Did you never think of marrying? That's an impertinent question. You might not be interested . . . in women, I mean. I've got my tenses wrong. You might not *have been* interested. We've already talked about this, haven't we? Wasn't she called Elisa? And anyway it's not my business to inquire. But I *was* interested in men, obviously enough I guess, *a* man in particular, like a good little Catholic girl, although there were one or two others before Jack, and now I'm not."

And as she talked, she crossed the void, turned to look at him with a faint smile, but smiling *into* him not *at* him. No one had ever done that before. He had no experience of it. "What do you think I should do?" she asked, and Newman realized that he had not really been listening, or if listening had not really grasped what she was saying, like someone trying to follow a conversation in a foreign language where every word is understood in isolation but the import of the whole is missed. The whole is more than the sum of its parts.

"Do?"

"Yes, *do*. About Jack. You've not been listening, have you?" She grinned suddenly, amused at having caught him out. "Fat lot of good you are. Or was it too boring for words?"

"Of course I was listening. Your marriage has grown stale. But isn't that to be expected? Isn't that the kind of thing you just have to struggle through for a while?"

"And what about *your* marriage? To Holy Mother Church. Does that grow stale?"

"Are we talking about you or me?"

"I'm sorry. Of course I shouldn't pry. Me. I. We were talking of me. But the problem is, you are the only person I can talk to. Do you realize that, Leo?"

"Me?"

"You see, you were one thing . . . and you've become another."

Anxiety. Anxiety is fear spread out thin, a thin coating of fear on the face of every action. "Another? I don't follow."

"You were a priest, and you've become a . . . friend. I'm sorry, perhaps there shouldn't be a distinction. This isn't a confession, Leo. I'm just a woman confiding in a friend."

And he thought: woman, *'issâ*, because she came forth from man, *'is*. Women get a mixed press in the Bible, starting with Eve, of course. Snakes weave their way into the discourse of women, holding out the fruit of forbidden knowledge, knowledge of the fruit that lies there, below the folds of cloth, between those heavy, quite unmasculine thighs. Difficult, women. Consider her namesake, Mary of Magdala, the woman from whom seven devils were cast.

"But Father Leo is now plain Leo," she was saying, "to whom I can talk not as a confessor but as an ordinary, I hope sympathetic, fellow human. And I hope he doesn't find it an intrusion." Leo fumbled some kind of reply, but she took little notice, merely smiled at him with her direct and careless smile, and confessed to crisis. "Oh, big crisis, Leo. Faith, love, the whole thing. Am I incoherent once more? You have before you someone who is destitute." She laughed. On the surface it seemed her usual, open laugh, the laugh that bore within itself the sharp, acerbic flavor of self-mockery. An acquaintance would never have detected anything untoward in it, no despair, no anguish. But those things were there. Somehow he knew them, and the very intimacy of knowing them disturbed him. "I have no more faith, Leo. It's gone, vanished, *puff!* in a little cloud of dust. Can you bring it back with your subtle, Jesuitical arguments? I no longer love God, because I have ceased to believe in his existence, and I no longer love Jack, who, I might say, has long given the impression of no longer loving me, because in a way I no longer believe in *his* existence either. Do I sound very like a silly teenager?"

"A little."

"But there's a difference. *I* am liable to act. With teenagers often enough it just blows over. But *I* may act."

"And do what?"

She shook her head. "Don't know yet. But it's there, the possibility. I feel it. You see, you've only got one chance, haven't you? I know you won't be so foolish as to give me the party line about treasures in heaven, or saving yourself for the Day of Judgment or whatever. When you're my age you've only got one chance left. There's a certain obligation to take it, isn't there?"

"Obligation?"

"To yourself. There's no one else, is there?"

"I thought there might be a few others. The children, for example."

She considered this idea thoughtfully. "Do you remember Saint Crisogono?"

"What about it?" Anxiety deepened, focused, became plain fear. Panic rose in his throat like gorge.

"Our visit there?"

"Of course." The sensation of her in his arms, the fragile presence of her, her shoulders beneath his hands, her head a mere hair's breadth beneath his face, the breadth of her hair, the breath of her hair; the focus of being in total darkness, so that she became the only thing, or rather her touch, her tactile presence became the only thing in his universe. Panic.

"I'm just as I was then, Leo. In the dark. Total." And she began to weep, quite suddenly, almost as though nothing had gone on before that ought to have given notice of this possibility, this organic manifestation of whatever emotion it was that coursed beneath her calm outer surface. He got up and went over to her and put his hand on her shoulder, awkwardly, as one might with a male friend who has suddenly and unexpectedly displayed embarrassing emotion; and she raised her own hand and clasped his softly, squeezing it, stroking it, and saying all the while that grown-ups don't just cry for nothing, do they, not like children?

Hysteria. Of course he had been warned against it. Hysteria, from *hystera,* a womb. It was, he understood, something that besets women. Jezebel, Susanna, their names stalk the nightmares of the celibate. Salome tosses the veil aside and gyrates her hips while Herodias calls for heads. Delilah strokes the male head of hair and reaches for her scissors while speaking in tones of blandishment and seduction. Judith reaches down the scimitar.

"I'm all right," Madeleine said after a while. "God, how embarrassing. I'm quite all right." She shook her head, shook tears from her eyes, found a handkerchief and dabbed at her face. "Has my makeup run? What a sight I must look. I have been an unconscionable imposition on you." She smiled through bruised, inflamed eyes and asked if she could use the bathroom—and it occurred to him that someone who could use the word *unconscionable* in those circumstances could hardly be considered hysterical.

He waited while she splashed around for a while, and when she came back her former equilibrium had been restored. She spoke in a quiet, matter-of-fact voice: "And now I'm going to say what I didn't dare the other day in that bloody church."

The censorious priest spoke, probably for the last time: "*Bloody?*"

"Well, they *are* bloody. The whole Faith is bloody—look at the stations of the cross, or the Sacred Heart of Jesus, or the Blood of the Redemption, or almost anything else you care to mention. The whole Faith is floated on blood. 'The multitudinous seas incarnadine.'" She had lost her fugitive beauty and now looked merely dull and determined, her face clenched into a kind of smile, a humorless smile, as though it were battened against the wind, against the rain, against whatever the elements might throw against her. "I'm going to speak and, out of pure, human compassion if nothing else, you're to hear me out without interruption." And he knew what it was even before she spoke, for the thing was obvious, really.

"I have fallen in love with you," she said. "I'm not hysterical. I have never been more serious in my life. And I know that it is all hopeless. I know, Leo. I *know*. But there it is." With care, as though balancing on the edge of a precipice, she opened her hands to show that she had given up all support and security and was ready to plunge over the edge. Her face was pale. The freckles across her nose stood out like blemishes. He could see the creases at her eyes, the dry brushstrokes of her eyebrows, the uneven texture of her skin, the lines that age had etched there.

He went over to her and he put out his hand and touched her cheek. Physically, that is what he did, just touched her cheek, and thereby did what had been denied him for so long, for almost three decades: made intimate contact with someone. You shake hands, yes; maybe you even embrace and exchange kisses. But you never touch another's cheek. An act of intimacy, a carnal act, feeling the flesh, the downy fabric of the other, surprisingly, startlingly soft. He touched her cheek and she made a small noise, inarticulate and mouselike, like the cry of a small mammal in distress. She made this sound and she came nearer him and they embraced, just as they had done in the darkness of the Church of San Crisogono, her head turned and pressed against his chest. But this time they were out in the light and the terms of endearment were clear between them, and he could not do anything else but lower his head and press his face clumsily—practice, how do you find practice in such things?—against her hair, against the silken down at the nape of her neck.

The scent of her presence, a strange, alien scent, flooded through him. It seemed as important as anything, more important than any cerebrations, more vital than any rationalization—her scent, with its blend of the mammal and the floral, the warm perfume of her skin and hair mixed with the sharp scent of fruit, the irrational chasing out the cerebral. He felt something akin to panic, something of the excitement associated with fear, something of the terrifying abstraction that might be associated with madness; and something of the dangerous conviction of heresy.

"Leo," she murmured from deep against his chest, "what are we going to do? Whatever are we going to do?'

Malaria—1943

S he is talking to Leo, of her childhood, of the days in
Mähren, Moravia, near Buchlowitz. She sits askew on the
side of his bed, and leans back against the propped-up pillow, and her arm is around the child's shoulders and her hand is
playing with a lock of his hair. The boy listens with wide eyes, as
though she is telling fairy tales, fantastic fables from long ago, and
indeed there are wolves and wild boar and dwarfs in the forests of
the Chřiby Hills—she pronounces the awkward Slavonic name with
ease—and great, black castles high among the trees; and she does
talk of a fabulous world, a lost world that lives on only in memories
and posed photographs, a world of horses and carriages, of lamplight, of long winter evenings when whole villages were cut off from
each other and from the city by drifts of snow, of the house where

she was born and lived until she married—"the *Zamek,* we used to
call it. It was said that Marshal Kutuzov himself stayed there before
the battle of Austerlitz. Oh, it was a wonderful home. And the gardens! The gardens, with the peacocks and the arboretum and the
fuchsarium—which was Papi's favorite. He always said that a man
ought to have an occupation, and growing fuchsias was his—and
we used to make a hideout in the arboretum, your uncle and I, and
no one could find us for hours, and . . ." And her tide of words turns
and begins to ebb, the memory of adulthood taking the place of the
fantasies of childhood:

"And in 1926 I met your father. We were in Marienbad. We
used to go to Marienbad every season for the waters. Papi said he
preferred it to Karlsbad because it was quieter and less claustrophobic—Karlsbad in the ditch, he used to call it—and we took
rooms at the Weimar where everyone went, and that was where I
met your father . . ."

Things change. We grow old. The center—that is, childhood—
cannot hold.

"It was summer. He was on leave from the Foreign Office, and
staying with friends who had a house somewhere nearby. The
borders meant so little then, you see. You could cross them at will,
and going from Bavaria to Austria to Bohemia was as though you
were still in the same country. And I came down the great staircase, looking, oh, so young and beautiful—sixteen, that's all—
and there was this man, standing with a group of friends,
smoking, and he just turned and looked . . ."

A lost world. The center cannot hold, *Mitteleuropa* cannot hold.

". . . walking with him in the Kolonada, taking the waters and
laughing at the horrid taste of it—rust, it tasted of rust, or blood,
like when you cut yourself and you suck the cut—concerts and
dances in the casino, and walks up through the woods—we went
chaperoned by my aunt—and, oh, what days they were, Leo.
Always sunny, always bright and sunny. He wrote me a poem,

do you know that? A poem about me in Marienbad. Gretchen in Marienbad, it was called. Imagine having a poem written about you!"

Thus Frau Huber to her child. The Zamek is now a state museum with a ticket office in the gatehouse, and a shop in the fuchsarium. What happened in between is what happened to the whole of middle Europe: the apocalypse.

"Everything seemed so safe in those days, that is the strange thing. Everything seemed so safe. And yet it was the most danger-ous place in the whole world."

"*Mutti,*" the child asks, a precocious child with words that are older than his years. "What will happen now?"

"Happen?"

"Will the war come here?"

She laughs. Frau Huber laughs. For this city seems as safe as anywhere in the whole benighted continent, a refuge from the bombs and the guns, protected by the presence of a small man with an ascetic face and a smooth command of German: the Pope, Eugenio Pacelli. "Of course the war won't come here." But she laughs because she doesn't believe it.

A disturbed night, a night of air-raid sirens and the sharp crack of anti-aircraft guns, a night played out against the drone of bombers, invisible in the darkness over the city. A hot night of flares bursting in the sky, apparently right over the Villa, and light-ing up the dark streets and the churches and the palazzi with flashes of summer lightning. An airless, sultry night during which the Huber family spends hours in the shelters beneath the Villa along with others of the embassy, wondering when and where the bombs will fall. The anti-aircraft fire seems distant and desultory. "These Italians have no stomach for a fight," someone remarks. To Leo it seems an adventure, to the adults little more than an incon-venience. "It is a bluff," someone remarks, a third secretary whose previous posting was in Washington. "They will never bomb the city—the Catholic lobby is too powerful for Roosevelt to dare."

Herr Huber's report the next morning seems some kind of confirmation of this. "No bomb damage," he announces, coming into the apartment from his office while his wife and son are at breakfast. "No bombs at all, in fact. Aerial photography. They were photographing the city. The Americans. They seem to be interested in the railway station."

It is chilling, this cold, analytical war in which invisible airplanes fly in the night and take photographs at will. "What do they want photographs for? How can photographs help them?"

"They will use them as a guide when they bomb the city."

"Bomb Rome? But how could they *bomb* Rome? Francesco said . . ."

"The man doesn't know what he is talking about."

The morning is a disturbed one, with messages and departures, and vague reports that are then denied. There are conflicting reports about the situation in Sicily, there is a rumor of a letter from the Pope to the American President, there is a report of contacts between elements of the Italian government and the Allies. Amidst it all comes a telephone message, taken by one of the secretaries—a domestic matter, an ordinary moment among the rumor of war: Leo's tutor is ill and so cannot come today.

"Is he injured?" Frau Huber asks. Bombs, even nonexistent bombs, haunt the collective mind of the city.

"Ill, *gnädige Frau*," the secretary says. "A fever, he told me."

"He told you himself?"

"He sounded unwell. He sounded very weak."

There is no reply when she calls the number. She wonders where the phone at the other end is ringing, in what apartment, behind what closed doors, ignored by whom.

"He's shirking," is Herr Huber's judgment. "I never did quite trust him from the moment he started. He was frightened by the raid last night and fancied a day off. What do you call it? Pulling the lead?" *You* means *the English*. It is a jibe, a faint provocation, an accusation: *you have one foot in the enemy camp*.

"Swinging," she corrects him. "Swinging the lead."

"Ah, yes. Of course. Swinging the lead. A *nautical* term. You have the sea in your blood. Whereas *we* are people of the land." He is in the mood for taunting her. They are absurd taunts, for she has lived all of her life in the very heart of Europe, as far from the Atlantic as from the Urals, as far from the Baltic as from the Mediterranean. She knows the sea from childhood vacations to the Côte d'Azur, that is all; and a single visit to her grandparents' home near Brighton. "Anyway, as Signor Volterra is not here, *you* can teach Leo, can't you? After all, you have teaching in your blood as well."

She ignores that further taunt, but gives life to it by setting her son to work despite his protests. So the morning drags past, the telephones ring, people come and go, Leo complains. Later she goes to the Villa and practices piano for a while, all alone in the reception room with the curtains half drawn against the heat, while the city lies splayed out beneath the sun, the summer sun beating on the asphalt like a hammer beating on brass, and cicadas shrieking in the trees, an insistent, nagging sound like the screaming of newborn babies. Shortly after lunch, a meager unappetizing lunch, she summons a car.

The embassy car, conspicuous with diplomatic plates, carries her away from the Villa and up Via Merulana to the summit of the Esquiline Hill where the Basilica of Santa Maria Maggiore stands sandbagged in the hot sun. Pedestrians glance around as the car passes, with dull expressions that may signify resentment, may imply simple indifference. Italians have long learned to be indifferent to strangers in their midst. At one point the driver has to stop to ask the way. He is from the Alto Adige, the German-speaking Südtirol, and is a stranger to the city, a stranger to most things

Italian. "Don't trust these people," he advises Frau Huber, but whether he is referring to the directions he has been given, or to the people's fidelity in general is not clear. Yet they find the street where Francesco lives easily enough: a long, narrow road leading down from the Esquiline Hill, paved with basalt, a ravine between two lines of buildings whose façades are rust-red and decaying, like the old red sandstone faces of the ancient men sitting outside the wine shop just opposite where the car draws to a halt. The street itself is awash with paper, sheets of paper lying in the dust, some of them crumpled underfoot, one or two torn, most of them entire and bright white in the sunshine: a summer snowstorm, like the legendary summer snowstorm that fell on the hill in the fourth century to mark the place where a church should be built to the name of the Virgin Mary. One of the men is reading aloud to his companions; Frau Huber picks up a leaflet and glances at it. The page is covered with bombastic, bellicose words, ugly threats:

. . . The war is at the gates of your country. The Italian people have the power to bring peace. You have the choice! If you want war, we will bring total war. Africa is ours. Our warships can shell the Italian coastal cities. Airplanes will darken the sun of Italy. Our soldiers can come ashore anywhere . . .

The leaflet is signed by the Allied High Command.

She folds the page into her handbag and turns to the door of number 26, a massive door like the entrance to a church. It opens onto a marble hallway, dark against the sun, dark and cool compared with the heat outside, as dark as the confessional. On the far side of a grille sits the *portiere* (does he comply with the secrecy of the confessional? Doubtful, because all *portieri* are rumored to be Fascist spies), who directs her to the top floor, by the stairs because the elevator is not working, Signora, what with the war and the electricity cuts and everything. They say they will bomb the city, but I don't think they can, do you, Signora, what with His Holiness here and everything? They wouldn't do that, would they? They're not barbarians.

"Aren't they?"

She climbs the stairs slowly, out of the cellarlike cool of the ground floor toward the roof, toward the heat. Finally, sweat-stained and breathless, she is standing outside apartment D, *piano* 6, and knocking in the hope—what hope? why a hope?—that Francesco's voice will answer. But there is no sound at all, and nothing from outside, from the street. Just the still and silent heat of a Rome midday.

"Francesco? Francesco!"

She pushes, and the door yields to her push. There is still no sound. For a moment she hesitates, looking into the shadows of the apartment. All she can see is a square meter of floor, and the corner of a table and the edge of a closed door. "Francesco?"

And then comes a noise, muffled and vague, as though some-one is speaking through some kind of gag.

"Francesco?"

She steps across the threshold into a small hallway. To the right a half-open door shows the kitchen (plates unwashed on a draining board, saucepans on the gas stove, an empty bottle on the table). To the left a closet stands open to display two brooms and a water heater.

"Francesco?"

A sound, if it is a sound, comes from the closed door directly opposite. She tiptoes up to it and listens.

"Francesco?"

The sound is nothing more than a low moan, as of nightmare. Frau Huber grasps the handle and turns it and the door swings open to reveal a darkened room, a carpet, a bed against the far wall, a washstand with a basin and a jug of water, a chest of draw-ers, a crucifix on the wall in this city of crucifixes, and a figure lying on the bed, wrapped in a sodden sheet, twisted into a sodden sheet, a figure that is barely sensible in the heat.

"Checco?" There is an edge of panic in her voice, and a flicker of anger at the words that her husband used—*swinging the lead*. Standing at the bedside, she can feel the heat from him, the heat radiated out from his fever, a heat that reaches over and above the heat of the summer day. His face glistens with sweat, his mouth is rimed with saliva, his hair is damp and matted. Sweat stains the gray pillow. He moves vaguely, as though trying to rid himself of something, and his eyes stare upward, perhaps at the ceiling, perhaps at her, seeing little or nothing. She places her hand on his forehead to feel the sharp burn of fever, and he mumbles something almost as though he is aware of her touch. She makes more sense of his mumbling than there actually is: "Some water, you need some water." The jug is empty. She carries it to the kitchen and opens the tap. You might expect nothing in this chaotic city in the middle of summer in the midst of a war, but ever since the Romans built the aqueducts down from the hills there is one constancy in Rome: water, limpid water, cold once she has let it run.

She returns to the bedroom and pours some water into a glass and crouches beside him, lifting his head for him to drink. The smell of his body comes up to her, rancid and sour. "Water, Francesco. Water." Water floods over his lips and down his unshaven chin, around the curve of his neck, into the grimy pillow. She lays his head back, as one might lay the head of a corpse, and looks around. A sponge. She grabs the sponge from the washstand, pours water into the basin and carries both to the bedside, placing the basin on the floor, soaking the sponge and holding it to his lips, to his brow, to his cheeks. She wipes his face with cool water, and then his neck. He moans and turns vaguely, as though searching for the light and not finding it.

More water, the sponge laden with water like something live in her hand. She pulls the sheet down and sponges his shoulders and his chest and his upper arms. More water. His chest is flushed beneath the tan, his nipples as sharp and dark as damsons, circled by a few strands of hair. She sponges him gently, sponging the fever down, her hand circling his chest, circling the nipples, running over the ribs. More water. The water is tepid now, and she takes the basin to replenish it, returning with it laden, setting it down beside the bed again, kneeling down herself and pulling the sheet down to his abdomen. His torso glows in the sultry shadows of the room, glowing with the amber glow of suntan and the flush of fever, a hot and heady mix. She blows gently across the damp skin, breathes in and blows again. He moans and turns his head and seems to look at her with focus for an instant while she loads the sponge once more and begins to bathe him again, first the face and chest, and then his flat belly, around the small knot of the umbilicus, down to the thin line of hair that vanishes beneath the sheet.

"Checco?" she calls, and he moves his head as though in pain. Kneeling beside him she takes the edge of the sheet and pulls it off him, and stays there motionless for a moment, looking down on him, at the lean and naked legs, the narrow hips, the dark mass of hair and the crumpled penis with its lucid purple cap. She breathes deeply, as she does when she is about to play, when she sits in front of the keyboard and composes herself, hands folded into her lap, as though waiting patiently for something to happen, some small surge of energy that will enable her to proceed. And then she reaches out and touches the small crumpled phallus softly with the tips of her fingers, as she might touch the keys of a piano in an adagio passage, merely stroking them, so softly that any sound they might make seems to have some other cause.

He stirs faintly under her touch. She starts and snatches her hand away. Her heart is beating, so loudly that she feels the sound in the room, reverberating like a drum. She kneels there beside the bed and waits while the young man stirs and moans and returns to some kind of rest, and then she takes up the sponge once more and begins to bathe his hips, his thighs, his chest again, anointing the thin, strong body as it lies there insensible in fever.

6

Limbo. Limbo is neither one place nor the other, neither heaven nor hell, neither paradise nor punishment, neither ecstasy nor execration. Limbo was invented by medieval theologians to overcome a problem—where to put those people who died unbaptized, particularly the innocent, particularly the dead babies. Limbo was where Leo Newman found himself. In limbo he lived out a new routine that was yet surprisingly like his old one, as though you might die and find the afterlife no different from your earthly existence: he lectured as he had always lectured to a motley audience of students on the Development of the New Testament Canon. He argued for an earlier establishment of the canon rather than a later, proposing that the Papyrus Egerton 2 was evidence of a four-gospel canon in the second century, rather than an independent gospel as suggested by Mayeda and later by Daniels, and positing the En-Mor papyri as evidence of this. "Here we have the teachings of the Lord and the teachings of his cousin John the Baptist recorded by a small group of adherents before the disaster of the Jewish War, written down sometime in the eighth decade of the common era. Perhaps earlier." And the students nodded and scribbled, as though what he said was proven and doctrinal rather than mere speculation. He spent afternoons in the library or in the document rooms working through the texts, unpicking them, arguing the words this way and that; and in the early evening he returned to the apartment, to make some kind of supper out of the few things he had gathered together. He felt like a hermit in a cave, a hermit who was hoarding the few fragments of his faith lest they too be swept away by circumstance.

Night was a desolate time, a darkness beset by dreams he could not recall when he awoke, and fears he could not enunciate when he confronted them in the cold light of dawn. Daytime painted over the fears of the night with a thin wash of immediacy.

The telephone rang.

It would be her. They had spoken on the phone but seen each other only twice, once when all three of them, Jack and Madeleine and Leo, had gone to some concert together and she had sat between the two men and Leo had sweated in his narrow seat, knowing her presence beside him, the contact of her shoulder, her knee against his, the quick, covert clasp of her hand. He wondered if he was the subject of some complex game, a game of finesse and sacrifice, the rules known only to her. Perhaps known to Jack as well. As they left the concert hall and walked down the wide triumphal way that leads toward the Basilica of Saint Peter's, she clung to his arm and extolled his virtues to her husband. "My favorite confessor," she called him. "Saint Leo the imperturbable."

"He doesn't look imperturbable to me," Jack had remarked.

"He looks damned embarrassed, you clinging to him like that, and only a hundred yards from headquarters."

The telephone rang.

Their phone conversations had been cautious and oblique, as though each was concerned that someone might be listening, someone else on the line, someone else hidden in the fabric of the world around them like an actor behind the scenery, a third party looking over their shoulders—God, perhaps, reduced to the status of an eavesdropper.

The telephone rang.

He was hurrying with his breakfast—the alarm clock that she had bought him showed the time as nine-thirty, and he had a seminar at ten.

The telephone rang.

Who else phoned him here? The phone lay on the floor in the living room, the cable snaking across the floorboards. It had been abandoned by the last occupant and activated only after arguments with the phone company, only after that rendezvous at the Church of San Crisogono, when she alone had turned up and they had been precipitated together by circumstance or chance or whatever it was that governed the pure caprice of the world.

The telephone rang.

And they had met, just the two of them together, just once. They had driven up in her car and parked on the Janiculum Hill with the whole of the city splayed out before them. There were tourists up there to see the view, and puppeteers performing for groups of shrieking children, and a trick cyclist and a fire eater, a stall selling ice cream and another selling trinkets, all this around the refuge of her car. "Safety in numbers," she said. She sat half-turned toward him, her knees up on the seat so that if he wished he could put out his hand and touch the smooth, silken mound of her patella. He felt a delight in her presence, something of the delight of juvenile love, the breathless longing to be the other, to be subsumed in the other. There were snatched moments of rapture that were no more than a clasp of hands (mature hands, these, lined with sinew and vein, their knuckles wrinkled; mature hands, but clinging to each other like children's). There was confusion and anguish. "If we were any other couple," she said, "we'd be deep into adultery by now. Do you realize that?"

"Of course I realize that."

"And instead we're here, meeting like children who don't quite know what to do."

"Maybe that's what we are in a way. Children."

"*You* are," she said sharply. A sudden anger bubbled up within her. "Not me. *You* are like a child. Retarded, for God's sake."

"That's unfair."

She laughed, but there was no humor there. "What the hell do you know about unfair? What do you know about having to live with someone whom you no longer love, having to show affection for him, having to tell him how fond you are of him—I use the word *fond,* do you know that? So that I won't actually have to lie about *love.* What do you know about having to let him fuck me when I no longer want it, when I want only you?" And the word *fuck* hung there in the air between them like a threat, the scabrous issuing forth from that articulate arabesque of a mouth, while her expression trembled, shook, collapsed slowly into tears.

"I'm sorry, Madeleine," he said pointlessly. "I'm sorry. God, I'm sorry."

She shook her head, as though trying to shake the tears from her eyes. "I'll just disappear from your life if you want that. Do you want that? I'll just vanish. I won't give you any trouble, Leo, I promise you that."

He felt panic at the idea of her absence, a desperate, physical panic, a shortage of breath, a constriction in the chest, the emotional manifested in the organic, a plain, bewildering attack of panic as though he needed to come up for air, as though stricken by asthma, as though felled by shock. "I don't want you to go," he said. "I love you, but I don't understand *how* I love you. I've no practice in the thing, that's the trouble. I don't know which way to turn."

"You can turn to me," she said quietly. "You can always turn to me."

The telephone rang. He knew it would be her. His mind trembled as he lifted the receiver. "*Pronto?* Madeleine?"

There was a silence.

"Is that Leo? Leo Newman?" A man's voice, an American accent.

"Who is this?"

"This is Steve, Leo. Steve Calder. I'm glad I found you." There was something about his tone, some wavering hint of shock that was detectable even over the line. "You've moved, is that right? We called your old number. They said you'd moved, and I had one hell of a load of trouble getting them to part with your new number. I'm his long-lost cousin from Wisconsin, I told them. Look, Leo, there have been developments. Pretty big ones, if you want to know. I've booked you a flight. I hope your passport is up-to-date. You pick up the ticket at the desk at the airport."

"What the devil are you talking about?"

"Tomorrow morning. Didn't I say that? There's a problem? What time is it with you now?"

"Half-past nine."

"Right. We're one hour ahead. Look, someone'll meet you at the airport, is that OK? Tomorrow morning. Your flight leaves at nine your time, that's ten here."

"What's all this about?"

"I told you. There's some new stuff from En-Mor. Didn't I say that?"

"You didn't say anything. What is it? What have they found?"

There was a silence, a hiatus in the rush of words, a carefully constructed pause. Calder knew how to do these things. At last he said it:

"They've found a scroll."

Madeleine phoned later, when he had got back from lecturing at the Institute. Her familiar voice, the small hesitations, the slants, the quick, nimble tones, the anguish that lay behind it, and the anxiety: "Can we talk, Leo? Can we do that? Jack goes away this evening, Leo. Can I come round tomorrow? I promise . . . God, I don't know what I promise. I promise I'll not pressure you. Nothing like that. But I must see you."

"I can't, Madeleine. Not tomorrow."

"Why not tomorrow?"

"I've got to go away."

There was a silence on the other end, that strange hollowness on the line when you know someone is listening but saying nothing, a faint electronic questioning. When finally she spoke her voice seemed far away, a small, fragile thing far away. "Why so suddenly?"

"This business in Israel. The excavation. They've asked me to go."

"Tomorrow morning?"

"Tomorrow morning. An early flight."

"Why didn't you tell me before?"

"I didn't know before—"

"Why do you spring it on me like this?"

"I told you—" Their words trampled across one another, contrasting words clashing where once their same words had echoed.

The flight to Tel Aviv was half empty. There were a few tourists, a few kids heading for the kibbutz experience, one or two businessmen, a group of orthodox Jews. In the departure lounge he encountered two Dominicans he knew, one of them a scroll scholar, a Frenchman of fierce and skeptical expression who had worked under Father Roland de Vaux at the Ecole Biblique.

"Father Newman." The Frenchman examined him critically, as he might have examined a text, and appeared to find him corrupt. "You look as though you are going on *holiday*. Surely this cannot be so."

"There's a meeting," Leo told him.

"A meeting? I know of no meeting."

"It's a *private* meeting."

They made their way out to the bus. Hautcombe's French intonation smoothed out the path, made the rough places plain. "You are making quite a stir at the moment, aren't you? These papyri from En-Mor. Perhaps now you will remove your opposition to my reading of 7Q5?" 7Q5 is a Qumran papyrus fragment that had been identified by Hautcombe and others as being part of an early gospel, a proto-Mark. Most authorities doubted it and doubt it still. Leo doubted it. A mere twenty letters, ten of them damaged, on five fractured lines. An academic quibble over whether the letters *nu-nu-eta-sigma* could be the middle letters of the name Gennesar, which may be the Gennesaret of Mark 6: 52–53. Things rankle in the minds of celibates. Ideas are your children, for you have no others. Ideas are your contribution to posterity. There had been an exchange of acid letters between Hautcombe and Newman in specialist journals, an embarrassing stand-up row during a conference of papyrologists in Switzerland.

"Perhaps," said Leo in a conciliatory tone. "But perhaps it doesn't matter any longer."

The bus drove them far across the airport to a distant hardstand where the Tel Aviv plane stood, corralled by two police vehicles and an armored car. The laughter of the orthodox Jews rang inside the cabin as the passengers took their seats. "They want to show that they are used to this kind of thing," Hautcombe said as he and Leo shuffled down the aisle. "Searches and questions, police and guns. They want to celebrate the fact that the Promised Land can only be gained by blood and sweat and tears."

"Isn't that our line as well?"

They took off into a spring sky. And as the plane climbed up over the Mediterranean the chaos of Leo's life in Rome receded, thoughts of Madeleine diminishing as though fading along lines of perspective toward some far vanishing point. In the seat beside him the French priest turned to reading his breviary. Outside the icy wind of 30,000 feet howled across a glittering silver desert.

When he emerged from the arrivals section at Lod airport he found a familiar figure waiting for him beyond the barrier.

"Remember me?" the man said.

"Patron saints," Leo replied.

"You got it. Hole in one. Saul Goldstaub." He held out a heavy paw to be shaken. When Leo had last seen him the man had been wearing collar and tie, sitting awkwardly at the Brewers' dinner table; now he was absurd in shorts and sandals, with a straw hat that would not have looked out of place on a croquet lawn. The T-shirt stretched tight across his belly was embellished with the slogan THE CONTENTS OF THIS PACKAGE ARE KOSHER.

For a moment Leo toyed with the possibility that this was all some ridiculous plot of Madeleine's. "I don't understand."

"I'm with WBC now," the man explained. "Press and public relations."

"What a strange coincidence."

"Not strange at all. You know I once did an article on the human nexus?"

"What's nexus?"

"Nexus, plexus, sexus," the man said, incomprehensibly. "Here, let me take your bag." They walked to the parking lot, Goldstaub prattling away. Spring in Rome, it was summer in Israel, the light burning hot and white outside the airport buildings and cicadas shrieking from among the agave plants. "You see, there's this one professor in Boston who has demonstrated that everyone in the developed world is linked to everyone else through a maximum of about six acquaintances."

"So?"

"So there's nothing at all strange about you and me coming up against each other like this. Happens all the time. It's this professor's theory of the human nexus."

"So tell me what the excitement is all about," Leo asked as he climbed into the car beside Goldstaub. "What's all this secrecy?"

But Goldstaub only laughed. "You'll find out soon enough. Steve Calder looks like he just got the tablets of the law from Moses himself."

They left the heat of the coastal plain and drove up to the cool of the city in the hills: Jerusalem, *Yerushalem,* whose Hebrew name was born out of the Canaanite god Shalem but over the centuries has become conflated with the Hebrew word that everyone knows, the word for the one thing that they have never had there in that dusty corner of the Mediterranean—*shalom,* peace. Approaching from the west they saw nothing of the Old City, nothing of that view that the prophets wept over. They straggled along behind buses and trucks into the sprawling suburbs. New housing projects were startling white in the sun, their buildings scattered like dice across bare hillsides where before only lizards had licked their chops and shepherds had tended their flocks. "How are the Brewers?" Goldstaub asked. "How's Madeleine?"

The Brewers were fine, just fine. Madeleine was fine. Her name, her words, danced through Leo's mind as Goldstaub weaved the car through the traffic.

"You see much of them?"

"A bit," he replied evasively. "Every now and then."

"A difficult woman." Goldstaub shook his head and laughed,

but there wasn't much humor in it. "Crazy. All that patron saint stuff . . ." Something obviously rankled with him.

"Just her idea of a joke," Leo said. He stared away from Goldstaub, out into the alien streets, and guilt seeped through his mind like a thin and corrosive fluid. *Keep away from fornication. All other sins are committed outside the body; but to fornicate is to sin against your own body.* They passed the bus station and the central markets, and the song of the police siren was loud in the land. Outside the windows of the car soldiers slouched along the pavements toting guns, like children with toys. *Your body is the temple of the Holy Spirit. You are not your own property; you have been bought for a price.*

"They found a bomb in a supermarket bag," Goldstaub said as they slowed for a roadblock. The soldiers peered at them through the windows but it was only Arab cars that were being flagged down to be searched. "Round up the usual suspects. Where the hell does that line come from? Round up the usual suspects."

"*Casablanca,*" Leo said.

"How does a priest know a thing like that?"

"A priest watches films."

Signs pointed the way to the Old City, but Goldstaub turned aside and swept along a boulevard that had been carved through the northern suburbs toward the Arab quarter of east Jerusalem.

"Why can't you tell me about the find?" Leo asked.

"Steve would kill me. He wants to keep the surprise all to himself." They crossed the desolate spaces where once the city had been divided, the Mandelbaum Gate that was no more, the Damascus Road that still was and always would be. Finally the car emerged from the buildings and Goldstaub brought it to a halt. Before them the ground fell away down a slope of scrub and bare limestone; and there across a mile of luminous air lay the Old City, cupped in the palm of the hills. All the familiar sights: the dark, funereal green of the Mount of Olives running down into the valley, the wall of Suleiman the Magnificent draped like a golden curtain across the stage, and behind the wall the crowded rooftops with the Dome of the Rock rising in the midst of it all like a turquoise jewel box capped with a bubble of perfect gold. This was, perhaps, the view that the prophets had wept over.

And I John saw the holy city, new Jerusalem, coming down from God out of heaven, prepared as a bride adorned for her husband.

"You want to get out and look?" Goldstaub asked.

"No."

"Seen it all before?"

"It's not that."

Goldstaub sniffed. "Trouble is, it means too many different things to too many different people. One place cannot bear so much devotion. That's the trouble." He shoved the car into gear and pulled away from the curb. They turned up the hill and into a driveway past a plaque that announced WORLD BIBLE CENTER.

The Center was one of those institutions that float like an ocean liner on a flood of funds from the United States. Part museum, part conference center, part temple, part university, it sat on the slopes of Mount Scopus in east Jerusalem and looked out over the Kidron Valley and the Old City with a modern, complacent smile. It housed a major collection of finds from the Second Temple period, relics from the times of King Ahab, important fragments from the ancient city of Jericho, scrolls from the caves of Qumran. It had access to the latest techniques and the most astute minds; it was one of the front-runners in the world of textual analysis. The building itself was an uncomfortable blend of styles, a pillared and pedimented body that looked something like a courthouse, with, on either side, low-lying wings of a vaguely oriental cast. It had once been an annex of the Queen Augusta Hospital, later, during the Mandate, a British military establishment. In front of the steps was a sculpture of an open book with the word LOGOS carved across the double page and the motto of the institution inscribed along its base: WORDS WITH KNOWLEDGE. Bougainvillea climbed over the main entrance. The blossom looked brilliant and festive, but it was the exact color of priests' vestments at a funeral.

So what did Leo Newman find there on the slopes of Mount Scopus, behind the golden limestone walls of the World Bible Center? Understanding? Revelation? Expiation? He found a shaded room that hummed with the faint reverberations of air-conditioning and held within its shadows a soft, aquatic coolness. He found the director himself, his face tanned, his hair a fine silver, his manner that of a business entrepreneur; he found a middle-aged woman with the no-nonsense manners of a nurse, and a tall young man who might have been a doctor. And he found a scroll.

"The day before yesterday, Leo," Calder said. The lighting was subdued. It gleamed on his platinum hair. "We found it just the day before yesterday. I called you right away."

There were cabinets along the side of the room. There were binocular microscopes and a pair of computer terminals. And in the center of the room was a table on which the roll lay. Beside it in a second dish lay a filthy rag, like an ancient, stained bandage. "It was wrapped," the young man said. "Wrapped and tied off with some kind of twine. We're sending pieces of the cloth for radiocarbon dating, of course. And the bundle was inside a jar. The jar is still at the site."

Leo peered at the roll. It looked like a dried-out piece of turd, like something excreted from the bowels of history, from the fundament of the earth, which is the Valley of the Dead Sea. He peered at the frayed edges, at the dumb, blank verso. "Well?"

"It's the first literary papyrus ever recovered from the Dead Sea area," the woman added. She was named Leah, Leah the daughter of Laban and wife of Jacob. Was she, Leo wondered irrelevantly and absurdly, the plain-looking one of two sisters, the other named Rachel? "When we opened the cloth we found that the first sheet was fragmented. It had come detached from the rest of the scroll. But we have all the pieces and it seems there are no significant lacunae."

"You've read it?"

"Koine is not my specialism," she replied.

"But you could read it?"

"More or less. There were some problems, but I could get the sense."

Calder spoke. "Leo," he said portentously, "this may be the greatest text discovery there has ever been. It could make the Dead Sea Scrolls look like a picnic in the Garden of Eden."

"Why? What the devil is it?"

The little group had gathered around. They were like a medical team gathering around a patient in a hospital ward. Almost as though delivering a fatal X ray, the young man leaned across and placed a sheet of glass on the table beside the scroll, a sandwich of glass, two pieces held together with black tape. In between the panes were eight fragments of papyrus. They made a crude jigsaw, the edges in approximate juxtaposition like a collage assembled out of old, discolored fragments of newsprint. "The first page," he said. "Have a look."

Leo sat. He turned the glass toward him. Greek cursive script straggled across the pieces, leaping brightly from one fragment to another along the line of the fibers, the strokes of lampblack almost fresh despite their two thousand years' entombment. "Different script, different hand from the other En-Mor fragments," he said. You learn to remember hands. You get to know them as you might recall your own mother's, the particular shape, the idiosyncrasies, the quirks. He glanced up at them. "It'll not be easy. I'll need time."

"All the time you need," said Calder. The others of the group were silent, as though their collective breath were held.

Leo began to read. He adjusted the light over the plate, put on his reading glasses and began to trace the lines of script with his finger, like a child reading the Torah at a bar mitzvah ceremony, tracing out the holy scripture with a *yad*, a silver pointer that is made in the form of a pointing hand, for the word of the law is too precious to be defiled by human touch.

It is Youdas son of Simon of Keriot known also as Youdas the sicarios who writes this, he read, *and he writes that you may know this to be true.*

He glanced up at them, at the girl named Leah in her sharp white blouse and blue skirt, at Goldstaub looking ridiculous in T-shirt and shorts, at Calder with his expansive smile, at the young man named David, who smiled nervously from the background, perhaps just as his namesake had smiled at the giant Goliath as they confronted each other in the Valley of the Terebinth. Then he looked back at the papyrus and read through the lines again, almost in case he had made some absurd error:

> *It is Youdas son of Simon of Keriot known also as Youdas the sicarios who writes this and he writes that you may know this to be true.*

Youdas, Judas. Somewhere within Leo's skull a voice called: *Who is worthy to open the scroll?* Absurdly, for there could be no doubt, he read over the words a third time. Judas.

Had he always been dreading a moment like this, Leo wondered, ever since his first plunge headlong into the warm ocean of belief? Had he always feared that as soon as he teased at the words that made up his faith, the whole fabric would unravel? Names, and the meaning of names. Judas Iscariot. He has always been a problem, has Judas. Even his name, being part patronymic—Judas Is'Qeriyot, Judas from Kerioth—and part nickname—Judas

Sikarios, Judas the knife—even his name is a problem. And here was this scrap of papyrus crowning the academic debate with a simple pun.

"Is this some kind of joke?" Leo asked.

"It's as serious as sin, my friend."

"And who else has seen it?"

"No one but us. The archaeologists did no more than recover it, just two days ago, as I told you. As you know, any paleographic finds are coming directly to us. You're the first . . ." Calder hesitated, the sentence incomplete.

"The first what?"

"The first from the other side." He smiled. The expression sat loosely on his face, as though it might easily slip off and reveal the embarrassment behind it. "The first Catholic."

Leo turned back to the page. The motion was everything, the act of turning seemed to occupy his whole body to the exclusion of any thought or any emotion. Merely to act was enough. He called for paper and pencil and then read slowly and methodically down to the end, transcribing as he went. He skipped some dubious readings, went back and revised, crossed out, erased, rewrote. He took three hours, while Leah moved around in the background, bringing him a glass of water when he was thirsty, and a sandwich when he was hungry, and her view of an occasional doubtful reading when he asked. Goldstaub came and went, Calder looked in from time to time; no one else stepped into the room. He could hear sounds outside, the coming and going of the Center, the slamming of a door down the corridor, vehicles maneuvering in the driveway, a radio playing in the distance, but none of this deflected him from the text:

I write for the Jews (of the dispersion?) . . . the Hellenes and those that live in (Asia?), and for the God-fearers (theosebeis?) among the nations (ethne) that they may know the truth about

Yeshu the Nazir that he was a branch (blastos) of the family of
Mariam that took power to Israel from the hands of the Gentiles
that was destroyed by Herod that he died and did not rise and I
myself witnessed the body in its corruption . . .

He took a deep breath and looked around. Calder and
Goldstaub had come in, sensing perhaps that he had reached the
end. David and Leah were watching him impassively as though
expecting a judgment.

"It's a forgery," he told them. "A piece of propaganda. Early
propaganda, of course, but propaganda nevertheless."

Calder wore an expression of quiet satisfaction. "It's a first-
century site," he said. "You know that. We've got coins of the
Jewish revolt."

"It's earlier than the Bar-Kochba papyri," David added, referring to one of the most implausible chances of his specialization,
the survival intact of certain letters from the leader of the second
and final Jewish revolt, the Son-of-a-Star himself. "I'm certain of
that. This is first century."

"It's forgery," Leo repeated. "It must be."

7

L eo didn't sleep that night. He needed no nightmares.
Inured to solitude, he had never felt so lonely in his life.
He lay in bed—an anonymous hotel bed with a mattress
as hard as in a monk's cell—and he battled with the text that he
had deciphered. The words ran through his mind, driven by their
own impetus, pulled and pushed by his manipulations. He listened to them and found nothing wanting—he believed them,
and believing them he found the remainder of his beliefs (a fragile
fragment of what had been) crumbling to dust. Maybe he could
hide behind academic caution; perhaps for the rest of his life he
could erect barricades of learned reticence, could argue and debate like the Pharisees in the Temple, could twist this way and
that, posing trick questions, finding pat answers just as had been
done with the Shroud of Turin, for example. But he knew. The pa-

pyrus had about it an awful, dull truth. It convinced by its plainness. He felt an awful void around him. The refuge he had learned to seek over the years—the refuge of prayer—was vacant.

Our Father, if there is a father, who art in heaven, if there is a heaven, hallowed be thy name, if you have a name . . .

He abandoned prayer as though it were a sinking ship and found himself seeking comfort elsewhere, in the memory of Madeleine Brewer. Bereft of spiritual comfort, he searched for material comfort, the fugitive, evanescent comfort of the flesh.

Goldstaub came early in the morning, before dawn, when the air was still cold. "You look as though you've been dragged out of bed with a hayfork," he said. "The mattress too hard for you? I thought you guys were all about mortification of the flesh."

"These days the flesh is out," Leo told him wryly. "These days it's mortification of the mind."

They drove through still dark, silent streets, a place where the ghosts were at liberty. The walls of the Old City were shadows blocked against a lightening sky, the Dome of the Rock was dull as lead. They drove down into the Kidron Valley, the Land Rover's headlights cutting a chalky swath through the darkness. Leo felt a strange detachment, as though this were an absurd dream pasted onto his normal life, a gray and colorless *she'ol* from which he would soon awaken. He would get up. He would wash and dress and have breakfast. He would make his way to the Pontifical Institute; he would celebrate mass in the chapel; he would give a morning lecture on the Development of the New Testament Canon; he would continue his work on the forthcoming publication of another of the En-Mor papyri. A life would continue as a life was planned to continue from days long ago in the seminary when his tutors had identified in him a certain dogged application to the trivia of language, an obsession with New Testament Greek, a quiet horror of the intrusive nature of parochial work.

He thought of Madeleine; and at the thought of her something inside him gave a small convulsion, the emotional manifest-
ing itself in the physical; a disturbing, subversive thing.

"You fallen asleep?" Goldstaub asked.

"I'm awake."

"Daydreaming? What does a priest daydream about?"

"I was thinking of Madeleine."

"Her?"

Why had he mentioned her? She smiled at him from memory,
Madeleine holding out comfort of a kind, the comfort of a fellow
human being to replace the terror of the abyss. "How all this
would affect someone like her."

"If the scroll is true," Goldstaub reminded him. "You called it
a forgery."

They drove beneath the silent hulk of a tank—a memorial to
the Six-Day War—and passed the olive trees of the Garden of
Gethsemane where, in the dead of night, in the reign of darkness,
Judas had led the cohort of Roman soldiers to arrest the man
called Jesus. And Leo summoned up the words from deep inside
him, from a small hard core of disbelief that had always been
there, throughout childhood, throughout the years of training,
throughout the years of fulfilled vocation. "It's true," he said. "In
my heart of hearts I fear it's true."

Goldstaub nodded. "I thought so," he said. "I thought so from
the start. When you first saw the thing you looked like the guy
who's gone into the clinic with strep throat and come out with
lymphoma."

They drove on in silence. The road led around the Mount of
Olives beneath the village of El-Azariye—which is the village of
Lazarus, which is the village of Bethany where Jesus was anointed
before his triumphal entry into the city. From Bethany it dropped
down past the Inn of the Good Samaritan with refreshments and
holy pictures and camel for photographs, down into the bowels of

the earth, down into a dawn of gray and silver and flushed rose where the Dead Sea, the Salt Sea, lay like beaten pewter beneath a high shield of cloud. On the far side of the water, drawn in two dimensions against the light, were the Hills of Moab, where Moses had looked across at the Promised Land that he was never permitted to reach. Above the hills dawn bled through like blood and lymph from a wound.

Down on the valley floor a sign pointed left to JERICHO, THE OLDEST CITY IN THE WORLD and right to nowhere. Goldstaub turned the Land Rover right, skirting the bluff on which the ruins of Qumran lie and the cliffs where the Dead Sea Scrolls were found. A battered, salt-rusted sign pointed the way to En-Gedi and Masada. The vehicle drove between the sullen sea and the crumbling ramparts of rock that are the ridges and gullies of the wilderness of Judaea, a place of lizards and jackals and prophets, a place where the man called Jesus passed his forty days and forty nights amid the terrors of solitude. And as they drove there was a sudden disturbance in the morning light, a sudden intrusion of the twentieth century into this inert and timeless landscape, a sudden sound above the whine of the Land Rover's transmission—two jet fighters sweeping down the valley, trailing their engine sound behind them like coattails. The aircraft tilted as they passed by, keeping to the Israeli side of the border, aware no doubt of the Jordanian radar watching them all the way. The Star of David was visible on their fuselages. Leo thought apocalyptic thoughts. *Who is worthy to open the scroll?* he thought as the aircraft shrank to mere specks on the sheen of the morning.

"Not far to go," said Goldstaub. A withered, parched landscape, a place of scrolls that was itself the color of scrolls: dun, the color of desiccation. They went on past the brief flowering of En-Gedi, where David hid from Saul and cut a lock from the jealous king's hair, and fifteen minutes later they reached Masada. For a few deceptive moments the grim mesa—where Herod had built a pleasure palace, where Mariamne, his queen, had once walked the terraces to admire the view, where the last of the Zealots held out against the Roman legions and finally committed mass suicide rather than surrender—was tinged with a delicate, coralline beauty by the dawn light. On the left was Lisan, the Tongue, the salt flats where the waters of the Jordan finally evaporate into the languorous desert air. Beyond was only the salt waste where once the cities of Sodom and Gomorrah had stood.

Ten minutes later Goldstaub brought the Land Rover to a halt. "This is it." A track led off to the right. There was a barrier manned by a couple of bored soldiers. A sign said that the place was called En-Mor and a notice announced that the area was under the control of the Antiquities Authority. A rough ridge rose up to the plateau, a skeletal limb of the wilderness of Judaea.

"This your first visit?" Goldstaub asked.

Leo peered through the window, craned to see up the slope, up into the gullies. "That's right."

The soldiers exchanged some words with Goldstaub and then raised the barrier to let them through. The vehicle lurched off the road and Goldstaub shifted down into low range for the long, slow climb from shore level, up the side of the ridge, winding up like the snake path to Masada itself, clambering over tortuous rocks. Yellow dust billowed behind them. There was dust on the windows, dust on the dashboard, dust on his arms and on his lips. *For dust thou art and unto dust shalt thou return,* Leo thought. Who came here at the pivot of history, he wondered? Who was it who stumped up this thorny slope with a bag of scrolls on his back?

Finally the vehicle breasted a horizon and reached the summit of a narrow bluff. They had arrived at the excavation camp. There was an army truck parked on a cleared area and a couple more Land Rovers. Beyond was a row of tents and a large marquee with the sides furled up. A group of volunteers was already moving around the dig, youths in T-shirts and shorts, mammary girls burned and blistered by the sun, boys with unkempt hair and rudimentary beards. The place had the atmosphere of a youth camp. Someone was at a bucket washing potsherds and distributing them to wooden boxes that had once held oranges. A radio announced the news in Hebrew. In the background a generator throbbed into the morning air. The excavation itself was little beside all this: a few lines of wall footings in the dust below the camp with surveyors' stakes laid out in a grid.

As Leo climbed out of the vehicle the director came over. He owned one of those glum, monosyllabic Jewish names—Dov. Dov Agron. His eyes lit up when Goldstaub introduced Leo. "*Father Newman*, that right?"

"Leo will do."

As they shook hands Agron's grip was dry and tough. His voice was a hybrid of accents, part Hebrew, part American, with an undertone of central Europe. "You should have been here earlier. You've seen the scroll?"

"I've had a look."

"Any ideas?"

Leo shrugged noncommittally. "It'll take time."

The man nodded. "I mean, the first fragments were important enough, but this is something else. What do you reckon, eh? Early Christian is it, like the other stuff?"

"Perhaps."

They clambered around the dig while Agron pointed out the features, the storerooms, the living quarters of whoever it was who had occupied this place of dust and rock, a dull place squatting on its small promontory in the wilderness, a kind of hell under the sun. One of the volunteer diggers looked up from her labor as they passed by. Her skin was battered by the sun and the wind. She wiped her hair away with the back of her hand and called out to them in an Australian accent: "Over here." They climbed down over the low masonry to where she knelt in the dust. Her dugs hung loose in her shirt as she bent to brush dust aside, and Leo remembered Madeleine in the Church of San Crisogono: the same gesture, the same sly glimpse, the same potent sense of womanhood. *Time for your fish lecture.* But this time, there on the ground, exposed like a guilty secret by the Australian girl's hand, lay a bronze coin.

Agron picked the thing up, blew on it and handed it to Leo. "The Tenth Legion, Fretensis. Judaea Capta. We've found a couple of dozen so far."

Leo peered at the bronze disk, at the familiar engraving: the Jewish woman seated at the foot of a palm tree with her head in her hands and the Roman soldier standing over her. *What woman with ten drachmas,* he thought, *would not, if she lost one, light a lamp and sweep out the house and search thoroughly till she found it?* He handed the coin back. "So what was this place before the Romans came?"

Agron shrugged. "That's the key question, isn't it? Zealots? Somebody who got out of Masada before the end of the siege? Refugees from Qumran? Who knows?" His voice trailed away into the uncertainties of excavation. "You can always make up a convincing story, that's the problem. If you are Arthur Evans at Knossos you can even rebuild a site in your own image. Who knows about this one? Judging by the papyrus finds they were some kind of early Christian sect. You should know about that better than me."

Leo shrugged. They went along the ridge to the uppermost part of the dig where the ordered stones faded away into the rubble of the hillside. Agron pointed up the slope to the cliff that blocked off access to higher ground. "Up there," he said. "The cave."

A spoil of boulders had spilled out from the cliff like the waste from a mine working. Around to the right, perched over the gully, there was a dark cleft in the rock, bearded with scrub and thorn.

"Pure luck," Agron said. "There was an earth tremor not long after we started the excavation. Common enough in these parts. It caused a rockfall and exposed the cave . . ."

They clambered up to the entrance, Agron leading the way, Goldstaub huffing and puffing at the back. They had to crouch to get into the cave, but the space inside was high enough for them to stand. There was a cable running up from the generator in the camp below, and the darkness was punctuated by the light from half a dozen lamps. Three volunteers were at work there, picking through the debris of dust and rubbish like fastidious tramps at a trash can. Their shadows loomed vast across the ragged ceiling. They barely took any notice of the visitors, just muttered among themselves as though reciting some arcane religious liturgy.

"We reckon that the Romans found this place when they took the camp," Agron explained. "There's no real evidence, but that's what seems likely. They found the cave and these jars inside and they smashed everything to pieces, tore the documents up, that kind of thing. Set light to some of them. And then they just pushed off. And that's the stuff we've been getting over the last few months. Just fragments."

"And the scroll?"

Agron smiled. This was his moment. This was the thing that would promote him into the hall of archaeological fame. "Over there. It was hidden away and the soldiers must have missed it. We missed it for weeks as well. It's been sitting there for almost two thousand years."

He led the way to an opening in the back of the cave, a narrow cleft in the rock that went through into a further chamber. They had to get down on hands and knees. Leo felt the weight of rock above him, the weight of rock all around him, pressing on him. Panic rose in his throat. *Rock of Ages cleft for me, let me hide myself in thee,* he thought. But there was no hiding, not even here in the breathless bowels of the earth.

Just ahead of him Agron clambered to his feet. The inner chamber was just high enough to stand in with your knees bent and your head tucked down into your shoulders. Two figures crouched over a pit in the floor of rock. They had the only lamp. The light glowed beneath their figures like the light in a Caravaggio painting, light issuing from what they were examining. Leo peered over Agron's shoulder. There was a little assembly of pieces in a crevice: the curved lip of a jar and shards of brown pottery like fragments of broken cranium. Battling with panic, he tried to concentrate on Agron's words.

"There must have been a land movement at some time. The earth fell across and crushed the jar." Agron gestured to show the movement, like a crushing of skulls. "We got the papyrus out almost entire, and now they're trying to excavate the rest. We thought we could make out names on the papyrus," he said. "Youdas, we thought. And possibly Simeon. But there's no one with Greek here. You've had a look. What do you reckon?"

"It seems possible."

"Who were they, then?"

"Common enough names."

The excavators were like surgeons at the scene of an accident attempting first aid, trying to ease broken bones, trying to lift trapped limbs out of the wreckage. They worked with brushes, painstakingly sweeping the dirt away, cleaning up the wound, searching for any other survivors of the disaster of time.

"Is there anything more?" Leo asked. "I think I'd like to get out into the fresh air." Panic welled up inside his chest, a tangible, physical thing. The press of rock against his head, the press of circumstance all around him.

Agron looked around. His face was harsh in the lamplight, a structure of light and shadow, almost biblical, almost the face of a prophet. "Thought you'd like to see the actual place."

"It's fascinating. But I'd rather get out."

The prophet grinned. "It gets some people like that."

Outside the cave the light was dazzling. Leo felt a surge of release as he emerged, a tide of relief flooding through his body. He dusted himself down and looked around with all the delight of someone who has just come back from the dead. The sun was up now, shining through the high cloud like a malevolent eye glaring through a thin gauze. The temperature was rising. A radio blared pop music. Dust shifted above the balks and hollows of the excavation where the small volunteer army grubbed in the dirt. Was it here, Leo wondered, in this place of dust and rock, a dead place beside a dead sea, that the history of Christianity would finally come to an end?

"It's bloody important, isn't it?" Agron said, following him out. "They wouldn't have flown you out like this if it wasn't important." He looked anxious, as though it might not be. Leo nodded and patted him on the shoulder, a gesture that he would never have made in the past, a physical, companionable gesture. "It's important," he assured the man. "Very important."

The sheet lay in the document room of the World Bible Center, bathed in a soft, effulgent light, looking quite innocent. Leo sat before it once more, examined it with the cold and objective gaze of reason. Part of him even began to formulate a commentary on the text, a gloss on the word *nazir*. *Nazir, nazaraios, netser, blastos*. Root, shoot, offspring; and *Nazarene*, the word that has always worried the scholars. An academic debate teased at the edges of his mind.

"It must be a piece of propaganda," he said. "The other possibility doesn't bear contemplating."

"Contemplate it," Calder retorted.

"The idea that it might be an autograph? The Gospel of Judas?"

"If you like."

"It's absurd."

"You discount the possibility? On what grounds?"

"On the grounds of common sense."

Calder considered the idea of common sense as though it were a piece of evidence. "Nothing else?"

Leo felt himself casting around in desperation. "Common sense is pretty powerful. There are dozens of apocryphal books, you know that as well as I do. The Gospel of Mary, the Acts of Pilate, all of them little more than pious tracts. I imagine that this is another, written from a rather different point of view. Surely that's what we must assume. We don't want to leap in with both feet and then look complete fools, do we?"

"And what about our dating? What about the site? You've seen it now. Doesn't it convince you?"

Leo shrugged the question away. "Even if the dating were certain, how would that change things? There were plenty of reasons for writing an anti-Christian tract in the first century."

"And what about the content? What about the matter of family?" Calder was no fool. Showman, entrepreneur, but no fool. It was like the questioning of a prosecuting counsel, the cogent questions carefully inserted among the merely circumstantial. Or like a soldier carefully dusting earth over the land mines. "What about *Mariam?*" he asked.

Mariam, Mary. It was a common enough name. Mary the mother of Jesus, of course. Everyone knows the story: dressed in a motley assortment of bathrobes, old sheets and costume jewelry, the whole cast traipses across the memories of most of the Western world. The Three Wise Men. Gold and frankincense and myrrh. The ox and the ass and the baby in a manger and the murder of the Innocents. And she sits there at the focus of it all, her composed face hooded in blue and white: Mary Mother of God, Mary Queen of Heaven.

But Calder knew, of course. He knew because it was so

damned obvious. You could talk about Mary the mother of Jesus as much as you pleased. You could dress her in blue and gold and adorn her with the sun. You could stand her on the moon and put the twelve stars on her head for a crown. But there was one family and only one family that had done what the text claimed, only one family *that took power to Israel from the hands of the Gentiles* (and) *that was destroyed by Herod.* That family was the family of the Maccabees, the Hasmonean dynasty, the descendants of Judas ben Mattathias who had driven the Seleucid Greeks out of Israel in the second century BC. And there was a prominent member of that family with the name of Mariam.

Calder left it to Leo:

"Mariamne I, the second wife of Herod the Great."

Herod. The name sounded in the hushed atmosphere of the document room, a name that has passed into the language. Herod. Herod the Great, Herod the Edomite, Herod the local warlord who played things right, befriended the right men, pandered to the right men, killed the right men, and finally found himself elevated from warlord to king—*King of the Jews,* to be precise, a title conferred on him by the Roman senate in 40 BC. Once he had acquired the title of king, Herod abandoned his first wife and took a new one: Mariamne the Hasmonean. It was a dynastic marriage. Mariamne's family had given a line of kings to Israel and a line of high priests—the one never being far from the other in the Jewish mind—and the Hasmoneans still possessed the kind of legitimacy that Herod himself could never hope to acquire. Yet, going by the account of Josephus, he came to love her.

"Each man kills the thing he loves," Leo murmured. He sat in front of the papyrus fragments and he smelled the reek of blood, the stink of the abattoir. Herod's rule had been the exercise of pure, incontinent power, a tragedy in the Elizabethan mold, where, by the end of the final act, bodies lie strewn across the stage. He had loved Mariamne, and yet he lured her own grandfather, the onetime high priest Hyrcanus II, out of exile in Babylon and had him murdered. He loved her, and yet he murdered her uncle. He loved her, and yet her young brother Jonathan, a mere seventeen years old and newly appointed to the high priesthood, was taken by the king's personal bodyguard and drowned in the swimming pool of the royal palace in Jericho. Herod loved Queen Mariamne, and yet finally, crazed by sexual jealousy, he had killed even her.

"Jesus as Herod's grandson?" Calder shook his head. "I don't know how we're going to handle this one, Leo. I don't know what we're going to do about it."

Leo looked up from the papyrus. "It would explain one set of New Testament stories, wouldn't it? The coming of the Wise Men. An embassy from Parthia comes to visit the new heir to the throne. Perhaps Herod had even recognized the child when it was born. Perhaps someone smuggled the infant out of the royal palace and hid it somewhere in the countryside. Bethlehem. Why not Bethlehem? It would have fitted in with the Messianic prophesies."

The logic of dynastic murder is implacable: sometime after the queen's death, her two sons by Herod were duly garroted on the orders of their own father. The date of their murder—7 BC—is instructive: it was about that year that the man we know as Jesus of Nazareth was born.

"And when Herod got to hear about it he ordered the murder of every infant in the village. Which has come down to us in Matthew as the Massacre of the Innocents."

"Something like that," agreed Leo. The stories fitted like parts of a jigsaw puzzle, like the fragments of papyrus pieced together between the sheets of glass before him. "Maybe we'll find out. Maybe the rest of the scroll will tell us."

* * *

That afternoon Goldstaub drove him back to the airport. They argued about the scroll, about how the work should be conducted, who should know, how it should be made public. "The thing is," Goldstaub said, "you've got a stake in all this, haven't you?"

"Haven't we all?"

"Sure. Sure we have. But the Christian Church especially. It has always made a historical claim, hasn't it? I mean, look at your creed. You've actually *got* a creed, which is more than the Jews have. It even mentions Pontius Pilate. I mean, what other religion sticks its neck out that far?"

"It's a complex story, the origins of the Nicene creed," Leo said. "The refutation of Gnosticism, things like that."

"Yes, but it's there. Almost a contract. You won't get a Jew signing a contract unless he can look the other guy dead in the eye. But the Christians have kind of signed up on trust, so to speak. They've rooted the whole thing in history." He glanced across at his passenger. "What happens if we show the history's bunk?"

The road dropped down off the heights, down through the gorges that guard the way to the Holy City. The Trappist monastery of Latrun appeared on the left of the road, placid in the sunshine. On the hill behind the monastery are the ruins of a crusader castle, the Toron des Chevaliers. The name Latrun is a corruption of El Toron, but it used to be believed that the name came from *latro,* a thief, and that Latrun had been the home of the good thief who was crucified with Jesus.

Leo sat in silence. He thought of faith and he thought of doubt; he thought of vocation and he thought of Madeleine. Maybe Goldstaub was reading his thoughts; maybe he could do that. When they parted at the airport he shook Leo's hand and told him to give his regards to her and Jack. "You will see her, won't you? I guess you see quite a lot of her, don't you?"

"Yes," Leo replied warily. "I suppose I do."

"You want to go carefully."

Leo had to suppress an absurd desire to tell Goldstaub every-thing, a ridiculous temptation to confess. "It's not easy," he admitted.

Goldstaub nodded. "Not easy for anyone."

The plane lifted off the runway and climbed up over the office blocks and hotels of Tel Aviv. It passed over the fawn-colored hem of the shoreline and the blue fabric of the sea, rising up over the glittering satin, away from the Holy Land, away from the Gospel of Judas with its skeptical whisper from the past.

Leo thought about Madeleine, thought of Judas, thought of faith and belief, of doubt and disbelief. The airline magazine had a story about the Dead Sea Scrolls. There were glossy pictures of the Shrine of the Book and the usual shots of the ruins of Qumran. "A monastery of the Essene sect," the caption said and the text agreed, falling into the trap that had been set, with a mixture of naïveté and ignorance, by the old goat Roland de Vaux all those years ago when the State of Israel barely existed and you could buy a priceless scroll for twenty-five pounds sterling. There was also a mention of the first finds from the dig of En-Mor: *The Dead Sea area continues to reveal the profound truths of our religious past,* the article said.

He dozed fitfully, waking with a start to a dream that receded from memory even as he tried to recall it. Madeleine had been part of the dream, Madeleine in some public place confessing her love for him while Goldstaub and Calder looked on, laughing. At times both he and Madeleine had been naked, but although they were ashamed of the fact, none of the onlookers had seemed the slight-est bit concerned. Jack had been there, watching from a distance, a detached and cynical figure.

Peering out of the window for distraction he saw an island lying 30,000 feet below like a fragment of papyrus laid out on a blue cloth. Crete. The aircraft's wing moved along the line of the south coast like a pointing finger, like a *yad*. Or like the finger that drew out the fiery letters *Mene, mene tekel upharsin,* thou hast been weighed in the balance and found wanting. The place down there was Kaloi Limenes, Fair Havens, the final shelter on the route that the apostle Paul himself took almost two thousand years earlier on his journey to Rome and to death. Leo knew Paul. He knew him intimately, had always known him ever since the days in the seminary, ever since his first unsteady steps into the dogma of Christianity. He knew Paul from within—the pain, the prejudices, the poetry, a dangerous combination that has never let the world rest. And he knew Paul's own moment of panic as he lay convulsing in the dust of the road to Damascus.

But he also knew Judas.

An air hostess came down the aisle and asked if he was all right, did he feel unwell, was there anything she could do? "I'm fine," he said waving her away. "Just fine."

Later the aircraft circled Rome in a bright evening sky. You could see the meanders of the river and the great cupola of Saint Peter's like a bubble blown out of the stone. You could see the streets radiating from piazzas like bursts of light from a dozen suns, and you could see the churches, dozens of churches, hundreds of churches, over four hundred churches. But Rome was no longer a place of triumph or refuge. The chaotic city that had known every sin on earth was no longer a bastion against doubt. The vandals had swept through and sacked it. It was a brash, noisy, pagan place on the edge of a volcano. The taxi from the airport drove along a wide avenue where transvestites strutted their stuff in the dusk. *Malakoi,* Paul called them: soft men. Along with sodomites and fornicators they are there in his litany of the damned: fornicators, idolators, adulterers, soft men, sodomites, thieves, usurers, drunkards, slanderers and swindlers. The cars cruised past and the girls, men, creatures midway between the two states, opened their coats to display what was on offer. There was haggling over the price and the cost.

The Palace of
the Caesars—1943

⌒

I will show you something, if you agree to come with me."

"Something? What?" Mock suspicion. A bubble of laughter there, just below the surface, a rich bubble of corruption.

"A treat. But you must agree first."

"How can I agree if I don't know what I'm agreeing to?"

"That's the risk you must take." Francesco laughing at her, teasing her with his look, smiling at her with that ironical and twisted smile, daring her to refuse.

"All right. I agree."

The treat comes the next day, with his Alfa Romeo waiting at the gatehouse at the bottom of the drive, and him standing to open the passenger's door, sweeping a bow for her as she climbs in, the pair of them feeling the eyes of the guard on them and not caring. "Where are we going?"

"A secret." The car roars away from the gates and turns toward Santa Maria Maggiore then left down Via Nazionale toward the road that Mussolini has newly carved through the city in order to lay bare the relics of the first Roman Empire, the one that worked. The Road of the Imperial Forums, it is called. There is little private traffic about. Overladen buses, trams clanking and swaying, flocks of bicycles swarming like starlings, but few private cars. Shoddily dressed pedestrians watch the passage of the brave little car with its handsome driver and the blond woman beside him holding a straw hat to her head, letting her silk scarf fly in the wind. *Tedeschi,* they assume. "*Tedeschi,*" one or two of them even say. Germans. "*Puttana tedesca!*" a cyclist shouts as the little car swerves past him and careers around the Colosseum, which was built by the Emperor Titus after his return from the Jewish War and has now become the largest and most imposing traffic island in the world. *Puttana* has an ancient etymology. Ultimately it derives from the Latin *putidus,* rotten, decaying. *Puttana* means a whore.

The little car passes the Arch of Constantine, heads down the Via San Gregorio and draws to a halt at a gateway halfway down the road. Behind the gate is a grassy slope with umbrella pines. Outcrops of brown brickwork breast the summit of the hill. "The Palatine," Francesco says, handing her out on to the pavement. "I will show you the Palatine as you have never seen it before."

The park is closed to the public. A notice announces as much. But Francesco merely smiles. "You must always know someone," he explains. "That is the source of power and status in Italy." With a flourish he produces a key. "This, *mia cara* Gretchen, is one of the keys to paradise." He unlocks the gate and holds it open for her, then follows her in and locks the gate behind them. They possess the Palatine Hill.

*   *   *

Figures in a classical landscape, wandering beneath the porticoes, creeping into tunnels and out into the sudden sunlight, stepping over fallen columns, playing hide-and-seek like children among the marble relics, posing behind a headless statue so that the flesh-and-bone head, the living skull and all its tissues, smiling, grimacing, laughing, takes the place of vanished marble emperor or looted marble empress. And the sound of laughter echoes from the cliffs of brick and sends their voices back to them in a kind of mockery.

"Tell me what it is like . . ." he asks as they contemplate a Venus standing in the long grass. The Venus gestures with half an arm, like an amputee. Her face, part ravaged by time, still contains within its worn features a strange modesty. Her thighs enclose her glabrous pudendum tightly, so that men may look but not see.

"What *what* is like?"

"To be a woman."

She laughs. "How can a woman explain that to a man?"

"Tell me how it feels when you make love."

"Don't be silly."

"Or when you have a baby."

"Painful. You're being idiotic."

"I want to understand you."

"Men cannot understand women."

"Italian men can. Maybe not German men, but Italian men can."

"German men are no different from Italian men."

"They are very different. German men murder children."

"They do not!" Her voice has risen now. The ghostly, mangled Venus has ceased to matter. She is suddenly angry, her face flushed, her nose, that not-quite-classical nose, sharp and white with a kind of tension. "That is a disgusting thing to say!"

He is grinning at her reaction. "Oh, but they do. Jewish children."

"Lies! I will not have you saying that kind of thing!" Momentarily, guiltily, she thinks of her husband. The argument flares and dies, but the mood is ruined just as the stadium around them is ruined. She turns and hurries away from him. There is an opening in the wall ahead, and a tunnel. He follows her into the darkness and through into another bright sunlit space. "Gretchen," he calls after her. "Gretchen . . ."

She stands in the middle of the space on the patch of dusty grass, looking up and around. Cliffs of brick rise up like the walls of a prison compound, up to the bright sky and the scudding clouds, a Poussin sky of flake white and ash gray and ultramarine. "Where are we?" And the question is flung back by the walls—"Where are we? Where are we?"—the senseless echolalia of stone because they know exactly where they are, on this Roman day of 1943 with the *tramontana* blowing and the clouds shifting overhead: the peristyle of the Palace of Augustus. They wander through the maze, climb stairs that might have been built for Augustus Caesar, enter rooms awash with shadow where Domitian may have dined, where Nero may have fiddled, where Titus may have lain with Berenice, come back into the great peristyle once more.

"What if . . ."

"What if what?"

He has regained the mood, recaptured the sense of game. "What if you were an empress . . ."

"And you?"

"And I were your slave."

Laughter, and the sudden catch of a hand. "Francesco!"

"But what if?"

"Let me go."

The place is silent but for the two of them, a wilderness of derelict flowerbeds sunk below the level of the plateau as though sunk back into the past. "Tell me," he demands, and pulls her toward the side of the space, toward the shadow of the columns that encircle it.

"Let me go!" No longer is she laughing.

"Tell me! If I were your slave . . ."

And despite her pulling away from him they have reached the shadows. There is a vault of brickwork over their heads and the exhausted air of the centuries around them and dust on the floor two thousand years old. "Do you know where we are? We are in a nymphaeum, a place where the nymphs used to play throughout the hot summer months. And you are my nymph." He grins as she tries to pull away from him. "Come on, tell me. If I were your slave and you were a nymph . . ." And he has stopped against the wall and pulled her toward him so that from the waist downward their two bodies are pressed together. "Francesco!" Her tone is of subdued panic, the panic of the captive, the panic of the claustrophobic, the sharp panic of a victim.

"You touched me," he says suddenly, startlingly. "When I was ill and you came and found me, you touched me."

She is still, as motionless as a captive bird, only her breathing giving her movement: the soft, subdued breathing of panic. "I bathed you. You had a fever. Only what a nurse would have done."

"You touched me. *There*."

She is silent. She has not denied the fact.

"You touched me," he repeats, and now he has pulled her hard against him, so hard that she cries out: "Please!" She says the word in English. And "please" again, and it is not clear by her tone whether she is pleading with him or not, whether she wishes to deny him or beseech him to continue. "Please, Checco. Please." Does she move her face so as to avoid his mouth? Or is she merely allowing him to explore her cheeks, the line of her jaw, her neck, the wisps of hair at her temples, her eyes? Matters are equivocal. "Please," she cries again. Does she struggle as he pulls her skirt upward, over silk stockings and white, shameless garters?

"Please," she says again. But her hands are powerless to push him away, if that is what they are trying to do. He grabs her against him, supporting her buttocks on his hands (no great weight, and he is strong), turning and holding her against the wall, ignoring what may be faint whispered protests, thrusting his hips against her as she seems to wrestle with him. The act that began by possessing a kind of athletic grace, such as you might see in two dancers involved in a complex and intense modern dance, ends up looking plainly absurd and rather sordid, he with his trousers around his ankles, she with her skirt hitched up around her waist and her legs up around his thighs and her panties pulled open. It began with a sinuosity, a certain tension and drama, it ends with cries and grunts and an awful discord of body and body, and Gretchen calling to her god, repeatedly, a drumbeat in the claustrophobic space—"Oh God, oh God, oh God!"—the sound going nowhere, merely absorbed by the ancient brickwork.

How often in those rooms and corridors, one wonders? How many blows, how many cries, how much overflowing desire?

And then it is all finished, and he lets her down slowly as though she has become a burden to him, and she turns away, averting her eyes from his and wiping at herself with a fragile scrap of lace handkerchief, distractedly pulling at her clothing and trying to get it back into some kind of order.

"What have we done, Checco?" she whispers, and the collective pronoun is plain to both of them. *We.* "Oh God, what have we done?"

If she is looking for consolation in his answer, she finds none. "It is only what we have both wanted."

"What if someone saw?"

He smiles and touches her cheek. "There's no one. The place is closed to the public. The Palace of the Caesars is ours."

She shakes her head, runs her fingers through her hair, and the gesture lets fall the short sleeve of her frock so that he can see into the shadows, see the deft curl of hair in her axilla. "And what happens now?"

Herr Huber and his wife, confronting each other in his study. Herr Huber is a powerful man. He seems to dominate his wife across the carpet. The carpet is Persian, silk, woven with exotic and sinuous patterns within which one may descry things sensual and organic, the writhing of limbs and the twining of tendrils. A face that is not a face peers out through foliage like a Bacchus half glimpsed in a garden.

"Where have you been?" Herr Huber demands. His voice is not loud. It is a cold, sharp thing, like a knife. "Where did you go with that . . . *teacher?*"

The Alfa Romeo is outside, parked near the entrance to the Villa. The owner is nowhere to be seen.

"Francesco took me to the Palatine. We have been exploring the imperial palaces."

"His job is to take Leo to such things, not you."

"I don't see why he can't do both."

"Because you should not go out alone with a man!"

"I go out with precisely whom I please."

"You are behaving like a silly little girl who has lost her head to a gigolo."

"I am *what?*" Outrage is written all across her face. How can this man, twelve years her senior, be so appalling, so insensitive? "How *dare* you impugn my honor?" Oh, a good response, a fine use of language—a shade archaic, reminiscent of gentlemen and ladies and duels—coupled with a most satisfactory disposition of expression: wide-eyed disbelief, stark with outrage, fiery with fury. Her mouth, often lovely, often a thing that can express amusement and affection, is ragged with anger, as though it has been carved out of the lower part of her face with a blunt instrument. "What in God's name are you accusing me of?"

"The way he looks at you."

The shift of emphasis has not been lost on her. It is *he* not *she*. But her expression does not relax. "What do you mean by that? How can you blame *me* for how *he* looks at me?"

"He looks at you as though—"

"Yes?"

He is forced to formulate his idea into words. "As though he wants you."

The dismantling of her expression is a careful process, as though, were she to make a false move, the whole thing might collapse and reveal the vulnerable interior. A smile metamorphoses out of the anger like a delightful butterfly emerging from a dull, dry chrysalis. "He *wants* me?"

"He lusts after you. Impure thoughts. I see it in his expression."

She laughs. The amusement is genuine. "And you think that they don't all do that, Hansi? Your colleagues, for example. When they see me play, don't you think they are all taking my clothes off as they watch? Don't you realize that? Why should Checco be any different?"

"Checco, is it?"

"Oh shut up." Her tone is bantering now, teasing him in the way she teased him from the start, when they made their first assignations in the spa gardens in Marienbad, she a mere sixteen-year-old and he almost thirty, pursuing some attractive widow and finding instead a young girl who could taunt him into doing exactly what she pleased. "You just mustn't be jealous, Hansi, don't you see that? Jealousy clouds your mind. They *all* want me, they all wish to see me . . . as only you are allowed. You have married an attractive woman, that is the simple truth of the matter." And she puts her head on one side to regard him with the look she used on him from the very start of their acquaintance, the one that has a hint of invitation haunting it, a hint of bruised innocence, a hint of dissipation. "And now, if you are very good, and only if you are very good, I will let you kiss me . . . *there*."

Two figures on a narrow bed, swathed in shadow, glowing with heat and sweat—a writhing laocoön of limbs, a living, lucid laocoön, the twin bodies strangled by the serpents of their own creation, the struggle finally yielding no victor but two vanquished figures, lying apart like spent swimmers, their shared seed glistening like pearls, her ragged hair matted with it, his belly wet with it. Their fingers, only their fingers now, are entwined on the ragged pillow.

Her breasts slop across her chest as she turns to him. "I must go. He will be wondering where I've been."

"We could go to Switzerland."

"Don't be idiotic."

"We could be there the day after tomorrow. I have a friend who has an apartment in Geneva. I could get the key."

"You expect me to believe that? And anyway, what would we live on?"

"You could play."

"On the streets?"

"You could teach."

"And what would be your contribution?" She gets off the bed and goes to the basin in the corner of the room. He watches as she splashes water under her arms and washes herself between the legs, watches the heavy shift of her buttocks, the absurd clumsiness of her hips. "What am I going to do about my hair?" she asks as she rubs herself with his towel.

"I could write my memoirs. 'Women I have known.' You could help me with the technical details."

"You're absurd." She pulls on her panties and shrugs herself into a thin, sweat-stained slip—both of them gifts brought back from Paris by her husband. Peering into an inadequate mirror she tries to do something with her hair, combing it, pulling it back from her face and fixing it with hairpins.

"I'm in love with you," he says.

She has hairpins between her lips. "Damn," she mutters as her hair escapes from her control. There is something businesslike about her manner as she peers into the mirror and curses her errant hair. She feels quite normal, as though all this were a mere matter of course, even a transaction of some kind. Looking into the mirror and seeing her unconcerned reflection, she wonders where remorse lies. "You are in love with no one but yourself," she tells him.

Gretchen in church, the German church, Santa Maria dell'Anima, Our Lady of the Soul, with the marble glistening and the woodwork gleaming and candles flickering in the shadows like small bright tongues, the tongues of Pentecost, tongues of fire, tongues of gossip. Overhead the decorated vaulting smiles with the dull gleam of gold. The two-headed eagle of the Holy Roman Empire is perched up there in the shadows.

Gretchen is not praying, not even kneeling; she is merely sitting in the back of the church in the incense-scented atmosphere, looking. She is wearing modest gray. Her hair, that splendid, golden hair, is demurely covered by a veil (black lace with gold edge, Neapolitan, a bit of a treasure). She looks at the distant altar, at the sanctuary light glimmering like a ruby in the dull velvet of the shadows, at the tortured Christ. She looks, and her eyes are glistening in the subdued light, brimming with tears, clouding with tears. It is all most satisfactory.

8

Where have you been?" Her voice on the phone, quiet and anxious.

"You know where I was. In Jerusalem."

"What was it all about? Why the mystery?"

"A scroll. They've found a scroll."

"It's always a scroll. Scrolls, papyrus, God in heaven, can't you get your mind away from it?"

"It's devastating." The word seemed both inadequate and absurdly overstated. The scroll was no more than a piece of rag, a scrap of plant pith, a mere scrawl of letters.

"Devastating? You don't know what devastating is. Leo, can we meet?"

He saw an abyss before him, and the ground beneath his feet sliding down into the gulf like the scree on the crater of a volcano. The volcano shook faintly and grumbled far away in the depths.

"Meet?"

"Oh, for Christ's sake! Look, I won't give you any trouble, please believe me. But I must see you."

And in some vaguely defined way, he had to see her. When you stand on the edge of the abyss you need someone there beside you. So they arranged to meet on neutral ground, outside a bar tucked in a medieval alley in the center of the city, just opposite the Palazzo Taverna, 14° secolo. Leo got there first and settled down at an outside table with a glass of beer and a copy of a magazine. Behind a small barricade of potted laurel bushes, the aromatic laurel that the English call bay, the pagan laurel that crowned the heads of heroes, he sat and watched and waited.

The occasional tourist passed by. So did the minutes. The owner of the café—a languid, middle-aged man with a carefully cultivated bohemian look—began a discussion about vacations with the girl who was serving behind the bar. Would she go away with her boyfriend or with him? It started as a joke and metamorphosed into a bitter little argument.

And then Madeleine appeared: a bright, sharp figure at the far end of the alley, walking down the gunmetal gray paving stones toward him. Leo waited to be disappointed in her: in her purposeful stride, upset momentarily as her heel caught between the setts and she almost tripped; in her manner, which was of nervous laughter, the kind that speaks of anxiety and insecurity; in her look, which was pale and tense, as though smiling were a strenuous exercise; in the way she pushed a strand of hair from her eyes and smiled at him with desperation. He wanted to be disappointed, but he wasn't. He was frightened of her, but he wasn't disappointed.

"I'm late," she said, sitting at the table. "I took a bus and the bloody thing broke down, and we all had to get out and catch the

next one, which of course was already full, and then there was this
gypsy that someone said had picked his pocket, and God knows
what . . ."

"What would you like?"

"Coffee. I want a coffee. Or a stiff gin. I think I want a coffee,
but I *need* a gin." She laughed, shaking her head and running her
fingers through her hair in a gesture that was purely, startlingly female. "I'll take a coffee. Just a coffee."

The conversation between bar girl and café owner broke off
long enough to provide the coffee, and was then resumed in
slightly louder tones now that there was competition. Madeleine
drank the thimbleful of dark liquid and replaced the cup on its
saucer with care. "I thought you'd run out on me," she admitted
quietly. "I thought I'd frightened you away and you'd run out on
me. I wouldn't have blamed you, you know that? I'm sorry, Leo.
I'm sorry about everything. I mean, I could have just kept quiet,
couldn't I? I should have. I should have shut up and continued to
see you as a friend of the family, a guide round the holy places, all
that kind of rubbish, and instead I had to do the full confession
thing. That's the Irish in me. Can't resist offloading her troubles
onto a priest . . ." Her mood lurched dangerously from misery to
laughter, so that the bar owner and his girl paused in their argument and looked across. "I'm sorry," she repeated. A caricature of
confession, a travesty of an act of contrition: "I'm sorry, I'm sorry,
I'm sorry. Christ, I told myself I wouldn't do this sort of thing. I
told myself I would be contained and collected and all those other
anal-retentive things that a well-bred diplomat's wife should be,
and now look at me. I'm crying." And to his surprise Leo saw that
she *was* crying, that her eyes were blistered with tears, so that she
turned away toward the laurels in a pathetic attempt to keep the
fact from him. "Damn, damn, damn," she whispered to the laurels.
"Damn, damn, damn."

He wanted to touch her, that was the unexpected thing, that

this need could be so plainly and simply physical. He just wanted to touch her, even shifted his chair around so that their knees could meet, so that they sat almost side by side and his hand on the arm of the chair could reach out to hers. She smiled and returned the grasp clumsily and tightly, patching her composure together as though out of component parts. "There," she said. "Better. Much better. A big grown-up now." Her eyes—mere organs, mere globes of gristle with a reflective costume jewel in the very center—considered him. "Now tell me."

"Tell you?"

"Your bloody scroll. If that's what it was all about, tell me what it was. Devastating, you said."

It seemed ridiculous. In the face of this woman, this table, this narrow Roman street, the matter-of-factness of hundreds of years of material history, the whole thing seemed suddenly absurd. "It's an account of the life of Christ."

She laughed. "I thought that had already been written."

"This is different. It claims to be a true eyewitness account."

"Claims."

"I've read it. The prologue anyway. It's enough."

"Enough for what?"

"Enough to undermine everything. My faith. The whole Faith, perhaps." The capital letter sounded in his ears. The Faith. Faith is the substance of things hoped for, the evidence of things not seen. There was silence there behind the laurel hedge with tourists going past and the couple behind the bar arguing about their summer. He looked at Madeleine's faintly freckled skin, at the delicate, precious flaws in her complexion, at the eyes that wavered between green and brown and watched him with an intensity that he had never known before, as though by looking they were possessing. And offering as well. And exacting something in return.

"It's Judas," he said finally. The name lay in the air between them like a threat, a name with all the emotional baggage of two thousand years of opprobrium. "Judas Iscariot. The scroll claims to be the writings of Judas Iscariot. It gives his name. Partly it is in the first person. It claims to be an eyewitness account of the Crucifixion."

She frowned. "Are you serious?"

"That's the claim."

"It's genuine?"

"Difficult to see how it could be a forgery. It hasn't been opened yet, but—" He shook his head. But what? It would be opened. He would read it. The whole ornate and arcane edifice of Christianity would come tumbling down. There were tears in his eyes, sharp, acid tears. "It claims . . ." His voice faltered, for any claim was surely absurd, fantastic. Yet Judas whispered in his ear, his voice quiet and measured as it sounded across the centuries of faith: . . . *he died and did not rise and I myself witnessed the body in its corruption* . . . "The author claims that he saw the decaying body of Christ, and that he didn't rise from the dead."

He felt the touch of her fingers on the back of his hand. "Poor Leo," she whispered. She picked up his hand and held it against her cheek as though it were the dearest thing that there could be, his dry and sinewy hand that was a mere machine of tendon and ligament and bone. "Poor, fragile Leo." She kissed him in the palm. He felt the press of her face and the intensity of her presence, just there within his literal grasp, and it seemed to him the most startling of intimacies. "Poor poor Leo, learning at last the only lesson that life has to give."

"What's that?"

"That there is nothing else. That there is only you and me, now, at this moment and this place. All else is no more than empty hope."

The apartment high up under the roofs of the Palazzo Casadei, the Palace of the House of Gods. She took his hand as they went inside, kissed him lightly on the cheek, helped him make tea neither of them really wanted, talked all the while, a light, bantering talk that he couldn't manage. Could the mundane intrude on the momentous in this way? She complained about the disorder in the kitchen, the lack of decent equipment and that kind of thing. She had gathered up her hair to keep it out of the way as she worked, and he stood behind her and watched what he had never really seen before, the hidden, secret intimacy of the nape of her neck, the subtle hollow between two taut tendons, fragile wisps of hair. The saucepan of water came to a boil and she plucked it from the flame.

"Jack's away until tomorrow."

"What's that meant to mean?"

"Whatever you want it to mean. There you are." She turned and handed him his tea, as though that were the reality, that and her presence here in his home, and all matters of papyrus scrolls or belief or faith or husbands were just nonsense. "So tell me," she said. "How do you feel?"

"About what?"

She eyed him over the rim of her cup. "Don't be idiotic. About *this,* us."

The volcano shuddered somewhere far beneath his feet. "Bewildered, I suppose. As though nothing is quite real."

She nodded in agreement. Perhaps all this was familiar to her, coming as she did from the foreign world of sexuality. Perhaps bewilderment was one of the symptoms, part of the etiology of the disease. They sipped at their tea, more to justify the making of it than out of any need, and then without another word, as though things had already been rehearsed, they got up from the table and went through into the other room, his bedroom, a room that until now had been as desolate as any abandoned attic.

The sound of cars came up from the street outside. Twin Madeleines, one real, the other reflected in the wardrobe mirror, crossed the room to crouch down and close the shutters. A sudden twilight descended. "Are you all right?" she asked as she turned back. "Leo, is there anything wrong?"

He told her that he was fine. He told her that he loved her and that he wanted to be there, and that he was fine. He told her this as, smiling, she unbuttoned his shirt and held her face against his chest. And he was shocked how his own body—something toward which he had learned to show nothing but indifference—could matter to her, and how she could matter to it.

A motorbike scoured the length of the street below the windows. There was the complaint of trapped cars, the grumble of a bus. In the shadowy room Leo and Madeleine undressed modestly back to back and then turned toward each other at the same moment, almost as though they were taking part in some preordained ritual, the liturgy of love, perhaps. The act of looking at her seemed a heresy. There were freckles scattered across her chest. Her breasts were large and blunt and scrawled with veins like pencil lines; her belly was pleated with the marks of childbearing. Clothed she had seemed small, small and precise, an artifact beautifully made, a thing to marvel at; naked she filled the space beneath the sloping roof, her flesh luminous in the false twilight. Close to, her flesh gave off a smell, a blend of her own scent and perfume, of memory and dream, of fantasy and nightmare, the smell of his mother lying in his bed when he was ill, the smell of the little pianist as it clung to his fingers, the smell of flesh and fur and feces, a confection of desire and revulsion, a blend of all those things that he had never dared imagine and those which, imagining, had repelled him. And her breath was in his ear, the rasp of her breath, the muffled voice of her heartbeat; and she was whispering absurd and childish words, as one might to a nervous animal: "My lion, my strong lion. I'm not going to eat you. You mustn't worry. It'll be all right." As though the breath of her body didn't frighten him, the lucid texture of her skin, the incontinence of her hands, as though all this didn't terrify him. As though her breasts, soft and warm against his face, didn't hold between them the warm smell of motherhood. "It'll be all right," she whispered as she lay beneath him in the hot, still anonymity of his bedroom with the traffic mumbling in the street below. "It'll be all right. It'll be all right." As though mere repetition would make it so.

She found some tissues in her handbag and wiped her belly. The room was hot, hot and airless. Their fragile, fragmentary unity was gone and they lay apart, slick with sweat, limned with guilt. He looked at her lying naked beside him. She was flesh again; for a few, treacherous moments she had been something else, something evanescent that he couldn't now recall, but now she was mere flesh once more.

She lay on her back, her breasts slopping sideways under the insistence of gravity. When she spoke she directed her words to the ceiling. "It must seem a disappointment. Does it seem a disappointment? Anticlimax, perhaps. That's the right phrase, isn't it? Apposite."

What is done cannot be undone, he thought. You can confess, you can ask forgiveness, you can expiate your sins, but you cannot undo anything. He thought of how her small tough hands had guided him knowingly; how she had whispered imprecations; how her hips had writhed, like the antics of a whore. None of that could be undone. "Your fish," she had whispered as she clasped him in her fist. "Your big, shiny fish." Another vocable from the Brewer family lexicon, no doubt. Doubtless Jack had a big, shiny fish. The thought thrilled him and appalled him. Fish, *ichthys, pisces,* pisser: an absurd concatenation of words. He had spent his life with words, with the texture of them, the precise intent, the significance. Another one floated up out of the wreckage: fornication—a tortured word. *Fornix,* an arch, a vault, the vaulted arch of a brothel, no doubt, the arch of the legs, the crotch, the crux, which is the cross on which we all hang. *Keep away from fornication,* Saint Paul whispered to him. *All other sins are committed outside the body; but to fornicate is to sin against your own body.* The fluid guilt was manifested in him, in the sharp start of tears in his eyes, in the awful incontinent flood from his body. *Your body is the temple of the Holy Spirit. You are not your own property; you have been bought for a price.*

She turned and kissed him chastely on the cheek. "I'll go and wash."

He watched her roll off the bed and pad, plump and clumsy, across the room to the door—her pale, awkward buttocks with their dark dividing crease; her thick waist and loose thighs; the way she moved, which was hers alone and which, at that moment, repelled him.

"I'm sorry," he called after her.

She looked back at him lying on the bed. "Forget it. For God's sake, don't worry. The last thing I need is apology." There was an edge of anger in her tone.

"What *do* you need?"

She laughed humorlessly. "Who knows? You, I suppose. The thought frightens you, doesn't it?" She turned away and went to the bathroom without waiting for him to answer.

9

T he phone rang the next morning. He didn't have to get to the Institute before eleven o'clock and he was at home doing little or nothing, just reading an article that he was reviewing for *Papyrology Today*, taking refuge in the quotidian. The phone gave its intrusive petulant sound that would never take no for an answer, and he assumed it would be her. He picked up the receiver. "Madeleine?"

There was a silence on the other end. "Is this Father Leo Newman?" A voice of limpid, crystalline tones, the tones of Oxford and the English College, the tones of the hierarchy. "Am I speaking to Father Leo Newman?"

He felt a small spurt of panic, something physical just below his diaphragm. He closed his eyes. "Yes, this is Leo Newman."

"I have Bishop Quentin on the line for you, Father."

The voice left him to sweat in the stillness of the morning. After a while someone else came on the other end, the tones of Maynooth this time, urbane, jovial, threatening. "Leo, my dear, how are you?" They'd had trouble tracking him down. They hadn't been sure where he was. They were concerned, worried, anxious about one of their number who had strayed in the wilderness, less concerned over the ninety and nine who were safely in the sheep pen. "I think we ought to meet for a chat, Leo," the Bishop said. "To talk things over. I think you owe it to yourself, and to me."

"I'm waiting for a call from Jerusalem. I don't know that I can get away."

"I think perhaps you ought to."

Madeleine came over that afternoon. She had called during the morning to fix a time. "Jack's flight gets in this evening," she had said. "We can be together for a bit." But when she let herself into the apartment her manner was hurried and distracted: things had gone wrong with her arrangements; Jack was due back earlier. She had telephoned the office to check and she had discovered that he had got a seat on an earlier flight, so she couldn't stay long. "The best laid plans of mice and men . . ." she said, divesting herself of coat and bag of shopping.

"It's 'schemes.' The best laid schemes . . ."

"Pedant. I'll have to make up some story if I'm late, shopping I'd forgotten to do or something. Here, I've brought you a present."

He watched as she unwrapped one of her packages. It contained different blends of tea—Lapsang souchong, green gunpowder, absurd names like that.

She came up to him and wrapped her arms around him and pressed her face against his chest. "Am I forgiven?" she asked. As though they were in that stuffy confessional once again and she was asking for absolution.

"Forgiven for what?"

"I was unkind yesterday."

"Were you?"

"It was the first time. First times can be difficult."

"Can they? You sound as though there have been many." Was she practiced in all this, he wondered—the hurried telephone calls, the assignations, the gifts? Did she know about it all?

She was very still, holding herself against him and not daring to move. "A few. Does it shock you?"

"There's not much that shocks me," he said. "Priests are remarkably unshockable. What would Jack do if he found out about us?"

"Jack?" She seemed surprised by the name. She looked up at him, her faintly furrowed brow with its scattering of pale freckles mere inches below his face. "He will eventually, won't he? I mean, we can't keep up this kind of deceit forever. People get a sense of something being up. They know."

"Do they?"

"Oh yes, assuredly they do."

"And then?"

She shrugged, releasing him from her arms, turning to the table and putting things in order, the things that she had brought with her. "He'll probably be awfully understanding. He is, you know. It's a dreadful word to use, but Jack is awfully *nice*. I suppose I should say decent. Very decent, very civilized, very English. He'd probably comfort *me* if he knew."

The word *know*, that strange biblical euphemism. Leo knew her, knew the smell of her and the taste, knew that imperfect concoction of flesh and fur that was her body; but with surprise he realized that he no longer knew the person within. Intimate physical knowledge had somehow chased away any previous understanding he had of her. What did he know of her life with her husband? What did he know of the secret life that was hers and his, the affective life that drives a marriage, the libido that drives a woman? What went on between the sheets? He noticed that her accent had become more accentuated as she spoke about her husband, as though in the act of praising him she was also distancing herself from his supposed Englishness, his decency. To go with the scent of exotic tea there was the pungent smell of hypocrisy.

"Calder phoned me this morning," he told her, wanting to move away from such dangerous ground.

"Calder?"

"The people in Jerusalem. They want me back. I put them off for the moment, but I'll have to go sooner or later."

"Have to?"

"This papyrus. If I want to be involved."

"And do you?"

"Of course I do."

"So you'll abandon me."

"Don't be ridiculous."

She laughed, as though to diffuse the fear, as though to show that it was no more than a joke. "I must go now. I'll give you a ring as soon as I can."

He had kept his real news until last, until she was halfway to the door. "And I've been summoned to London," he said. "Tomorrow."

She stopped. "Summoned?"

"By my bishop."

"They can't know about us."

"I think they feel I'm straying from the straight and narrow."

"And they're trying to pull you back."

"Something like that. There's the scroll too. Maybe they've heard about that."

"Why can't they leave you alone?" Her eyes seemed bright with tears, her composure fractured. "Why can't they leave you to make your own decisions?"

"They have their rights, don't they?"

"What in God's name do you mean by that?"

"Nothing. It's their duty, that's all. You can't blame them."

"Meaning you can blame me?"

"I'm not blaming anyone. I expected it sooner or later and I've got to face up to it."

"What'll you say to them? What'll you say about us, I mean?"

"I don't know what I'll say."

"When are you going?"

"I told you. Tomorrow. At eleven."

"Tomorrow! Where will you stay?"

"With the Jesuits at Farm Street. They're good with apostates."

"Is that what you are?"

He shook his head helplessly. "I don't know, Madeleine. I just don't know."

She watched him thoughtfully, brow puckered, lower lip gently bitten. He himself had bitten that lip and tasted its determination. "Leo," she asked, "do you still believe?" The question was quite unexpected, quite shocking, in fact. Their relationship has been built on a shaky foundation of allusion and joke, not on a substantial discussion of matters of faith.

"Believe?"

"In God, in Christ, in any of what you are still wedded to. You know what I mean. That scroll. Me. Has all that blown everything away?"

He shrugged. "Belief doesn't just evaporate."

"Doesn't it? That's exactly what it seems to do in my experience. Evaporate, like a lake or something drying up, leaving nothing behind but mudflats and a few dirty puddles and a musty smell of superstition. You remember that time I came to make my confession? Well, that was almost my last moment of faith. I guess the lake had become a small pond but hadn't yet degenerated into a puddle."

"So I let you down in your moment of need?"

"Not at all. You gave me something new to believe in. And you haven't answered my question."

"Perhaps that's because I don't know the answer."

"Can't tell pond from puddle, is that it?" She laughed, but it was one of her humorless laughs, a bitter thing. "We can't go on like this, Leo," she said. "You know that."

"What alternative do we have?"

"Oh, there's an alternative, all right. You leave the priesthood, I leave Jack."

"You couldn't."

"Of course I could. I think maybe it's you that couldn't."

He ignored the barb. "What about the children?"

"I can see the children during the holidays. That's almost all I do anyway."

"How can you *say* that?"

"Because it's dead simple, Leo," she replied, and the faint touch of her accent was sharpened by emotion. "The children take second place. Does that sound dreadful? But it's true. Underneath it all there's you, and there's only you. That's what love means."

"I thought love was selfless."

"That just shows where you are wrong, you poor deluded fool. Love is the most selfish thing in the world. That's why the Church still demands celibacy." She smiled at him and shook her head sorrowfully. "You don't want this, do you, Leo? You don't want this to go any further."

Leo breathed. He was startled by the difficulty, the physical effort required. As though he had lost the knack. He breathed deeply and watched her watching him, and he felt that in some way, absurdly, his new knowledge of her made her less accessible, less familiar. She was no longer a friend, a companion, someone with whom he could share his amusement. She was an unknown territory into which he had intruded, an island of conceit and concern. He had no reference points, no landmarks, nothing to guide him in this confused place of desire and revulsion. Love, he understood, was a Janus emotion. He loved her and loathed her at one and the same time. "Can't we step back?" he asked absurdly. "Can't we go back to where we were?"

But there is no going back, there is no undoing. He knew that without her having to say it for him. You cannot unremember, you cannot unravel the warp and weft of experience. You cannot unbury your dead. He knew that well enough, knew it even as she laughed derisively at his idea. "Is that really what you'd like?"

"It's not a matter of what I'd like," he said.

"What is it, then?"

"It's a matter of what I *am*. Maybe I'm crippled, perhaps that's it. Damaged by a lifetime of celibacy. Maybe some part of you atrophies. Love of one particular person is a very different thing to manage than love of humanity in general."

"But I don't think you *do* love humanity in general. I think you rather despise humanity. I think that over the years you have learned to love only Leo Newman, that's the trouble. And trying to love Madeleine Brewer is a bit of a shock." Her eyes were sharp and bright, and her smile sat awkwardly on her face, as though it might suddenly slide off and fall to the floor. "Leo Newman," she said, "do you love me as I love you?" Her words had a strange echo about them, a sense of ritual. She might have been quoting from an obscure liturgy with which he was only half familiar.

"I don't know. I don't *know* how you love me."

That little laugh had once intrigued him. "That's always been the way. That has always been the whole problem between a man and a woman. No one ever does know. You just muddle along and hope, and every now and again you have the fleeting illusion that you *do* know, that you both love each other in the same way and to the same extent." She came over to him and put her hands up to his shoulders and reached up on tiptoe to kiss him, very softly, on the lips. "I'll take you tomorrow if you like."

"Take me?"

"Yes, take you. To the airport. Can't I drive you to the airport?"

"Yes," he said. "Yes, I suppose you can."

"I'll come round first thing."

She kissed him again. He tasted the wetness of her lips and the bitterness of her saliva, and felt the flagrant intimacy of her tongue inside his mouth. And then she was gone, and he could hear her shoes clipping down the stairs.

10

He had barely dressed when she arrived next morning. She came in announced only by the sound of her key in the door, as though the place were hers as much as his, as though she belonged. A banal greeting. A kiss on the cheek.

"You're early."

She shrugged. "I thought I'd get here in good time. I guessed the condemned man would be up bright and early."

"Is that what I am?"

"Aren't you about to face the Inquisition?"

"The Inquisition, what's left of it, is here in Rome. I'm just going to speak to my bishop."

"But it's only the beginning, isn't it? The beginning of a long and complicated process. *Auto-da-fé,* isn't that what it is?"

Opening the window she climbed out onto the terrace. She made the same little gasp as she emerged into the view, the same sound that she had made when they had first looked the place over together—mere weeks ago in measured time but an eon, a light-year, infinity in any other dimension. She stood at the parapet with her back to him, like a passenger at the taffrail of a ship looking out over the pitching, tossing ocean. The breeze caught her hair and threw it about, so that she put up a hand to control it. He could see cords of tendon beneath the pearly skin of her hand, and the thin lines of veins as blue as smoke. "You can see right through the lantern on Saint Peter's," she said. "Have you noticed that? You can see the sky through the lights."

"That's exactly where the sun is setting at the moment. It shines right through just as it goes down. I suppose that's just for one or two days in the year."

"Maybe that means something."

"What? What on earth *could* it mean?"

She stood looking at the view. Perhaps she was trying to picture this sunset behind the lantern, shards of light throwing the delicate structure into silhouette, the flare seeming to consume the stonework for those few moments. Then she turned around and confronted him across the small terra-cotta strip of terrace. "We have plenty of time before we need to go," she said. "I came early on purpose, don't you realize that?"

"On purpose?"

"Don't be naive," she said, and went inside, leaving him standing there with the whole city circling around him, the clouds cascading across a spring sky above his head, starlings surging in strange and convolute arabesques across the blue, the domes and towers turning around like parts of some great mechanism, pieces of machinery, cogs and cams and wheels in a great piece of medieval apparatus. He stood without moving. He heard the sounds of the day coming up to him, the groaning of this machine, the roar of traffic, the noise of people, someone calling from across a street, a door closing. And Madeleine was inside, waiting.

By the time they drove to the airport the sky was covered by broken cloud and there were fat spots of rain on the asphalt. She drove with dangerous distraction, talking all the time of matters of family, matters of common interest, as though there was nothing between the two of them and they had not shared the bittersweet flesh of the fruit of the tree of knowledge of good and evil; as though a moment's fleeting ecstasy had never been theirs. "Jack's back in London next week." That kind of thing. "And the girls, oh, they don't get back for the holidays until after that. They'll go to their grandparents for a few days first. In Surrey, that is. Jack's parents, of course."

But in the anonymous shadows of the multistory parking garage her mood changed. She turned to him and clung to his hands and she looked bewildered, like the survivor of an earthquake picking over the wreckage, the fragments of a ruined life. "I love you, Leo," she whispered, and her hands clung to his as though to life itself. They were closer than in any confessional, barricaded from the prying world, shuttered together with only their thoughts. Passengers came and went. Cars cruised by in the shadows. "Do you love me now? Do you?"

"Of course I do. I showed you."

"You don't. You don't even understand. I *love* you."

"Of course I understand."

"You don't," she whispered. "You are just like in the confessional. You don't have the faintest idea. But I can't go on like this. You never say anything. You're so bloody bound up. Costive." She giggled. It was a strange, uncertain sound, the sound of something fracturing inside.

"I'm sorry—"

She shook her head as though in disbelief. "Don't apologize. For God's sake, don't apologize."

They got out of the car. There was a silent walk along Plexiglas tunnels, past advertisements for expensive shoes and bottles of perfume with curious, organic shapes. She had set her face against the future like someone confronting a blizzard. She was almost ugly like that, her sharp and luminous expression worn down by the elements. He wondered what she was feeling, what currents lay behind her distant expression, her distracted manner. He had never known this paradox, the sense of distance that intimacy brings with it, a sensation that the same shared things had different meanings for the two of them, the same words held different significance. They picked up his ticket at the airline desk and walked aimlessly among the crowd for a few minutes. The departures hall was as wide and impersonal as a railway station. "It'll be a relief to get away, won't it?" she said.

"Don't be silly. It's just two days. Less. Less than two days."

"And when you come back?"

"We'll see."

She nodded, as though she already knew. At the departure gate she held his hands and raised herself on her toes to kiss him chastely on the cheek. Each action, each gesture seemed to carry with it a ritual significance that he couldn't fathom. He let go of her hands and turned away and went through gates to passport control. There was a security alert in effect. Had he packed this bag himself? they asked. He had. Had anyone tampered with it since he had closed it? They hadn't. Had it been out of his sight since he had packed it? Would he mind opening it . . . ?

She had given him a photograph. She had brought it with her to the apartment that morning and he had had to open his case and pack the thing away. Now it lay there among his shirts and underpants like a votive object, a quiet, composed portrait framed in silver. Leo looked back for a moment and saw the same face watching from the other side of the glass partition, from beyond the X-ray machine, from the other side of the Styx. She waved, like someone bidding farewell to a lost soul. Then the security guard indicated that he could go, and he was through into the departure lounge and he couldn't see her anymore.

On the flight to London he was a figure in gray among the tourists, a solitary figure in gray amid the colored interlacing of the rest of the world. Picture him there, crammed between a nodding, smiling Japanese and a middle-aged American in a button-down shirt and Nike sneakers. "I'm from Rome," the American kept saying to people. "Can you imagine that? Rome, Georgia, mind you. Not Rome, Italy." Picture Leo sitting there smiling and agreeing with his traveling companion and trying not to listen. He is at a turning point in his life: more than just a turning point, a veritable multiple intersection. In Jerusalem they are beginning to open the Judas papyrus; in Rome (Italy, not Georgia) Madeleine is awaiting his return; in London his bishop is awaiting his arrival. He sits there uncomfortably, between the sacred and the profane, between the devil and the deep, between the past and the present. And he looks quite relaxed and normal, almost composed, in fact. Within there is turmoil, and a welling sense of claustrophobic panic; outside there is only the patient face of the cleric. Within he essays a brief prayer, rather in the manner of a child, to see if there is anyone there to take his call; outside he smiles at an account of Rome, Georgia, Floyd County, as a matter of fact, have you ever been there, Pastor? Within he sees Madeleine lying naked before him; outside he thanks the stewardess profusely and accepts her offer of *The Times*. Within he wonders what he has wondered for much of his life but has rarely allowed conscious space to: is there a being, transcendent or immanent—either will do—that one might call God (or Dio, or Allah, or Yahweh, or Bog, if it comes to that), and if there is such a being, does he (He?) care one jot or tittle for the spiritual or physical life of this speck of dust crammed into tourist class on an Alitalia flight to London, Heathrow? He reads his breviary, possibly for the very last time. His question remains unanswered, but his body (embarrassingly: he has to shift in his seat to make things comfortable again) answers all too readily to the persistent vision of Madeleine, which exists in a separate but simultaneous part of his mind and has by now opened its legs. The sight shocks him again in retrospect, just as it had shocked him in hot and fetid reality, for he had never imagined it like that, never that gaping wound, that stigma that women bear, and all that tangled hair. "Priests are fairly unshockable," he had told her. But it wasn't so.

Only on the train from the airport did he open the newspaper that he had been given. He leafed through the pages in search of distraction. There were the usual stories, the usual stalled Middle East peace initiative, the usual floods, the usual political scandals. And there on an inside page was the first hint of a different disaster, a different catastrophe:

ARCHAEOLOGICAL FIND
QUESTIONS CRUCIFIXION STORY

There was little substance. He could hear Goldstaub's voice behind the words, his superlatives mixed with his evasions. *While work proceeds on the painstaking task of opening the scroll,* the story finished, *Church sources are said not to be impressed by claims that may run contrary to the gospel account.*

Apparently the Gospel of Judas was in the public domain. That was how Goldstaub would have put it.

*   *   *

Leo's interview with the bishop was good-mannered on the surface, but beneath there were undercurrents of acrimony and fear. "Did you seen that article in yesterday's *Times*?" the man asked.

"I've read it. They were all talking about it at Farm Street."

"They're calling it the Gospel of Judas. Aren't you tied up with the thing?"

"I've been over to see the scroll," Leo admitted.

"And what did you think?"

"It's very early, possibly first century."

"But so are the gospels, for God's sake. Why should we give any greater credence to this thing? The Gospel of Judas. I ask you. Can it really be what it claims?"

Leo shrugged. "It's pretty convincing."

The bishop shook his head. "Things are bad enough as it is, without some priest calling the whole story of Christ into question. You know what I think? I think all this'll just blow over, and you'll be left looking a bloody fool."

The accusation rankled. "It's one of the most sensational finds in the whole history of New Testament studies. Whatever it turns out to be, even if it's second century and a piece of anti-Christian propaganda, it's a sensation."

"And if it isn't?"

"Isn't what?"

There was a spurt of anger, a sudden, electric hint of fear. "Oh, for God's sake, Leo. If it turns out to be first century and what it claims to be—an eyewitness account, a contemporary account of the life of Christ by someone outside the gospel tradition. What then?"

"The Church is going to have a lot of explaining to do."

The bishop shook his head. "It does no good to explore the Faith too minutely, Leo. It isn't that the Faith is not true, even factually true, if you like, but surely it is not susceptible to the methods of science. One man's hallucination is another man's transfiguration. Who's to say which is the *true* account?" He attempted a smile. He was a genial fellow, really, popular with the press, who could always rely on him for the smart smack of common sense. "And will anyone believe yours?"

"What do you mean by that?"

"There's been talk about you, you know that? Quite apart from this Judas thing, there's been talk. It's bound to affect how people view what you say."

"Talk?"

"You moved out of the Institute, didn't you?"

"Is that against Canon Law?"

"Of course it's not. Don't be contentious. But there's talk of a particular friendship. Particular friendships are dangerous things, Leo. You know that. An English couple. A diplomat and his wife."

He had expected something, of course, but still he felt himself flush. "Oh for God's sake!"

"I have to tell you that their reputation goes before them."

"Their *what?* The Brewers are a respectable married couple. Mrs. Brewer is a Catholic."

"Lapsed, I understand. Not that there's anything wrong with lapsed. Half my congregation is lapsed these days. But I believe that when they were in Washington she was involved in—"

"This is a disgrace." Fury. A kind of fury, something that was visceral more than intellectual, like a tumor lodged just below the diaphragm and sending its fragments throughout the body.

"Rumors, of course. Only rumors. But still. There were those in the Foreign Office—"

"How can you deal in this kind of filth?"

"—who were concerned to post her husband away—"

"I'm in love with her," Leo said. He spoke quietly, but the fury was just below the surface. "You are talking about a woman that I love."

The bishop was silent. They could hear the tapping of a keyboard in the office next door. "Leo, I strongly advise you to take a long rest," he said at last. "For your own spiritual well-being. I suggest somewhere that is truly holy. The Trappists, perhaps—"

"No."

"Or the Benedictines if you want something a little less demanding. Somewhere where there is no argument and no debate, but only the plain certainty of the eternal truth of God. You need time for reflection. Do you want me to get in touch with an old friend of mine at Subiaco?"

"No."

The bishop shrugged helplessly. He glanced around his dull bachelor's room as though somewhere he might find a silver lining. "At least it's not choirboys. I couldn't take choirboys. Not again." The conversation spluttered on, the two men edging around issues of faith and love like dogs circling around a disputed bone. There was talk of suspension from priestly duties, of laicization, of apostasy. "Maybe we should say a prayer together," he suggested finally. Prayer seemed to be the last resort, a sign of desperation.

After leaving the bishop's rooms Leo went into the cathedral. He went past the exhortations to contribute to the upkeep of the place, past the program of services, the notices about concerts of sacred music, the rack of books, the rack of pamphlets, the thermometer that showed the health of the roof fund. He went into the purple shadows of the place with their faint hint of incense, their sense of the numinous. There were people in the cathedral, a few tourists wandering around, but mostly worshipers just sitting in the pews or kneeling in prayer—surrendering in their own way to the broken, pinned figure hanging in the air above their heads. Someone began to play the organ. The sound drifted up into the shadows of the vault as though passing through the very bones of the building, making the whole place shudder in protest. Leo felt at the end of so many things: his faith, his vocation, his tether. He had exhausted prayer. Now he stood at the back of the central nave looking up at the great Christ figure hanging in the shadows over the crossing, and he was Judas. He knew all the pain of betrayal, how compelling it was, how necessary. Betrayal stemmed from belief, that was its compulsion. It stemmed from belief and conviction and it carried with it the certainty of knowledge.

It was raining outside. He crossed the little artificial piazza outside the cathedral and he felt a terrifying sense of freedom. A taxi waded past through the rain. He hailed it and to his surprise it stopped. The driver set the meter going with a flick of his hand. "Where to, guv? *Father,* is it? Where to, Father? Quick round trip to heaven?"

"Farm Street," Leo said. "The Jesuit house."

"Jesuits, eh? Near enough."

A Picnic—1943

picnic. *Eine Landpartie* is what Herr Huber calls it, but Gretchen insists on the English word. A *picnic,* with friends, the fortuitous friends created by the exigencies of war or diplomacy, men and women thrown together by chance. A picnic at the amphitheater of Sutri, in the countryside north of Rome, a beautiful place hedged around with holm oak and approached along an avenue of umbrella pines, the Roman *campagna* at its most secretive and seductive, heavy with the echoes of its Etruscan past. It is her picnic, her small reminder of days long gone by when they used to go on picnics in the forests near Buchlov Castle, her small treat and Leo's too, with Jutte and Josef invited, and the amusing von Klenzes, and of course Checco, so that she can feel his eyes on her. As she sits on the rug that the servants have spread out in the amphitheater she even lifts her knees for him to see beneath her skirt. Just a glimpse of hidden, secret silk; no more. Just sufficient to make him uncomfortable as he sits in front of her, managing plate and knife and fork and the bulge in the front of his trousers with a certain lack of competence. "Are you quite all right, Signor Francesco?" she asks mockingly. He looks hot and awkward, but answers that he has never been better.

"Because you look most uncomfortable."

"I am perfectly comfortable, Frau Huber."

There is some banter about the wine. They eat *prosciutto crudo* and figs, and Herr Huber decides that this particular variety of ham is not as good as Viennese *Schinken*.

"I prefer Prague ham," someone says. It is Josef, who was in Bohemia in 1938 where he met Jutte, in fact, in those distant days when the State of Czechoslovakia still existed and he was with the embassy in Prague. He does tend to go on about the city rather, its beer and its food, but his reflections on the matter of Prague ham, which the Führer himself ate on that momentous day when he visited the city in 1939, are interrupted by a sound, a sudden and intrusive sound like the fabric of the blue sky being torn apart. The picnickers pause, forks frozen halfway to mouths. They glance upward.

"What the devil?"

Something dark and silver, something awkward, cruciform, loud, flashes overhead from behind the fringe of holm oak and roars away over the road and above the umbrella pines, tearing at the sky as though doing it a great hurt.

"*Amerikaner!*" Leo cries in excitement, getting to his feet and running to the entrance to the theater as though he might catch the great, dark machine.

"Nonsense," says Josef. "Luftwaffe! A Messerschmidt."

"Leo!" shouts Gretchen. She gets to her feet and runs after the child. The noise is background now, a distant roar against the spring day. "American," agrees one of the men, and Herr Huber begins a lecture, directed mainly toward Signor Francesco, a lecture about how the great tragedy of the war is that it has given the Americans an excuse to get into Europe, and things will never be the same again, whatever happens. And whatever happens is this: the sound of the cruciform creature grows louder in the sky once more and the people of the picnic stand transfixed in or about the entrance to the amphitheatre, with Gretchen calling "Leo! Leo!" and Herr Huber impatient to develop his argument.

And there is the machine once again, sudden over the umbrella pines, not cruciform now but a swollen face with outstretched arms, raging in fury at the soft spring day and the picnic party on the turf below. There is a racket and the anguished whine of metal and an explosion of rock dust from the tiers around the theatre, and the sour stench of sulphur in the air. Then the thing has gone and all is quiet.

The disposition of the picnic party is this: Herr Huber is picking himself up from the grass (his hat has been dislodged and lies some distance away; his crown is fine and arched and devoid of hair) and brushing himself down as though he has just been splashed by a passing car. Jutte is crying softly and Josef curses softly, as though that way he might comfort her. And Gretchen is running through the entrance toward the cars, calling "Leo? Leo?" with a faint upward intonation, as though she is taking part in a game of hide-and-seek and is getting rather tired of it and wants to hand victory to the boy.

"They've hit the damned Mercedes," cries von Klenze, going to investigate. He reaches Gretchen just as she gets to the entrance, where she halts for a moment as though waiting for her whole world to collapse just as the Mercedes has collapsed onto its suspension and two flat tires, just as Leo has collapsed in an awkward heap, his face in the dirt, one arm twisted beneath him, his legs lying anyhow just as though they have been dislocated, and a dark puddle spreading into the rough grass around him.

He is still moving when his mother gets to him. That only makes it more distressing. It's the hope that is so distressing. A fait accompli, a certainty, the inexorable and contingent hand of fate, that's easier to deal with. Hope is the destroyer of things.

But he soon stopped moving. She was soaked in his blood by then, calm and detached, trying to hold his right shoulder together, and soaked in her child's blood. Later the dress will have to be thrown away, along with so much else.

Magda—now

Y our family?" Magda asks me just as Madeleine had once asked.

"My family was like yours, less than yours. There was just me and my mother."

"No father?"

"No father."

"My father was a big man, always drinking. Maybe you were better with no father."

"Maybe." I watch her working at her pictures, watch that narrowing of her wide features, that puckering of the black mouth that accompanies the brushstrokes as though it were her lips rather than her hand that marks the lines on the canvas. She works with acrylics and oils. Sometimes there are other things there as well, sand, for example, mixed into the paint to give a harsh and abrasive texture.

"And there was my brother."

"Your brother? You said there was just you and your mother."

I shake my head. "There was always my brother."

Today with Magda I visited the city of the dead. The city of the dead lies behind the Basilica of San Lorenzo *fuori le Mura,* Saint Lawrence Outside the Walls. In that place outside the walls, beyond the pale, in the place where the Romans lay their dead, one sultry August day in the year 258, they buried the scorched and scoured body of Saint Lawrence. I feel for Lawrence, the martyr who had a taste of hell before he ascended into heaven. The authorities didn't throw him to the lions or anything like that. They didn't stick him with spears or crucify him or any of those things. They tied him to a gridiron and roasted him over a fire. The night sky weeps meteors on the day of his death—*le lacrime di San Lorenzo,* the tears of Saint Lawrence, they call them—but I just feel the flames.

The city of the dead has a street map and bylaws. Cars cruise solemnly along its tree-lined avenues. Taxis pause at the curb, waiting for their fares with their meters ticking over. Pedestrians walk the streets like ghosts, flitting beneath the cypresses and the umbrella pines with armfuls of flowers—chrysanthemums, which are the flowers of the dead.

The city of the dead has quarters, districts, zones named for the inhabitants—an Evangelical quarter, a district for the Muslims and a ghetto for the Jews. There is a military area with barracks and parade ground and monuments. There is a zone where the rich reside, there are spacious villas for the bourgeoisie and apartment houses for the poor, with steps leading up to glass entrance doors and elevators to take the inhabitants up to the top floors. The city of the dead has running water and electricity and its lights burn all night lest the inhabitants awake and cannot see for the dark.

"Why are we here?" Magda asked, but she needed no real reason. She wore funeral black, of course—black jeans, black jacket, clumsy black shoes like army boots. She crossed herself at the gates of the city and she wore the composed face of a mourner as she walked with me along the paths. She is an artist and she understands such places. The place will live again under her pen and ink and brushes and paint: the dead will awaken and their fingers will grab the marble slabs that lie on top of them and slide them aside. They will lever themselves out of ditch and sarcophagus, and stand finally before the judgment of history or God, whoever happens to be around at the time.

There is no saying whom you might meet in such a place as the city of the dead. I half expected to find my own mother there among the marble and the travertine, to bump into her on the pavement much as you might bump into someone on the street. "Good God! Fancy seeing you here!"

How would she be? Aged, as she is whenever I recall her; or a youthful shadow of that young woman who first conceived me? How are the dead when they arise at the last trump? Which version of them survives for all time: the first bloom of youth, or the victim of age and Alzheimer's? That's the problem with bodily resurrection, isn't it? Is it the child or the adult, the youthful sinner or the aged repentant, who gets to emerge from the tomb?

But of course there was no real risk of meeting my mother. She lies safely buried in the cemetery of Saint Mary's, Kensal Green, where I helped inter her amid the comforts of Holy Mother Church. *I am the resurrection and the life: he that believeth in me, although he be dead shall live: and every one that liveth, and believeth in me, shall not die forever.* She wanted the rite in Latin; of course she did. It was there in a codicil to her will, along with the details of the bank account in Geneva and the deed to the apartment: "I wish to be buried using the Latin form of the mass."

Ego sum resurrectio et vita . . .

Or we would encounter Madeleine, walking in that quick, determined manner that she had, as though she always had somewhere to go and was just fractionally late for the appointment. She would halt in surprise at the two figures coming toward her, her surprise transforming into an ironical smile: "What, you here? And who *on earth* is this?" Looking at Magda with a knowing expression, as though she understood how things stand.

"This is Magda. She shares your name."

"Does she, indeed? I wonder what else she shares with me."

There are jokes, you see, even in the city of the dead. Let me give you another one, an inscription on a tomb:

Angelica Tomassini, Vedova Contenta.

Can you manage it? Why should I explain it? I don't explain my miseries, so why should I explain my jokes? And when explained, does it remain a joke? I had to explain it to Magda, though. "Roughly," I told her, "it means: Angelica Tomassini, the Happy Widow."

A frown, the frown Magda makes when confronting linguistic difficulties. "*Roughly?*"

It was a lesson again, a lesson among the lessons that the dead themselves teach. "Approximately. That's *approximately* what the inscription means: the Happy Widow."

"So she was *happy* that her husband die?"

"That's what it says, but not quite what was intended. Her husband's name was Contenta. Her married name was Contenta. She was the widow Contenta."

Magda pondered the matter, and then laughed, too late. Madeleine would have been the first to see the joke, of course. She would have pointed it out to me and made the most of it: "I'll bet she was," she would have said. "The wicked old thing."

But there aren't many other jokes in the city of the dead: an elevator for the exclusive use of coffins is worth a chuckle, I guess.

Tomb doors of anodized aluminum like the doors and windows of a vulgar modern house evoke a wry smile. But

Quello che siete fummo
Quello che siamo sarete.

is not a joke. We found it inscribed on one of the memorials and it's perfectly true: *That which you are, we were; that which we are, you will be.*

Or *Mors Ultima Ratio* carved above the portals of a vault built like a modernist house in the style of Le Corbusier: *Death is the final reckoning.* It is curious how little overt religiosity there is in the city of the dead. The dead know, I suppose. They know the truth, they see through the lies.

Remember Man that thou art dust, and to dust thou shalt return.

That fragment of the ritual that always struck me as being the most plainly honest was the administering of the ashes during Ash Wednesday. I remember it so well when I worked in a school for a few years after my ordination: the progress around the classes with the small bowl of gray ashes. The bowed brows, the smear of ash, like a smear of pigment, the rough brushstroke of an artist: *Thou art dust and to dust thou shalt return.* Perhaps that is when the priest is most near to his true purpose: when he enacts the ritual task of an artist.

There are cross-connections in the city of the dead, associations known only to the inhabitants. There are secret mistresses entombed whole streets away from their clandestine lovers. There are bastards buried distant from their parents. Chains, links, bonds, concatenations. There are murderers and their victims, rapists and their prey, libertines and their catamites. There are enemies buried in pious proximity and friends buried far apart. There are only secrets in the city of the dead.

Magda the artist standing in an open space among the monuments and memorials. Before her an area of grass, an urban square, the kind of place you might find the children playing, dogs with balls, mothers with baby carriages. A car drifted past along the road behind us, heading toward the high-rises of the newly dead. There were pedestrians on the pavement, their arms laden with shock-headed chrysanthemums.

"We're here," I told her. She followed me along a gravel path between the gravestones and stopped where I knew to stop, before the slab that said *Leo*.

"We're here," I repeated.

Leo Alois Huber. 1932–1943. Geliebt.

And a small spray of fresh flowers, their shaggy yellow heads like a mop of curls, with a printed message: *Dal Ambasciata tedesca.*

Magda's forehead puckered in a frown. "Who is he?" she asked. "Eleven years. Who is the boy with your name?"

Who indeed?

"Who is this Leo?" Magda insisted.

They have taken my Lord and I know not where they have laid him.

But I knew.

"Who is he?" she repeated. "Who is the boy called Leo?" She seemed confused, bewildered, perhaps frightened by this city of the dead and the forgotten. She rarely took much notice of me, painting me with the indifference of a surgeon stitching. She rarely showed any glimmer of emotion. But now her voice rose among the silence of the tombs like someone crying for the dead, crying to waken the dead. "Who is the boy called Leo?" she cried.

Magda paints. She works in acrylics and oils, deftly, with cunning, smoking as she works, her eyes half closed against the smoke and her head held tangential to the line of vision so that the thin wreaths of gray will not annoy her. There are things embedded in the paint: sand, bits of plants, bits of twig, spines of cactus culled from the rooftop terrace, toothpicks like shards of bone. She even works with chicken wire rolled and molded into shapes like limbs, heads, creatures that come out of the paint as though perhaps they might fly. But nothing flies. Flight is beyond it all. Everything is trapped in the intricate web of her creation.

She sits, hunkered down and leaning against the low wall on the terrace, observing the paint dry (acrylics dry fast, she tells me) and rolling stuff into a loose cigarette, and smoking calmly as she looks. She keeps her things in a leather wallet hung around her neck and pushed down the front of her T-shirt, hanging between her narrow breasts. "You want a smoke?" She smiles, not caring one way or the other. She doesn't care, one way or another, about anything.

She paints Leo among the tombstones, Leo among the memorials, Leo on fire in the anteroom to hell.

11

It was raining in Rome, the basalt paving slick with water and glistening with lights. He paid off the taxi. The porter's cubicle was closed, like a market stall that has been shut up for the night. He took the elevator up to the top and climbed the remaining stairs to his apartment. The smell of freesias greeted him, the vivid smell almost overpowering in the closeted air. There was a bunch of the flowers in a vase on the table in the living room. They must have been put there by Madeleine. She must have come to the apartment during his absence, let herself in and left the flowers for him to find on his return. He could hear her saying it: "You need some color in here. You need a woman's touch."

Women were color; men were gray—clerical gray.

He smiled at the mute message of the flowers. A plea? A question? A statement. Say it with flowers. But what exactly was she saying?

He washed approximately and went to bed. Exhaustion edged around his thoughts, eroding their coherence, dragging them down into the idiocy of dream and nightmare, a nightmare in which Madeleine tried to tell him things that he didn't understand, Madeleine and Judas, the one faithful, the other betraying. But which was which?

He woke early and showered. The smell of freesias was still heavy in the air, a smell which now seemed almost sickly, like the scent that his mother had worn, something old-fashioned and redolent of a past that could never be captured, never conquered. Eating breakfast he tried to turn his thoughts to the lecture he would deliver that morning. Banal, ordinary thoughts to dispel the demons. But Judas whispered in his ear, his voice quiet and measured as it sounded across the centuries of faith and doubt:

. . . he died and did not rise and I myself witnessed the body in its corruption . . .

And other thoughts crowded in. Madeleine and freesias. Madeleine in that loft under the sloping ceiling, padding on bare feet into the bathroom to wash the evidence of their lovemaking from her body. Her matter-of-factness, her acceptance of what he was and what he wasn't. He drank coffee and ate some cheese that he had found in the fridge and tried to place her within the chaos of his mind. Madeleine naked beside him, her flesh soft and warm, a negation of faith and vocation, a fragile grasp on humanity.

Who is worthy to open the scroll? he thought.

It was only after he had eaten that he found the note lying on his desk. He unfolded the paper with trepidation, without knowing what to expect, without even recognizing her handwriting: with a flash of inconsequence he realized that he had never seen anything in her hand.

Dear Leo, he read, *I think you had better telephone me.*

But it was not signed Madeleine, nor even Maddy, nor, as he supposed it might have been, merely initialed *M*. It was signed *Jack*.

A terrible stillness. The words again, their careful grammatical accuracy, their diplomat's caution, hiding everything and betraying nothing: *Dear Leo, I think you had better telephone me.*

But he didn't. The telephone lay there on the floor, but he didn't pick the receiver up. He made his way down the stairs to the entrance of the palazzo. There were many things to face: a lecture theater of students with varying degrees of interest, a woman with whom he might or might not be in love, a future in which he might or might not be apostate, a husband who knew everything. His world was, perhaps, on the edge of dissolution. He would face the various fracturing parts in his own time.

The porter was in his cubicle. His face hung in the dusty pane of the window like a piece of dirty material: an expression of concern and suspicion was scrawled across the fabric. "Signor Neoman." That was how he managed the name, emphasising the novelty of it, accentuating the raw newness. Neo-man. What did the man want? Something about the electricity? Something about the water, or the cleaning of the stairs? What could it be?

"Signor Neoman, there's been an incident." *Incident* is the word he used. *Incidente*. There are shades of meaning. Accident; incident. Leo paused beside the sign that announced to a waiting world that the Casadei Palace was open to the public during the hours of 10.00–13.00 and 16.00–17.30, but not on Monday. The man came out of his cubicle. Perhaps it was the first time Leo had seen him outside his box. He was surprised to find that he was small, reaching no higher than Leo's chest. Leo barely even knew his name. Mimmo, he was known as Mimmo. "The police were here," the man said. "The day before yesterday. In the afternoon. The signora . . ."

"Yes?"

"She fell. That's what they think."

"*Fell?*" Tripped on the stairs. Fell over a chair while she was in his apartment putting the freesias in the vase. Sprained her ankle. Broke something? Her wrist, perhaps. Perhaps she tripped and in trying to save herself she put out her hand and broke her wrist. But why, in heaven's name, *the police?* The speed of the human mind is remarkable. So is its inability to face the obvious.

The porter laid a confidential hand on Leo's arm. He was a lugubrious character. In the time that Leo had known him—no more than a few weeks—he had never demonstrated a glimmer of emotion: but now he contrived a glistening of the eyes. Now he even squeezed Leo's arm, as though to show some kind of solidarity. "She came to put flowers in your apartment. I said *buongiorno* to her and she smiled at me and said *buongiorno* back and she had a bunch of flowers in her hand. She looked like she always does. Happy, you know what I mean? And she fell."

"What do you mean, *fell?*"

The man looked anguished, as though it were his fault, as though he were somehow to blame, as though it was all owing to his carelessness, his dereliction of duty. "From the roof. Signor Neoman, the signora is dead."

Panic. Panic manifested in the flesh, the panic of the agoraphobic, the panic of someone who cannot bear the void of the open street, who stands on the edge of the pavement and fancies himself on the edge of a cliff with emptiness below and a clear sensation that the whole world is tilting in order to thrust him over the gulf. Fear like an ache in the bones, deep and hollow, the kind of pain you know you are going to have to live with for months and years.

He ran out into the street, distractedly, as though looking for something. It was a day of scirocco, the south wind that comes from the Sahara Desert laden with heat and damp and sand. There was a high blanket of cloud, a cloying warm blanket above the tilted roofs of the city. The alleyway behind the Palazzo Casadei was a narrow canyon between the old, crumbling cliffs. One of the outer reaches of the ghetto. Around the corner from the small grocery store—*Minimarket,* it announced hopefully— there was nothing, no shops, no bar, no trattoria. There were only drainpipes and mute back doors and the uneven ribbon of black paving stones like the scales of a snake's back. A cul-de-sac led off the alley into the body of the Palazzo Casadei. There was a barri- cade across the entrance, a barrier of galvanized steel with a battered notice in baby blue saying POLIZIA. He pulled the thing aside. There were trash cans at the far end and a rusted fire-escape ladder that led upward to nowhere. On the ground he found a smear of sand and some dark substance in the fissures between the stones. Someone had placed a small bunch of flowers against the wall.

He walked. Rome lay exhausted beneath the cloud, like a corpse beneath a shroud. It was a place where everything imagin- able happened and presumably would happen again, a place where nothing was remarkable. Madeleine was not remarkable, Leo was not remarkable, their poor, stunted relationship was not remarkable, death was not remarkable. He walked without direc- tion. He walked unsteadily over blocks of basalt, down between the ocher and umber walls of the Campo Marzio, the Field of Mars, where bits of the ancient city show through the medieval like bones poking though the flesh of a corpse.

Panic is a pagan thing born of the great god Pan, that mysteri- ous deity who stands in the shadows behind the cold light of Olympian reason. Leo felt pure, pagan panic: a shortage of breath, a sensation of tightness in the chest, as though his sternum were gripped in a vise, a feeling of enclosure and exposure at one and the same time; a feeling that he must be somewhere else other than here. He walked. For an hour or more—whatever happened to the restless group of students awaiting his lecture?—he just walked. And then he fetched up near a post office where there was a line of telephone booths. He had the number on a piece of paper in his wallet.

Over the phone Jack's voice seemed perfectly calm. "I was wondering when you'd get back," he said. "Where were you? Maddy said something about London." She might have been still there, just there, standing right beside him at the phone.

"That's right," Leo said. "London. Jack, what happened?" People walked past the booth, an anonymous street crowd. Tourists, kids, a gypsy woman with a baby at her breast.

"I thought of you," Jack's voice said. "Of course I did, considering where it happened. Your apartment, I mean. I'm sorry, I'm maybe not quite as articulate as I should be. But I thought of you and I didn't really know how to get in contact."

"That's quite all right." Why should it be quite all right? Why should Jack be half apologizing, and Leo refusing the need for apology, as though some kind of solecism had been committed?

"I don't know if the magistrate will want to see you . . ."

"Jack, what happened?" Leo repeated. "In God's name, what happened?"

"In God's name, is it?" There was the faint breath of a laugh on the other end of the line. "I wonder if that's quite accurate."

"Just tell me what happened."

There was a pause. "I suppose you'd better come round."

Jack was entirely calm, that was what was so terrifying. He was as calm as if he was in the midst of some diplomatic negotiation, with the police, with the embassy, with the magistrate's office, with some officially constituted body for the management of corpses. The phone would ring and he would pick it up with a faint frown and stare at the floor as he spoke, and issue instructions in measured tones as though making important but passionless decisions, the kind of thing one might do when buying a house, or taking a new job, or negotiating a new trade agreement. "I can't come for the moment," he said to one of the callers. "I'll be with you as soon as possible, but I can't at the moment."

Leo looked around the familiar room. Madeleine watched him from a silver frame on top of the piano. She seemed to smile, almost as though she had this all planned. On the floor beneath the piano was a copy of an English newspaper. He saw the small headline down at the foot of the page: DIPLOMAT'S WIFE IN ROOF PLUNGE. He felt renewed panic, a sense of the pure randomness of things.

There was a pause and the phone rang again and quite suddenly Jack was talking in a different pitch, with a softer, gentler tone. "Mummy's hurt herself," he said in this counterfeit child's voice. "Yes, I'll be coming to see you soon. Meanwhile, you look after Boot for me. Will you do that, Katz? Yes, everything's quite all right. You two just be good, and soon I'll be there." He replaced the receiver with infinite care.

"What happened?" Leo asked. "Can't you tell me what happened?"

"She's dead. That's what happened."

"But how?"

There was someone in the kitchen, a dutiful and earnest woman whom Leo vaguely recognized. She came out now and asked Jack if he wanted anything and he said no, thanked her courteously and denied that he wanted anything at all, even a cup of tea. "I wish they'd stop fussing," he said to Leo when the woman had retreated. "I know they mean well, but I wish they'd stop fussing. This is the FCO pulling out the stops, you see. Rallying round, they call it, as though . . . as though what? The flag, I suppose. Rallying round the flag. The fucking Gatling's jammed and the square's broken and they're all rallying round." He looked away, toward the piano with the pictures of the family, toward the window, beyond which lay the rest of the world.

Toward the bluebottle that hammered its head against the pane with a desperate insistence. "Did you know she had a key?" he asked suddenly.

"Key?"

"To your apartment."

Leo found himself measuring his answers, wondering where they might lead. He couldn't read the shifts and allusions of this situation, the matter-of-factness of it all, the undercurrent of familiarity. "From when you helped me move in, I suppose."

Jack nodded. "They found the apartment locked, you see. The police got the porter to open it. And they found the key on the table. Of course they call it an accident for the moment. That's what the magistrate said. Incidentally, she'll want to interview you."

"Who will?"

"The magistrate, Leo. The magistrate." Jack's tone was of studied patience, the kind of tone he might have used with a stupid child.

"And you don't think it was an accident?"

He smiled the smile of a diplomat who knows he has scored a point in the negotiations. "My dear Leo," he said quietly. "I *know* it wasn't."

"You *know*?"

Jack looked at him. Leo wondered, what goes on behind the face, behind the eyes? What goes on in the gray jelly that lies behind that fine forehead? In the confessional one never saw the face. There was nothing more than a dim shadow laying bare its soul without ever revealing its features. Gender you knew. And social class. And sometimes, but not always, you could guess at intelligence and education. But you never saw the face with its look of panic, its mask of shame. "I'm surprised she never told you," Jack said, "seeing how close you were. I would have thought she would have confided in her great friend, her father-confessor . . ."

"Confided what?"

"This wasn't the first time that Maddy tried to take her own life. Didn't you know about that? Didn't you? Hadn't she told her confessor?" He laughed faintly. His expression was drawn in gray and white, a composition of disaster and despair, but his tone was of amiable patronage, a tone born of Winchester and Cambridge, of years of effortless superiority. "Maddy wasn't the kind of person who needed the comforts of a priest. She was *ill,* Leo. What she needed was a doctor, a psychiatrist, but of course she wouldn't have anything to do with them. So she found you instead. And she never told you."

Leo tried to say something, but Jack trampled easily over his words. There was a relentless quality to his manner, as though he were standing there in the alley and looking up the ocher side of the building and watching the woman balanced for a moment on the parapet way up there, five stories up there, high up against the sky, just watching and waiting for her to make the small step into the void. "Maddy was the survivor of half a dozen previous suicide attempts, Leo. Mostly pills. Once she cut her wrists—wrist, singular, to be precise: she only managed one. And there was another incident that involved booze and one of my ties round her neck. You can make what you wish of that one. But mostly it was pills. She said to me, 'You think I'm just messing around, don't you? You think I'm just seeking attention. But one day I'll do it properly.' That's what she said. And now she has."

There was a silence. Jack looked steadily at Leo and the smile had gone from his face, like snow from a bleak winter landscape. Was there accusation in that look? Did Jack Brewer hold Leo Newman, the innocent Leo Newman, the naive Leo Newman, to *blame?*

"She was ill, Leo. How stupid can you priests be? I've never really believed in priests as confessors, do you know that? It has always seemed to me like giving a child a hand grenade to play with. She was ill, a depressive or whatever you want to call it. She lived part of her life on the edge of despair and part of it in some idiotic state of excitement, like a five-year-old child at a party. Just like an overexcited child being sick at a party. Except she was an adult and so she didn't throw up all over the carpet. She just fucked other men instead." He paused, as though for effect, as though to let his words strike home. "Didn't she tell you that either? Didn't she confess it in all its squalid detail? Perhaps she didn't. Perhaps it had all gone beyond guilty secrets in the confessional. Perhaps she fucked her pet priest as well."

Leo got to his feet. The ground seemed to shift a fraction. For a moment he had to concentrate on keeping his balance. "You're distressed, Jack," he said. "You're overwrought and you don't know what you're saying. Maddy and I were friends, you know that. Close friends." Why was it so easy to lie, not to lie directly, but to lie by implication? Why did the words come so easily to hand? He paused for a moment as though to let his assertion find its mark. And then he turned and made his way to the front door, leaving Jack alone in the sitting room. A face looked out of the kitchen to see what was going on, then darted back out of sight. He opened the door. Shame coursed through his body like a chill tide, guilt and shame in equal measure, the one seeping into the other, both denied the means of atonement, for atonement is at-one-ment and the one was gone, extinguished in a moment's plunge. *She fucked other men.* He went out onto the landing and closed the door behind him. She padded across his mind, her buttocks moving clumsily as she walked. She turned toward him and her dark, untidy delta of hair pointed to things he could not comprehend. He even spoke her name as he walked down the stairs, as though she herself might answer him and explain. "Madeleine," he whispered. "Madeleine."

*   *   *

That evening he went around to the narrow alley behind the palazzo to look again. The flowers were still there, ragged and bruised now, a sorry litter of yellow and red. He looked upward, up the cliff of burnt ocher, up the receding lines of perspective toward the distant parapet. What happens on the way down? he wondered. Mere seconds. A decision made and just as soon brought to its conclusion. Consummation of a kind. What happens during that momentary plunge? What do you think? Of whom do you think? He saw the kick of her legs. Her skirt billowing. A sudden glimpse of white thigh. And then the blow. Something soft and heavy. Things breaking inside.

12

T
he magistrate examined Leo's identity card, glanced at the photograph, considered his profession—*sacerdote*—thoughtfully. *"Prete,"* she said. Her tone was carefully edged with contempt.

"Priest," Leo agreed.

"And your relationship with the Englishwoman?"

"A friend."

The office was high up in the ministry building with a view over plane trees and the dark flow of the river. The magistrate herself was brisk and smart, impatient to resolve one case and move on to the next. Manila folders were piled on her desk. In one corner of the room, hedged about with box files, a man sat behind some kind of word processor. There was the patter of a keyboard.

"Where were you when she died?"

"I was out of the country. In England."

"You can prove this?"

"Prove it?"

"Can you demonstrate when you left the country?"

And suddenly, quite suddenly—for only a moment before the idea had been beyond consideration—Leo understood that he was a suspect. "Of course I can prove it."

"How?"

He cast around. How do you prove things? How do you know what happened, when? How do you know who the man Youdas was, and what kind of relationship he had with Yeshu? "Airline tickets. People, for God's sake. The people I was with in London." He thought of the bishop and his heart sank. The keyboard tapped in the background, the hesitant touch of evidence. The magistrate looked down at the desk in front of her, examining a report or something. Her voice was neutral, informed with the indifferent tones of bureaucracy. "At what time of day did you leave Italy?"

"In the morning. She drove me to the airport."

A sudden upward glance. "The signora *drove* you?"

"Gave me a lift. Drove me."

"So she was at your apartment in the morning when you were there?"

"She came to my flat that morning. To drive me to the airport."

"So you were the last person to see her alive?"

"Was I?" Some kind of nightmare. Not a nightmare with Madeleine, not a nightmare with Judas. A nightmare of absence, the lack of someone, a void where once there had been a presence. "I don't know. I don't know when she died. I don't know who saw her. How can I answer that kind of question?"

"Signora Brewer"—the woman struggled to pronounce the name; it came out with the vowels widened and emphasized:

Breu-where—"died during the course of that morning. She was not found until the afternoon, but she died during the morning."

"But when?"

She ignored his question. "Can you provide evidence that she took you to the airport at the time you say?"

"Of course I can. The time of my check-in."

"Tell me. Tell me the time and the airline and the desk."

He told her, and the keys pattered at his back, footsteps hurrying after his account of the morning, a morning that was merely two days ago but a whole world away, a whole eon away, projected now into a new significance: the last moments of Madeleine on earth, her last moments anywhere, perhaps. Madeleine letting herself into the apartment with her light familiarity, her smile, her gentle hands touching his hands, his face. Madeleine begging him, that was what was so disturbing, Madeleine begging him for consolation, for consummation, for that fragile communion that they had shared, the communion that gave them an impoverished glimpse of the eternal. "She must have gone back to the flat," he said. "After she left me at the airport she must have gone back. Didn't the porter see her come in?"

The magistrate was impassive. "We will need material evidence of all this. Airline tickets, receipts, that kind of thing. What was your relationship with this woman?"

"I've already told you. We were friends."

"What kind of friends? Close friends? Were you her confessor?"

"I had been, some time ago. When we first met. But no longer."

"How was she that morning? How did she seem?"

Leo shrugged. How did Madeleine seem? She was dead, for God's sake. How did she seem? "Normal. She was a woman of moods. She seemed happy, she seemed sad. Sometimes both at the same time."

"And that morning?"

He was silent. The magistrate looked at him, saw something there, picked up with her magisterial antennae some vibration. "Were you and Signora Brewer lovers?" she asked.

"What an extraordinary question."

She looked at him bleakly. "My job is extraordinary, Mr. Newman. The death of a woman in this way is extraordinary. Falling from a roof is extraordinary, suicide is extraordinary, murder is extraordinary, therefore my questions are extraordinary. I repeat: were you and Mrs. Brewer lovers?"

"I am a priest," Leo said.

The magistrate made a small noise, a noise that was part laugh, part snort of contempt. Evidently she did not think much of priests. "I will have to ask you for a blood sample."

"A *blood* sample? Why in God's name a blood sample?"

The keys pattered in the background. "Because Mrs. Brewer had sexual intercourse shortly before she died. The pathologist found semen inside her body. We want to know whose it might be." Her words seemed to hang in the still air of the office like an exhalation from the tomb. *Inside her body.* And Leo saw Madeleine lying broken on a slab, an approximate collection of limbs and ribs, a bag of bruised and ruptured organs. And probing, latex fingers working their way inside the depths of her belly, intrusive impersonal fingers searching inside her. Desecration. He heard his own voice in the room, his voice being chased by the chatter of keys, by the scream of swifts outside the open window, by the awful hurrying footsteps of guilt. "What possible business can it be of yours whether Signora Brewer made love to someone before she died?"

"Did she have sexual intercourse with you, Mr. Newman?"

"Her husband. Why not her husband?"

"Mr. Newman, will you please answer my question?"

"Why is it your business?"

"Because a woman is dead, Mr. Newman. A woman is dead and it is my job to discover how and why she died."

"You think I might have killed her? This is ridiculous. You think I killed her?"

"I don't think anything yet. She was a woman with a family. Possibly she was a woman with a lover. She was a woman who might have been a danger to one of the people in her life. She was a woman who died. She may have fallen, she may have jumped, she may have been pushed. She may even have been killed by a blow to the head before being thrown from the roof. All these things are possible. Some of them are more probable than others; one of them happened. My job is to find out which one it was."

Leo said, "She was a woman with a history of attempted suicide."

The magistrate smiled, as though mere knowledge were an admission of guilt. "Did you *know* that, Mr. Newman?"

"I was told so by her husband. This morning."

"But you did not know about this before? Your close friend never told you that she had a history of . . . mental instability?"

"Never."

"And you never suspected anything?"

"She had moods. Nothing particular."

The woman nodded. "And now will you answer my question? Did you have sexual intercourse with Mrs. Brewer on the morning that she died?"

"What about her husband?" Leo repeated. He almost shouted it. He raised his voice and the magistrate looked back at him and smiled a humorless smile because she was used to being shouted at by men and she had learned to use it to her own advantage.

"Her husband denies having any sexual relationship with his wife for the last two months," she said.

Leo Newman was silent. The tapping of keys paused, waiting for his answer. Pointedly the magistrate looked down, consulted the pathologist's report as though she might discover something new there, some small, organic detail that she had overlooked.

"I did," he said quietly. "Yes."

A quick glance up. "And did she consent to this?"

"Do you mean, did I rape her and then throw her body off the roof and make my own way to the airport? Don't be absurd."

"I mean just what I said. Did she consent to having sexual intercourse with you?"

Leo was silent. He closed his eyes. You might close your eyes in the confessional and no one would notice. Here the magistrate watched, and put her own interpretation on things. He closed his eyes and Madeleine touched his face with her fingers as though discovering him in the total darkness of the Church of San Crisogono. "Yes, she did. She wanted it."

"Meaning that you didn't?"

"Meaning nothing of the kind. We were in the middle of a love affair. It was difficult, not the kind of thing you can summarize easily in a couple of words."

"But you wanted the affair to end?"

"Perhaps. I don't know." He cast around for an answer, as though such things as answers and explanations were lying around somewhere in this cramped and shabby office. And in a sense they were, bound up in dozens of manila folders: answers and half-answers and lies; the truth, the whole truth and nothing like the truth. What is truth? Pilate asked. The Greek word *aletheia*. "I don't know," he repeated. "Then I thought, maybe yes, I wanted it ended. Now . . ." His voice faltered. Something took over, some awful tide of emotion that for a moment he couldn't control. He shook his head as though to rid himself of it. His eyes smarted and his heart pounded and sweat stood out on his forehead. He needed to swallow. There was something stuck in his throat that would not go down. Perhaps these organic manifestations were all symptoms of guilt. Perhaps they signified that he *had* killed her.

The magistrate nodded as though she understood everything. She called for water and a plastic cup and she waited while he drank. And then she went on: "You had sex with her and when it was all over you killed her and threw her body over into the alleyway behind the palazzo, and then made your way to the airport? Was that it?"

Some part of him, a small, fragmented part watched all this from a distance and knew that he ought to laugh. It was a joke, an uproarious, absurd joke. He should have roared with laughter, wept with laughter, wet himself with laughter. It should have hurt his sides and made his ribs ache. He just shook his head. There were tears there, of course; but they were not tears of laughter. He saw his tormentor through a blur of tears, as though she were painted in watercolors and the paint had run in the rain. "Of course I didn't kill her," he said quietly. "This whole thing is mad. I didn't kill her. I love her."

"But you didn't expect her to take her own life, did you?"

"Does anyone expect such things?"

"Apparently her husband did."

"So why don't you listen to him?"

"Because my job is to listen to everyone." She paused, considered the papers in front of her, considered the man in front of her, considered matters of guilt and innocence. "I would like you to make a formal statement, Signor Newman. You are obliged by law to state what you know of the events surrounding the death of Mrs. Madeleine Brewer. You are, of course, entitled to have a lawyer present if you wish."

"I don't need a lawyer," Leo said.

"Are you sure of that?"

"Yes, I'm sure."

"Very well. I suggest you begin from the very start, when you woke up."

And so they rehearsed the trivial, intimate events of that morning once more. Yet again he moved through the apartment getting his breakfast, getting things ready, listening for a footfall on the landing outside the front door. Yet again Madeleine fitted her key in the door and opened it and walked into the apartment. Yet again she greeted him with a flat "Good morning" and took his hands in hers, kissing the tips of his fingers, touching them to her face. They talked, they went out onto the terrace, he followed her back in. "Love me," she whispered once more. "Love me."

"Can you tell me the time that this happened?" the magistrate asked.

Leo cast around vaguely. "About eight o'clock. My plane was at midday. She came about eight, I think. I hadn't expected her so early."

"Why not?"

"I didn't know what time she'd come."

Again she took his hands and led him into his bedroom. Again they lay down on the bed and her hands held him, drew him toward her, drew him into her. Not like that first time, not the awful fumbling and the shame. This time she held him there while the small explosion took place inside her, his explosion and hers: a small organic miracle. The keys pattered at his back. "There," she whispered to him. "There." He felt her breath in his ear, felt the small impulse of air as much as he heard the words. "There," she said. "You've loved me."

"And what time did you leave the apartment?"

"After ten o'clock. I remember hurrying. I remember hurrying Madeleine because we would be late. I think perhaps . . ."

"What do you think?"

What did he think? He thought perhaps he had killed her. "I think perhaps she wanted me to."

"To what?"

He raised his voice in anger: "To be late. To miss the flight. I think perhaps she wanted me to miss the flight."

And then the drive, the sudden change of mood, from the small, intimate triumph, to silence and withdrawal. She didn't speak much on the journey, didn't speak much at the airport, stood silent beside the check-in desk as he went through the business of ticket and passport, watched him with a neutral face as he disappeared beyond the metal detectors and the television screens.

"That was the last I saw of her."

"What time was that?"

"About eleven o'clock. I don't remember exactly but it was about eleven o'clock. Eleven-fifteen. We were late for the check-in."

The keys fell silent. A printer whirred back and forth and rolled out four pages of typescript. Leo read through words that were a mere skeleton of that morning, a mere simulacrum of reality, a mere shadow of Madeleine's presence there in the apartment beside him, her body on his, her mind enveloping his. *She fucked other men,* said Jack.

"I must ask you to surrender your passport, Mr. Newman," the magistrate said as he signed the document. "You must not leave the country until such time as the preliminary investigation is at an end."

The entrance hall of the ministry was a space of marble and travertine. It had the atmosphere of a station concourse. There was the same shifting crowd, some people with purpose—a train to catch, a hearing to attend—others with nothing to do but hang around to see what might happen. There was the same sense of randomness, of strangers thrown together by the arrogant and ridiculous hand of chance.

"You are Mr. Newman?" One stranger among many, a young man with a sharp nose and a prominent Adam's apple. He spoke English of a kind.

Leo frowned. "How do you know that?"

"Press," the man said. "*Il Messaggero*. You can tell me of the woman's death? The wife of the English diplomat? You can tell me?" He brandished a small tape recorder. Leo saw wheels turning within the thing. He brushed the youth aside. "I can tell you nothing."

The man hurried after him. "You can confirm the things that are being said?" And suddenly, from nowhere that Leo could see, there was the stark flash of a camera.

He hurried through the huge doors, out into the dazzling light, down the steps to the pavement. Buses trundled by, swirling around the square pursued by shoals of mopeds.

He walked across the river. The water slid beneath the bridge in a soft and pungent organic flow. There was the smell of asphalt and exhaust fumes, a miasma like the shifting mists of Hades or Sheol or wherever it was that the dead went. Madeleine walked beside him, his own image of Madeleine, Madeleine sharp and acerbic and normal, not a hysterical woman who would throw herself at men or from rooftops. She accompanied him through the narrow streets of the old city, all the way to the Palazzo Casadei, where she slipped quietly away from him as he went into the entrance. From his glass box the porter watched. Leo climbed slowly up to the attic and let himself into the apartment. The place was as desolate as it had been on that first occasion when he had looked it over with Madeleine. But then she herself had filled it, made it bright with her presence. Now it was as empty as a tomb.

He found her photograph, the one she had given him before she took him to the airport. It had taken on a strange votive power, the potency of an icon. He placed it on the table. It was like one of those pictures on a gravestone, a solemn image of a person who never was, a Madeleine he had never known. There was nothing else, that was the problem. He wanted her to walk in the door and greet him in her manner. With a kind of panic he even tried to imagine the event, the key turning in the lock, the door opening, Madeleine appearing there in the sudden space. But she had no face. *She fucked other men.* She had no face. Not the face of the half-smiling woman in the photograph, not any face at all. He had lost her and he had lost even the memory of her. *She fucked other men.* He picked the freesias out of their vase and threw them away. They were faded and withered and the water was foul.

The tyranny of the telephone. It rang throughout the day, bleating like a tiresome child. Would he confirm that . . . ? Did he deny that . . . ? Voices sounding across a spectrum that ran from perfect English to native Italian with all the hybrids in between. Was he available for interview . . . ? Was it true that . . . ?

In the evening Goldstaub called. "Is it true?" he asked.

"Is what true? Can't I have a moment of peace?"

"Madeleine, Leo. It's all over the English newspapers. Is it true?"

"If you mean, is she dead? then the answer's yes. I don't know what else you may have been reading."

"Christ alive, Leo—"

"I doubt it, I truly doubt it."

"Stop trying to be clever. Is there some kind of problem?"

"The authorities seem to think I may have killed her."

"That's ridiculous."

"The ridiculous is what they deal in."

Later Jack called. His voice was dull and expressionless. "You'd better get hold of the English papers tomorrow," he said.

"Why? What are they saying?" But Jack had already hung up.

* * *

Next morning he found the letter. It was there in his mailbox beside the porter's lodge, the envelope addressed in unfamiliar handwriting and franked with a Rome postmark. He tore it open, thinking that it might be anything, a letter from a sympathizer, a letter from an accuser (plenty of phone calls from that kind already), a letter quite unconnected with the matter of Madeleine's death. He never really expected a letter from beyond the grave. The expert in the handwriting of two thousand years ago, of the uncial and the minuscule, could not even recognize Madeleine's handwriting.

I've tried this before, she had written.

An unpleasant sensation. A sensation of nausea, just below the breastbone; and dizziness, and a chattering in his mind as though a dozen voices were speaking to him all at once, a dozen whispers on the edge of audibility. He looked around for somewhere to sit, there in the shadowy entrance archway of the Palazzo Casadei with the porter watching curiously from his glass cabinet. It was easier to go through into the courtyard beyond, into the pool of daylight and the faint dribble of the fountain where papyrus grew green and bright. He sat on the step of the pedestal and peered at the page.

I've tried this before. Oh yes, I'm practised in this kind of thing, didn't I tell you? That's being disingenuous. I didn't tell you because I didn't want to frighten you away. This may be just another practise, in which case I'm writing it for no one but me. I want to apologise, of course. I want to ask forgiveness for imposing on you (who else can forgive but a priest?) and I want to say I'm sorry. You mustn't blame yourself, that's all. You mustn't blame yourself. Just tell yourself it's better like this. Good, clean break. Snap.

Maybe I won't be brave enough. Maybe I'll sneak round and

retrieve this letter before you see it. I've done that before. There's a lot you don't know, I'm afraid.

M

He almost laughed when he read it. Through the mess of emotion he almost laughed. Certainly he smiled. But it really posed more questions than it answered, for still he could not find a reason within the words of her scrawl (written awkwardly in her car, he guessed, shortly before she bought a bunch of freesias and took them to his apartment). Why hadn't she left the note there for him to find? Another part of the joke? Did you joke when you were about to kill yourself? What did you feel? Leo Newman, ex-priest (let's be honest about it now), ex-lover, ex-everything, felt no inclination to kill himself, so why did Madeleine Brewer, who had so much—husband, children, friends, even a lover, should she have wished to continue that little diversion—why should she? And not he?

He, who had always been able to answer every question, argue every point, suddenly had no answers at all.

He delivered his evidence to the investigating magistrate by hand. He was forced to wait for almost an hour to see her because she was in court. "There's this," he said when finally she received him, and she took it from him and read it with difficulty, being unfamiliar with both the English handwriting and the language.

"What is this word?" she asked, pointing.

"Disingenuous."

She tried it in Italian—*disingenuo*—and seemed to find sense in it. She read on down as far as the final, ironical salutation. "And it is certain that this is from the Englishwoman? This is her handwriting?"

"I can vouch for the fact that it is not mine. You'd better ask an expert to say whether it is hers."

"This must be deposited as evidence. It must be examined. We must obtain attested examples of her writing."

"It means that she killed herself," Leo said.

The magistrate smiled on him as though he were being naive. "It means there is further evidence in the case. What the evidence *means* is another matter altogether."

In the dead time of the afternoon he went out to the nearest newspaper stand. The English newspapers were just in. He tucked them under his arm and returned home, where he sat at the table in front of the photo of Madeleine and rifled through the pages until he found it, down at the bottom of an inner page, a different photograph of her looking quizzically out of the past, questioning him from beyond the grave, beneath a headline that said:

SCROLL SCHOLAR PRIEST AND
DIPLOMAT IN LOVE TRIANGLE

It was like one of those children's games, a tongue-twister. Peter Piper picked a peck of pickled peppers. Scroll scholar priest. The authorities were still making inquiries. There was no evidence to say whether it was an accident, or suicide, or worse. The article was carefully evasive. Body fluids were under forensic examination. And the article used that phrase beloved of English journalists but used nowhere else in the entire Byzantine edifice of the language: *Foul play has not been ruled out,* it said.

Later that day there were reporters camped outside the Palazzo Casadei, a small clutch of them with tape recorders and cameras. The next morning the story really broke, a synergy of stories, the sexual and the theological conspiring to make front-page news in the British papers: self-righteous outrage among the tabloids implying that they were guardians of the true faith no less than the Holy Father himself; a thoughtful leader in *The Times* that betrayed sophistry and priggishness in equal measure; sober, salacious details in the *Daily Telegraph* along with a photograph, snatched from some family album, of a smiling, faintly freckled face which had not the slightest hint of the wanton about it. SCROLL EXPERT COVETS HIS NEIGHBOUR'S WIFE, ran the headline. Below it came the photograph of Leo, captured as he stepped out of the gates of the ministry, appearing to glare suspiciously at the camera when in fact he had merely been surprised by the flash.

The Italian papers carried it in the sections devoted to *chronache,* the chronicles, the stories that are not the serious matter of politics but the prurient business of sex and violence and corruption. *Cronache di Roma,* one of them had: Chronicles of Rome. It might have been from the classical corpus, something written by Tacitus.

The next day Leo had a brief, acerbic conversation with the rector of the Pontifical Biblical Institute, a conversation in which self-righteousness trampled on the heels of outrage. "You will have to go before the Congregation for the Clergy," the rector said. "You face excommunication and disgrace. You will have to make peace with your conscience." But Leo Newman had other matters with which to make peace: his loneliness, for one. The void within him. The sensation of dispersion, that he was mere scattered atoms among the awful chaos of the city and the world. That evening he stood on the terrace and watched the sun set behind the dome of Saint Peter's. It no longer shone right through the lantern. The earth had shifted and the sun now went down fractionally to the right.

And Madeleine was dead.

A Funeral—1943

A funeral. A quiet, private affair tucked away in the narrow streets behind Piazza Navona. Weeping openly is for the Italians. The protagonists here weep silently. They sit in the pews before the draped catafalque as if in a courtroom, waiting for the words of the priest with all the composure of people waiting for sentence to be pronounced. They will not contest the sentence. They will not appeal to any higher court. They are under authority and they understand these matters.

During the service Frau Huber faints. The heat, the oppressive presence of the mourners, the clouds of incense like the smoke from a funeral pyre have all contributed. Fainting is, perhaps, a forgivable lapse although, again perhaps, it is also a sign betraying her imperfect breeding, the alien genes that lie behind her apparently perfect Aryan features. She faints and falls against her husband, who does not let her down but holds her upright for the chant of *Miserere mei, Deus,* his left arm holding the missal, his right arm around her shoulder and his hand hitched under her damp armpit to prevent her slumping on to the pew:

> Have mercy on me, O God,
> According to Thy great mercy.
> And according to the multitude of Thy tender mercies,
> Blot out mine iniquity

He will not let her sit. She must stand. It is a kind of expiation.

Amplius lava me ab iniquitate mea, chant the choir: Wash me yet more from mine iniquity; And cleanse me from my sin.

And the Hubers, husband and wife, stand there in the face of the psalm like a couple facing a blizzard, the one with his face clenched tight against the storm, the other pale and staring, as though battered by the gale and almost beyond caring. She looks dramatic in black, a mourner for all times and all seasons, her hair like gilt decoration on the canopy of a hearse.

After the funeral there is the interment, across the city in the great cemetery of Campo Verano beyond the railway sidings, beside the Basilica of San Lorenzo, outside the walls where all Rome's dead lie among the umbrella pines and cypresses. It is a place of marble and travertine, a place of dried flowers and dying flowers, a place of memory and regret, of guilt and remorse. It is a place that has been much in use of late: as the cortège draws up outside the front of the portico of the basilica there are already two funeral processions there, impoverished ones with horse-drawn hearses and wailing women. The shining automobiles pause in the heat of the square and wait for the way to be cleared, and then it is their turn at the gates of heaven or hell, their turn to drive in through the portals and process at walking pace down the main street of the city of the dead to where, amid marble and porphyry, a grave lies open. Bearers—soldiers from a pioneer unit drafted for the occasion—shuffle the coffin out of the rear doors. Leo's cap, the cap of the Jungvolk, is arranged carefully on the top of the coffin. The soldiers lift the coffin onto their shoulders and carry it toward the open grave.

The burial ceremony is a brief, almost cursory affair. Clouds of incense drift around the grave like smoke from a bomb crater. There is a sprinkling of holy water and a scattering of earth, a dull drumbeat on the wooden coffin; and then the deed is done, the child has been consigned to eternity, with hopes of fellowship with the choirs of angels.

The mourners walk away from the scene uncertainly, as though unsure whether it is all over: first the Hubers, then the von Klenzes in anxious attendance, and then Jutte and Josef and some others from the Villa. Francesco Volterra hovers nervously at the back. As the funeral party breaks up he goes up to the parents and solemnly, with a small, brisk bow, shakes hands with Herr Huber; then he raises Frau Huber's gloved hand to within a half inch of his lips, inclines his head for a moment and clicks his heels.

"*Sono desolato,*" he says.

The Hubers' expressions are impassive in the face of his distress.

Guilt. Grief and guilt. A powerful combination. Guilt like a liquid, a thin liquor, seeping everywhere, informing everything, saturating the whole—corrosive, like seawater, scented with the rich stench of ordure and corruption, and carrying with it hard, abrasive shards of grief.

"Bless me, Father, for I have sinned." She makes a full confession, baroque in its fullness: a minute description, a count of the times, an explication of the things done, the actions performed, the minor brutalities, the major betrayals.

"I cannot pretend that what you tell me is not very grave," says the shadow beyond the grille.

"Yes, Father."

"It will take time to atone, time and discipline. You must never see this man again. You understand that?"

"Of course, Father."

She meets him on neutral ground, one of the cafés on the Via Veneto that has remained open despite everything, a place that attempts a poor imitation of a Parisian café with tables out on the pavement underneath a glazed shelter like a conservatory. She watches his approach warily, as though expecting him to snatch her handbag or make a pass at her, but when he is finally standing in front of her and raising his hat—a rather absurd straw boater— she barely looks at him, merely makes the shape of a smile, crosses her legs carefully away from him, and gestures to him to sit.

The waiter comes with a cappuccino made of ersatz coffee and powdered milk. When the man has gone Francesco asks, "How are you feeling?"

She looks up the slope of the street toward the red brick of the wall that forms a barrier across it at the top of the hill, a stretch of the Aurelian wall that once encircled the whole of the classical city. How is she feeling? How ought one to feel? She feels dispersed, scattered. "I am going away," she says, almost as though talking to someone else. "There is nothing for me here any longer. I am going back home."

He laughs. "Home," he repeats. "The Russians will be there before long. And then you'll see."

"Do you suppose I care about that?"

"Come away with me. Your country is finished, my country is finished, and your marriage is dead. We can go to Switzerland. I know someone who can get us both a visa. Someone at the Swiss embassy."

She shakes her head. "I cannot go with you, Francesco," she says quietly. "I *cannot* be with you. It would be wrong."

"Wrong?" He raises his voice. She hushes him, glancing around to see if people are listening. But there are just some army officers two tables away, four officers with a couple of Italian girls. The girls are laughing at something that has been suggested to them. Elsewhere a woman in a wide, feathered hat, the *principessa* Casadei, delivers a lecture to a wizened man who is her father, the prince, a Knight of the Order of Saint John, a member of the papal noble guard. "Wrong?" Francesco repeats. "We did nothing wrong. We were in love, *are* in love—"

"Shh!"

The Princess Casadei looks across to them and inclines her head toward Gretchen. Her expression is one of polite inquiry. How is Frau Huber after her great personal tragedy?

"We *are* in love and so we did nothing wrong."

"For God's sake keep your voice down. And if it is so, that we did nothing wrong, then why did Leo die?"

It's a good question under any circumstances: why *did* Leo die? The German officers are laughing loudly; the *principessa* Casadei is talking in subdued tones to her father; an army staff car is cruising slowly down the street with men inside looking for women—even at ten-thirty in the morning they are looking for women—and Gretchen is asking why Leo died. It is a question that never ceased to exercise her mind, but which never received a satisfactory answer. "Because of an act of war," is Francesco's reply. "That is all. Unless you pretend that God works through the hands of an American pilot, then it was no more than that— chance, fate, whatever you want to call it."

"It is a punishment."

"A fairly odd way of punishing one person, to kill someone else. What kind of God is that? Hardly the God of loving kindness."

"You are a Jew. What can you know of God?"

"I thought we invented him."

She chooses her words deliberately, as one chooses a weapon that will do the most damage: "You may have invented God," she says, "but you also murdered him."

There is silence. There is a sensation of the irrevocable about those words. She cannot unsay them. Just a moment's vibration in the air, but that is enough. They have been said.

Francesco gets slowly to his feet. Surprisingly there is an air of dignity about him. He gets to his feet and leans forward and places something on the table. The object, a key, gleams in the sunlight like a piece of bright, tawdry costume jewelry. It has a small tag attached to it. "The key to the apartment in Geneva, lent to me by the friend you do not believe in. That is where we would have gone." He straightens up and stands over her, for a moment proud and rather impressive. "Maybe we will meet there one day, who knows?"

And then he turns and walks away. Gretchen waits for a moment. She picks up the key and looks at it, as though wondering how it came to be there. Rue des Granges, it says on the tag. And a number. She slips the key into her handbag, gets up from the table and crosses to the table of the Casadei father and daughter. The prince rises and kisses Gretchen's hand. "My dear," the *principessa* says comfortingly, "how good to see you in public so soon. I can never abide these long periods of mourning which we Italians indulge in."

"Hansi," she whispers.

He says nothing. There is light coming in through the shutters, the faint monochrome of the moon. He lies on his back in the shadows, a large still figure whose grief has no expiation.

"Hansi?"

There is no answer, but nevertheless she speaks: "Francesco Volterra is a Jew," she says.

He speaks upward toward the ceiling, his silhouette unmoving. "Now how can you possibly know that?" He laughs faintly and without humor. "No, don't bother to answer. You will only lie."

"I won't lie to you, Hansi," she whispers. "Ever again."

"Perhaps even that is a lie."

"No lie," she says. She reaches beneath the sheet and takes his hand, and moves it to her belly, to the rough hairs, to the warm folds.

"Then you must do one thing more," he says. "To purge your lies."

"One thing?" She moves herself against his fingers. "What thing?"

"You must take me to him."

The two black cars gleam like a pair of patent leather shoes, court shoes with silver buckles. They pace slowly down the narrow street and come to a halt outside one of the anonymous apartment buildings. Five men and one woman get out. The woman leads the way, in through the entrance archway as far as the *portiere*'s glassed-in booth.

She turns away from the elevator and instead she takes the steep steps that wind upward, turning at each floor where there is a landing and a small window like a porthole, up toward the roof of the building. The men follow her, pausing uncertainly when she reaches the topmost landing. It is hot, almost stifling up here under the rafters. There are dust motes in the air. One of the men—his face glistens with sweat—slips past her and stands against the wall beyond the door. The others wait down the stairs, just below the level of the floor.

She knocks, a piece of practiced syncopation: four raps on the wood, three in rapid succession and the last after a breathless pause.

After a while the door opens a fraction, like legs reluctantly yielding to an insistent pressure. "Gretchen," he says quietly. He is there in the doorway, standing on the threshold, his face moving swiftly through a whole complex of expressions, from surprise to delight to something like dismay as she steps toward him and says the name "Checco" and reaches up to kiss him on the cheek.

"Gretchen," he repeats. His hands are poised in midair perhaps to grasp her shoulders, perhaps to keep her at bay. But just as quickly as she stepped forward she has stepped back, stumbled back, turned for the stairs while men push past her.

Behind her there is a cry, slammed shut by the door. She walks carefully back down the stairs to the ground floor. Her face is set in marble, not beautiful, not classical. Her husband is waiting for her on the pavement.

Gretchen at the spinning wheel, spinning the web of fate. Gretchen at the keyboard, playing soft and sullen, the plangent chords of the Beethoven C minor piano sonata opus 111, which has no name but might be called the Innominate, expressing as it does nameless things—the anguish of mere existence. Gretchen weeps. She weeps for Leo and she weeps for Francesco, the one dead, the other damned, and the music wanders between the solemn and the reflective and the angry—a meandering, pensive threnody, a celebration of life and an elegy of death. She doesn't play accurately. Sometimes she loses her way in the serpentine complexities of the *adagio* with its absurd tempo marking *molto semplice e cantabile,* very simple and singable; but the mistakes do no more than bring a faint smile to her lips as she pauses and returns and gathers up the fragile pieces and fits them together like someone repairing a piece of fractured porcelain. The notes swell out of the great Bechstein, out through the long windows and across the Italian garden, at times like a dirge, at times like a cry of something approaching joy, but at the end nothing more than a fading into silence.

Magda—now

M agda pads through the apartment. Although she is tall, she treads as softly as a cat. Her feet are long and white, with uneven toes. Sometimes she takes her folder of sketches, occasionally a pile of paintings; more often none of these: just herself. I imagine a bus ride out into the suburbs—some place of reinforced concrete and ill-kempt shoulders—where she poses in front of a camera in a tawdry makeshift studio, her limbs contorted and splayed so that the lens can see everywhere, pry into every nook and cranny. Knowledge without understanding.

"Do you want to see?" she asked, and tossed a magazine across the room at me. Magda's mag, a lurid, multicolored creature as cheerful as Christmas wrapping. SUCK ME, it was called. I opened the thing and leafed through the coarse pages. There, sure enough, was Magda: Magda wearing a startling blond wig and posed in a variety of awkward convolutions across a bed in what seemed to be a cheap hotel; Magda with legs apart, and flesh raw and glistening; Magda showing folds and declivities and delicate ravines; Magda called *"Krystal, our own Velvet Revolution from the Czech Republic,"* but Magda nevertheless. Unmistakable.

"Disgusting." I can hear Madeleine even now. "I think"—that *th* sound that lingers midway between two fricatives, the dental and the palatal, half *th* half *d,* whole Irish—"I *tdh*ink that something should be done about it." Something? What?

A final turn of the page, and there was the centerfold spread, Magda peering around from behind her buttocks like a housewife opening the back door to the milkman.

She was watching me. "What do you say?" she asked. "It pays the rent?"

"You don't pay any rent," I said.

She laughed.

Magda paints. She watches me when she paints, watches with the narrow, possessive gaze of the artist. She watches me as she paints and I watch her as she goes about her ordinary life: Magda sitting naked on a chair, her knees drawn up, varnishing her toenails a funereal black; Magda in the kitchen boiling water for the coffee that she calls Turkish but isn't; Magda lying in the bath like a Bonnard woman, her breasts floating like poached eggs in the scum, the froth of pubic hair like seaweed at low tide, kelp in the foam of low tide, dark and mysterious and home to thousands of secrets. Magda is black and white—the black of her hair, the black of her eyes, the black of her lips, and the nude white of her skin. I watch her, and watching her I possess her.

"You were not always a teacher," she said to me one day. Her words had the intonation of a plain statement of fact, not because of unfamiliarity with the language but because she knew that she was right. "You were something else."

"A priest," I told her.

"I knew. Something else, I knew. Do you say that? Something else?"

"Yes, you say that."

"A priest." She shook her head as though she had imagined something, but not that. "*Katolicky?*"

"*Katolicky,*" I agreed.

"And now you are not."

"No."

Every Sunday, as dutifully as a village girl, Magda goes to church. Around the corner from the palazzo there is an undistinguished baroque church sited on the edge of the ghetto like a watchtower. She walks quietly into the church and slips into one of the pews at the back, and watches, as though consigning everything to memory in the manner of someone playing a parlor game: the plaster saints, the elaborate altars, the dusty gilt of the ceiling, the aged and doddering celebrant, the few old ladies, the occasional young woman with an earnest Evangelical expression—all of this is consigned to memory.

When she gets back from church she paints the scene as an amalgam of things: the dome of the church, the bowed heads, the ornate plasterwork, the priest in his vestments with his arms outstretched as though he is not merely celebrating mass but actually in the throes of crucifixion. And the face is no longer the ancient face of the priest, but mine.

One day walking through a street nearby she saw a monstrance in the window of an antique shop. She happened to have money on her (perhaps she had just been paid for posing beneath the camera lens in the grip of some phallic, faceless man) and so she went in and bought the thing. It stands on the sideboard in the sitting room, a great tarnished brassy sunburst. It appears in many of her paintings floating over the crucified priest like an explosion, the fires of inferno, the holocaust in which the Lamb is sacrificed.

"My mother went to church," she said when I asked her. "I think she did not believe, but my father was a Party member and she could make him hate her that way. To go to church was bad for the Party. They asked him questions. Why does your lady go to church? You understand? As soon as he left she didn't go more."

"But you believe?"

"Believe?" A shrug of her bony shoulders. "I believe there is God. What else can be?"

"And what does he think of what you do?"

"I don't think he care. He does not care much of anything, does he?"

"I don't know," I answered her. "I used to know, but I don't any longer."

Then unexpectedly she asked, "Are you frightened?" and I agreed that yes, I was frightened, and the shared fright seemed to please her. "I am often frightened," she said. "But I think that life has to be frightening, and that is why people go to church, to not be frightened."

"Something like that."

"But you are frightened and you do not go to church."

"That's right."

In bed that night she crept closer to me and drew my hand between her thighs. "Don't be frightened," she whispered. And the warmth of her hair and the touch of her secret flesh, the part that she exposes to the camera without compunction and yet which is entirely hers, the quick of her, the warm mammal focus of her, gave me some kind of comfort. I love her smell. It is a warm, floury smell, the smell of grain and grass underlain with the tang of sweat. Her bones are strong and her flesh doesn't have the soft, yielding quality of Madeleine's. Magda's flesh is tough. Two women with the same name but at the opposite end of every spectrum of femininity that there may be.

Two bus rides across the city and a walk down the Via Merulana and there we are. She recognizes the type of place well enough: a narrow defile between tawdry, jerry-built apartments, something that would have been familiar to her from the suburbs of any city in Moravia. The products of fascism and the products of the People's Republic are very much the same; it is the banality of terror that is so striking. "Where is this?" Magda asks. "Where are we, Leo?" The uncertain air of amusement which she has brought to the journey gives place to one of tacit fear, like a bright joke suddenly turned sour.

"We are in Via Tasso," I tell her. "Number one hundred and forty-five, Via Tasso," I add, to get things exact. Does she recognize the name? I doubt it. History for Magda began a mere decade ago.

The woman in the ground-floor office is earnest and helpful, like a nurse administering to the sick. There is a small library where we can consult the documents. There is a booklet in English. We can go up to the next floor whenever we wish.

"What is this, Leo?" Magda asks again. "What is this place?"

I don't tell her. Perhaps I want to imbue her with a tremor of disquiet. Perhaps I want to make her afraid.

"Tell me," she asks. "What is it?"

We go silently up to the next landing, to the dull doors, to the patina of grime and the smell of disinfectant. Public housing, that is how it seems. It reminds me of the couple of years I spent in a parish in south London, before the texts claimed me. Linoleum floors and tasteless flock wallpaper, narrow corridors and exiguous rooms and a shared kitchen and bathroom.

"What is it, Leo?" Magda repeats as she joins me at the front door, where you might ring the bell and the woman of the house might appear, her hair bound up in a scarf, her body bound up in a floral apron, slippers on her feet. But no one guards the entrance: as though something has happened, some domestic disaster, perhaps, the door to the apartment stands open.

"What is it?" Magda looks in at the narrow corridor and the dull rooms, the ventilation grilles above the lintels, the peepholes in the doors. "What is it?" she repeats, but she understands well enough.

Uninvited, we step over the threshold. No nice cup of tea here. No peas for your tea, no sausage and mash or whatever it is. One of the rooms, the one facing the door, is windowless. Oh, they were all windowless then, but that was because the windows were bricked up and clever little ventilators fitted to the outside walls so that the inmates would not actually suffocate. But the room facing the door is narrow and bare and windowless by nature—a mere storeroom, a box room, what is called in Italian *un ripostiglio*. "In there," I tell her, gesturing. "In there."

The room is six feet wide by sixteen long. The floor is bare. The walls are plastered with thick blue paint, an ugly, utility color. Magda stands in the doorway, looking in reluctantly, not knowing what she might see.

"Look." Scratches of desperation and defiance are gouged out of the paintwork. I know the place well and know where each word is, each phrase, each pious hope or pathetic testimony. "Look."

She steps in and looks where I point—at the Greek word ιχθυς, fish.

Time for your fish lecture.

"And there."

A date, a scratched calendar, a curse, a message: *Dio c'è. Camerati non dimenticarmi.* There is a God. Comrades, don't forget me.

"And over here." White plaster showing through the scrap-ings, like flesh showing through a wound, like bone showing through a burn: *Addio pianista mia. Non serbo rancore. Un bacio Francesco.*

The reality of the text, at one and the same time evidence and witness.

Addio pianista mia. Non serbo rancore. Un bacio Francesco.

What do you scratch such things with? Your fingernail? The buckle of your belt? No, they'd take that. A paper clip found in the dust in the corner of the cell? A nail from your shoe? What?

"What does that mean?" Magda asks. She grabs at a word, one word among many, the word made flesh. "*Serbo?* What does it mean? Serb?"

"*Rancore* is rancor, grudge."

"What is that?" There is an edge to her voice, a brittle fracture.

"*Non serbo rancore.* I don't bear any grudge. I don't blame you, you understand?"

She looks at the words scratched into the plaster. "Who was Francesco?" she asks. "Pianist, who is pianist?" And she shakes with the terror of it all, the enclosure, the entrapment, the sense that here the past presses onto the present and allows no one any freedom. "I know what this place is," she says softly. "This place is prison."

Magda paints just as I knew she would paint: Leo crouched in the corner of a blue room. Scratches on the wall, pictures and words in gray paint. Leo in prison.

13

At the World Bible Center in Jerusalem they worked on the scroll with the infinite care and patience of surgeons picking at someone's brain. A video camera stood behind them and peered over their shoulders as mute witness to the events. There was the woman named Leah who had come from the Israel museum; there was the man named David Tedeschi, who had worked on the papyrus collection at Duke University and was one of the foremost experts in papyrus conservation—foremost in a world in which there are no more than a few dozen practitioners. "This is unique," they murmured to each other as they humidified the scroll with a gentle mist of water and picked at the edge with forceps and lifted it up to peer within. With care, with infinite care, they unfolded the papyrus as one might unravel a winding-sheet to discover the corpse inside, the secrets of two millennia. "Just amazing," they said as they worked. "Fantastic."

The banality of words.

The opened scroll resembled a piece of coarse cloth, some ten feet long. Gnawed, bitten, chewed at by mites or by time, eaten away in places and blurred and damaged in others, yet it was substantially whole. There were uncertainties, there were lacunae, but the text was more or less complete—squads of regimented letters without pause, without break, with barely a hesitation, marching down the length of the scroll as though they had been ruled by an unseen hand. Sixteen sheets beaten and glued together. An average of twenty letters per line and twenty-four lines per page. Sometimes a slight space seemed to indicate the start of a sentence. Otherwise there were no punctuation marks, no accents, no breathings. The language was the plain, muscular language of the eastern Mediterranean, Koine.

"A good documentary hand with elements of cursive about it," Leo explained to Calder as they examined the unraveled scroll for the first time. "Careful writing, but not by a professional scribe."

Calder was searching along the strip, peering at the maze of lettering, hoping that something would leap out at him, the solution to a puzzle coming with the suddenness of revelation. "Can there be any doubt?"

"Doubt?"

"That this Yeshu and Jesus Christ are one and the same man."

Yeshu the Nazir. Leo could pick the name out of the manuscript almost as he might recognize his own: ΙΕΣΟΥΤΟΝΝΑΖΙΡ, *iesou ton nazir.* Jesus the nazirite. He crouched over the text, examining the lettering with a binocular microscope. Broken fibers floated in the brilliant circle of the microscope field. They carried flecks of pigment that were invisible to the naked eye, so that an *omicron* became, within the bleak circle of magnification, the fragmentary relic of a *theta*. "Maybe with time."

"How long?"

He answered without taking his eyes from the lenses: "You need method. First a diplomatic transcription, then the translation. Don't muddle one with the other, not if you can help it." On a notepad he wrote, *theta-rho* and then peered once more, as though peering down through the centuries. Painful, painstaking work. "It's *thronon,* throne," he muttered. "Surely it's throne." But the following letters were damaged beyond recovery.

"What's throne? What the devil's throne?" Calder cried impatiently.

"Nothing. Nothing's throne. Just an idea."

"What about date? Can you give an estimate?"

Leo moved the microscope onto another patch of damage, cross-referencing to photographs they had taken, impatient with Calder's questions. "No one can be certain. Early, I'll say that. A consistent use of the iota adscript, for example, the general simplicity of the letters, the lack of breathing marks, other things. First century. I don't think anyone can deny it's that early. But they'll deny that it tells the truth. Sure enough they'll deny that, and no amount of paleographic or carbon dating will tell them otherwise. Now please—"

"I'll leave you in peace," Calder said. "I'll leave you be."

They had housed Leo in an annex to the Center, a building that had once been a private villa and now accommodated visiting scholars. There was a garden in which he could walk, a place of thorn and cactus, of century plant and prickly pear, of silvery olives flickering in the breeze. The soil was reddish-brown, the color of dried blood. They were days circumscribed by work and nights by thoughts of Madeleine. He lived in the annex and he walked in the garden during the evening and he labored throughout the day in the artificial peace of the document rooms. He dreamt. Sometimes he had seductive dreams of life and resurrection, so that he awoke to the dull dimensions of reality and the bathos of mere existence. Sometimes his dreams were nightmares of falling through the air, of plunging toward the ground, of plunging into a pit that had no bottom; and then he would wake in relief to find that the nightmares were true. She was dead. Not a presence in some other dimension, a shade in Hades or a soul in She'ol, but dead. Her broken body had been packed up and dispatched to England for a private funeral and now she herself lived only in the impoverished memory of those who had known her, a strange, fragmented afterlife, like a familiar face glimpsed through a dozen different, cracked lenses, not one of the images the real woman who had lived and loved and just as surely died.

"A terrible, terrible tragedy," Goldstaub had said when he met Leo at the airport. "But at least you've got your faith." He had been trying to help, that was what made it so ridiculous. He had been trying to alleviate the pain. "Leo, at least you've got your faith."

But Leo's faith lay anesthetised on the slab before him and at the mercy of his own careful intervention:

This is the inheritance of Yeshu the Nazir. He was son of Aristob(ulus, son of ?) Herod. When the king had Aristobulus put to death his[1] son Yeshu was (. . . hidden away?) For a prophecy had been made that this son would . . . (ascend to the) thr(one?) Aristobulus was son of Mariam[2] the Hasmonean and his[3] mother was Mariam (daughter) of Antipater (son) of Herod and (daughter)[4] of Antigonus the Hasmonean. He swears that this is true who knows it.

[1] read: "Aristobulus's." Aristobulus was the second son of Herod

the Great by Herod's second wife Mariamne I. Aristobulus was executed on Herod's orders in 7 BC.

[2] i.e. Mariamne I.

[3] read: "Yeshu's."

[4] The text is confused over these precise relationships. Possibly read: "Mariam (the mother of Yeshu) was daughter of Antipater and his wife, who was herself the daughter of Antigonus the Hasmonean." Antigonus was the grandson of the last Hasmonean high priest/king. This family tree would mean that Yeshu was a Hasmonean *and* a Herodian on both his mother's and his father's side.

He peered through an image of Madeleine at the even, measured strokes of lampblack:

And this prophecy was in this manner, that out of Jacob would come a star, a scepter to rule the world. And this was foretold by the scriptures.[1] *And Yeshu was given to Joseph as his father and hidden from Herod that the child might live and take the throne as prophesied. And this Joseph came from Rama-thain. He was a trusted man and member of the Great Sanhedrin and longed for the return of Israel.*

[1] Numbers 24: 17.

"The star prophecy from the Book of Numbers," Leo told the committee. The Judas Committee, they called it: it had been established to oversee the work, to decide how the destruction of a faith should be communicated to the world. There were half a dozen members—Leah, and David Tedeschi, and someone from the Israel Archaeological Authority, and a government nominee from Hebrew University, and Calder as the chairman. "The star prophecy was one of the most popular messianic foretellings. Bar-Kokhba springs to mind, of course."

"Maybe that dates the scroll to the Bar-Kokhba revolt," Tedeschi suggested. He was a thin, bony man with a prominent Adam's apple and the stooped posture of the very tall.

Leo shrugged the suggestion away. "Bar-Kokhba wasn't the only messianic hopeful. And then there's the matter of Joseph, Yeshu's adoptive father . . ."

"Surely that's where the Joseph of the New Testament comes from," said Calder from the head of the table. "Adoptive father; just right. Kind of confirms the gospel story, doesn't it?" The ceiling overhead was studded with small, recessed lights, like a galaxy of stars. His silver hair gleamed in their reflected glory.

"In a sense," Leo agreed. "But not quite the way you mean. This Joseph is Joseph of Arimathea."

There was a silence. "It's *who?*"

"Joseph of Arimathea." The matter was obvious, beyond surprise. "Arimathea—Rama-thain. The identification was first made by Eusebius, and also by Jerome. I don't think any Bible scholar would doubt it."

"Joseph of Arimathea was Yeshu's *adoptive father?*"

"That's what it says." He smiled bleakly at Calder. "It's the confirmation you've been looking for, isn't it? That Yeshu the Nazir is the same man as Jesus of Nazareth. It has the dull ring of truth about it, doesn't it? Explains a whole lot of the New Testament story—who Joseph was, why he had this interest in Jesus, why he gave his tomb to be used. A whole lot."

They all looked up the table to Calder for some kind of response. He rearranged the papers in front of him, his movements quick and nervous as though he didn't have much time. "Who the hell *wrote* all this?" he asked of no one in particular. He seemed helpless. He wanted answers, and there were none. "What in God's name was he trying to *do?*" The irony seemed to have escaped him.

"We've been over this time and again," Tedeschi said wearily. "It's just idle speculation. The historians and the archaeologists can make of it what they like, but really it's only speculation. All we have, the only *concrete* thing we have, is the text."

244

Calder seemed to cast around for the right words. "It must be kept utterly secret," he decided. The word *secret* appealed. *Secretus,* set apart. There is the secret of the mass, a prayer murmured by the priest at the offertory. Secret knowledge is the knowledge that the initiates of Gnosticism possess.

"Doesn't this kind of thing belong to everyone?" Leah demanded angrily. "I've spent most of my professional life battling for the full publication of the Qumran scrolls. I don't want to find myself caught up in another dubious academic cover-up."

There was a rancorous argument between her and Calder. "The thing's dynamite," he said. "Worse than dynamite. Fissile material. Plutonium. The apocalypse, for crying out loud! We cannot just let it out into the world."

"We must publish as we work," she insisted. "Working papers, provisional findings. We must keep the outside world informed. Otherwise all we'll get is rumor and speculation. There's enough of that as it is."

It was the man from the Archaeological Authority who brought some kind of peace. He had offered little to previous discussion and there was the vague sensation that he was an intruder from a different world, some kind of spy. "We're not talking about academic freedom or anything like that," he pointed out. He smiled coldly at Leah. "What we have here is politics, plain and far from simple. As Steven says, this thing is more than dynamite. The last thing that the government of Israel wants is conflict with the Christian Church. And this scroll is the property of the Israeli government."

There was an awkward silence. After a while the members of the committee rose from their chairs and began to pack their papers away. Whether any decision had been reached was unclear, but outside the walls of the Bible Center a storm was on its way. Goldstaub took Leo aside as they left the committee room. He laughed at the idea of secrecy. "You think we can bottle up a thing like this? It's already out, Leo, the story's just about to break. You remember that *Times* story? Well don't think for one moment that's the end of the thing. The rumors are already out there and they aren't going away."

Rumor is the wrong word. Rumor means noise, but whatever it was that percolated out through the walls of the Bible Center was more of a caustic, insidious fluid, the first trickle of flood waters. It was as though the world's journalists were poking at the dike, watching and waiting for the thing to burst open. *Will the World Bible Center release the full text of this scroll so that the academic world can judge for itself?* the *Tablet* demanded in its next edition. *Can we be assured that this work is in the hands of objective Bible scholars, rather than mavericks with a desire to create sensation?*

"What the hell's the *Tablet*?" asked Goldstaub. "Sounds like something to do with Moses."

"A Catholic journal," Leo explained. "Intellectual, rather smug."

"How the hell do they know anything?"

"You said it yourself: the story is out there. It's just waiting for the fullness of time."

He returned to his work. Isolated from the world, insulated from the world, he returned patiently to the dissection of two thousand years of his faith: letter for letter, word for word, eye for eye, tooth for tooth; burning for burning, wound for wound, stripe for stripe. He appended notes, he added glosses, he tiptoed through the intricacies of conjugation and declension, of syntax and accidence. Outside, it was summer. Outside, the heat battered on the ground and the light shattered the world into white and bronze, into sun and shade. Outside, the rock was too hot to touch and the cicadas screamed in agony as though at the contact. Inside was the limpid coolness of a cave, the cavelike cool of a scriptorium, the cool of the mortuary.

What kind of man was Yeshu? A waverer,[1] a reed (that bends with the wind?) . . . the Galileans rather than the Pharisees . . . (he was known?) by the leaders of the people (as) Jesus Bar-Abbas, Son of the Father, that (his ancestry might be?) known to all; but the common people[2] called him Jesus Bar-Adam, which is Son of Man. I knew him and I loved[3] him.

[1] *plagkteros,* possibly with the sense of misleading, leading astray.
[2] *am-hares,* (Hebrew) in the original.
[3] *agapa.* Exceptionally the writer resorts to the first person in this passage.

I knew him and I loved him. He closed his eyes against the strain of the light and the nagging of the intricate letters. *I knew him and I loved him.*

Greek has a plethora of words for love, and even then probably not enough. Love of God, love of man, love of woman, love of life, love of parent, love of country. Leo crouched over the text and struggled with love. Love of Madeleine, he thought. Too difficult to explain, this last love, being made of *eros* and *agape* and *philia,* the three of them blended together in uneasy combination. *Agape* was the love of man for God and God for man, and through this, the love of one's fellow beings. It was *agape* that Paul included in his famous triad—along with *faith* and *hope*: *agape,* which the translators of the King James Bible famously and unfortunately rendered as *charity.* But which kind of love destroyed Yeshu? Which kind had destroyed Madeleine?

I've tried this before, she had written. *Oh yes, I'm practised in this kind of thing, didn't I tell you?*

In what kind of thing was she practiced? What was the import of her ambiguous words? Leo tried to talk to her. Bereft of a God to address, absurdly he tried to talk to Madeleine, attempted to magic her out of his own mind, tried to create her out of the ether or the air or whatever substance it was that still bore her imprint;

just as once, as a child, he had tried to conjure up the living Christ from the assembly of images and illusions that were all he had to go on. And as with Christ, she didn't appear before him. Madeleine remained mute. He thought of her and the more he thought of her, the less substantial she became; he imagined her and the more he reached out to grasp her image, the more elusive it was. There were moments when he dreaded recalling her, in case the very act of memory should expunge the record from his brain, as though memory were finite, a thing used up at each re-membering.

> *This was the teaching of Yeshu, that you should love God above all things and that you should despise the powers that rule you who are not of God but of man. This was the teaching of Yeshu, that you should renounce your family and your friends and follow him to salvation. This was the teaching of Yeshu, that if a man has riches, he should sell everything and give the worth to those who follow God's way.*

David Tedeschi invited Leo to supper. The Tedeschis lived in a cramped house in one of the new developments on the outskirts of the city, an area where the buildings were laid out in concentric circles like the walls of a citadel around an inner keep—a super-market and a post office and a police station. It was as though the inhabitants were expecting a siege.

They ate supper in the tiny garden at the back of the house, with the two children running amok around the barbecue and the dining table. David's wife was named Ellen. They were devout Christians, the pair of them, struggling to match their faith with the rest of the world, members of a quiet and convinced American Baptist congregation. They had moved to the Holy Land to fur-ther David's career in the obscure art of papyrology, but also to be nearer the center of their faith. They had learned Hebrew. They attended services with a group calling themselves Jews for Jesus. "And now there's this scroll," Ellen said quietly. "Isn't it heretical?"

Leo tried to reassure her. "Many early texts are heretical in one way or another. The Gospel of Thomas, for example. Some of the Oxyrhynchus papyri. The early Church was riddled with dissent and disagreement."

"But this is different, isn't it? David says this is different."

"It's older, that's all."

She wouldn't let go. She was a big, beautiful, untidy woman. Her brow was furrowed, with concern for her children, concern for the faith, concern for the future of the world. "It's not just older than other noncanonical texts, is it?" she insisted. "It's older than *anything*. It's older than the gospels themselves."

Leo agreed that, yes, it was. It appeared to be older than any New Testament text, older than the oldest relic of the gospel, far older than the Chester Beatty, older than the Rylands fragment. The oldest text in Christendom.

"And it denies the resurrection?"

There was a silence. David brought hamburgers from the barbecue and got the children to sit down.

"Yes," said Leo. "The writer claims that he saw Yeshu's body in its corruption. We haven't got to the end of the scroll yet, but that's what he says at the start."

Ellen said softly, "I believe that my Redeemer liveth."

"So do millions of others."

"And now you're telling me that he died like anyone else. What do you think, David?"

But her husband was silent. The thing disturbed him. The whole matter of the scroll, with its plain, insistent voice, its lack of appeal to the miraculous or the fantastic, its plain historical witness, all of it disturbed him.

Finally Ellen turned back to Leo. "I remember in the days of the Cold War," she said. "My father was in the Air Force. We lived on air force bases, surrounded by bombers and missiles. I remember I used to have dreams about the whole thing going wrong, the airplanes taking off and the missiles being launched. And the others coming in. Great silent flashes in the sky. Looking out over miles of countryside and seeing the mushroom clouds rising. I would wake up panicking in a sweat, but I never told anyone about it, not my mother, not my father. I feel like that now. The same panic, the same sense of pure, unmitigated disaster."

David reached across the table and took her hand. She shook her head, but let him hold her hand just the same. There were tears in her eyes. "Would you like to say grace?" she asked Leo. "Weren't you a priest once? Didn't David tell me that?"

"I still am. Technically I still am."

She smiled, and her eyes glistened. "Aren't we all priests in Christ?"

So Leo said grace for his hosts, and the little family bowed their heads over the food as though they all believed that what he said carried some kind of moral weight; and in the act of making that small and unimportant prayer Leo felt something of the power that had once been his, the power and the glory that had deserted him.

Later, when the children had been put to bed, Leo talked about Madeleine. It was the first time he had ever talked to anyone about her, apart from oblique comments to Goldstaub. But now he sat in the Tedeschis' garden in Jerusalem and told them the whole story, more or less. It was a kind of expiation. Merely to talk about those days in Rome put some of the ghosts to rest.

Afterward they walked to David's car. The sky above the houses was blurred with the lights of the city, but still they could see the stars. "There's a moral in that, isn't there?" David said.

"Moral?"

"Something to do with still seeing the stars even through a

polluted sky. Man is in the gutter, but he's looking at the stars and still seeing them despite the pollution."

"I suppose there's a moral in most things if you look for it."

"What's the moral in the Judas scroll?"

Leo had no answer. They drove back to the Bible Center in silence, through the darkened suburbs of the city where Jews waited for the coming of the Messiah and Arabs waited for the call of Allah, and as they approached the gates of the World Bible Center they found parked cars and flashing lights and armed, uniformed men. Policemen flagged the car down.

"What the devil's this all about?" David exclaimed. That was the nearest he would ever come to blasphemy. He would never invoke the name of God, but in moments of surprise or stress he might invoke the devil. "What the devil —?"

Flashlights shone in their faces and voices from beyond the lights shouted at them. "Get out! Identity cards! Keep your hands in sight. Identity cards! Papers!"

"How can we do both those things at once?" Leo asked. He was grabbed and pushed around so that he stood with his hands on the car roof.

"Are you being funny?" the voice asked just behind his ear. "You think you're funny guy?" There was a hint of America in the disembodied voice, a suggestion of American movies. Guns were hard against his ribs. Hands ran all over him, under the arms, down the chest, into the crotch, down the legs. "What you doing here? Where you come from?" they asked.

David looked across from the other side of the car, his face thrown into harsh relief by the lights. Leo was reminded of a face painted by El Greco, the long, lean lineaments, the dark and agonized eyes. He had the patient tone of a parent admonishing children. "We've just come from my home. Mr. Newman lives here. We're on the staff of the Bible Center. May I ask what's going on?"

"Can you provide evidence of that?" the policeman asked.

"Of what?"

"Your movements this evening,"

"Of course we can."

Calder appeared. He looked as though he had just been dragged from his bed. His hair was awry and his eyes were wild. In sharp contrast to Tedeschi he was shouting. "What the hell has been going on? What in God's name is happening? What are you doing with my colleagues? These men work with me."

There was a pause around the two figures and the car, and then an apologetic dusting down. Identity papers were restored to their owners. "You never know," the man in charge said helplessly. "You never know."

"It seems there's been some kind of break-in," Calder explained as they went up the drive and into the main building. "Someone got over the fence and forced a window."

In the entrance hall the custodian was explaining to anyone who would listen that he had been doing his rounds in another part of the building, that he was always alert, that he never slept on duty. They went around the building with him, opening doors, turning on lights in empty, expectant rooms. In the manuscript rooms a door was open that ought to have been closed, a cabinet was unlocked that ought to have been locked, but there was nothing else. The scroll lay sealed beneath its panes of plateglass, like a winding-sheet on display in a museum. Nothing of significance had been taken, no particular damage was done. But the curious event itself and the subsequent investigation by the police brought an air of disquiet to the Center. Suddenly it seemed that the place was in the front line of a battle whose motives were unclear and whose combatants were undeclared.

"We must be vigilant at all times," Calder announced to the assembled staff the next morning. "We must be always on watch." On the table in front of him lay a copy of that morning's *Jerusalem Post*. BIBLE CENTER SCENE OF MYSTERY BREAK-IN, the headline announced. Had the intruders been after the new scroll? Journalists contacted the Bible Center to ask for confirmation or denial throughout the morning. Could the document be examined? Could the director make a statement, not about the break-in but about the scroll itself? Were stories true that this was the testimony of the disciple who betrayed Jesus? Was it a forgery? Was it a hoax?

The international press followed on the heels of the national. Could they take photographs, could they do interviews? Telephones rang at the Center, in the annex, at people's homes. JUDAS DISCOVERY ROCKS CHRISTIAN CHURCH, was the headline in the London *Times*.

"We must control the information," Goldstaub advised the committee. "Press releases, official interviews. We must manage the information flow. We must pro-act, not react." His voice had about it a hint of desperation, Canute advising on how to stem the tide.

"Can you confirm rumors about this text?" an interviewer asked Calder in front of the baleful eye of a television camera. "Can you deny that it calls into question some of the basic tenets of the Christian faith?" Calder smiled urbanely into the lights and evaded the question. "I would call it another witness," he said. "An alternative witness."

It was in those days that the Children of God first appeared. No one quite knew where they had come from, but they gathered on the road outside the Bible Center with placards and banners and a clear determination to pray for the souls of the damned locked up inside the building. Their camper van had *God is Great* painted in crude lettering along the side.

Leo went to speak with them. The weather had broken and there had been rain that afternoon. There were blue-gray clouds hanging like dirty linen over the city; the asphalt still had the slick of wetness. On the far side of the road were the protesters, six or seven of them, women and men. One of the women carried a baby on her hip. The adults were young, but their skin had the tanned and weathered look of parchment and somehow that made them seem older than their years. Their hair was plastered down and they smelled of damp.

"What do you want here?" he asked. But they looked past him, through him, tangential to him. "The Word is God's," they told him. "You have no right to the Word. The Word is from God and the Word is God and there is no other Truth." You could hear the capital letters in their speech. One of their number, a young man with a beard and glazed eyes, came up to Leo. "All other words are the words of Satan," he said loudly. "You will burn in hell for what you are doing."

"All we're doing is reading a text that has been discovered at an archaeological site," Leo said helplessly.

"It is all written," the man said. "It is there in the Apocalypse." And he raised his eyes heavenward and began to quote. " 'So I took the scroll from the angel's hand and swallowed it and it was as sweet as honey in my mouth. But when I had eaten it my stomach turned sour.' " He glared at Leo. "Who can doubt that he is God's creature and will suffer God's wrath?"

The work of translation continued, the writing and the revising. The committee pondered the words, pulled things this way and that, argued, criticized, debated, speculated. There was an edge of anger to the debates, as though each member were fighting for his or her own interests.

After one such meeting Goldstaub approached Leo and handed him a copy of the latest edition of *Time* magazine. The cover showed a reproduction of the Crucifixion by Mantegna, the one with the Holy City brooding in the background and the unrepentant thief hanging on a forked tree. The picture was overwritten with a mighty question mark. SCROLL QUERIES JESUS STORY, the title said. Inside was a short, sharp summary of the whole story with an information box about all the extant papyrus texts of the New Testament. There was an item on the current state of Christianity in the world. There was a photograph of Calder and the same photograph of Leo that had been snatched at the Ministry of Justice in Rome. *As the world begins the third millennium, the story asked, does it also face the end of the religion that, more than any other, has marked those two thousand years? In the nineteenth century Nietzsche declared that God is dead. Perhaps, in the company of an ex-American Baptist and a renegade Catholic priest, we are about to witness His burial.*

Meanwhile the translation continued, the unpicking of the text, the careful knitting together of the pieces:

In the week before the great feast he was anointed by the woman (Mary?) . . . he came into the city as it had been prophesied, riding on a donkey's back; and the people hailed him as their king. The cohort[1] was amazed.[2] Youdas witnessed this. He believed in the rebirth of the nation (and the) (restoration?) of the house of Israel. He wished for the cleansing of the Temple in the name of the Lord. But the man Yeshu believed that he had become like a god[3] and had the power of kings and was the Messiah[4] of God.[5] His band(?) waited outside the city for the word to be given by the elders to enter the city, for his demands were the throne and the crown and the destruction of the forces of Rome. And the elders of the people argued over his manner of taking power.

[1] *speira*. The Roman garrison in Jerusalem.

[2] *ekplisso*, struck, astonished, amazed.

[3] the anarthrous noun *theos*, "a god" in all probability signifying "godlike." cf. John 1:1.

[4] *massia*. The Hebrew word transliterated.

[5] *El*. Again, the Hebrew word for God transliterated.

"The anointing at Bethany and Palm Sunday," Calder said from his place at the head of the table. "The triumphal entry. Even with the donkey. The Zechariah prophecy." The members of the committee bent over the transcript and Leo's translation. "Does it mention Mary? Is that what it says here?"

"The text is damaged." Leo's tone was almost apologetic, as if he were somehow to blame for any defects. "The name, if it is a name, begins with the letter *mu*. David and I are working on the damaged letters. It's not easy, for goodness' sake. It's not easy to be objective."

"Who needs objectivity with those barbarians at the gate?" Calder asked.

David flushed. "They're just people with a strong faith," he protested.

"Friends of yours, perhaps?"

"People with many of my beliefs. You can't just trample over people's faith."

"Who's trampling? I'm sorry, David, but the only person who's trampling here is Yeshu." Calder turned from the young man's concern to the page before him. "There's an insurrection of some kind . . . that right? The cohort was 'amazed.' Amazed, confused, what good's that?"

"The word in the original is *ekplisso,*" Leo explained. "It's ambiguous. It could mean *struck,* literally struck as well as metaphorically."

"Maybe it's literally struck. Maybe Yeshu has a whole army and they've defeated the Roman garrison and got the survivors holed up in the Antonia Tower. Maybe that's what it was."

Another voice, the man from the university, said, "There's the cleansing of the Temple, just like the gospel account."

"What I want to know is, what has this Yeshu got waiting outside the city? *Band,* it says here. What's a band?" Calder looked up at Leo with a smile. White teeth, evenly capped, like a row of shining trophies on a shelf. "Has he got sousaphones or what?" There was the momentary relief of laughter.

"The word is *strateuma*," Leo said. "You can see from the transcription. It appears to be *strateuma*, although there's a bit of damage there. You may see the photographs if you wish. *Strateuma*, maybe *stratopedon*. *Strateuma* goes best with the stichometry, but the difference is minimal. And they both carry the same meaning."

"But *strateuma*'s not a *band*, is it?" Calder said. "It's an army, for God's sake. This Yeshu's got a whole damned *army* waiting outside the walls."

"Maybe."

"I'll say maybe. What's 'band' in the New Testament?"

"It depends on the translation."

"Of course it depends on the translation, Leo. For God's sake, I know it depends on the translation. I'm not stupid."

"*Band* is usually *speira*, which is what I've translated as *cohort* earlier in the same passage. Technically cohort is likely."

"So we have the two words in the same passage, army and cohort. The contrast's significant, isn't it? Jesus, *this* Jesus has frightened the Jerusalem cohort away. He's got a whole damned *army* with him waiting outside the city. And that's the difference from the gospel story. A rebel army. Galileans, I guess. This is only a supposition, but I guess they're Galileans. And he's waiting to see whether the Sanhedrin wants to call him in, go the whole hog— sorry, Daniel, that's not too appropriate, is it?—and occupy the city."

"It'd be the Jewish War scenario but half a century earlier."

"Thirty-three years earlier. Get your chronology right. If this is, what, thirty-three AD? then the Jewish War is just three decades in the future. And this Yeshu is nothing but another power-hungry military leader. Or that's what he seems."

"Or that's what he's *become*," Leo suggested. "Youdas implies that it was not always so."

"Of course. The guy has changed. Of course he's changed. Power corrupts. We know that. What's going to happen at the end, that's what I want to know."

"The final two sheets are detached from the scroll," Leo said. "There's some damage."

"Well let's find out. We're in the home stretch and Leo's doing great."

The meeting broke up and the members dispersed. David followed Leo along the corridor toward the manuscript rooms. "I don't feel happy about this," he said. "I don't feel happy with Calder, I don't feel happy about anything."

"Many people are going to have to rethink their ideas after this. Even Steven Calder."

"He gave you a bad time back there."

"He's nervous. Worse than that, he's frightened." Leo held the door open for David to go through into the manuscript rooms. There was the familiar hush of the air-conditioning. "Like a cigar humidor," someone had described the atmosphere. It wasn't much different from keeping cigars: the same vegetable matter to be conserved, the same worry about humidity, the same threat from mold and bacteria.

Together they stood looking down on the scroll as it lay there in its long glass case. The letters, the regiments of letters, the ranks and the columns, the squads and the cohorts, seemed to move to a rhythm, as though someone were calling the orders, someone were marshaling the troops. And they had marched with them down to the final, fragmented end of the scroll. The translation was almost complete.

"What on earth is it going to tell us?" David wondered aloud. He didn't wait for an answer, but went off morosely into one of the other rooms to look for something to do. Leo found the place where he had left off and took up his pencil again.

> *Youdas went with the Temple guard to treat with him at Gat Semen . . .*

He was inured to surprise now, hardened to the dramatic resonances that sounded throughout the scroll. *Gath Shemen (Aramaic: the oil press),* he wrote as a gloss, *becomes Gethsemane in the gospel account (cf. Matt. 26: 36; Mark 14: 32). Youdas makes no mention of this being a garden.* After the name there was a damaged patch of a few lines before the sense picked up again:

> *. . . his own followers let him into the presence of their leader and . . .*
>
> *. . . the elders would call the people[1] to war in the name of the House of David. And Yeshu embraced him and agreed to go with him to the elders, that all of Israel might speak with one voice for the (destruction of the power?) of Rome . . .*
>
> [1] Hebrew, *am ha'ares,* in the original. The significance of this familiar biblical phrase is difficult to interpret here. Perhaps merely "people of the land," i.e. peasants, perhaps "people who were not in complete observance of the law," a sense which certainly had become common by rabbinical times.

"How's it going?" David called from the doorway.

Leo shrugged. The question had no answer. "There's some damage here you need to look at. I don't know if there's anything to be done." The young man leaned over Leo to see, and Leo remembered Madeleine looking over his shoulder in the Biblical Institute in Rome. He felt for a treacherous moment the soft touch of her hair and the breath of her scent. But Rome seemed so far away, as far away as it would have seemed to the two men meeting there in the garden of the oil press: a distant, ill-defined threat. "Look at that," he said, pointing to the text. "It's the Judas kiss."

David was silent, reading Leo's rough translation. "There's something sinister about it all," he said finally.

"No there's not. There's nothing sinister. Nothing at all. That's what makes it so disturbing. It's just so matter-of-fact." He took up his pencil and returned to the task. He worked silently and without break through the afternoon, and by the time he had finished he had reached the broken end of the main roll:

> *. . . arguments in the Sanhedrin and among the elders and the priests. Youdas witnessed this . . . arguments among his own followers, between the Hellenists and the Hebrews . . . Yeshu himself stood up before the Sanhedrin and asked which they wanted— Jesus Bar-Abbas[2] or Jesus Bar-Adam[3]*
>
> *. . . but the . . .* (high priest?) *. . . stood up and said, It is better that one man dies than the whole nation. For if this man lives and this revolt (continues) then surely we shall die[4] . . .*
>
> *. . . the cohort from Caesarea and the revolt was crushed and the man Jesus was handed over . . .*
>
> [2] Bar-Abbas, Son of the Father. It is unclear whether this term refers to God the Father, as in the Christian gospels, or the man Jesus' actual father, the Hasmonaean Aristobolus (see above).
> [3] Bar-Adam, Son of Man.
> [4] cf. John 11: 50, 18: 14

And all that remained was the final fragmented sheet.

Later that evening Leo stood outside the Bible Center and watched the sun setting below the clouds, saw the domes and towers touched with a momentary fire. Nothing in the whole span of that view was as old as the Church, nothing but the skeleton of the landscape itself: neither the golden dome that belonged to the Umayyads; nor the walls of the city, that were Suleiman's; nor the dark olive trees down there in the shadows of the Garden of Gethsemane; nor the cluster of cupolas among the crowded roofs of the Old City that marked the Church of the Holy Sepulchre, nothing. Only the bones of the landscape were as old as the Church, only the slope of that hillside on his left descending into the shadows: the Mount of Olives, where something like a rebel army had gathered before its final entry into the city a distant nineteen centuries ago, while the power brokers of the province of Judaea argued and debated and wondered which way to jump.

What had happened down there in the shadows of the garden? Who had betrayed whom, and for what motive?

The broad bulk of Goldstaub loomed up in the half light. "We're almost at the end, aren't we?" he asked.

"I suppose so."

"You know when I read a book, you know what I do?"

"You read the last page first."

"Hey, how the hell did you know that?"

Leo smiled.

"But you haven't, is that right? It's been sitting there all the time, and you haven't even taken a peek?"

"I've transcribed it. That's all."

"But you *know* this damn language. You must have gotten some idea of what it says."

Leo shrugged. "No more than a vague hint. No breaks between words, no punctuation of any kind, remember that. You don't know where one sentence finishes and another starts, or even where a word begins and ends."

Goldstaub hesitated. He sensed the other man's mood, wondered how to react. Finally he clapped Leo on the shoulder. "I'm sorry about Madeleine, you know that? I've told you before, but that doesn't mean I don't mean it. I'm just sorry. For her, yes. But more for you."

He went away after that and Leo stood there on his own.

Among the sterile stars overhead—mere clouds of hydrogen exploding in the void—his only comfort was memory of Madeleine, a fragile woman with a sharp sense of irony and a hard streak of selfishness, a woman who had forgiven him for being a sterile, wasted thing, a woman who had claimed to love him above all things, a woman who had killed herself for reasons that he could not clearly fathom, a woman who left him with a plain and unblemished sense of guilt.

He watched the light fade and the stars begin to come out over the hills and the city, stars whose names he did not know cast in patterns he could only half recognize. Rigel, Sirius, Antares; the Great Bear, the Swan, the Scorpion. The pagan past still riding high over the present. He felt the solitude of the stars and the awful emptiness of space.

14

L eo rose early and breakfasted on yogurt and fruit. He glanced at the newspaper as he ate. There had been a raid into southern Lebanon the day before, a unit of Hezbollah destroyed, an Israeli soldier killed. Arab shops in east Jerusalem were closed as a protest about something. The Pope had made a statement on the relationship between the Jewish faith and Christianity, a statement that was already being dissected, analyzed, argued over, dismissed, applauded. He hadn't mentioned the Gospel of Judas by name, but he would soon enough. *Those who would seek to destroy faith in the name of historical research,* he was quoted as saying, *are anathema to both our religions. Anathema* was a strong word in papal pronouncements. It smacked of the Inquisition and the *auto-da-fé.*

After breakfast Leo made his way through the garden of the

villa to the gate that gave onto the grounds of the Bible Center. Shadows still lapped at the bottom of the valley below the garden, but on the far side the walls of the Old City were touched with light and the Dome of the Rock was a brilliant, golden flame. There was that limpid morning cool, with the threat of great heat to come.

Today he would decipher the last of the scroll, the final hours.

He walked up the drive to the Center, where purple bougain-villea hung down the wall: Tyrian purple, the color of kings. Outside the main gate were the Children of God with their banners and their slogans. He went through the main entrance of the building into the hall where there was a mosaic on the wall showing the plants of the Bible—vines and fig and olives—intertwined with symbols from Christianity and Judaism: a cross and a menorah, a fish and a Star of David, and a bipartisan chalice. Self-conscious and didactic, it was not a successful work.

The door to the manuscript rooms allowed NO ENTRY TO UNAUTHORIZED PERSONNEL. His magnetic card—a new notion of Calder's—let him through. The rooms beyond the door were bathed in a perpetual twilight; the only sound was the hum of the air-conditioning and a faint buzz from the lighting. It gave the place a womblike, amniotic atmosphere.

He turned on the lights and opened the lid of the cabinet that held the scroll. A host of letters, a multitude of letters, an ant march of letters down a dry and dusty pathway, the road to hell, perhaps. The pathway came to an abrupt halt just before it reached its goal, and the final sheet, long ago glued to the rest of the scroll with starch paste, was now detached. He took the page from the drawer where it was kept sandwiched in glass and laid it on the desk beside the computer terminal.

Madeleine stood at his shoulder, bright, acerbic, skeptical. Her namesake had been there at the discovery of the opened tomb, of course, the enigmatic Mary of Magdala. Appropriate then that

Madeleine, his memory of Madeleine, should be with him now, at the rolling back of the stone.

He settled himself in his chair, put on his reading glasses, turned on the computer, picked up a pencil and drew a sheet of paper toward him. He let his eyes move along the lines of letters. The hand was so familiar now that he could read it as he might have read his own mother's writing. There were no gaps, no caesuras, no pauses in the careful monotony of the pen strokes. He searched the lines (some damage in one place, a tearing of the fabric, some rough shreds of plant fiber and a blurring of some letters) until he found the combination that he sought: ΠΕΙΛΑΤΩ.

There was that snatch of excitement, a thrilling, treacherous emotion. He paused and took breath. The letters were split between two lines, but they were clear enough: *P-e-i-l-a-t-o.* Pilate. The dative case: *to Pilate.* He moved backward as far as the damaged patch, and then read forward:

... ΚΑΙΠΑΡΕΔΩΚΑΝΑΥΤΟΝΠΕΙ
ΛΑΤΩ ...

Then he transcribed the line and divided the words with pencil strokes:

... ΚΑΙ / ΠΑΡΕΔΩΚΑΝ / ΑΥΤΟΝ / ΠΕΙΛΑΤΩ
and they handed him over to Pilate.

He went back above the damaged area. Immediately before the script became indecipherable there were the letters Σ-Υ-Ν-Ε. The prefix *syne-*. It means "together with," "along with"; but it could also form compound words—ΣΥΝΕΔΡΙΑ, ΣΥΝΕΔΡΟΣ, gatherings, councils, congregations of men and birds. And the preceding letters were ΤΟ. Τ-Ο-Σ-Υ-Ν-Ε. The definite article: *The syne-*. The *synhedrion,* the Jewish council.

He picked up his pencil. *The Synhe(drion?) . . . (lacuna c. 25 letters) . . . and handed him over to Pilate,* he wrote.

Standing at his shoulder just as she had stood at his shoulder in the manuscript room of the Institute in Rome, Madeleine smiled. He almost looked around to find her. Then he shrugged and went back to the text, working steadily throughout the morning, scribbling with his pencil, tapping into the computer, leafing through books. A few people came and went. Calder looked in for a moment, but no one disturbed the figure crouched over the fragment of papyrus, the figure with the lexicons and the concordances, the figure with the flickering computer screen, the figure with tragedy at his back.

The Synhe(drion?) . . . and handed him over to Pilate to be judged, and Pilate . . . (put him to death?) . . . that night. It is Youdas who tells this, a man who wept over the body of the man who . . .

. . . and the night of his death they went to the tomb that was the tomb of Joseph . . . The witness of this was Youdas who writes. Joseph and Nicodemus and the same Youdas were there, and Saul . . .

Leo stopped.

ΣΑΟΥΛ. Saoul.

He went over the letters again. No doubt, no damage. He continued, his pencil elucidating the letters: ΣΑΟΥΛΤΑΡΣΕ . . . Then the fabric of the page let him down: there was a blemish, a sore, a hole eaten away at some time during the centuries by some infinitesimal animal gnawing away at random in the cold tomb of the cave. But he had enough.

ΣΑΟΥΛΤΑΡΣΕ *saoul tarse . . .*

The incomplete word was *tarseus,* Tarsian, an inhabitant of the city of Tarsus. Saul from the city of Tarsus.

His bowels turned. A good biblical phrase? It'll do. Bowels in the New Testament, the Greek *splanchna,* has a meaning altogether beyond the obvious, the merely anatomical, the merely alimentary, the sorter of flesh from feces: the cognate verb *splancnizomai* means to feel compassion for someone. The Good Samaritan *felt it in the bowels* for the wretched man he found lying in the ditch. Leo Newman, adulterer, apostate priest, felt it in the bowels for the whole of Christendom that is and was, and might never more be. Saul the Tarsian could only be one man. Surely he could only be one man.

He sat for a long while, bringing his thoughts under control. Even in the artificial cool of conditioned air, sweat rimed his forehead. Finally he summoned up some kind of calm and went on to the end, the final letters, the final words, the final statement from the last witness:

> *. . . and Joseph wept over the body that had been his son and anointed the body with his tears. And they took the body away that the jackals should not have it.*

And then there remained only the final sentence of the whole testimony, the last utterance of Judas the man from Kerioth, known as Judas the knifeman:

ΤΟΣΩΜΑΤΟΗΡΜΕΝΟΝΕΤΣΦΗΛΑΘΡΑΠΑΡΑΠΟΛΙΝΙ
ΩΣΗΦΗΤΙΣΚΑΛΕΙΤΑΙΡΑΜΑΘΑΙΜΖΟΦΙΜΕΓΓΥΣΤΟΥ
ΜΟΔΙΝΕΩΣΑΡΤΙΓΙΝΩΣΚΕΙΟΥΔΕΙΣΤΗΝΤΟΠΟΝ
ΤΟΥΕΝΤΑΦΙΑΣΜΟΥΑΥΤΟΥ

He went painstakingly through the letters, marking the word divisions, checking for possible alternatives, convincing himself that this is what was written, that the sequence would bear no other interpretation:

ΤΟ ΣΩΜΑ ΤΟ ΗΡΜΕΝΟΝ ΕΤΣΦΗ ΛΑΘΡΑ ΠΑΡΑ
ΠΟΛΙΝ ΙΩΣΗΦ ΗΤΙΣ ΚΑΛΕΙΤΑΙ ΡΑΜΑΘΑΙΜΖΟΦΙΜ
ΕΓΓΥΣ ΤΟΥ ΜΟΔΙΝ ΕΩΣ ΑΡΤΙ ΓΙΝΩΣΚΕΙ ΟΥΔΕΙΣ
ΤΗΝ ΤΟΠΟΝ ΤΟΥ ΕΝΤΑΦΙΑΣΜΟΥ ΑΥΤΟΥ

He wrote out the translation, hearing the last words of Judas as he did so, the final weary, matter-of-fact declaration:

The body that was taken was buried secretly by the town of Joseph that is Ramathaim-zophim beside Modin and to this day no one knows the place of his burial.

Leo stood among the litter of a thousand different popular beliefs, among the rubble of nineteen centuries of faith, amid the ruins of a myriad of treasured illusions. He knew now for certain. There had been no resurrection on the third day. He knew that on the night of the Sabbath, a group of men, men who had no doubt believed in something, had gone to the tomb and struggled in the dark to roll the stone aside. And that one of them was the man known to the world not by his Hebrew name of Saul, but by his Greek name, Paul: Paul of Tarsus. Saint Paul the apostle.

He was there at the tomb. He saw the flickering of the lamps and heard the urgent voices. He saw the figures enter the claustrophobic chamber where the broken body lay. He followed them into the smell of damp and the stink of blood, into the heady stench of myrrh and frankincense. They knew that they were defiled. They knew the words well enough: *Anyone who touches a man who has been killed, or a man who has died, or human bones or a tomb, shall be unclean for seven days.* They knew that merely by being there, they were defiled.

Lamps guttered in the cold air, throwing ugly shadows across the walls. Leo saw them. The body would have been awkward, rigid in death, its limbs like the branches of some rotten tree. He felt them. There would have been muttering and arguing, the urgent arguing that comes with fear. He heard the sound, felt the rigid flesh, smelled the myrrh and blood, the frankincense and corruption.

"Leave the cloths. Get hold of him. For God's sake don't drop him."

Still *him* no doubt. A man they had known and followed, loved in their own way, worshiped even, because worship is *latreia,* the act of service, the act of obeisance of a servant toward a master. They would not leave him to the jackals.

"Lift him across. Now go back. I'll guide you. Duck your head now." Edging the awkward corpse through the doorway and out into the blessed cool of the night where a cart was waiting, the horses snorting and shifting in the dark. The bump and slither of the limbs as they lifted the corpse and slid it across the boards. And then the nightmare journey away from the Holy City, down through the gorges, down over the paved road that the Romans had built, down to the foothills as the dawn came up over the heights of Judaea, a dawn that saw a woman from Magdala coming to the tomb and finding the stone rolled away.

The body that was taken was buried secretly by the town of Joseph that is Ramathaim-zophim beside Modin and to this day no one knows the place of his burial.

Then they had gone back to their lives, doubtless sworn to secrecy over what they had done. And a few years later one of them turned his back on Judaism and spread the Christian faith into the Gentile world; a man whose thoughts were etched with guilt, a man whose brain was on fire, a man whose lean and hungry Greek has thrilled every person who ever read it:

> *Behold I show you a mystery: we shall not all sleep, but we shall all be changed, in a moment, in the twinkling of an eye, at the last trump: for the trumpet shall sound, and the dead shall be raised incorruptible . . .*

Who can unweave the motives of the past? Who can divide warp from weft? Leo sat for long while before the final page of the scroll. Someone looked in and asked how he was doing. One of the technicians came through whistling a mindless tune, some song that had just won a contest and now blared out of every radio, every open café door. Leo waited; but what he was waiting for was not clear. He waited and Madeleine stood at his shoulder and waited with him.

Finally he acted. He reached down and opened his briefcase and slipped the sheet of papyrus inside. Then he stood up and made his way out of the Bible Center and went back to his room.

15

One man among many at the Damascus Gate. An ordinary man, getting down from a bus at the grimy bus station, clutching an envelope to his chest, looking vaguely around as though uncertain where he is or what he is doing among the crowds. "American?" someone asked him, and he smiled and shook his head. "English." They nodded with something like approval. The English were friends of the Arabs, they told him.

He crossed the road to the gate. The gate was a place of focus now as it had always been, a place where demonstrations were held, where camera crews from news agencies kept desultory watch, a place from where, long ago, a young and intransigent man called Saul had set out on a journey northward on a mission to stamp out the embryonic Christian Church. The young man had ended up groveling in the dirt of the road, with his brain exploding with light and a voice ringing in his ears. *Saul, Saul,* a voice had called, *why are you persecuting me?*

He joined the tide of people passing through, a mixed and muddled tide passing in and out of the Old City, El Quds, the Holy One. In the narrow alleys beyond there was a *suk,* a shamble of stalls selling vegetables and fruit, chickens and quails in tiny cages. A pair of soldiers toted their guns through the throng. He pushed past the traders and the customers, past a man cooking lamb's liver on a large and fire-blackened hot plate, past a shop that wanted to sell him rosaries made of olive wood and crucifixes of mother-of-pearl, past a coffee shop where old men sat and smoked narghiles. Farther on, at a junction of the ways, a ceramic sign high up on the wall announced the *Via Dolorosa,* but of course he knew that it wasn't. He knew all the arguments. *Station VII, Jesus Falls for the Second Time.* But he hadn't. Not there anyway. Assuming the gospel account to be true the actual route would have been in the other direction, from the Roman Praetorium which lay beside the Jaffa Gate. Probably. Everything was probably. A group of pallid pilgrims were reciting the rosary in the company of an earnest priest. Women in floral dresses and open sandals, men in straw hats against the sun. As he passed he turned his head away from them in case—the thought was ridiculous really—in case he should be recognized.

Narrow alleys of dark shadow and sudden shafts of light. The storm of the day before had cleared the air and the sun was bright and sharp even among the constricted streets of the ancient city. Around the corner from the pilgrim group was a narrow space where Arabs sold religious trinkets and leather handbags stamped with images of camels and palm trees. "Rosary?" the traders asked. "Holy crucifix from olive wood of Garden of Gethsemane? Holy picture?"

Daylight burned the margin of a small courtyard. There were

twin Romanesque arches and a narrow door in the back. He went through the yard and into the door, out of the glare into the shadows, into a darkness that was like the darkness beneath the Church of San Crisogono. He stood for a while to let his eyes accommodate to the light. A stone slab emerged from the darkness as though materializing out of the past, a slab where a body had been laid to be anointed with oil. On his right, steps led up to a raised chapel where you could look down through plate glass at a lump of rock as gray as an elephant's back and a posthole where they had jammed, so the story went, the pole that formed the upright of the Cross. Once long ago, on his first visit to the Holy Land as a senior seminarian, he had stood up there and wept for the blessed misery of it all. Now he ignored the steps and went on into the rotunda of the building where there was scaffolding to prevent the whole place from collapsing into a heap of rubble, and where, in the midst of the circle, the tomb itself stood, a cave that had long ago been cut away from the bedrock by the engineers of the Emperor Constantine, long ago been dressed and decorated and clad with marble, long ago made the opposite of what it was, the cavity become a prominence, the cave become a hut.

The warm, amniotic smell of candles was all around him. An Orthodox priest stood there like a shadow, his lips moving faintly in the depths of his beard. There was a coming and going at the tomb. Pilgrims knelt in prayer, people ducked in and out of the opening. In some sense just there, in those exact coordinates of space, Mary of Magdala had stood and seen the stone rolled aside and the black maw of the tomb. If you could move through time as you can move through space, if you could shift along the single dimension of hours and days and years and centuries, back almost two thousand years, she would be there still, on a silent morning in a garden outside the city walls, with the smell of death in the air.

Paradise is a garden.

Leo walked around the little hut, to the back where you can

still see the actual rock, the place where the Copts have their pitch. The least favored of the various sects who squabble for control of the Holy Sepulchre, the Copts have trumped the whole lot by removing a bit of the marble cladding to reveal the bare limestone beneath. For a dollar or two they will draw a curtain aside for you to see the living rock behind. "Candle lit at the tomb of God?" they ask. "One dollar." And before you can move, a new wand of wax has been lit from their own lamp, and just as swiftly blown out and handed over. It is like a conjuring trick, a sleight of hand so fast that you are not quite certain what has happened.

He stood up with his still smoking taper and looked down at the crouching monk and a voice behind him said, "It adds a certain drama to the proceedings." He turned and there was the Frenchman standing in the gloom of the rotunda with a faint and ironical smile on his face and his own taper (but no telltale curl of smoke) in his hand.

They walked. Out of the Church of the Holy Sepulchre through the narrow alleys of the Old City, past Jews in ringlets and homburgs, past Arabs carrying bales of cloth and bags of beans, past Christians overburdened with guilt, beneath arches as old as Islam itself, past a battered sign that warned the orthodox that it was forbidden by the Chief Rabbinate to trespass on this ground because of the utmost holiness of the place, to a gate where police officers were checking documents, searching handbags, running hands over pockets. There was a bright light ahead and an air of suppressed excitement among the waiting people, as though something startling were about to happen, the Prophet about to descend from heaven on his steed Burak, perhaps, or the Messiah come down on clouds of glory. Leo Newman and Father Guy Hautcombe passed through the gate and climbed wide stairs onto the great open space, up out of the tunnels of the dark city into the sharp sunlight where, mounted on a box inlaid with turquoise and ivory, the golden dome dreamed of the ineffable glory of God.

They found a stone bench in an avenue of cypress trees and sat down. "So tell me," said Hautcombe. "Tell me what you have to say."

So he told him. Was the Frenchman his last chance? He told him, and the Frenchman heard him through without interruption, with an expression of calm consideration on his face. It might almost have been a confession, the one failed priest opening his soul to the other. "And you think this is all genuine?" Hautcombe asked at the end. He pronounced the word *genuine* as though it were French, with a soft *g*.

Leo opened the envelope and took out a cardboard folder. The Frenchman raised his elaborate Gallic eyebrows. Leo opened the folder, and there was the final sheet, the broken ragged thing the color of biscuit, the color of tobacco, the color of the earth. With its straggle of gray lettering.

He held it for the Frenchman to see. "I am sure it is genuine," he said. "I am sure that the scroll is more or less what it purports to be."

Hautcombe shifted on the bench, partly to see the thing, partly to shield it. "The light, for God's sake be careful of the light," he cried. He craned to see. "How can I make a judgment like this? I need time, time."

"You don't have time. And I'm not really expecting a judgment. I have made a judgment already."

Hautcombe's finger glided along just above the surface of the sheet. Without looking up he asked, "Does anyone know you have taken it?"

Leo ignored him. "Look," he said; and he leaned over the Frenchman's shoulder to point to the word ΠΕΙΛΑΤΩ. Pilate.

Hautcombe nodded.

"And here." Leo pointed once more, and caught the smell of the man, the fusty smell of celibacy that surely he himself had once possessed. He read the lines out loud rapidly in his clumsy,

Anglicized Greek: *"The body that was taken was buried secretly by the town of Joseph that is Ramathaim-zophim beside Modin and to this day no one knows the place of his burial.* Maybe they wanted to stop the tomb becoming a focus for further disturbance—"

"It did not work, did it?" There was a note of defiance in the Frenchman's tone.

"They couldn't possibly have foreseen what would happen, could they? They couldn't have predicted a resurrection story. The god who rises from the dead is not a Judaic myth. There's no precedent for that idea in the whole of Judaism."

There was a long pause. Tourists herded past toward the Dome of the Rock, towards the El Aqsa Mosque, Japanese with bewildered expressions, Americans with an air of studied piety, people consulting guidebooks, people listening to guides, people preserving everything on videotape and seeing nothing with their eyes: a motley collection of witnesses up there at the navel of the world.

"There's another thing."

Hautcombe looked up from the text. "Another thing?"

Leo pointed. "There. One of the helpers at the removal of the body. One of Judas' assistants. Saoul." The Frenchman looked back at the letters. "Look where it is damaged: Saul the Tarsian, it says. The final couple of letters are damaged, but there's no doubt about the first five. Tau-alpha-rho-sigma-epsilon . . . Tarseus, the Tarsian. Paul of Tarsus."

Hautcombe sat with his lips pursed, almost as though he were tasting something. Maybe he was trying to change the meaning, alter the wording by dividing the line differently. Maybe he was praying. Probably that is what it was: he was praying, praying for guidance, for help, for wisdom, all those things that every one of us needs and so few get. "A piece of anti-Christian propaganda," he said eventually. It was as though he were delivering a judgment after due consideration. "If it really stands up to critical examination, that is how it will be judged. A piece of early anti-Christian propaganda. Probably Ebionite. Written in Greek, trying to damn Paul, so probably Ebionite. Important, of course. But not truly significant except insofar as it confirms the gospels."

"Confirms the gospels?" Leo almost shouted. There on the Temple Mount, a place charged with the beliefs of three religions, he almost shouted. "This scroll is older than any fragment of the New Testament. It is virtually complete. Yes, of course there are holes in the story. There are bits that don't add up. There are lacunae. But that is only what you might expect. The overall impression is *conviction*. And it's older than any gospel fragment and older than the whole gospel story. It even reads as though it might be the *source* of much of the Synoptic account. For God's sake, this is a nightmare!"

"It won't hurt people with a powerful faith," Hautcombe replied. "It won't hurt the educated. From what you tell me they will be able to find ways around the difficulties."

"They'll always be able to do that. But what about the rest? What about the ordinary life of the Church?"

The Frenchman looked at him. His expression was a deliberate blend of surprise and accusation. "What do you care about the Church?" he asked.

And Leo wondered, what did he care? Why should he care about the Church, he who was excommunicate and had accepted excommunication? He cast around for some kind of answer. "It's what Paul said, isn't it?"

"Paul said many things, not all of them to the taste of the modern liberal."

"Or the orthodox Catholic. Perhaps one passage in particular, from Philippians." Leo recited it, and the words stung hard, stung his eyes and stung his mind, so that he couldn't tell what he believed or thought any longer: "Whatsoever things are honest, whatsoever things are just—you know the passage."

"Of course."

"Whatsoever things are pure, whatsoever things are lovely, whatsoever things are of good report; if there be any virtue and if there be any praise, think on these things."

The Frenchman laughed at him. "Newman, you are one of those sentimentalists, who see Jesus Christ as a kind of social worker and the Christian faith as a series of conveniently liberal moral precepts. No wonder you abandoned the Church." He got to his feet. "The Almighty is not a liberal, Monsieur Newman," he said. "The Almighty is the driving force for the entire universe and the universe is not a very liberal place. That is what the modern world seems not to understand. I don't give a moment's credence to your papyrus, Newman. Go ahead with it. Publish it and be damned. The Church will survive this just as it has survived every other attack throughout the centuries. The Church will survive you." And then, in the act of walking away, he paused. "Do you know what they call you? Your former brothers in Christ, I mean. Do you know?"

Leo tried to shrug the question aside, but Hautcombe warmed to his theme, coming back toward him to deliver his parting shot: "You know how important names are in our work. You know that. Jesus means *Yahweh is salvation,* doesn't it?" He reached out and pointed his finger at Leo's face. "They call you Judas, Newman. That is what they call you. A second Judas. And do you know what they do?"

"What do they do?"

"They pray for you."

Solitude up there on the Temple Mount, on Mount Moria, at the axis of the world. He walked out of the shade and into the sun, out onto the platform that surrounds the Dome of the Rock. The dome dazzled in the light, a great golden blister, a ball of fire, golden, liquid fire. Looking up he saw the clouds and the sky circling around this point, as though the whole world were turning on this pivot, the place where the Temple had stood, the place from where Jesus had driven the profane, the place where Mohammed's steed Burak had planted a single hoof before leaping up to heaven, the place where Abraham had grabbed his son's neck and held him down against the rock. The sky swirled. Leo looked up and the sky swirled around him and voices babbled in his ear, a hundred voices, a thousand voices, babbling just behind him, just out of sight so that when he turned there was no one there. The light glared at him like a single, malevolent eye. He couldn't tell if it came from outside or from deep inside his brain. The light glared and the voices babbled and the sky turned around and around overhead, and the polished pavement, polished by thousands and thousands of pilgrims, polished and burnished in the sun and the wind and the rain, came up to meet him . . .

Voices babbled. Hebrew and Arab and English. The word *American* came out of the noise, the word *English,* the word *doctor.* A blue uniform stood above him and hands struggled him into the shade.

"My envelope," he said. "My envelope."

"It's all right."

"It is here."

Something was thrust into his hands. They shuffled him into the shade and asked questions of him, as though he were under interrogation. Where was he staying? Was he a visitor? Was he German? Did he understand English? Did he have a telephone number? Did he want a doctor? How did he feel? Someone pushed a glass of water into his hand, the friendly one, the one that gains your trust while the other rants at you, the one that gives you comfort while the other rails against you. A face looked right into his, bearded, mustached, the eyes dark. All right? Did he feel faint? Did he want a doctor? Did he want to call anyone? Did he want anyone?

"I want Madeleine."

"Where is she?"

"She is your lady wife?"

"Is she here?"

"She's dead."

Later he was in a bar, a small, dark place with three or four indifferent customers. There were two soldiers outside the bar and a policeman, some kind of Arab policeman, watching him. "I'm all right," he said. He clutched his envelope to his chest. "I'm all right."

"A doctor is coming."

"I'm all right."

"The sun. You Americans don't know the heat of the sun. Because here is high up and the air is thin."

"I'm all right." He got to his feet and this time they let him. The customers just watched. "I'm all right." In the background someone babbled on the radio, voices babbling, someone singing that bloody song.

"You all right?" the policeman asked.

"I'm all right. Just a headache. I want to go home."

"You get a taxi or something."

"A taxi, yes."

He walked out of the bar and into the narrow space just inside the gate, a gate he recognized, the Sheep Gate where they had brought in the sheep to the sacrifice, thousands of sheep, hundreds of thousands of sheep, and the paving running with blood and the smell of blood and the burning of flesh. Saint Stephen's Gate, where the first of the martyrs had been led to his death outside the walls in a hail of stones, with Saul watching. The Gate of the Blessed Virgin. The Lion Gate. So many names for one hole in the wall.

He stood outside the gate looking out over the Kidron Valley with his envelope clutched to his chest and his heart pounding. Was he dying, he wondered? There were graves on the hillsides, white tombs like teeth or pearls. And a dusty Mercedes taxi coming up the hill toward him.

16

An ordinary day in the world of textual analysis, if you could ignore the graffiti scrawled on the walls outside the Bible Center, the exhortations to repentance, the imprecations, the cries for damnation, and the clutch of protesters camped on the pavement. The Children of God. They changed in identity but not in appearance, these guardians of the true faith: four or five adults, each face dressed in the drab and sanctimonious uniform of belief. Opposite them there was the usual security van. The police had taken their own guard away after the first few days of protest. The government had decided that there were more important security issues in the Land of Israel than a squabble over the origins of the Christian faith. The World Bible Center would have to pay for its own protection.

There was a small stir of interest among the protesters as they caught sight of Leo beyond the gate. They knew him. They know that it was he who had given voice to the Judas scroll, that he was the figure of the seer in the Book of the Apocalypse. BEHOLD THE BEAST, said one of their placards; the numerals 6–6–6 were written on another. They began to sing a hymn:

Were you there when they crucified my Lord?

they sang.

Were you there when they crucified my Lord?
Sometimes it makes me want to tremble, tremble,
  tremble;
Were you there when they crucified my Lord?

He went up the steps into the main entrance of the World Bible Center. "Beast," they called from behind. "Beast."

Or was it *peace?*

A face nodded at him from behind the glass cubicle just inside the door. "*Asalamu aleikum,*" it said. Peace be with you. Under the circumstances it seemed to carry a heavy burden of irony. Leo turned down the corridor toward the manuscript department with its NO ENTRY signs and its warnings about alarms and security, with its lipless mouth that took his security card and mulled over it and spat it out with a grunt from the locking mechanism.

The heavy doors closed behind him. Within the manuscript rooms all was quiet. You couldn't hear the chanting from outside, the praying and the ragged hymn that the protesters cobbled together. You couldn't even hear the interior noises of the building itself. There was nothing more than the hush of the air-conditioning and the heavy stillness of double glazing and fireproof doors. A digital clock on the wall gave the time as five fifty-nine. His own clock—that old-fashioned mechanical thing

that Madeleine had given him—sat beside his keyboard and con-
tradicted the electronic age: eight minutes to six. *Carpe diem,* it ex-
horted him.

He went about his work as usual—the comfort of the quotidian, the consolation of ritual. He turned on the radio to listen to
the morning news on the BBC and then turned on the computer.
Powered up. Goldstaub had taught him to say that. He *powered up*
the computer. The words *Welcome to the World Bible Center* appeared
in an arc across the screen, like the rays of light from a great sunrise. The Center's logo, the open book with the word LOGOS inscribed across the pages, took the part of the world. On the radio
the newscaster spoke in measured terms of protest and demon-
stration.

How long now? A month? Time seemed an elastic, malleable
dimension. Only a month since Madeleine's death? As much as a
month since the first words of the scroll? He dreamt about her
often. Sometimes she was remote and inaccessible, sometimes she
was all too vividly present, suave and naked against his own naked
body so that he exploded into her and woke up with the shock to
find his belly wet and glutinous with his own wasted semen. And
other times she just seemed so plainly, simply *there* that when he
awoke he expected to find her in the room with him; and the discovery that she was not was like the loss all over again.

RANDY PRIEST BETRAYS HIS VOWS, the *Sun* newspaper had
written.

Leo opened the file directory on the computer, and selected
the folder named Judas. What had happened yesterday? He
couldn't remember exactly. He had experienced something, some
kind of panic, some kind of breakdown, perhaps. Was that it? A
notice on the wall warned that YOU were responsible for any document taken from the shelves, that YOU must enter your name in
the logbook, that NO DOCUMENT was to be removed from the

room, that NO IMAGE of any part of the Judas scroll was to be made with the intention of removing it from the manuscript rooms of the Center. He recalled speaking to Hautcombe, showing him the evidence, begging him to do something about it all. But what? What could be done now that the beast was unleashed?

The newsreader was talking about a group of fundamentalists holed up in a log cabin in Montana, waiting for the end of the world. The Beast of the Apocalypse is at large, one of them had declared. The tone of the report was of faint irony, a hint of BBC amusement. The group was reported to have antitank weapons with them and assault rifles.

He opened the drawer where the photographs of the text were kept and took them out. Thirty-five of them, each showing a different page, a different view, a different light. He placed them on the desk beside the computer, then he turned to the cabinet that held the scroll.

A discussion program had started on the radio. *Focus on Faith,* the program was called. There was the Anglican Archbishop of York and the Roman Catholic Archbishop of Liverpool, allies in the battle against a representative of the British Humanist Society.

"What exactly does the discovery of this scroll mean in the post-Christian age?" the chairman asked.

"I don't think we *are* in a post-Christian age," one of the archbishops retorted. He had an ingratiating voice, a voice that sounded as though it had been strained through a dozen layers of abstract reasoning. "The Christian message is as relevant today as it has ever been . . ."

Leo turned the key in the lock and opened the lid of the cabinet.

"But we haven't even been allowed to see this so-called scroll," the Archbishop of Liverpool was complaining. "All we have is a whole mélange of rumor and half-truth. The so-called

World Bible Center must release the text for all of us to assess. At the moment it appears to be the exclusive property of an apostate priest and a renegade Baptist."

"I must take issue with that description . . ."

Leo looked down on the scroll, the winding-sheet, the long, faded banner from some distant war. His hands did not shake. His bowels did not churn. His mind did not balk. He thought of Madeleine, of course. Yes, he thought of her. Two minutes past six. The manuscript rooms were still and silent. No one came in, no one would come in for two hours or more. He opened the glass lid that covered the scroll.

The radio was saying, "If this scroll is what it purports to be—and I may say I am *extremely* skeptical about that—but *if* . . . ," and there was a small bright splutter, a sharp, cheerful spurt of flame.

". . . a genuine account by a hostile witness, then why should we worry . . . ?"

There was a concussion, a soft warm wave of heat like a belch from some deep and fiery maw. Leo made a sound, lifted his hands perhaps in protection, perhaps in benediction. As though it were possessed with an inner life, the length of papyrus blackened and coiled. And then a great body of flame emerged from the cabinet, a transparent liquid body out of whose heat claws reached out to tear at him, to tear at his clothing, to tear with talons of pain at the back of his hands as he raised them to his face.

Madeleine. Somehow he thought that she might save him. The claws tore and scoured, the arms reached out to embrace him. Madeleine. And the last thing he heard was the prattle of the radio and above it the sound of screaming, the screaming of the beast, the wailing of the souls of the damned deep inside the pit into which he was being pulled.

In Via Tasso—1943

I want to see him." She has found her husband in the top garden, the formal Italian garden, among the box hedges and the gravel paths, where he is reading an official document, the word *Geheimnis,* secret, in red across the top. She is distraught, her hair awry, her eyes—those blue, innocent eyes that captivated the older man all those years ago in Marienbad—wide with anguish. "I want to see him."

A tired smile and a weary glance up from his newspaper. "My dear Gretchen, why on earth?"

"I want to see him." The repetition is dull, mechanical, as though she has steeled herself to do this but the effort has strained her beyond the point where she can bring any arguments to bear. "I just want to see him."

"It is out of your hands now. Out of *our* hands."

"I want to see him."

"But it is all over. You have promised me."

She bites her lower lip. "I want to see him," she repeats.

During the 1930s the building in Via Tasso was conveniently near enough to the Villa to turn it into the German cultural center, where Teutonic and Aryan values could be transmitted to the people of Italy. But now another use has been found for it: the roadway is blocked at either end by steel chevaux-de-frise and barbed wire, and pedestrians pass down the street with reluctance, under the eye of armed soldiers. Only the long, black Mercedes belonging to the embassy is allowed through the barricades, to slide as slowly as a barge past the reefs of steel and dock alongside the pavement beside number 155. A soldier holds open the nearside rear door and the passengers emerge. There is the tall, stooping form of Herr Huber. The figure behind him shows a flash of blond hair beneath the black scarf that she clutches around her head. Black scarf, black dress, gray stockings. The two hurry up the steps and inside the door.

The entrance hall is ill lit and poorly ventilated. A smell of disinfectant pervades the stairwell, and beneath that something organic: the faint and putrefying scent of drains, perhaps. In the first room there is a ledger to fill in with name and rank and time of entry, and then an escort to show the way upstairs. Little deference is shown to Herr Huber and his wife. They have left the world of embassy and diplomacy and tact and crossed the threshold into another realm where all is different: relationships are different, rank is different, manners are different, logic itself is different. This is a realm that stretches unbroken from border territories such as this, right across Europe to the heartland of the East, where the names of Treblinka and Sobibor and Belzec are whispered. Outside the limits of Via Tasso it is a hot Roman day, pregnant with the past and with fear of the future; within the limits of this tawdry apartment building Herr Huber and his wife are in one of the antechambers of hell.

Frau Huber's high heels clip briskly on the marble stairs behind her husband's heavy tread. They pause on the landing outside a closed door while the escort knocks and whispers to the guard inside. The door opens. Beyond lies a hallway, a narrow, darkened domestic hallway with five doors giving onto it. The smell is stronger here—the pestilential smell of sepsis—and Frau Huber pulls a handkerchief from the pocket of her jacket and holds it to her face. Before they enter the apartment her husband bends toward her and says softly, "You will *do* nothing, you will *say* nothing." Above the lace edge of her handkerchief her eyes stare back like the terrified eyes of a rabbit. She nods her head. The pair of them step over the threshold.

The door on the left of the hallway is painted dark green. It is marked with nameless stains and inscribed with the plain number 5. In the center of the door, at about five feet from the floor, there is a disk of thin metal. The guard flips this aside and reveals a hole in the wood. He puts his eye to the hole for a moment and then stands aside and indicates to the visitors that everything is ready.

Huber is the only one who smiles. He cannot help smiling. It is smiling that has got him where he is; but this is a thin, nervous smile as he points his wife to the door. "Don't breathe a word," he says in her ear as she presses her eye to the peephole.

She can see part of a tiled room, illuminated by a bare bulb set in the ceiling. The tiles are pale blue. There is a sink opposite the door and a galvanized bucket beneath the sink. There is no other fitting in the room. Where there might once have been a window above the sink there is now a rectangle of bare brickwork. Her single eye allows no depth to the view, but the angles between floor and wall create perspective lines that converge into the vanishing point of the far corner. At this focus a man crouches, speared by the lines of perspective, crucified by the angles. The figure wears pajama trousers and a collarless striped shirt. The front of his shirt is stained rust-brown. His feet are bare. The face—slick with sweat, gray with two days' growth of beard—is a slack, lifeless caricature of the face of Francesco Volterra. He has his hands in the front of his trousers and he is massaging himself gently, like a child comforting himself with a favorite shawl.

Without raising his head, without moving anything but his eyes, without ceasing the rhythmic massage, Francesco looks up at the door.

Has he sensed their presence? What does he see? The blank back of the door. A single, blue, anonymous eye framed by the peephole, an eye as vacant and without expression as the lens of a camera. And then the eye has gone and there is the small and secret sound of the disk falling back into place. Nothing more. No sound. No hope.

On the landing outside, Gretchen is being violently sick into a corner. Her husband stands beside her, holding her narrow waist and turning his head away in disgust. A cleaner stumps up the stairs carrying a bucket and a mop. But there isn't much to clear up, for she hasn't eaten for days.

On their return to the car Herr Huber orders the driver to return to the Villa, but Gretchen shakes her head. She wants to go to the church, the Church of Santa Maria dell' Anima. She wishes to go there to pray. Her husband accedes to her request, directing the driver through the center of the old city, among the bicycles and the pedestrians, amid the people scratching an existence from the relics of grandiose days—the days of Bernini and Borromini, of rebirth and counterreformation, when these people had a genius that Herr Huber really cannot understand. "Monkeys in the ruins," he says of the Italians as the car eases its way into Piazza Navona, where the great fountain is dry and sandbagged. A policeman waves them on. The car noses its way through the square, like a barge nosing through the flotsam of a harbor. "Monkeys in the ruins," he repeats, acknowledging the policeman's salute with a regal wave of the hand.

The car halts outside the church entrance, which lies in a narrow street, the ironically named Vicolo della Pace, behind the buildings of the great square. "I'll wait here," Huber says. His wife passes through the entrance, through the tiny courtyard beyond where one of the Franciscan fathers is watering the plants, through into the shadows of the church where incense lies on the air like a promise of things ancient and ineffable.

There are a few figures kneeling in the stalls, young men in uniform mainly. There are heads blond and heads brown, uniforms black and gray, all bowed before the ornate baroque of the high altar, each one praying, no doubt, more or less the same thing: God, let me survive. But given the normal run of things, the pure, incontrovertible nature of statistics, some of them are bound to be disappointed.

Frau Huber edges into a pew right at the back. She kneels and, like the figure in front of her, she begins to pray—but unlike them she is praying for something that she will never grant herself for as long as she lives, even if her God does. She is praying for forgiveness.

Magda—now

Magda is a habit. In the morning I watch her every move—watch her wash, watch her towel herself dry, watch her dressing, which she does with something of the casual purposefulness of an athlete preparing to compete, watch her squat to urinate and then wipe herself with a scrap of tissue paper. She seems indifferent to my watching, as though her body is no more her own possession than is the street down below our windows, or the view of the great dome across the rooftops.

Madeleine was not like that. Madeleine seemed to possess herself when anyone looked at her, as though by seeing her you were joining the ranks of the privileged. "It'll be a relief to get away, won't it?" Her last words to me, probably her last words to anyone at all. "And when you come back, what then?" The Irish lilt of inquiry, as though whatever might happen was of little consequence. For a long time I wondered how I might have acted to make it different, but now I no longer care. I have borrowed Magda's fatalism and cloaked myself in it.

In the narrow bathroom Magda leans forward toward the mirror to apply her makeup. She has that minute attention to detail that she brings to her painting, creating of her pale face an artificial mask.

"Where are you going?"

A shrug. "To see a friend."

"Who is this friend?"

"A friend."

"Is it a man?"

Lipstick delineates a curve of blood. Her lips pucker. "Perhaps there will be a woman." She gathers up her things — her shoulder bag, perhaps a folder of her drawings — and leaves the apartment. There is no particular affection to her farewell, a half smile and a gesture that is somewhere between a shrug and a wave. No more than a hitchhiker bidding good-bye to a useful lift.

Today I followed her. My motives were, are, uncertain. Jealousy, of course. Jealousy is from *zēloō:* jealousy both good and bad, God's jealousy and man's, the beginning and the end. But there was also something else: possession, the desire to possess her as she possesses me, to *know* her. I feel that, unlike Madeleine, Magda is *knowable*.

I waited as she left the apartment and went down the stairs. Then I got up and followed, keeping out of sight above her, then hurrying down past the porter's cabin and out into the street. I saw her angular figure thread its way through the traffic and head toward the river. When she walks she moves like an athlete, with a casual grace. None of Madeleine's hurry. A certain languor. A confidence. Perhaps she feels that she has nothing to lose. Men turn their heads to watch.

On the embankment she waited for a bus. The trees that grow along the river provided cover for Leo the lion as he stalked his prey. When the bus came it was packed with people. Magda climbed on at the front along with the season-ticket holders, while I pushed in through the rear doors. As the vehicle moved off I could just see down the car, past heads and arms, to where her narrow hand grasped the rail. Her face was in profile. She stared indifferently out of the window, her jaw moving to the thoughtful rhythms of gum. It was like one of her artworks, an assemblage of bits and pieces: figure in a crowd, a mere shape among the press of passengers.

The bus crossed the river and ground its way uphill, shedding people as it went. The crowd thinned. I took a seat and faced half away from her, keeping sight of her reflection in the window so that when she reached across to press the stop button, I was ready. She slipped off at the front—against the regulations, against the complaint and argument of a tide of passengers trying to climb on board—while I stepped off at the back.

The bus had dropped us somewhere out in the suburbs, on a street with tattered apartment buildings and an automobile show-room and a ragged collection of shops. I walked away from the stop and paused at a safe distance to look back. Magda was still there beside the stop, leaning against a low wall, chewing thought-fully and watching the traffic go by. The grimy youth at the gas pumps across the street seemed to know her. He called some-thing—I heard the word *fica*—and she looked in his direction and made a quick gesture with her right fist, an equivocal gesture that might have been dismissive, might have been obscene. His laugh-ter sounded above the traffic noise.

About five minutes later a car—a steel gray BMW—drew up to the curb just beside her. She went over and leaned in at the window and there was a brief exchange with the man in the driver's seat. Then she climbed in and slammed the door behind her. The car moved away and disappeared among the traffic.

I felt helpless, a diluted version of the helplessness that I had experienced when I discovered Madeleine's death. Where had she gone? What was she doing, on this dull morning in suburban Rome with desultory traffic passing by and an aircraft grinding down through the air overhead? A dozen possibilities floated like scum to the surface of my mind.

There was a bar—Bar dello Sport—among the shops nearby. I sat at the counter, watching the street outside through the window and drinking a beer. The place was busy. People came in to play the lotto or the lottery or the football pools or pinball. Old men sat and stared into the past while youths with shaven heads and rings in their ears talked in obscenities about the merits and demerits of the city's two soccer teams. The words *cazzo* and *culo*, bright, cheerful Latinate expressions, sounded loud in the land. A computer game in the corner roared and shrieked like a motorcycle grand prix. I felt like a castaway, thrown up by mere curiosity on a foreign shore and devoid of any point of contact with the inhabitants.

And then, quite unexpectedly, when I was looking the other way and taking no further notice of the street, she walked in.

Why was the sight of her a shock? Why should I have been so surprised to see her suddenly there, standing at the bar with the bartender smiling at her and saying *buongiorno, signorina* in a manner that seemed an exaggerated politeness in that place of casual obscenity? She ordered fresh orange juice, *spremuta di arancia*. To clear her palate, I supposed. But clear it of what? Where had she been? What had she been doing? A dozen questions, a hundred lurid answers bubbled up to the surface of my mind. I sat mere feet away as the bartender pulped oranges and then, with a flourish, presented the glass to her: bright red blood-orange, as red as her carefully colored lips, as red as any hemorrhage. She stirred a heaping teaspoonful of sugar into the juice just as I knew she would, and leaned forward just so, with a faint and inward smile, to suck the surface scum of pulp from the juice beneath. Then she replaced the glass and looked around. It took her a moment to make sense of what she saw. She frowned and leaned forward again. There was an edge of anger. "What are you doing here?" she asked, in English. The bartender turned from the coffee machine.

"I'm watching you," I replied stupidly.

"You *follow* me?"

"More or less."

Sitting back and sipping her drink, she considered this. A pinball machine shrieked and jibbered in the background. There was the precise and ordered click of pool balls from the back room, geometric precision in the face of an irrational world. "You *spy* me?"

"*On* you. I spy *on* you."

"So," she said with a hint of impatience. "You do *that*. You spy."

"I suppose so."

She ran her tongue across her teeth to gather up the flecks of orange, and then repeated the operation with a single, clawed finger. "Why?"

"I'm frightened for you."

"Frightened of me?"

"For you. Frightened *for* you. I want to know what you do, where you go. I worry that you aren't safe."

She looked faintly perplexed. "I am not frightened. It is not frightening. They make pictures of me. That is all. You have seen."

"Yes. But still I'm not happy."

"Why? You don't like the pictures? They give me money. My paintings do not give me money." She shrugged, as though it was obvious.

"I like you more than the pictures."

She pursed her lips at this. A tight little bud of concentration. Or maybe that was just to allow her tongue a better purchase on the flecks of orange sticking to her teeth. "You *like* me?" she asked, as though to be sure what we were talking about.

"Yes." Absurd, this confession at the bar, with the bartender as witness. "I like you," I repeated.

The bartender felt a need to explain. "*'E laike you,*" he said.

"And if I leave?" she asked, ignoring him. "I have money, you know that. Almost I can buy my ticket to America."

I felt a wild moment of panic at her words. "I would be very unhappy if you leave."

"What you mean, *leeve?*" said the bartender. "She *is* leeving. Very leeving lady."

She turned to him. "*Sta zitto, stronzo.*" He shrugged resignedly and went back to organizing cups on top of the espresso machine. "Then I will not leave," she said to me, and laughed to show that it had been a joke, a clumsy child's joke. "We are a bit like man and lady," she decided. We drank for a moment in silence, united by this shared joke, this awkward declaration. Then, for the first time she told me something, something more than the merely circumstantial, more than the quotidian and the mundane: she told me about her husband. Until that moment I had not realized that there had ever been such a person, that Magda Novotná had once been a partner in whatever passed for marriage in the People's Republic. Perhaps she felt that some boundary had been crossed, some barrier of intimacy, and she could now reveal a little more of her past. Sitting there in the Bar dello Sport, with the bartender trying to make out what we said, she told me about her husband. "Jiří," she said. An awkward sound, like an expletive. She shrugged. "We had three years. We were maybe happy. There was also," she added, "my girl."

"Your *girl?*"

Her smile was a fragile thing, part misery, part defiance. "Milada. Her name. Milada. We name her for a hero. Milada Horakova. I tell no one about this."

Magda as mother, a new concept. "Where is she?" I asked. I imagined adoption, a foster home, something like that.

"She die," Magda said flatly. She added some words, a small clutch of brittle Slav consonants. "*Zanyet,*" she said. Something like that. *Zanyet.* And touched her head.

"How old was she?"

"Two years. After that Jiři leave. So I am alone."

"You never told me."

She gave a desolate little laugh, a sound that was just a small exhalation of air, like a final breath. "So I tell you now." That seemed to be the end of it. She drained her glass and put it sharply down on the counter. I paid the bill. The bartender thought he understood the score. As we went out he winked at me and made an eloquent and encouraging gesture with his forearm. "He is *stronzo,*" Magda said without turning. It wasn't clear quite how she knew what had gone on behind her back. Maybe she just assumed. Maybe she knew that every man followed her with his eyes, everyone wondered about the possibilities. "How you say *stronzo?*"

"Shit," I told her, although this was hardly on the syllabus.

"I thought *merda.*"

"That as well. Italian is a rich and evocative language."

At the bus stop she held my hand. "You like me," she said, and the thought seemed to please her. "Perhaps you love me a bit?"

"Perhaps," I agreed. And she laughed and leaned toward me and kissed me on the cheek. I admit to delight, childish delight. Not like with Madeleine, not the awful racking pain of loving, but something that dances on the surface of the emotions.

*   *   *

When we got back to the apartment Magda got her dictionary out and found the words. She pointed them out to me: *zánět mozkových blan*. Inflammation of the membranes of the brain. Meningitis. She mouthed the word in English, as though it were an important addition to her vocabulary.

17

People padded around, murmuring to each other like undertakers at a funeral. They prepared the body as for burial. They dressed it and anointed it with balm and wrapped it in shrouds. They inserted tubes and dripped in fluids. The scent of frankincense and myrrh filled the chamber.

He thirsted. He thought of Madeleine. He drifted to and fro on the shifting surface of consciousness and he thought of Madeleine. "Will I die?" he wondered.

They drugged him. Morphine is the analgesic of choice. Morphine, from Morpheus, the god of dreams, who was the son of Sleep. And so he dreamt. Guilt, like a substance, pervaded his dreams. He dreamt of his mother talking to him, his mother incontinent and senile speaking to Leo, the living Leo and the dead

Leo, the loathed and the loved. She spoke to Leo and she spoke about Leo, her mind meandering through the tortured landscape of senility, the distant landscape of her childhood in Buchlowitz. "We are all punished for what we do in our lives," she assured him. "I am punished, you are punished. We are all punished." And sometimes his mother and Madeleine were one, and he dreamt them naked, touched the cool and lucid skin of their belly with its rough scrub of hair. They enveloped him and they gave birth to him: the acts were the same.

"You look terrible." Goldstaub bringing comfort. He was wearing a gown and a surgical mask, his beard showing ragged around the edges. "How do you feel?"

Leo peered through swollen lids and mumbled through swollen, blistered lips. "What happened?"

"You tell me." Goldstaub gestured at his dressings. "Does it hurt?"

A grimace that may have been some kind of smile. "The superficial burns hurt, that's what they tell me. The parts that don't matter hurt. It's the places where it doesn't hurt that the real damage is done."

"Sounds like life."

"Tell me what happened."

"Don't you remember?"

"Nothing. I remember nothing. I remember breakfast. That's it. And then fragments. Noise. Fear."

"Fire?"

"Fear," he repeated, his lips fumbling with the sound. "Fear."

They hustled the visitor away, with warnings about tiredness and shock, with assurances that he could come again later. They left Leo to dream and he dreamt of flames and he dreamt of Madeleine. He plunged through the air and into the fire, and

Madeleine was with him. "I'll come to hate you, Leo," she told him as they fell. He plunged through the fire and into her flesh, so that she enveloped him with her burning. This, he understood, was purgatory, the purging of the soul in flame, the cleansing of the spirit, the ejaculation of guilt into the fire. They burned together, Madeleine and Leo, and they lived together in the burning, and she hated him.

Later there were David and Ellen, with stark, concerned faces. David talked while Ellen merely sat and folded her hands in her lap and watched him. Dimly Leo understood that she was praying, praying for his recovery, praying for his salvation. The idea brought a painful contortion to his lips and an agonizing convulsion of his chest.

"Are you in pain?" David asked.

Leo shook his head. What must have looked like a grimace, like a fit of some kind, was laughter.

Later there was a man from the police department, speaking a kind of transatlantic English and frowning as he wrote things down. "Was there anything unusual that morning?" he asked. "Did you notice anything out of the ordinary, any strangers around, anything at all?"

"Why were you there so early?"

"Do you possess a clock?"

"Can you describe your movements in the previous twenty-four hours?"

"Have you ever met anyone from outside the Bible Center, anyone at all?"

"Did anyone give you anything to carry? Anything at all? A package, a gift, maybe?"

"Have you visited anyone's house during your time here?"

"Tell me."

"Tell me."

Later there was a priest. They warned Leo of the priest's presence as though the man might do some kind of harm. "Only if you wish to see him," they assured him.

"Of course. Let him come."

The priest entered the chamber with the solemn, processional step of a funeral mute: the Frenchman Guy Hautcombe, his hands clasped before him as though ready for some kind of self-defense, the defense of prayer. He sat by Leo's bed and rested a benevolent and benedictory hand on his shoulder, then withdrew it sharply when Leo winced. "Do you feel pain?" he asked, as though there were a possibility that Leo didn't.

Goldstaub returned with copies of a newspaper. There were photographs showing the blackened, toothless gums of the windows of the manuscript rooms. There were charred lumps, and glistening puddles. "They put the damage at a couple of hundred thousand," he said.

"What do they say?"

He held up the page for Leo to see. *Person or persons unknown*, was the phrase. "Why were you there so early?" he asked. "What were you doing so early?"

Leo didn't know. He knew only the noise and the light, the light of the sun, the light of the fingers of flame reaching out to touch him, Madeleine's fingers touching his frigid flesh, fingers that scalded.

"They say there was gasoline," said Goldstaub. "That's what the forensic guys are suggesting. Gasoline and mineral oil. And maybe some kind of timing device." He folded the newspaper differently and held up another picture: a close-up of the cogs and wheels of a clock, blackened and charred. *Carpe diem*. The alarm clock shrilled in Leo's ear and he awoke and Goldstaub was gone and there was his mother beside him, his mother's arms around him, his mother's flesh enveloping him, his mother's flesh that became Madeleine's, her slick suave flesh engulfing his, engulfing him so that he drowned in it, struggled for life in it, swam out of the flames and lay there on the shore beside her.

Someone else from the police department, a woman this time, a woman with black hair and dark eyes and the sympathetic smile of a nurse. But the same questions, exactly the same questions. "Did you meet anyone from outside the Bible Center?"

"Why were you there so early?"

"What was the normal time that you began work?"

"Was there anything unusual?"

"Tell me. Take your time. Tell me."

Later doctors talked to him in low tones of graft and granulation, of eschar and necrosis, of antisepsis and debridement. He liked the word *debridement*. He enjoyed its bitter and astringent irony. They injected him with anesthetic, and masked figures bent over his wounds and cut away dead tissue, and he saw Madeleine plunging into a lake of flame, Madeleine who became his mother: not his mother as he remembered her but his mother as a young woman, as naked as a blade.

People came and went: nurses, doctors, one of Hautcombe's minions, someone languid and thoughtful from the British embassy who reminded him of Jack, who *knew* Jack, of course, knew Madeleine, knew the whole damned story. "Terrible business," he said. And Calder. Calder wandered around the room, gazed out of the window and talked to the blue sky and the clouds. "What happened?" he asked.

Leo didn't answer him.

"They tell me you can't remember."

"No."

"They think it might have been those protesters. The Children of God or whatever they're called. They might have planted some kind of device. They've gone, of course, disappeared."

"You think that? You think it was them?"

Calder shook his head of silver hair. A vision against the window, a person with an aureole of light around his body. "I don't know." He turned away from the window and looked at Leo. He didn't like the look of the patient, you could see that by his expression. Leo understood. He knew what he was like because he had asked one of the nurses to bring a mirror. She hadn't wanted to and he had demanded that she do what he say, and she had said that it was orders, and then she had disobeyed the orders and brought the mirror for him to look. He was like a leper, with running sores. He was like one of the creatures whom Christ had cured. His flesh was swollen black and mauve and crimson. His hair was a charred stubble, growing in patches like weeds in a parched field, the Potter's Field, perhaps.

"What do you think?" Calder asked as he watched Leo, and his eyes were narrowed, as though by that means he might descry the truth.

"I don't know what I think."

Calder shook his head. "The sprinklers didn't work. Can you believe that? The alarms went off but the sprinklers didn't work."

"I remember the alarms. The noise. I dream the noise." Leo smiled painfully at him, turning his head slightly to see Calder better, willing him to believe. Calder was watching expectantly, as though waiting for Leo to discover more down there in the depths of his subconscious. But he wouldn't discover anything, he knew that. "I dream a lot, you know: souls in purgatory."

Calder's tone was impatient. "A Catholic fiction. I thought you agreed with that."

"Didn't anything survive?"

"*You* survived. Just. And a copy of most of your transcription, did you know that? Not the last part. I'd copied it onto my own laptop, you see. And there are some photos. Not many, but they're not bad. We can publish, of course. We *will* publish it. But what will it mean without the material evidence . . . ?"

He left after a while. He gave the impression of having left things unsaid, accusations unuttered, suspicions unvoiced.

Resurrection is not an instant thing. It takes time and pain. It proceeds by small steps and it is measured in millimeters, the millimeters of epithelium and epidermis and dermis. And when pain dies away it is replaced by itching, the ant crawl of pruritus, the exquisite torture of formication, the sensation of invisible fingers touching, stroking, caressing, perhaps as Madeleine had once touched him, touched the surface of him and through the surface, the very quick of him. Dreams awoke the itch of his love for her. She stood beside the tomb that he had left empty.

Later, days later, they flayed him alive and lifted layers of his skin like parchment from his thigh and laid them on his chest and neck like the priest spreading the corporal on the altar. Later still they buried him beneath anesthetic, and surgeons worked away with minute instruments to reconstruct the tendons of his hands, to give the claws something to move them. Percentages were noised abroad, the percentages of burn, the percentages of probability, the percentages of success. There was more flaying, more grafting. It was like a snake sloughing off its skin, shuffling its way out of its old integument, shouldering its way out into a new life where it would no longer have to crawl on its belly and be bruised, but could walk up and down a sterile corridor or sit in a chair and look out of the window at meager pine trees and a distant view of hills. A life delimited by meals and books, peopled by hushed doctors and nurses and rare visitors, punctuated by the agonies of compression gloves and the small and intimate flexure of the fingers with a physical therapist watching and advising. The therapist reminded him of Madeleine. Something about the way she smiled, the way she inclined her head. Sometimes he fancied that Madeleine herself might suddenly step forward out of the therapist's body, slough off her superficial therapist's skin and stand there before him with that faint and ironical smile.

But the metamorphosis never happened, the transfiguration never took place, the physical therapist remained immutably herself.

He was summoned to the official inquiry. The doctors didn't want him to be moved. "Grafts need time to take," they said. But eventually they assented. It was like a day release from prison, the shuffled walk out to a waiting car, the drive through a world that seemed bright and surprising and strangely unfamiliar. Outside the court a clutch of photographers waited. In the courtroom they sat him in a black leather chair and they asked him the same questions that the police officials had asked. More or less he gave the same answers.

The story made the headlines in the local press and merited a few inches of column space in the international newspapers: BURN VICTIM TALKS OF SCROLL FIRE, a headline said. Back in the clinic a psychologist came to talk to him, an expert in posttrauma therapy or some such. He wore bright and hopeful colors and talked of grieving, grieving for parts of your own body just as you might grieve for the dead. "What do you dream?" he asked, crossing his legs and leaning forward to examine the patient, steepling his fingers, fingering his notebook, wishing he could finger the patient's mind.

Leo dreamt of Madeleine.

Person or persons unknown was the official verdict of the inquiry.

Later, much later, weeks later, months later, they discharged him from the clinic with assurances of cure and care, with recommendations for the future. He still wore gloves to keep pressure on the scar tissue on the back of his hands. He still used wax to soften the slick skin and did exercises to prevent contractions over the joints and around the neck. They gave him an address in Rome where he could find help with whatever was needed, and he walked out into the world abraded and burnished, shiny with polishing.

Goldstaub drove him to the airport. "Why back to Rome?" he asked.

"Where else?"

"England?"

"But England's not my home." Why should he have been surprised by Rome? The city was Leo's home, or all he had of one. As overwhelmed by history as a bankrupt is overwhelmed by debts, and equally spendthrift, Rome was the perfect place. "I'm an exile," Leo explained. "Rome's a place of exiles. It always has been, perhaps it always will be. Foreigners and exiles."

"And what'll you do?"

"I've no idea."

Goldstaub's last words were these, just as Leo prepared to go through the security checks, just as he got into line for the ritual interrogation about whether you packed the bags yourself and where you were staying during your visit to the country and had you had any contact with people who lived here and that kind of thing: "Leo, did you do it?" he asked.

Leo paused. He had a bag slung over one shoulder and his suitcase on a trolley. With his gloved, clawed hands he could manage the two only with difficulty.

"Did you do it?" Goldstaub repeated.

Leo smiled at him. "Saul, I've told you," he said. "I've told you before: I've no idea."

The plane rose up into a bright, burnished sky. He felt like Icarus, who had flown too near the sun for his own good and been burned. Like Icarus he had fallen; but unlike Icarus he had survived the fall. The stewardess did her rounds with plastic dishes and plastic smiles. "How are you doing, sir?" she asked.

Luck, chance, the random element in nature, these things had always disturbed him. If God resides anywhere, he thought, looking at his bland chicken salad, surely he shelters behind barricades of pure chance.

"I was once in love," he told her. "But she died."

The stewardess looked embarrassed and eager to get away. "I'm so sorry," she said.

18

W|inter in Rome, the streets washed with rain, sodden
leaves clogging the gutters and creating local floods,
cars churning up bow waves. What else about this new
Rome, newly drenched, newly washed from the sins of the past?

> Owing to restoration work
> the Palazzo Casadei
> is closed to visitors

The *portiere* was out of his cabin, morosely sweeping water from
the paving of the entrance archway. There was an ancient drainage
hole in the center of the arch, but the thing was clogged with
leaves and a small lake had formed. He looked around with scant

attention as a taxi drew up outside. Perhaps he didn't recognize me. Perhaps he didn't care.

"Signor Mimmo," I called to him, "can you give me some help?" and the man rested his broom against the wall and came out onto the pavement.

"Signor Neoman," he said. It was more a statement of fact than a greeting. He seemed indifferent to my appearance there outside the palace in the middle of a wet and wintry afternoon, devoid of surprise, devoid of any appreciable emotion.

"Could you help me up with my things? I don't think I can manage . . ." I displayed my hands for the man to see, the white pressure gloves with their Velcro fasteners. As though he might require evidence. "Burns, you see. I was burned."

He nodded, as though burning was the most natural thing. Perhaps he considered it appropriate for a man like me. "I heard something," he said. "I don't listen to gossip, but I heard something."

"Is everything all right?"

He gave a shrug, and uttered the Roman expression for the ineffable and the inevitable: "*Boh.*"

"I was away rather longer than I intended."

He nodded again. With apparent reluctance he took up my suitcase—"I've got a bad back, you know? Shouldn't really be doing this kind of thing"—and made for the back stairs, the stairs which Madeleine and I had climbed in excitement mere months before. Maybe a year. Maybe as long as a year. In my reckoning now there seem to be two sets of time, two whole assemblies of events: before the flames and after the flames. Now was after and the world was a different place.

"There's mail," he called over his shoulder as I followed him up. "I've kept it down in my place. You can have it any time you want."

"Mail?"

"Letters, that kind of thing. Quite a pile." For a moment there was a glimmer of something beneath the dull exterior: interest, curiosity. He stopped and turned, and there was a hint of censure in his tone. "You created quite a stir, didn't you, signor? One way or another." Then he fell silent again, plodding on up the stairs past the window where you could see out over a stretch of roof, stumping up to the landing outside the front door to the apartment. I fumbled in my pocket for a tip. "I'll bring the mail up if you like," he said when he saw the money. He shuffled off down the stairs while I struggled with the door key, turning it with difficulty, opening the door with caution, fearful of what I might find beyond it. But the vacant space of the entrance hall was more or less what I expected: dusty, empty, with a faint hint of mold on the stagnant air. There were no ghosts at large beneath the sloping ceilings, no ghosts walking across the creaking boards.

I struggled the suitcase inside but I didn't bother to drag it through into the bedroom, just opened it inside the entrance and unpacked it there. First I took out the photograph of Madeleine and placed it with care in the living room over the fireplace. She looked back at me with habitual irony and challenged me to feel sorry for myself. Then I unpacked my clothes and carried them through into the bedroom.

Later I went through the bundle of letters that the porter brought up. He emptied them from a plastic sack that said *Posta Italiana* on it. They spread across the dining table, about fifty envelopes, a motley collection of sizes and colors. Some addresses were typed, some handwritten, one or two, the crazy ones, printed in a variety of colors. I sat at the table to sort through them. One, with a New York postmark, was addressed to *The Beast 666*. Another to *The Antichrist*. Most had *Father* Leo Newman, some plain *Mr.* And one was written in my own hand.

I paused. Froze would be an apt word: the sight brought a sensation of cold, like a chill fluid flowing through my body. It was a heavy manila envelope, stiffened inside with card. It bore Israeli stamps and postmark. And the handwriting was mine, indubitably mine. I couldn't be mistaken, not about that. I couldn't write like that any longer, not with my stiffened, awkward claw (writing exercises had been part of the rehabilitation program), but once that had been my own handwriting, a familiar, personal thing like a facial feature. I examined the date, and it was a date I knew well, a date of inferno, a date of flame, a time of burning. I turned the envelope over as though there might be clues on the other side, but I found nothing more. And memory offered nothing. Memory was an uncertain chart, with spaces devoid of symbol or character, gaps in the fabric of time like blank spaces on an ancient map: here be dragons. I recalled nothing.

I sat looking at the envelope for a long while. Then with some care I slit it open.

There was a ragged brown scrap inside, a mere fragment, stiff with age. I slid the sheet out on to the table: a piece of fibrous material that had long ago been spread out and beaten down and rammed and polished and pounded into an acquiescent surface. A few crumbled pieces followed, and a small shower of dust. I looked down on the sheet with something like amazement, something akin to fear. The letters taunted me, their precision making a mockery of the chaos I felt. I read, tracing the letters with the forefinger of my clumsy, gloved right hand:

ΤΟΣΩΜΑΤΟΗΡΜΕΝΟΝΕΤΣΦΗΛΑΘΡΑΠΑΡΑΠΟΛΙΝ
ΙΩΣΗΦΗΤΙΣΚΑΛΕΙΤΑΙΡΑΜΑΘΑΙΜΖΟΦΙΜΕΓΓΥΣ
ΤΟΥΜΟΔΙΝΕΩΣΑΡΤΙΓΙΝΩΣΚΕΙΟΥΔΕΙΣΤΗΝΤΟΠΟΝ
ΤΟΥΕΝΤΑΦΙΑΣΜΟΥΑΥΤΟΥ

The body that was taken was buried secretly by the town of Joseph that is Ramathaim-zophim beside Modin and to this day no one knows the place of his burial.

I sat back and stared at the piece lying there on the table, the page that had stepped out of my nightmares, the page from the Gospel of Judas that had preceded me across the Mediterranean, that had followed the footsteps of Paul and lodged here in the Holy City itself to await my return. Almost as though it were imbued with some kind of inner intention, or guided by an unseen hand.

The material evidence.

Outside I could hear the rain starting again, the heavy and persistent drum of fingers on the roof tiles. From somewhere within the apartment came the drip of water.

And the night of his death they went to the tomb that was the tomb of Joseph and took the body away . . . The witness of this was Youdas who writes. Joseph and Nicodemus and the same Youdas were there, and Saul of Tarsus.

There was fear there, of course. I recognized it now. I was practiced in it. Not fear *of* anything. This was a generalized fear, fear without a focus, the plain fear of existence. How did this page come to be here? How had it escaped the holocaust?

The floorboards creaked. I glanced around at the dusty room. Was there anyone there? It was growing dark now, the day sliding into twilight. The tick of rainwater, the soft creak of wooden boards was all around me. Absurdly I called out, "Madeleine?" and as though in answer she looked at me from the mantelpiece. Her eyes followed me as I rose from the chair and moved around looking for somewhere to put the envelope. "What would you do, Maddy?" I asked out loud. I had never called her Maddy. That was Jack's nickname for her. But now she was as much mine as his. "What would you do?" I asked her. "What would you do, Maddy?"

There was my trunk, the same trunk that had followed me from school to seminary, from seminary to my first parish, and from there to every other temporary home I had ever possessed. I opened the lid. There were papers inside: my mother's will, the deeds to the house in Camberwell, the statements from the bank in Switzerland, the diaries she had kept, the letters. I slid the page of papyrus back inside its envelope and laid it on top of all the things in the trunk and closed the lid. Then I went to look for the leak in the roof.

A Train Journey—1943

A train in wartime, a halting, crippled thing, with every seat taken and passengers crouching in the corridors, lying in the corridors, jamming into the connecting passage between the carriages. People are lying in the luggage racks over the seats, people are bedded down in the luggage car, people are crammed into the soiled lavatory. People and the press of people. The smell is rancid in the close air, the smell of unwashed clothes, of unwashed bodies, the stink of ordure and urine and cigarettes.

"Guardate come siamo ridotti," someone remarks. Look what we've been reduced to.

The train stumbles through the night and halts for hours outside stations with no more explanation than the paltry reason of rumor: an air raid, the track damaged by terrorists, the engine broken down, no coal, no crew, no sense. Frau Huber sits crushed into the corner of a first-class compartment, beside the window. A window seat is the last luxury the embassy could provide for her. Her face rushes by in the darkness at her side and through it she watches the shadowy world beyond, the hills and the villages fading into an autumnal dusk, the rivers, the bridges, the forests all disappearing into the night; while the other passengers in the compartment watch her, knowing she is German, not knowing what this means any longer. Her maid, an anxious woman from the Alto Adige who has been persuaded to make this journey with the promise that it will get her home, sits opposite and moans. There are eight other people crammed into the compartment: two naval officers, a businessman with the slick, affluent look of the black market about him, a woman with two children, and two young men who ought to be in uniform. The passengers eye one another with suspicion in this world of suspicion, where motives are always mixed and loyalties are various. The woman beside Frau Huber has been visiting a hospital in Rome. Her husband is dying, so she explains to anyone who will listen, of cancer. It seems absurd that in the midst of war someone should be dying of mere disease. She explains the details of his illness but doesn't explain the point of having him in Rome, where nothing will be done for him, rather than at home, where nothing can be done for him. "At least he's near the Holy Father," she suggests with a shrug, as though proximity to the Pope plays some part in the cure of malignant disease. "And where are you going?" she asks Frau Huber. She uses the familiar form *tu* as though speaking to a child: "*E tu, dove vai?*"

"I'm going home."

"*Germania?*"

"*Germania.*"

From Florence the train begins its climb into the mountains. The air in the compartment grows chill. There is no heating, or if there is, no one has turned it on. The train slams into a tunnel, the noise thrown back from the walls with a sudden ferocity. Frau Huber thinks of bombs falling, of landslides, of entrapment. Then there is the blessing of release and rain dashing like pebbles against the matte black of the window. She sleeps fitfully. In the snatches of sleep she dreams her own personal nightmare, only to awaken and discover this impersonal one, the packed bodies, the condensation running down the windows, her fellow passengers shifting and groaning in their discomfort. The journey over the watershed of the Apennines takes three hours, and when finally the train slides down out of the hills it comes to a halt in the periphery of a city, in the darkness, somewhere among the apartment buildings and the ruined factories.

"Where are we?" she demands as though she has a right to know. "What place is this? Why are we stopping?" Her maid is useless, reduced to mere whimpering and moaning. The carriages sit in the darkness and seethe, while beyond the windows the sky lights up with distant flashes that may be autumn lightning, may be bombs. The name *Bologna* is passed from mouth to mouth like a rumor. *Bologna.*

At last the train shifts, jolts, moves again through the desolate suburbs toward the station and rumor becomes fact and the signs saying BOLOGNA slide past the windows and steam rises in great gusts beneath the roof, like the vapors of inferno.

At Bologna there is a change of plan. Frau Huber has it all carefully worked out. She stands amid the currents on the platform and holds her maid's shoulders tightly as though to squeeze the stupid woman into comprehension. "You will continue on to Bozen," she says. Men in uniform push past them. Announcements are made over the loudspeakers in Italian and German about trains being delayed. "You will continue on to Bozen," Frau Huber repeats. "You will go home just as we have planned. But I will not be coming with you."

"Not with me, *gnädige Frau?*"

"You understand me, girl. Don't be obtuse."

"But Frau Huber—"

"I have other business to attend to. I may follow on later. Now get me a porter and then get yourself to the Bolzano train."

"But *gnädige Frau*—"

"Do what I say!"

People do. The maid does, so too does the young transport officer, a pallid asthmatic youth who doubtless will only make it into the front line when all else is lost. He has probably never seen a diplomatic passport in his life but he is shrewd enough to guess that to argue with it is to invite more trouble than any number of shouting Italians, and sharp enough to recognize a woman who demands what she wants and gets her way. A seat on the next train to Milan? He will write the rail pass himself. Of course it is not necessary for him to call the embassy. The *gnädige Frau* may do whatever she pleases. A soldier will see to the luggage. And if the *gnädige Frau* wishes, she may take shelter in their office, away from all these Italians with their noise and their smell and their sense of defeat.

"We will win, won't we?" the soldier asks her in a sudden wavering of conviction.

"Of course we will."

So there is a wait, a long and tiresome wait amid the stench of cigarettes and the furtive smell of schnapps. The station is a seething ferment of rumor: the Allies have landed on the Italian mainland; the King has run away; Mussolini, sequestered in a mountain prison, has been spirited away to Germany by special troops of the SS. Frau Huber dismisses such rumors as ridiculous fantasies when she hears them. She scolds the soldiers for listening to such stories and for diffusing them. "Such behavior does nothing but damage to the German people's morale," she tells them, and they feel chastised, like resentful schoolchildren. She waits for hours in the fug of the movements office while people come and go and phones ring and cups of ersatz coffee are consumed and, as a thin dawn begins to draw the platform outside in tones of gray and ocher, a train slides into view.

"This is it," the young officer exclaims. His tone suggests surprise and relief. Orders are shouted and soldiers come running. People, a struggling mob of people, are pushed aside and Frau Huber is handed up into her carriage. Doors slam and whistles blow, and at six o'clock the train leaves Bologna, bound for Milan, and beyond Milan for the town of Chiasso on Lake Como.

Magda—now

T he newspapers talk of a weeping Madonna. "I saw her shed tears of blood," one witness claims. "I held her in my arms as she wept," says another. The Madonna in question is a statue bought by a pilgrim at the shrine of Medjurgorje in Bosnia, and presented to the altar of some chapel near Rome. It is a glistening white plaster thing of no artistic merit, the product of an industrial process rather than a sentient human being. Works of artistic worth never attract the grasping mind of popular devotion. You can visit an ancient church in this country of ancient churches and gaze in awe at works by Perugino, by Pinturicchio, by Piero della Francesca—the tourists do, by the millions—but you'll never find such works attracting the adoration of the pious and the penitent. The glimmering flock of candles is always ranged before an ill-proportioned painting of crude primary-school colors, a meretricious thing with an incongruous and ill-fitting silver crown pasted to its head like a paper hat from a Christmas cracker. Pilgrims always pay homage to a piece of kitsch.

Magda saw the article about this weeping Madonna. She found the newspaper thrown aside and the photograph immediately caught her attention. I watched her pick the paper up and take it over to the sofa, where she curled up catlike and read the article slowly and thoughtfully, with the small pink bud of her tongue lodged between her lips in childish concentration. There is something childlike about her. She has the manners of a child dressed up in the disturbing garb of an adult. "Have you seen?" she asked when she reached the end.

"It'll be a load of rubbish," I said. "A bit of pious superstition and a lot of commercial exploitation."

My indifference seemed to annoy her. "We go there," she decided. The inclusive *we*. The uncertain present tense. "We go there and I am praying for you. And Milada."

It is a novel experience to be the subject of prayer rather than the object of damnation; it is novel, too, to be put beside an innocent child.

A train in peacetime, a stuttering progression through the Roman *campagna* in overcrowded, grimy carriages. One almost expects chickens in the luggage racks and pigs in the baggage van. A dull and expressionless countryside traipsed past the windows. Dull and expressionless passengers stared at us with a fine lack of discrimination: they would have stared at anything and anyone. Hunchbacks and gypsies would have been equal objects of their gaze. Respectable lawyers and dubious businessmen, anything would have been regarded with insolent curiosity. There was only us and so they stared at us. What did they see? An incongruous couple speaking in foreign words: he well into his middle age, with a dry and withered face; she with the blemished complexion and heavy makeup of a tart. He biting the inner surface of his lower lip, she chewing gum with the empty concentration of a cow chewing its cud.

Did the electric current of physical contact pass between this disparate couple?

No.

Did they show a fraction of affection?

Minimal.

Did they share the same bed?

Probably.

Were they man and wife, man and lover, man and mercenary?

Impossible to say.

The passengers stared.

We left the train at an anonymous station somewhere near the coast, a halt with a single station building and a single platform. Electric blue letters were blocked on the wall of the station by some spray-paint artist. They announced, in English:

THE BEAST

As we waited for a bus Magda produced a sketchbook from her bag and roughed out some pencil strokes on one of the sheets. A section of wall, the biblical slogan, the broken windows of the station building, emerged from the plain white paper. She has that ability, the strange power of the artist to take possession of the world, to possess it and remodel it in her own manner.

The bus finally arrived to take us and a few other lost souls to the Sanctuary of the Madonna delle Paludi (Our Lady of the Swamps). There was nowhere to purchase tickets and thus on the final leg of our pilgrimage to salvation we traveled illicitly.

The sanctuary lay among eucalyptus trees on reclaimed ground that had once been part of the Pontine Marshes. There was a large parking lot with a section reserved for buses, but on this indifferent autumn day in the middle of the week there were few vehicles—a single bus of Polish tourists, a few private cars, a van loaded with nuns. Beyond the parking lot was a small encampment of stalls selling trinkets and amulets. Things fluttered in the breeze like bunting at a fair: rosaries, crucifixes, medallions. Heads of Christ dripped blood from their thorns, portraits of Padre Pio held bandaged hands in prayer. Effigies of the Pope hobbled over his episcopal crook; Saint Francis fondled the wolf.

And there was the weeping Madonna. Everywhere there was the weeping Madonna. White and glistening she lay in careful rows like grubs in a beehive, like clones on a laboratory bench. There were pocket-size Madonnas and Madonnas for the mantelpiece and Madonnas for the hallway, and doubtless Madonna-shaped soap for the bathroom. There were Madonnas that glowed in the dark and others with internal lighting. They all had the same form, the same praying hands clasping the same rosary; and the same witness to the miracle: a smear of rust-red running down from sightless eyes over passive alabaster cheeks.

Magda picked over these items like a customer at a market stall looking for the best fruit. "Let's see the sanctuary," I suggested.

"Wait."

"We didn't come for this. We came to see the real thing." My tone was mocking, I knew that. I worked on my tone of voice, had always done so. Tone is 50 percent of the meaning. But Magda couldn't read my tone. Madeleine would have laughed. Madeleine would have touched my sarcasm with her irony.

"Nothing is real," Magda said. Whether she was speaking of this miraculous Madonna or of life in general, I couldn't be sure.

"I'm real," I said. "You're real. This whole awful place is real." I waited while she chose her statuette and handed over the money. She fed the statuette into her bag and turned to the business of the day with a solemn expression.

The sanctuary itself was a recent building of concrete slabs and steel joists, a modern place slung together as though in haste. Angles didn't quite meet: awkward gaps were bridged by slabs of colored glass so that the whole construction looked like something built by a child out of plastic pieces. The words *I am the Handmaid of the Lord* were inscribed in gold above the entrance.

Something like a crowd had developed around the paltry building. Where they had all come from was impossible to say, but there was something like a real pilgrim crowd edging toward the entrance. "You keep close," said Magda and her hand snaked into mine, her tough, paint-stained fingers lacing through my own. We shuffled through double doors of glass into an atrium where posters announced trips to Lourdes, trips to Fatima, trips to Medjurgorje itself. Portraits of Padre Pio smiled benignly upon us. Hidden speakers played Schubert's "Ave Maria" on instruments that had never been seen on earth. The expectancy of the crowd was a palpable thing, a substance in the air around which any ancillary noise had to edge its way. Stewards searched for naked shoulders or bare knees. Under their guidance the random herd of pilgrims coalesced into a line and shuffled forward into the body of the church like a single organism, a snake, a worm.

Magda clutched at my fingers like a child drawing comfort from a father. "This is pure nonsense," I whispered. She hushed me to silence. She wore a beatific smile, as though she had just seen the light. Her black figure was like the black of the old women in the line, a funereal, penitential black. "Strange," she whispered.

There were shadows and pools of colored light in the body of the church. Hunched forms knelt before the main altar. A disembodied murmuring seemed to be extruded from the tawdry fabric of the building, a muttering, a whimpering, something like the mumbling of the feeble-minded. The line snaked around the inner wall of the church and down a side aisle, edging toward a niche at the far end where a dazzling light splintered from edges of tinsel and gilt, where the Madonna awaited her supplicants, her poorly modeled hands fused together in prayer, her tears, the miraculous tears, mere workaday smears of rust-red like a poorly stanched but trivial cut. KEEP MOVING said the signs in four languages, but the snake tried to disobey, pausing and writhing as though in pain, bowing its head before the Virgin to allow it to be bruised. Old women and young women, men and boys, the halt and the lame all stumbled before the image as though they were witnessing a celestial vision and not a cheap and tawdry statue, a thing of pure spirit, not a machine-made lump of glazed plaster. Magda knelt and crossed herself, and pulled me down beside her. For a moment I was there on my knees beside her, her hand still clutching mine to hold me down. What passed through my mind? A faint glimmer of prayer, like a last ember in a fire that has otherwise died out? A mere emptying of the mind in the hope, the impoverished hope, that someone might speak there, into the space?

Madeleine, I thought.

Outside, the daylight was dazzling. Magda was solemn with the grandeur of the moment. She found a seat and sat down with her sketch pad to make some little intricate drawings from memory—figures hunched, figures shuffling forward like prisoners in a line for the latrines, broken figures with bent and twisted limbs. I stood beside her and tried to pray.

Beside the sanctuary was a trattoria announcing *pasta delle lacrime,* pasta with tears. We had lunch there before getting the bus back to the station. On the journey home Magda's face seemed heavy and coarse, like a clumsy, badly made carnival mask. At one point she took the plaster statuette out of her bag and looked at it thought-fully. I knew what she would do with it when she got back to the apartment. It would find a place out on the rooftop terrace, where it could see the whole panorama of the city, where she could watch it carefully, as though daring it to weep before her. And then she would pull out a canvas and some pots of paint, clotted around the lids like blood around the edge of a fresh wound, and she would begin to work, and the Madonna would float in the midst of a collage of newspaper and holy picture, of worshiping crowds and damned souls, a Madonna holding a child for all to see, a small, tortured baby. And a serpent would crown the whole scene.

"I've got something to show you," I told her as she worked.

"What?"

"Wait." There was the trunk against one wall of the living room, the battered old trunk that had followed me around my life before finally fetching up here like flotsam cast on some distant and unexpected beach. I opened the lid and took out an envelope. It was richly decorated with foreign stamps and postmarks. "This."

She watched, head to one side, mouth twisted so that she could bite the inside of her lip. I slid the page out and held it for her to see. Fragments of the thing came out with it. Bits, crumbs, dust.

"What is this?"

The dry and arid sheet, like rice paper, like rice paper grown discolored with age. The lettering crawled and writhed across its surface, an exotic, esoteric script. I saw **MOΔIN**: Modin.

Magda stepped forward and peered to see. "What is this? This is old?"

"Very old."

She put out a finger to touch it.

"You can use it," I said. "Here, take it. You can use it if you like."

"It is precious?"

"It is very precious, but you can use it. It is yours."

She smiled with delight at the idea of being given something precious. She took the sheet and held it on the palm of one hand and smiled down at it. "With my Madonna picture," she decided.

"You're holding it upside down," I told her.

I watched her work. I watched the quick, deft strokes, the way in which paint became object, the sure balance of abstract lines, the strange colors, the curious fragments pasted into the picture, the faded letters of Koine, that language that was the language of commerce and social interchange and scripture. The language that has had greater impact on the world than any other, painted now into the world of the weeping Madonna and Child. Fragments of newspaper and scripture arranged in delicate harmony around the lady with the drops of acrylic crimson that fall like jewels down her cheeks.

Lac Léman—1943

M rs. Margaret Newman, English, enigmatic, a foreigner in this city of foreigners, walks down the narrow streets of the old town toward the waterfront. Behind her, tucked beneath the eaves of an old and narrow house on the rue des Granges, lies the apartment. Ahead of her, visible between the narrow houses, Le Jardin Anglais and Lac Léman and the great plume of water that dashes sudden rainbows against the sky. Around her the insouciant bustle of a city that is not at war.

This will do, she thinks.

She is wearing a floral frock with a cardigan thrown over her shoulders against the cool breeze, and when she walks men turn and watch. One gentleman even approaches her and raises his hat and addresses her in French as *madame* and wishes her good morning. *"Voulez-vous venir avec moi?"*

She rebuffs him with that way she has of making the shape of a smile without any of the underpinnings of welcome. The man moves on. There are other more welcoming smiles, Frenchwomen who managed to cross over the border and are living as refugees, living in the only way there is to live in a country that is overflowing with the dispossessed and the displaced.

Mrs. Newman has just come from hearing mass. Mass in this city of Protestantism gives her a small stir of delight. She has already found a church and a priest to whom she can offer her delicate confessions.

She finds a bench in the English Gardens. She sits, crossing her legs and arranging her skirt modestly over her knees, and tries not to think too much. No newspapers, no wireless, no news from over the border. She takes a book from her bag and opens it at the mark and begins to read—Jane Austen, of course. Of course Jane Austen. It is possible to ignore a war. The characters in Jane Austen's books seem to spend much of their time ignoring their own particular war, the incessant war against Napoleon. She reads her book and feels the stirring inside her. She will find herself a doctor. She will have the tests done—they will inject her urine into toads—but she doesn't really need the tests. She knows. She knows everything: it will be a boy. It will be Leo; a kind of resurrection. Her atonement will be complete.

It is maybe twenty minutes later that another man approaches—young, slightly awkward, slightly effeminate with his soft collar and foppish hair. "Madame Newman?" he asks. He makes an awkward half bow, as though he is uncertain whether the gesture has quite gone out of fashion yet.

She marks her page carefully and closes her book. "*Oui. Je suis la Madame Newman.*"

The young man looks relieved. "I think perhaps we should go somewhere less conspicuous," he suggests. It is a curious sentence, beginning in poorly accented French and ending in perfect

German. "I am Paul Weatherby of the . . . ah . . . British Foreign Office. I understand that you wish to talk to someone about your . . . how shall I put it? . . . difficulties."

She likes the aristocratic hesitations, the hesitant manner. They are unmistakable. She also likes the fact that there is a car in the background, conspicuously manned by other, less effete men. "I think that is an excellent idea," she says. She gets up from the bench, puts her book into her bag, settles her cardigan over her shoulders. "You see, I wish to return home."